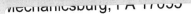

Liza saw the poster w........ ....pping for her mother. It was stuck in the window of Mrs Baxter's drapery shop near the market, and had slid a bit sideways. She stopped to read it, but had to ask a passer-by to explain the long words. The kindly old gentleman walked on afterwards, but Liza lingered, staring at the big black words and mouthing them again:

FEMALE EMIGRATION TO AUSTRALIA
SERVANTS OF RESPECTABLE CHARACTER REQUIRED
PASSAGE PAID FOR SUITABLE YOUNG WOMEN
REFERENCES ESSENTIAL

When a young man stopped to study the poster, she plucked up her courage and asked him where Australia was.

'Right on the other side of the world, love. You can't get much further away from England that Australia.' He stared at the poster longingly for a minute more than walked on.

He'd never be able to find me there, thought Liza.

Lancashire Lass

Anna Jacobs

CORONET BOOKS
Hodder & Stoughton

Visit Anna Jacobs' website at: http://www.annajacobs.com

First published in Great Britain in 2000
by Hodder and Stoughton
First published in paperback in 2001
by Hodder and Stoughton
A division of Hodder Headline

A Coronet Paperback

13

A CIP catalogue record for this title
is available from the British Library.

ISBN 978 0 340 74827 5

Printed and bound by
CPI Group (UK) Ltd, Croydon, CR0 4YY

Hodder and Stoughton
A division of Hodder Headline
338 Euston Road
London NW1 3BH

With many thanks to the following people for
sharing their expertise:

Lisa Chaplin, a writer friend who generously used her
Aboriginal background and studies to help me with
with the character of Dinny.

Peter Bamforth, ex-ship's engineer, who checked
through the sailing chapters and changed the word
rope to halyard and sheet and all sorts of
other puzzling things.

Ronald Richards, local historian, who checked that
I'd done my research properly and whose book
The Murray District was an invaluable research tool.

Part One

CHAPTER ONE

March 1857

Dorothy Pringle stood in the doorway, smiling as she watched her cheerful young maid working. The room was fragrant with polish and flowers, spring sunlight was glinting through the windows and Liza, unaware that she was being observed, was humming softly as she set the table, placing each plate carefully and aligning the silverware round each setting.

When the door knocker sounded, the girl looked up and jumped in shock. 'Ooh, I didn't know you were there, Mrs P.'

The knocker sounded again, demanding attention not asking for it.

'Shall I answer the door, ma'am?'

'No, I'll do it. You finish in here.'

Liza got on with her work. She loved making the table look nice, loved everything about working here for such a kind mistress. She heard conversation, the deep rumble of a man's voice, the soft tones of her mistress, and paused, frowning. It sounded like – but it couldn't be, surely?

Mrs Pringle reappeared, looking puzzled. 'It's your father.'

When Con Docherty followed her into the room, not waiting to be invited, Liza shot a worried glance sideways at her mistress. What was her father doing here? And pushing into the parlour, too, with his dirty boots on. It wasn't the last Friday of the month when he came to pick up her wages. Her heart began to thump with anxiety. Perhaps there was trouble at home?

Con threw a surly look at the lady of the house, who barely came up to his shoulder and yet always intimidated him. 'I've come to take my daughter away, I'm afraid, Mrs Pringle. She won't be able to work for you any more. Her mother's ill, so she's needed at home.' He turned to his daughter. 'Go and get your things together, girl!'

Liza looked doubtfully from one to the other, waiting for her mistress to speak.

'You can come back when your mother is better,' Dorothy said soothingly.

Con cleared his throat. 'I'm afraid we're going to need her at home from now on, missus, so if you can pay me what she's due, we won't trouble you further.'

Liza, who had paused at the doorway to listen, could not hold back a wail of disappointment. She saw her father glare at her and clapped her hand across her mouth. You didn't argue with Da, or go against his wishes if you knew what was good for you, but the last thing she wanted, the very last, was to leave here. She hated it at home.

Within half an hour she had her things packed and was walking towards the town with her da carrying on his shoulder the wicker trunk she could scarcely lift when it was full, but whose weight he hardly seemed to notice. Liza was worried sick about her mam, but he'd told her to shut up when she'd tried again to find out exactly what was wrong, so she walked along in silence beside him, fretting.

Once they were over the rising piece of ground that separated the village of Ashleigh from Pendleworth, the pretty lanes gave way to cobbled streets. The town was dominated by the huge mill with its tall, smoking chimney and by the two big houses, Pendleworth Hall and Rawley Manor, which lay to the north-east and north-west, overlooking everything from a safe distance. The Hall was the home of the Ludlams, who owned the mill – and a lot of other things in the district as well. The Rawleys had lived at the Manor for ever, but these days they did not bother much with the town, which had doubled in size in the past twenty years.

Back at Ashleigh you couldn't see the mill or the big houses. The air tasted sweeter out there and Liza loved the big shady trees round the house. Here the air had a sooty taste to it and everything seemed darker, with roofs of grey slate and square setts of grey stone paving the main streets. Even the red bricks of the little terraced houses, built by the Ludlams to house their

4

workers, had been darkened to an indeterminate murky brown by the smoke from the big mill chimney. Every month, when Da came for her wages and brought her home for her Sunday off, Liza felt the narrow streets closing round her like a vice. That hadn't worried her when she'd known she'd be going back to the Pringles' in the evening, but she was already dreading the thought of staying here.

She didn't try to speak again, just concentrated on keeping up with Da's long strides. She only came up to his shoulder because she and her sister took after their mam. Her two elder brothers took after Da and were burly men already, but it was too soon to tell with Kieran, who had only just turned nine.

At the lower end of Market Road they turned into Underby Street, where the shop stood with its faded sign above the window, DOCHERTY, SECOND HAND CLOTHING, and a grubby card in the door saying *Best prices given*. Liza's steps faltered. She didn't want to live here again, not when she'd tasted another sort of life, one where you had enough to eat every single day in a house where things were kept lovely and clean – and where no one shouted at you, let alone thumped you if you spoke out of turn.

As they walked through the shop with its piles of clothes and its sour smell, she wrinkled her nose and tried not to breathe in. Passing into the kitchen, she saw her sister standing in the scullery doorway, but Da muttered, 'Look sharp!' so she merely waved to Nancy and followed him upstairs.

Through the open door of the front bedroom she saw Mam sleeping restlessly but not looking as bad as Liza had feared, thank goodness. Da dumped the trunk in the back bedroom and glanced towards the front room.

'It'll do her good to have you here looking after things. And it'll do me good to have your help in the shop again. Get changed out of them fancy clothes and come downstairs. I want some food an' you're a better cook than our Nancy.'

'Yes, Da.' But when Mam was on her feet again, surely they would let her go back – if her place was still vacant. Liza crossed her fingers tightly. Please, let no one else be found to take her place! The Pringles didn't pay high wages, which was why they'd taken on a girl from Underby Street, so maybe there was a chance.

Da had vanished into the shop by the time she went down. In the scullery Nancy, who had only just turned twelve and was small with it, was washing the dishes half-heartedly. 'I'm that glad you're back. Da's been in a terrible mood all week, an' Niall hit me this morning.' She sniffed dolefully and rubbed at a bruise on her cheek with one wet, reddened hand.

'Well, never mind that now. You get that washing up finished. Mam would have a fit if she came down and saw this mess. We'll take her up a cup of tea as soon as she wakes.'

'I can't do everything,' Nancy muttered, scowling.

'Of course you can't. I'll feed Da first, then we'll clean up together.'

Only she had to go into the shop first to ask him for money to buy tea and food, because there was hardly anything in the house, which put him in a bad mood and made him shout at her. It was, Liza thought miserably, as if nothing had changed in the two years she'd been living away. Just her. And she'd changed a lot. This place didn't feel like home any more – and she didn't feel like putting up with things, either.

The next day Da went through her trunk and took her good working clothes to sell in his shop.

When she begged him not to, Liza got a clout round the ear. It was then she realised he really wasn't going to let her return to the Pringles. She wept into the pillow that night and when Nancy turned to cuddle her, whispered, 'I'm not stopping here! Whatever he does, I'm not stopping!' Once her mam was better she'd find a way to escape, then go somewhere so far away Da would never find her again.

When he nipped out for a 'wet of ale', Liza went into the shop, took some of her clothes from among the better stuff and hid them under the piles of old things that were going for rags, hoping he wouldn't notice.

For the next two weeks she hardly had a minute to think, because there was not only Mam to look after, but her elder brothers, Niall and Dermott, too. They expected her to jump to attention and serve their needs the minute they came home from the mill. As always they took the biggest share of the food except for Da, and that didn't leave much for the younger children.

Once again Liza knew what it was to go hungry and began to feel bitterly resentful of her brothers' greedy, bullying ways.

6

The younger members of the Docherty family did not starve, but they did not get enough to eat, either, and she had sharp words with Niall more than once, for he was far nastier than Dermott and always had been. When he hit her one day, she picked up the frying pan and threatened to retaliate if he touched her again.

Luckily, Dermott began laughing.

'What's so funny?' Niall growled.

'The size of it – threatening you?' And Dermott was off again.

Niall started to grin. 'You're going to beat me up, are you, our Liza? You and whose army?' He picked her up and tossed her in the air a couple of times, laughing as she shrieked in panic.

The two men were still chuckling as they walked out.

She watched them go, hands on hips. Well, she'd meant what she said. She wasn't going to put up with their rough treatment any more.

When Andrew Pringle came home from one of his long rambles round the countryside, Dorothy greeted him with, 'Liza's father's taken her away to help out at home. Her mother's ill, it seems. I'll have to get another maid. Just when I'd got the girl nicely trained, too.'

He pursed his lips and looked at her sideways.

She knew then that he was up to something and her heart skipped with anxiety. That look never boded well.

'Don't bother to look for another maid, my dear. We'd have had to give Liza notice soon anyway.'

'Give her notice – but why?' Had he lost more of their money in one of his silly schemes? Surely not? No, he was beaming at her like a village idiot, not avoiding her eyes and mumbling out a confession of his losses as he had so many times before.

He put an arm round her shoulders. 'I've got some good news for you, my dear.'

Heart sinking, she walked with him into the small parlour, asking, 'What is it?' before they'd even sat down, so anxious was she. His idea of good news and hers often differed markedly.

'I've decided that we're never going to do well here in Pendleworth. There simply aren't enough opportunities in an industrial district for a man like me.'

Dorothy felt her apprehension increase and thump down like a lead weight in her belly. 'Just say it straight out, Andrew,' she begged.

After another of his assessing glances, he took a deep breath and said quickly, 'Well – I've decided to emigrate to Australia.'

For a moment she couldn't believe she'd heard correctly and could only blink at him as she considered the words in her mind. But whichever way she tried it, they meant the same. *'Emigrate to Australia!'* she said faintly. 'But – but why should you go there?'

He was avoiding her eyes completely now. 'We're *all* going there, Dorothy. In fact – well, I've already booked our passages.'

'What?' The room spun round her for a minute, then settled down. She wanted to scream at him, but what good had getting angry ever done? In his own quiet way, he was as immovable as the Pennine Hills. 'I don't understand. Why should we want to go to Australia? It's a place for convicts, not gentlefolk.' And they were gentlefolk, however poor they'd become. That thought always consoled her.

'That's Sydney you're thinking about. Western Australia has far fewer convicts than the rest, and only got some because they asked for them. People mostly go out there as free settlers.'

'Well, I still don't want to go.'

'You must allow me to be the judge of that, my dear. I am, after all, the head of the family, and I sincerely believe we'll be able to make a better life for ourselves in the Antipodes. Things are going from bad to worse in England and people tell me there are great opportunities in the colonies if you're willing to work hard – which I hope I am.'

When Andrew gave her a radiant smile, like a small boy who'd brought her a present, her heart sank still further, for he only got that look in his eyes when he was well into one of his schemes. She should have guessed he was up to something because he'd been in a good mood lately. But he always cheered up as spring approached and he could spend more time outdoors

8

in his beloved garden, so she had thought nothing of it. 'Well, you can just go there on your own. Find out what it's like and if it looks promising, Kitty and I will follow you later.'

'I'm afraid I can't do that. You see, you'd have nowhere to live if you stayed here. Anyway, a wife's place is with her husband and a daughter should live with her parents till she marries, especially an only child like our dear Kitty.'

For a moment Dorothy could hardly breathe, then the words came out twice as loudly as usual. 'What do you mean, we'd have nowhere to live? We have this house.'

'Not any longer. I've sold it to Mr Ludlam. We're going to need the money to buy a piece of land in Australia, you see. A farm. My forebears were farmers and now I'm going to be one too. That's why things haven't gone well for me before. I've been going against my nature.'

Dorothy had difficulty putting words together and they came out in short, angry bursts. 'But – but what if it all – what if it goes wrong?' Most of his schemes did fail, but there had always been the house to fall back on – that and her small annuity. This time they would have absolutely nothing left except the fifty pounds she received every year, the legacy of an old aunt, which had been intended for pin money not household expenses. He always took it away from her immediately, anyway.

Andrew waved her objections aside. 'I won't *let* it go wrong. Now, I really must start clearing out my shed and you will have to start on the house because we're sailing next month. We can only take essential items with us – and no furniture. It's quite providential that Liza has left, really, but Maggie will be coming with us, of course. She's been with us for fifteen years and I'm sure she won't leave us in the lurch, so I've booked her a passage, too.'

Dorothy sat motionless for a long time after he'd left, feeling stiff and shocked. This was worse than anything he had done before, far worse. She decided to say nothing to Kitty yet, dreading her daughter's reaction, but went to confide in Maggie, who stared at her in horror and burst into tears.

'Mrs P., he never!'

Dorothy could only nod unhappily. 'You will come with us, won't you, Maggie?'

'How can I? I have Mam to think of – and my sisters. How can I?'

That evening, after their daughter had gone to bed, Dorothy tried once more. 'Andrew, I've been thinking. It'd make so much more sense for you to go out to Australia first and – and investigate the situation. Kitty and I can go and stay with my sister. You know how Nora dotes on the girl. She'll have us for sure.' And would make them pay for it in small services and regularly expressed gratitude, but it'd be worth it.

He glared at her. 'Certainly not! You're my wife and you're coming with me. So is our daughter. Have you told her about it yet?'

'N-no.'

'Then I'll tell her myself in the morning.'

The news made Kitty throw a tantrum and she continued to weep at regular intervals till her eyes were puffy and her nose red. Dorothy argued, scolded and cajoled, trying every way she could think of to make her husband see reason, especially as Maggie was definitely not coming with them. But nothing they did or said could move him from his decision.

It wasn't often she wept, but she did now, and just as bitterly as fifteen-year-old Kitty.

But although their tears drove Andrew from the house into the garden he loved and cared for himself, they did not make him change his mind.

When Liza's mother was well enough to come down and sit on the rocking chair in the kitchen, things improved a little in Underby Street. Mary Docherty was as gentle and ineffective as ever, but Con would not let anyone except himself bully his wife, so she was able to protect the younger children a bit from her two eldest sons and share out the food more fairly, too.

One evening a few days afterwards Da came into the back room, beaming broadly, and beckoned to Liza. 'Come into the shop a minute, will ye, girl? I've some good news for you.'

She brightened and followed him, hoping he'd got her place back. He hadn't found the clothes she'd hidden, and she was sure Mrs P. would understand if she didn't have all her old things.

'Come over here to the light.' He grabbed her and ran his

hand down her body in a way that made her yelp in protest and try to pull away. 'Stand still, will ye!' he roared, feeling the swell of her breasts in a dispassionate way, pinching the flesh of her upper arms, then turning her round first one way, then the other. After the initial shock she didn't dare protest, because Con Docherty was very much master in his own house, and even Niall and Dermott did not dare defy him.

As he pushed her away, he pursed his lips, put his head on one side and asked, 'How old are ye now?'

'Eighteen.'

He nodded. 'Thought so. You're a woman growed, that's for sure.'

What had got into him tonight? When had he ever cared about her? It was sons who mattered to him, not daughters.

'Teddy Marshall's wife has been dead these two months now. 'Tis hard for a man on his own. He needs a woman to look after things for him.' He smiled knowingly as he added, 'And, of course, to warm his bed.'

Liza stared at him in horror, guessing what was coming next.

'So I told him he could wed you. I could see he fancied you when he came into the shop last week. It'll be better for you than going off to work for that uppity Pringle woman. You'll have your own house and Teddy's a good provider. He's comin' over to see you in a few minutes. We'll fix it all up then.' He stared at her again, then added abruptly, 'You'd better do something with your hair, though, instead of scraping it back in a bun like an old woman. There's some ribbons in the bottom drawer. Use one of them.' His eyes softened. 'You've a fine head of hair on you. You're black Irish, like your mother's side of the family. Good lookers, the Brennans.' He made a fist and stared down at it admiringly, 'Though the Dochertys are built stronger.'

Liza didn't move for a moment – couldn't! – and when she found her voice again, it came out nearer to a squeak. 'But Da, Mr Marshall's *old*!'

He scowled. 'He's no more than thirty-five. Younger than me. A man's in his prime at thirty-five, let me tell you, young lady. It's women as fade after thirty. Look at your mother. She once had rosy cheeks an' bright blue eyes just like yours.'

He gazed into the distance for a moment, then added more softly, 'And Mary was prettier than you'll ever be – you're too sharp-featured, you are – though you wouldn't think it to look at her now.'

Liza sought desperately for some way to change his mind. 'But, Da, I don't want to marry *anyone* yet.' Especially not Mr Marshall. He was another large, heavy-handed man, very like her father only uglier. Mrs Marshall had died in childbed recently and the latest baby with her, but he had three sons and, young as they were, they were already shaping up to be bullies. Liza's little brother Kieran was absolutely terrified of them. She shuddered at the memory of how Mr Marshall had caught her in a corner and rubbed himself against her last time he came into the shop. It had made her feel sick and she'd expected her father to protest, but he hadn't. Now she understood what that had all been about. It was the real reason she'd been brought home from Mrs Pringle's. No doubt Mr Marshall was slipping her father some money to hurry things up. Well, she wasn't going to agree to it. Oh, no!

Her father nudged her. ''Tis the best chance you're ever likely to get. You'll be set for life. Young men don't have money like the older ones do.'

'I won't do it.'

He scowled at her. 'Don't be stupid, girl! Have a bit of sense for once!'

There was the sound of clogs on the road outside and the little brass doorbell on its wobbly curled spring tinkled wildly. Con turned round smiling. 'There you are, lad. I was just tellin' my lass that you're to wed her.'

Teddy Marshall nodded. 'Good.' But his eyes were on Liza, raking up and down her body.

She stared back at him in horror. He had thinning brown hair and a lumpy nose, and always smelled sour, as if he washed even less than her father did. He had beaten his other wife, given her many a bruise, broken her arm once – everyone knew that.

'I'm sorry, but I don't want to get wed,' she said as firmly as she could manage, because inside she was shivering with fear at the thought of defying Da.

Both men ignored her.

'I'll go and see the priest tomorrow morning, then, shall I?' Teddy said over her head.

'Aye. Sooner it's done the better. Our Nancy's twelve. She can take over helpin' me in the shop an' my Mary will just have to pull herself together.'

'But, Da—'

Con turned to his daughter. 'We'll have no more silliness from you, my girl. You'll do as I tell you or you'll be feeling the back of me hand, so you will.'

She shook her head. 'I'm sorry, but I don't want to marry anyone.' She nodded to the other man and tried to soften her refusal. 'Thanks all the same, Mr Marshall.'

Da came over and clouted her, then pushed her towards his friend. 'Stay here and talk to Teddy. He'll soon change your mind. I have to see your mam about something.' He was gone before she could protest.

Mr Marshall moved swiftly to grab her. Liza shrieked and tried to pull away but he ignored that and began to fumble with her body, his fingers tweaking her nipples. She wriggled and tried to kick him but he was so much bigger than she was that she felt like a toy in the hands of a clumsy child.

'I won't do it!' she panted, glaring up at him. 'No one can make me say yes in church. Let *go* of me!'

'You will do it,' Marshall said. 'And we can so make you.' Again his fingers nipped and tweaked, and she couldn't help crying out in pain.

When he started to lift her skirt, however, there was a cough behind them and her father said, 'That's enough, lad. A bit of a feel's one thing, but you don't get anything else afore you're wed. She's a good girl, my Liza is, an' she's staying untouched till Father Michael has married you.'

Teddy let go of Liza, breathing deeply and adjusting his trousers. 'Well, let's get it done quick, then.'

'Come away to the pub with ye and we'll discuss the details. A sup or two of ale an' you'll last out a bit longer.'

The two men laughed and went out together, but Marshall turned at the door to stare across at the white-faced, trembling girl. 'I'm looking forward very much to makin' a woman of you, Liza Docherty.'

She shook her head, holding herself upright until they'd left, then she drew in a long, sobbing breath. Mr Marshall's clogs make a loud clopping noise he walked away, her father's shoes sounding like a faint echo beside them. He always made a lot of noise, Mr Marshall did. And his sons used their iron-tipped clogs to terrorise other kids. They'd be hell on a young step-mother, those three would.

She couldn't seem to move again until the sound of the men's footsteps had died right away down the bottom of the street and only then did her mother slip into the shop to join her. 'He told you, did he, love?'

Liza smeared away the tears. 'You knew what he was planning, Mam – *You knew!*'

Mary's voice sounded weary. 'He only told me this morning.'

'Why didn't you warn me?'

'What good would that have done?'

'It'd maybe have given me time to think of something. I tell you flat, Mam: I won't marry Mr Marshall.'

Mary looked at her daughter. 'Your da will make you.' Her voice was toneless, as if she didn't care about that or anything else.

Liza stared at her. Married to Mr Marshall, she'd soon look like this. His other wife had done. Beaten. Hopeless. At that moment, she determined that she'd do anything, even run away from home, if necessary, to escape such a fate.

'Liza, love—'

'I won't marry him,' she said again, then shouted, 'I won't. *I won't!*' But the piles of old clothes muffled the words so that they faded to nothing and her mother had already shuffled away into the back room. 'I won't, though,' Liza whispered, then sniffed away the tears that were still threatening before following her mam.

14

CHAPTER TWO

━━━━◆>◆◇◆<◆━━━━

Josiah looked at his father and flinched from the expression of utter disgust on Saul Ludlam's face. That sonorous voice sounded good when reading the lessons in church, but battered at your ears like a hammer when it was used inside a house.

'Were it not for your mother, I'd throw you out now!'

Josiah drew in a breath in which relief that he was not to be disowned was mingled with the anger that had been building in him for the past few years. Damn his father anyway! Who did he think he was, forcing his sons to marry the women he had chosen for them, whether they fancied them or not, then keeping them all living at home, so that even a huge house like Pendleworth Hall seemed to be permanently overflowing with resentful adults and their frustrations?

To make matters worse, Saul Ludlam doled out money to his family in dribs and drabs, so that you had to ask him for extra when you had any big expenses. He seemed to expect his three grown-up sons, two of them fathers themselves, to behave like schoolboys still, and had them working meekly in the family businesses, obeying his every word. Matthew and Isaac did not appear to mind this, but Josiah hated the man who had sired him and the life he was forced to live here – and despised himself for not doing something about it.

His father's voice boomed out again, emphasised by a thump on the desk. 'Well, sir? Have you no answer for me?'

'I'm grateful for your – your forbearance.' Even as he spoke Josiah felt like puking at the hypocrisy of his father, who was a womaniser and had betrayed his gentle wife many a time, but still acted as if he led a blameless life. However, if a soft word or two would gain him some relief from his father's anger, then Josiah would bite his tongue till it bled, for without money of his own, he was helpless.

'Save your damned gratitude for your mother. It's she who went down on her knees to beg me not to throw you out.' Saul breathed in deeply. 'As I'd still like to do. As I may still do if anyone at the church finds out—'

The clock ticked loudly as Josiah waited for his punishment to be pronounced. There was always retribution when anyone upset his father. The man was an expert at devising ways of paying you back if you offended him.

'Are you listening to me, Josiah?'

'Yes, sir. And – and I'm grateful for the chance to make amends.'

Saul's voice became even louder. '*Amends?* There is no possible way you can make amends so far as I'm concerned. The only way to save this family from scandal and disgrace is to get rid of you. Which is what I intend to do.'

'Sir?'

'So I'm sending you,' he paused to prolong the agony, then just as the silence seemed to have been going on for ever said with great relish, 'to Australia.' He smiled in satisfaction at the look of shock and horror on his son's face before adding, 'It's the farthest place I know of. They'll take almost anybody as a free settler, it seems. Even you.' He was grateful to Andrew Pringle for giving him the idea.

Reeling in shock, Josiah forgot to mind his tongue. '*Australia!* What the hell do you think I'll do with myself there? I'll not go.'

'That's your choice. But you'll agree to go to Australia or you'll get out of my house today.' Saul leaned back against the soft brown leather of his high-backed chair, arms folded, smiling.

Again silence hung heavy between them, then Josiah burst out, 'Christ, you mean it, don't you?'

'Do not take the Lord's name in vain.' Saul Ludlam leaned forward, hands resting on the broad mahogany desk. He was clearly well satisfied with his son's reaction. 'I don't care what you do out there, actually, but be very sure, Josiah, that if you set one foot in this country again, I will myself denounce you to the authorities – who will no doubt jail you.'

Josiah's throat was laced with the acid frustration of not being able to disobey this command to go into exile, for even

16

his wife's generous dowry had been paid to his father by the Rawleys and then 'invested' in the family business. He could not speak, could not even think for a moment, as he fought for control over his anger.

Smiling broadly, Saul tossed another piece of information at him. 'I've booked you a passage next month on the *Louisa Jane* and I'll give you enough money to buy yourself a piece of land out there. You've always liked being outdoors. Farming should suit you.'

'Farming?'

'What else?'

'But I know nothing whatsoever about farming.'

'I'm aware of that, so I intend to send Benedict Caine out to Australia with you as well, if only for Catherine's sake. It's her duty to go with her husband, but I'll not see her want. He's a born troublemaker, Caine is, and I shall be glad to have him off the estate, but he knows about farming and can teach you.'

'Surely there's something else I can do, somewhere else I can go? America, maybe? There'll be much more opportunity for a man like me in America and—'

'It's Australia or nothing. And I've chosen farming because it seems to me a healthy sort of life.' Saul smiled, that tight smile which meant he had the upper hand on someone and was relishing it. 'You'll have to work hard, mind, if you expect to eat once your start-up money has run out – and don't think I'll be over-generous with you, either. You'll be given enough to manage on and no more.'

Josiah had to get away from the hatred in his father's eyes, so he moved over to the window, trying to speak calmly. 'Did it not occur to you that I might miss Pendleworth?' He stared out of the window at the landscape he truly loved, cursing once again the fate that had made him only the third son, the one who stood not a chance of inheriting the estate, especially now that both his brothers had produced sons of their own.

More words battered him from behind. 'It matters nothing to me what you do or do not miss, sir.'

Josiah closed his eyes, terrified he might start to weep. As usual, his father was making it impossible to do other than accede to his wishes. Only this time his wishes were quite terrifying.

'I'm also doing this for Catherine, who does not deserve a

17

husband like you. You might even try to make a fresh start in the colonies, build a decent life. Have children.'

Josiah could not think what to say to that. His father had chosen his wife for him and then appropriated the money that came with her. Neither of them had had any say in the marriage, though he had discovered later that Catherine had been willing enough. But *he* had not been willing, as he had made plain on their wedding night. That had upset her then and continued to hurt her, he knew and was sorry for. But although he still slept on a truckle bed in her dressing room, the two of them had become good friends, for they had known each other since childhood and she was more like a sister to him. Sometimes, when his spirits sank and the world seemed filled only with misery, she was all that kept him from ending his life.

'Are you paying attention to what I'm saying, Josiah!'

He nodded, wondering desperately how to get out of this. There had to be a way. His mother perhaps. Or Catherine's father. If there was, he'd surely find it.

'I shall supply you with seeds and tools, whatever a farmer needs to make a start out there. After that, it's up to you whether you survive or not.'

'Father, please—' Josiah's voice cracked and the plea died on his lips at the sight of the determined expression on his father's face.

'Of course, if you're short of money, there is one way you could earn more from me . . .' Saul paused and waited.

So Josiah asked, 'How?' because he might as well know the worst.

'On the day your first child is born, I'll send you five hundred pounds, with a further two hundred for every child born thereafter.' Saul gave a mirthless chuckle, his expression saying clearly that he did not expect this to happen, then pulled out his big gold pocket watch and consulted it. 'You had better go and inform Catherine of what has been decided. I shall tell your mother myself, and she will no doubt spend the rest of the day weeping.'

'And Benedict Caine? Does he know what you intend for him?' Was this a possible way of getting the arrangements changed?

No, Benedict was also a third son. His father had a lease

on Northbrook Farm, the largest property on the Pendleworth estate. Martin Caine would no doubt take over the farm when his father grew too old. Paul, the middle brother, had moved into Lancaster to work as a cabinet maker like his maternal grandfather. Benedict had a feel for woodwork, too, and had done clever carvings when he was a boy, but like his father he loved the land and so had stayed at Northbrook. He was a handsome fellow, much sought after by the local girls, but he'd not married. Wise of him. Women were more trouble than they were worth.

Saul Ludlam was already shuffling some papers. 'Caine has not yet been informed of my plans.'

'What if he doesn't want to come to Australia with me?'

'Oh, he'll come. I'll make it impossible for him to refuse – though I don't mind sweetening the pill a little if he does as I wish.' Saul stood up.

The interview was clearly at an end and Josiah knew he'd only make matters worse if he stayed and continued to argue, so he walked out and made for the rose garden to think things through before telling Catherine. There must be a way to get out of this. There must!

Over supper that night Jack Caine looked down the table at his youngest son. 'Mr Ludlam wants to see you tomorrow morning, Benedict. Nine o'clock sharp at the house.'

'Me?'

'Aye. Stopped his carriage to tell me today, he did.'

Benedict frowned. 'What the hell does that old devil want now?'

Jack shrugged.

'Eh, lad, what've you been doing?' his mother asked. 'You know how angry Mr Ludlam was when you started talking to the estate workers, saying they should be paid more money. You haven't been doing it again, have you?'

'I've done nothing. And he *ought* to pay them more. Every other employer round here does, even that old sod Rawley.'

'Mr Ludlam doesn't let his workers want. He gives them food and such when times are hard.'

'Folk could buy what they needed themselves if he paid

them a fair wage. It'd not cost him any more. He just does it that way because he likes to control what everyone on the estate does.'

'Now, don't you be speaking pertly to him tomorrow, son!' Jack Caine pleaded. 'He *is* our landlord and – and the farm lease is up for renewal next year.'

Benedict breathed deeply. 'He must have said something about what he wanted. Have you no idea at all?'

Jack shook his head, but Benedict could see that his father was avoiding his eyes. 'Tell me what you know, at least.'

But his father would say nothing. The thing Jack Caine was most afraid of in the whole world was losing his farm, so he took great care not to anger Saul Ludlam. If his landlord had told him to walk round the town naked, he would have done even that to keep the farm. The Caines had lived here for well over a hundred years, though the Ludlams had only been at the big house for fifty years or so, and Benedict knew it would kill his father to move elsewhere.

He sighed. 'All right. I'll go and see him tomorrow.'

'Well, see that you smarten yourself up a bit first,' his mother pleaded. 'Show some respect.'

Liza saw the poster when she went shopping for her mother. It was stuck in the window of Mrs Baxter's drapery shop near the market, and had slid a bit sideways. She stopped to read it, but had to ask a passer-by to explain the long words. The kindly old gentleman walked on afterwards, but Liza lingered, staring at the big black words and mouthing them again:

FEMALE EMIGRATION TO AUSTRALIA

*SERVANTS OF RESPECTABLE
CHARACTER REQUIRED*

PASSAGE PAID FOR SUITABLE YOUNG WOMEN

REFERENCES ESSENTIAL

She wished she could read better, but had not been allowed to go to school for long, just enough to learn her letters and fumble through a few of the easier reading books. Then she'd had to stay home and help out.

When a young man stopped to study the poster, she plucked up her courage and asked him where Australia was.

'Right on the other side of the world, love. You can't get much further away from England than Australia.' He stared at the poster longingly for a minute more then walked on.

'He'd never be able to find me there.' For a moment Liza allowed herself to dream of getting a position as maid to some nice family, sailing off across the sea and never seeing her father or Mr Marshall again – then reality hit home, as it always did. When you were the daughter of Con Docherty, dreams didn't hold up for long in the harsh light of day.

'I'd go if I could, though!' she told the poster. Balancing the heavy shopping basket on one hip, she lingered to spell through the details of the ship and the cost to migrants for a third time, anything to delay returning home. She had taken over the marketing for her mother and this was the only bit of freedom she had.

She sighed. Da and Mr Marshall had gone ahead and booked the wedding with Father Michael, in spite of what she'd said. Her da had thumped her a couple of times when she'd continued to refuse to marry his friend, but Liza wasn't going to change her mind. Oh, no. The priest had come to the house to see her, but Da had stayed with them and she hadn't been able to speak openly, and the Father had said children should obey their parents. Only she wasn't a child now, and she wasn't going to let Da ruin her whole life.

The words on the poster blurred as tears filled Liza's eyes and she scowled down at the new brown skirt and blue bodice that didn't match it in any way. They had smelt rank with sweat when her father tossed them at her, though she'd washed them since then. What was she going to do? Mam was no help, just kept begging her to do as Da asked, saying he knew best and Mr Marshall was a good earner, which was the main thing for a woman.

Liza could see nothing for it but to run away – only how did you do that without any money?

She glanced at the bank clock down the street. *Five more minutes*, she promised herself. *Then I'll go back.*

'Fem-ale ser-vants of re-re . . .' she began again.

'Respectable character.' A voice next to her completed the phrase.

She looked round to see Mrs P. standing there.

'How are you, my dear? And your mother? Is she better?'

'I'm all right, thank you, Mrs P. And Mam's a lot better now.'

'Are you thinking of going to Australia, then?' Dorothy tried to keep her voice light and teasing, but she had begun to hate the very sound of that word.

'I'd be off there tomorrow, if I could.'

'You would? I'm – I'm going there myself soon.'

Liza stared at her in surprise. 'You never said owt about that, ma'am.'

'Mr Pringle has – arranged it. He's set his heart on it.'

'Oh.' No need for further explanations. Liza had seen Mr Pringle get these sudden enthusiasms – and usually it was Mrs P. who suffered.

'Um – Maggie has refused to come with me, so I'm looking for another maid to take her place.'

'You are?' Hope flared briefly in Liza, then faded as she thought of Da's determination to marry her off.

'Yes. I need a sensible girl, not one with her head in the clouds. Did you really mean what you said, my dear?'

'Oh, yes. I'd love to go there.' Anywhere far enough from Pendleworth would do, actually.

'Would you like to come with us, then?' Liza was cheerful and hard-working; strong, too, for all she was so slender.

'I'd love to – only Da wouldn't let me.'

'I could come and see your parents myself. Perhaps if I talked to them?'

'No. You see, the reason Da took me away from you was because he wants me to marry his friend. Only Mr Marshall's thirty-five and,' Liza grimaced, 'he makes me feel sick when he touches me.'

Dorothy felt a surge of sympathy. She did not like the father at all. Con Docherty was a harsh, bitter sort of man. 'You'll have to say no to this Mr Marshall, then.'

Tears filled Liza's eyes and she couldn't stop them spilling down her cheeks. 'I have done, but they won't listen. They've gone an' arranged the wedding.' She shivered. 'Da said last night he'd *make* me do it.' She looked pleadingly at her companion. 'My only chance is to run away, Mrs P., but I don't have any money. You know how Da always took my wages. He never gives us a farthing, just spends all he earns on drinking with his friends.'

Dorothy looked at her thoughtfully. Liza was much thinner now, as if she wasn't eating properly. Her vivid blue eyes had lost their sparkle and even the dark, wavy hair, tied neatly back, seemed duller, with less bounce.

As usual, Andrew was leaving the practical details of selling up and packing to his wife. He was blithely certain they'd make their fortunes in Australia, or at least be able to make his small income go further for apparently the authorities sold land there very cheaply. Dorothy wasn't sure about anything and to risk all they owned on a wild venture like this made her shiver sometimes in the long, wakeful hours of the night.

She knew she shouldn't encourage any girl to run away from her family, but all the others she'd asked to come out as her maid to replace Maggie had refused point-blank. 'Would you *really* like to go to Australia?'

Liza's heart began to pound as hope surged through her. 'I'd go anywhere to get away from my father. And – and I'd work my fingers to the bone for someone who saved me from marrying Mr Marshall. Oh, Mrs P., do take me with you! *Please!* You know I'm a hard worker.'

'Well – I'll think about it. And you should think about it, too. Let's meet here next week on market day and you can give me your answer then?'

'I can give it you now. I definitely want to go.'

But Dorothy's conscience would not let her accept immediately. 'No, dear. You must have a really good think about such a big step. Perhaps you should talk to your mother?'

'I can't. She'd tell Da. She always does.'

'Well, I still want you to think things over carefully. You might never see your family again, if you went, you know.'

'That'd suit me just fine.'

Dorothy looked at her sadly. 'Oh, Liza, is it that bad at home?'

'Yes, Mrs P., it is. Worse.'

'Well, then, I'll see you here next week.'

Liza watched her former mistress walk away, then sent up a quick prayer that Mrs P. would not change her mind during the coming week, because as far as she could see, this was her only hope of getting away. She didn't care if she sailed to Australia or flew to the moon. A maid's life would be the same wherever she worked, surely? And she definitely didn't care if she never saw her father or elder brothers again as long as she lived. She hated them.

Hope continued to well inside her as she walked home. The wedding wasn't for another couple of weeks. With a bit of luck, she'd be well away by then.

CHAPTER THREE

After the interview with his father Josiah went up to his bedroom. His wife Catherine was resting on a chaise-longue near the window, staring out across the small lake at the immaculate gardens. The expression of underlying sadness that he had placed on her face soon after their marriage was plain to see. Her soft blond hair looked lifeless beneath the delicate lace cap and her face seemed thinner.

'Are you feeling all right, my dear?' he asked. 'You look tired.'

'Never mind me. What's happened, Jos dear? I could hear your father shouting from here.'

He walked across to fiddle with the ornaments on the window sill. 'He's found out about – about me.'

She gasped and pressed one hand against her breast, holding in the pain, concentrating on his needs. Heaven help her, she loved him and always had done, ever since she was a little girl. If the only way she could have him was by being his friend instead of a true wife, well, she was prepared to do even that.

When he looked up, she stretched out her arm and he came to sit on the edge of her sofa, clasping her hand in his large warm one. 'Tell me, Jos.'

'He's sending me away.'

Her voice was barely audible, a mere sigh. 'Where to?'

'As far away as he possibly can.' He hesitated, but she would have to know. 'To Australia, actually.'

Her face lost every vestige of colour. 'Jos, no!'

'I'm afraid so, and – and I doubt he'll change his mind, Cat. He wants me out of sight as well as out of mind. Permanently.' He began to fiddle with the wedding ring on her finger, frowning to see how loose it had become. 'Maybe this is the time for you to disown me? You're young enough to find yourself another husband.'

She shook her head, not needing to think about that. 'No, never. You're my husband, Jos. For better, for worse. And – and you're my friend, too. I don't want to marry anyone else.'

He raised the hand to his lips and kissed it, the only sort of kiss he ever offered her voluntarily. 'Oh, hell, Cat, what am I going to do? He intends to turn me into a farmer. A bloody farmer, for heaven's sake! What do I know about farming? Or want to know?'

Then he slid to the floor, buried his face in her lap and began to weep, great racking sobs. 'It will mean – Cat, I shall never see Pendleworth again.'

Her eyes were bleak, but she continued stroking his head. She had grown up on the next estate and she, too, loved the district: the stark moors that girded the eastern side of town, the patches of woodland in sheltered spots lower down, and the little moorland streams in which she'd paddled as a child. Going away would hurt her as much as it would him, but she didn't say that, didn't add to his burden. In some ways, Jos was like a boy, the son she would never have.

'We'll have to build a new Pendleworth out there in the colonies,' she suggested as his grief abated.

He looked up then, his cheeks still moist with tears but his interest caught by the idea. And although he grew gloomy again, settling into one of his darkest moods ever, she knew her idea had caught his interest and was relieved that she had given him something to cling to.

She dressed carefully for dinner that evening, although she was not feeling well and had intended to eat in her room. If anyone could get more money out of Saul Ludlam, it was she, and she meant to do her best. She'd approach her own father, too. Perhaps she could pretend she was carrying a child? Yes, that was it. Her family would be delighted and if she hinted a little, her mother would persuade her father to give her some extra money. It would be hardest to lie to her younger brother. She and Nick were very close and always had been, given the sort of man their father was, proud of his ancient name and place in the county and harsh in his treatment of anyone who fell below his exacting standards, which any lad as lively as Nick was bound to do.

If she could just help Jos make a decent start in Australia, she would feel better about everything else, would feel her life had not been totally in vain.

The following morning, Benedict watched the last cow's bony backside sway down the muddy path towards the shippon, where his sister-in-law and the dairymaid would be waiting to do the milking. He closed the gate, then leaned on it to set his thoughts in order. He knew he couldn't stay here much longer. He'd find out what Mr Ludlam wanted, do it for his family's sake, then look round for a small farm to rent. There must be somewhere he could get a start – but not on Ludlam land. He'd had enough of kow-towing to that old skinflint. And he didn't want one of those barren little moorland places, either. They were cheap enough to rent, for the obvious reason that the land was sour stuff where beasts didn't thrive and you couldn't make a decent living for your family. There had to be something else, some other way of getting himself a farm.

He'd been saving his money for a while now, earning extra by finishing bits and pieces of furniture for his brother, Paul, when they had a rush on. He also had the hundred pounds his great-uncle had left him sitting in the savings bank. And if he married Grace Newton, which he was seriously considering, he knew she'd bring him something as well. At twenty-six he was more than ready to leave home, but he would need a wife if he was to run his own farm. Grace was a skilled dairywoman and had a pleasant nature, even if she didn't make his blood run hot as one or two other young women had, usually women of the wrong sort for a farmer's wife.

A few years ago he'd seen Martin get wed in a hurry because Tabby was expecting, since when he'd watched the love between them fade and his brother settle down to indifference and even annoyance at a wife who had to be taught all her duties on the farm by his mother and who still had less skill in the dairy than the maid they employed. Hah! Martin had always been stupid. Paul had been wiser, getting apprenticed to a carpenter and marrying his master's daughter. He was independent now, the lucky sod. Well, Benedict wasn't going to get trapped by a pretty face, but was going to plan his life sensibly.

Over breakfast he looked down the table at his only sister and exchanged smiles with her. He'd miss Jenny greatly, wherever he went. She was a nice lass, his little sister, the child of his parents' old age, only fourteen and young for her age. Her sunny nature lit up the whole house and she was the only one he could really talk to. He'd already warned his father not to let her go into service at the Hall if she turned out as pretty as she promised, but Jack, who never visited the alehouse, simply wouldn't listen to gossip about the landowner and insisted Mr Ludlam wasn't like that. Well, other folk knew better and a few maids had left the Hall suddenly over the years with swelling bellies.

Later Benedict went upstairs to wash himself all over and change into his Sunday clothes. He wasn't going to face Saul Ludlam dressed like a farm labourer or smelling like one, either. He'd rather not face the man at all. The landowner was a shifty old devil, full of nasty tricks, and dealt as harshly with his own family as with his servants and tenants. Jack Caine was a far better father, for all his weakness.

Perversely, Benedict went to knock on the front door of Pendleworth Hall, not the rear servants' entrance.

The butler opened it, goggled to see who it was and hissed, 'Get round the back, you fool! Who do you think you are, coming to the front?'

Benedict put one foot in the door. 'I'm here by invitation of Mr Ludlam.'

'The master didn't invite such as you to use his front door.'

For a moment Benedict hesitated, then his anger at being summoned like a schoolboy overflowed and he pressed one hand against the door, holding it open easily. 'I'll come in this way or not at all. And then you can explain to your master why I'm not there, if you like.'

After a quick glance round and a hiss of indecision, Mattley jerked his head and held the door open wider.

Benedict strolled inside, staring round and enjoying the richness of his surroundings. What must it be like to live in such luxury, to have everything you wanted simply by ringing a bell and giving an order? When Catherine Ludlam came out of a room to the right, he nodded a greeting. He'd known her as a child, because they'd often met at the stream which divided the Caines' farm from her family's estate. She had loved to paddle in the clear water and been happy to talk to him in those days. Children were not as snobbish about who they associated with as adults were.

He frowned as he studied her blue silk gown with its huge bell of a skirt and the delicate lace trimming round the neck. When had she grown so thin? She nodded to him and disappeared up the stairs as he followed the butler towards the back of the hall. He was left waiting on a wooden bench in the corridor outside the office where the master of the house received his tenants.

Of course Ludlam was late. Probably on purpose. Benedict stifled a sigh, got up and went over to the window to look out at the beautiful gardens, famous in the district. Children were going hungry but Ludlam spent his money on lawns and flower beds, not to mention the folly of the new lake. He made a sound of disgust in his throat.

'My garden doesn't please you, Caine?'

He swung round. No matter how often you decided you wouldn't kow-tow to him any more, there was something about Saul Ludlam, some force or power, that made even the gentry tread warily with him. 'Aye, sir. It's beautiful. But it'd please me still more if it grew food for the hungry.'

'Well, it wouldn't please me to look at rows of cabbages. Come through.'

Benedict entered the large, comfortable study and moved towards the chair which had been set ready, waiting for Saul to sit down on the big leather-covered chair before he lowered his own backside on to the hard wooden seat.

Saul stared across the desk at him, looking thoughtful, saying nothing.

Benedict stared back at the handsome old face, with its mane of white hair, and waited.

In the end Saul broke the silence. 'Your father's lease is due for renewal next year.'

'Yes.' Benedict's heart sank. This was the only threat which might work and Ludlam had used it straight away. What could he want doing that needed prefacing by a threat?

'I am prepared to renew the lease only upon certain conditions.'

'What's that got to do with me?'

'Your agreement to a little plan of mine is one of the conditions.'

Benedict stilled. 'Oh?'

'Well, Caine?'

'I'm waiting to hear what the plan is before I agree to it.' He didn't say 'sir'. He was tired of saying 'sir' to this arrogant bastard.

'Nothing to your disadvantage. Come! I require your unconditional agreement.'

Benedict shook his head. 'I'm happy to listen to your proposal, Mr Ludlam, but I can't agree without knowing what your proposition is.'

'Even though your father may be dispossessed if you do not agree?'

'Even so. I'm not my father's keeper and it's not my inheritance that's threatened.'

Saul breathed in deeply and stared down at his steepled hands.

When he looked up again, Benedict felt a shiver run down his spine, so determined was the other man's expression.

'Listen, then. My son, Josiah, is emigrating to Australia. He is to take up some land there, since he can never inherit Pendleworth Hall. But as he knows little about farming, I have decided that you shall accompany him there to help him settle.'

Benedict gaped for a moment, then sucked in enough air to refuse on the spot. But before he could do more than open his mouth, Mr Ludlam held up one hand, so he waited.

'I hope you'll see this as a good opportunity. Like Josiah, you are a younger son with your way to make in the world.'

Benedict folded his arms. 'I have no desire whatsoever to leave England.'

Saul's eyes narrowed in calculation. 'If you do as I wish, I am prepared to give you enough money to buy a smallholding in Australia for yourself, though it will be on condition that you stay with my son until he has his farm established, say for five years.'

30

Benedict let out a long, slow breath. How had the old devil known he was hungry for land? Trust Ludlam to find a weak spot and push. 'How much money would that be?'

'A hundred pounds.'

'It's not nearly enough.'

Ah, Saul thought, caught him! But he didn't smile, merely continued to watch the young man who was one of the new breed of independent thrusters whom he heartily detested, men who didn't know their place in the world. 'And how much would you consider adequate payment, then, Caine?'

'I'd have to find out what land costs out there – and I'd need enough money for tools as well.'

Saul had not expected the man to accept his first offer. 'We might come to some agreement about that, though you needn't think you can push me too far. And I would require your written promise to abide by my conditions.'

'My word would be good enough if I gave it.'

'I prefer agreements to be made in writing. Go away and do your sums, then. Come back to me with a list of your needs as soon as you can – within a few days at most – and we'll talk again. The ship sails next month. I want you on it.'

As he was shown out of the back door, Benedict let out his surprise in a soundless whistle. This could, indeed, be an opportunity worth seizing. He'd seen a poster about emigration to Australia in a shop window in Pendleworth. He'd go and find it again, study it carefully before he went home. Tomorrow he'd begin gathering information.

Surely things couldn't be all that different in Australia? Surely you could grow to love a piece of land wherever it was if you worked on it – if it actually belonged to you?

Dorothy Pringle was packing the china from the parlour, studying each piece as she decided whether to take it to Australia. She had little idea what that distant country was really like, and wasn't sure her husband was much better informed. Hotter than England, people said. Well, she hated the cold, so that could be an advantage.

She sighed, admitting to herself how worried she was. Andrew's inheritance had never been large, but they could have lived on it in reasonable comfort if he had not lost it bit by bit on worthless investments and silly enthusiasms. She looked round the room, tears filling her eyes. She didn't want to go anywhere, but they couldn't have stayed here for much longer anyway because they simply couldn't afford to keep the place up. The roof needed repairing and every piece of furniture was old and worn. Only the gardens were in good condition because, though they couldn't afford a gardener, Andrew loved working outdoors and produced most of their fruit and vegetables himself.

Kitty came in. 'Maggie's weeping again, Mother. And she hasn't done the dishes yet.'

Dorothy pulled herself together and turned to her daughter. 'Then you can do them instead and send her to me.'

'But—'

'Do as I say without arguing for once!'

Kitty flounced out, her soft brown curls bobbing indignantly, her thin young body stiff with indignation. She had begged to be allowed to stay with her Aunt Nora, who was childless and would have loved to have her, but Andrew had remained stubborn. Kitty was *his* daughter, she was staying with him and that was that.

Maggie came into the little parlour, her eyes reddened and a damp handkerchief clutched in one hand. 'I can't believe you're really going, Mrs P! I wish I could come with you, I really do.'

'Oh, Maggie!' Dorothy's anger faded and she went across to give the other woman a hug. For a moment they stood there, then she pushed the elderly maid away and said with false cheerfulness, 'We neither of us have much choice, it seems, so please try to cheer up. I'll make sure you have excellent references. Get back to your work now.'

Once she was on her own, Dorothy's smile faded. She would have only Liza to depend on now. Someone had told Andrew that if they didn't take their own servants with them, they'd have trouble finding any once they got to Australia. She couldn't imagine life without domestic help, was dreading what she would find in the colonies. She would have to insist that Kitty do more to help, and that would undoubtedly lead to constant arguments, because at fifteen her daughter was wilful as well as lazy.

★   ★   ★

Niall strolled into the shop one evening just as Liza was thinking of locking the door. Her father had long since gone to the pub and there hadn't been a customer for a while. She was hungry, but there were only a few pence in the till and she knew Da would have counted the takings, so she didn't dare take any money to buy herself, Nancy and Kieran some food.

'Sold much today?' Niall mocked.

'No.'

'You'll have to marry old Marshall, you know. With luck you'll be left a widow while you're still young enough to have a bit of fun.'

Liza stared at him in surprise. When had he ever taken an interest in her doings? 'I'm not marrying him and that's flat.'

'Dad will make you agree.'

She couldn't help touching the bruised cheek Da had given her the previous night when she was rude to Mr Marshall, then she looked straight at her eldest brother. 'He can hit me as much as he likes, I'll not change my mind.'

He cocked one eyebrow at her. 'Marshall's promised him some money once you're married.'

'I'd guessed that.'

'It'll make a big difference to Mam.'

She wasn't going to be caught like that. 'No, it won't! Da'll only drink it away, like he drinks the rest.' Her stomach growled.

Niall gave a snort of laughter. 'You're a fool, Liza. If you had any sense at all, you'd be cuddling up to Marshall, making sure he treats you right. You'll eat well with him, if nothing else.'

'He doesn't know how to treat a woman right, that one doesn't. He'll thump me like he did poor Fanny, so I might as well stay where I am. Food's not everything. Now go away an' let me lock up.'

'Marshall wants to speak to you. He asked if you'd nip across to see him for a moment. His lads have gone out and you won't be disturbed. I'll mind this place for you while you go, if you like.'

'No, thanks. I don't want to speak to him.' Or have him

33

fumble with her body again. 'I've said all I need to say – which is no.'

Niall reached out and grabbed her arm. 'Just have a few words with him, you stupid little fool.' He began to pull her towards the door.

She tried to shake his arm off, but he only held her more tightly and forced her across the shop. She shrieked for her mother, then remembered with a pang of terror that Mam had gone round to the church, so shrieked for her sister instead.

Nancy appeared in the doorway with Kieran huddled behind her. 'What are you doing, Niall? Let our Liza go.'

He paused long enough to say, 'Sod off, you two.' When the children didn't move, he roared, 'Bugger off, or I'll make you sorry!'

They retreated to the back room.

Liza grabbed the door handle and tried to brace her foot against the frame, but he jerked her away, laughing at how easy it was. 'You might as well come willingly. He'd prefer that, treat you better.'

She slid to the ground without answering and he jerked her to her feet by the back of her bodice, which made one of the seams rip.

Outside it was nearly dark and the other shops in their street were closed. With no one around and only a single gas lamp at the far end, the place seemed suddenly sinister. Liza opened her mouth to shout for help, but Niall clamped his hand across it, and since he was as big as Da now, she could not dislodge his hand any more than she could help moving where he wanted her to go.

On the far pavement, he shook her and muttered, 'Have a bit of sense, will you?'

She quietened down as if heeding his words, but when he took his hand away, yelled for help again.

He smothered the sound into a gargle of panic with his hand and kicked the door. 'Open up, quick!' It swung open and within seconds they were swallowed up in darkness that smelled of wood shavings and iron and paint, all the bits and pieces of the clogger's trade, plus the tobacco, chewing twist and toffees that Marshall's also sold.

Teddy loomed beside them, a dark shadow against the faint

34

light from the street filtering through the sides of the blinds. 'Give her here.'

'Money first.'

Niall yelped suddenly as Liza bit his hand. He clouted her across the ears, but didn't let go.

Marshall thrust something at him and the girl was passed from one to the other like a package. Then the door slammed and she was alone with the man she hated.

He didn't waste time on words but carried her out to the back room and threw her down on the old sofa. Without speaking he began to unbutton his trousers.

Only then did Liza realise what he intended. She jumped off the couch and ran towards the back door, but he laughed, a deep throaty sound. 'It's locked an' I've got the key.'

She turned to face him, back pressed against the door, fear making her whole body tremble. 'I won't marry you, whatever you do to me.'

'You'll have to. I'm good at getting childer, I am. Never miss. Fanny were a weakling an' lost more than she bore, but you're a nice strong lass. You'll give me more sons, strong 'uns, an' a daughter or two, mebbe.' He tried a little coaxing. 'You'll have a better life here than you have at home. Good food an' a warm house. What's wrong wi' weddin' me?'

Anger welled up. 'If I wed you, I'd get thumped and knocked about like your Fanny. I won't marry you, Teddy Marshall, no matter what you do to me.'

'You will, you know.' He slid his trousers down and she looked away from his great swollen thing, snatching at one of the pans hanging on the wall. Before she could get it off the hook, he grabbed her and tugged at her bodice. The other seam parted at his second pull and Liza shrieked as it exposed her breasts.

'Aaah,' he said softly, and bent his head to chew at them.

She screamed and fought all the way, but no one came to help her. And hitting him had as much effect as hitting a stone wall. Indeed, he didn't seem to hear what she was saying or feel the occasional blow she landed, just carried on hurting her till he got his own satisfaction.

When he had finished, he stood up and stretched, smiling down at the sobbing girl. 'That's only for starters, Liza girl. I've

35

been missing it something cruel. I'll be good as new in five minutes.' He went and poured himself a glass of beer, taking a long swallow from it then holding it out to her. 'Want a drink? Aw, come on, girl. It's done now. No use cryin' over spilt milk. You can enjoy it, too, if you give it a chance.'

She ignored him, huddling in pain and humiliation on the floor, sobbing loudly. Her clothes had all been ripped off in his urgency, her body hurt, but worst of all was her terror of him touching her again.

Which of course he did.

After that, he carried her up to his bedroom and tied her to the bed head. Liza continued to weep noisily. 'Ah, shut up that caterwauling, you stupid bitch! I'm going to marry you, aren't I?'

She raised her head then and looked him right in the eyes. 'I'll never marry you, Teddy Marshall, *never*! I'd rather throw myself in the canal.'

He just laughed. Within a few minutes he was snoring beside her.

She waited a while, then shouted for help, screaming at the top of her voice. No one came, though the neighbours must have heard her.

But her shouting woke him up and with a grunt of annoyance he tied a gag across her mouth, then rolled over again.

Da must know about this or he'd have come to get her. Tears trickled down Liza's cheeks, but she held on to one thought. She wouldn't marry this brute, not for anything in the world, not if they brought a hundred priests to see her. She wasn't spending a lifetime with a man who'd hurt her like this.

In the morning, Teddy woke her, laughing so much he couldn't move for a few minutes at the shock on her face as she realised where she was and what he was doing. Then he proceeded to rape her again.

And still no one came to help her.

Con Docherty lay abed till noon that Sunday, snoring, farting from time to time, and getting up once to piss out the rest of the previous night's ale into the chamber pot. When he

36

eventually stumbled downstairs, he grunted, 'Food. An' a cup o' tea. Sweet.' Throwing himself into his chair, he leaned his throbbing head on his hands and groaned.

When Mary brought him the cup, he stared round. 'Where's Liza? She knows I'll not have her goin' out an' leavin' all the work to you.'

Mary could not hold back a sob.

Con grabbed the cup, took a gulp and cursed her for making it too hot. Then he realised she was still weeping, stared at her and asked, 'What the hell's the matter with you?'

'Liza didn't come back at all last night. You shouldn't have done that, Con. It was a cruel way to persuade her.'

'Done what?' He jumped to his feet. 'And what do you mean, she didn't come home? Where the hell was she?'

Mary blinked at him in puzzlement. 'Why, Niall said it was your doing. He said you'd told him to take her across the road to Teddy Marshall's, leave her there and . . .' She clapped one hand to her mouth and burst into noisy sobs. 'Didn't you know about it? Oh, no, no! She's been there all night.' And Mary had spent half the night weeping silently into her pillow.

Con heaved himself to his feet, rage twisting his face, meaty hands clenched into fists. 'Where is he, the young devil?'

'He went out. Said he wouldn't be back till late. But Con, you—'

He drained his cup, thumped it down on the table and stood up. A minute later, the bell on the shop door tinkled and the outer door was slammed shut so hard the whole house shook.

Mary clutched her hands together at her bosom and prayed impartially for the safety of her husband and daughter, crossing herself, then starting her prayers all over again.

Con stormed across the road, shoving a man out of his path, ignoring the rain and hammering on his friend's door. 'Let me in this minute, you sneaky, stinking rat!' When nothing happened, he began to hammer on the door again, making it rattle in its frame and yelling. 'Let me in or I'll break it down, so I will!'

When the door opened and a dishevelled Teddy appeared in the opening, Con did not ask questions, just slammed his fist into the other man's face and sent him crashing backwards to the floor, where he lay groaning and shaking his head.

'Where is she?' He pulled Teddy into a sitting position and

shook him. *'Where-is-she?'* And although the other man was as big as he was, rage gave Con enough strength to keep the upper hand.

Teddy jerked his head towards the stairs. 'Up there. But I—'

Con stormed upstairs and found a naked Liza still tied to the bed, her face chalk white beneath the bruises and her eyes swollen with tears. He undid the bonds, cursing fluently, and when Teddy stumbled up the stairs behind him, snapped, 'This'll cost you.'

'Aw, lad, it was the only way to get her to agree.'

Con wrapped a sheet round the trembling girl. 'Not with my daughter, it wasn't. I'd have brought her round to the idea without this. Where's her clothes?'

'They – er – got a bit torn.'

Con breathed deeply. 'Then find some of your wife's stuff for her. She can't walk across the street dressed only in a sheet.' He patted the sobbing girl's shoulders in a futile effort to offer comfort.

Liza couldn't stop weeping, couldn't think straight. And she hurt all over. Only one thing was clear to her. 'I'm not marrying him,' she announced through her tears. 'I'm not.'

Con's hands bunched into fists again at the sight of her distress. 'You'll have to marry him now, lass, but I'll see he treats you right, by hell I will!'

Teddy went to fumble in a chest and came back with a pile of dresses and underthings. 'Here, she can have them all.' Truth to tell, Liza's pallor was making him feel uncomfortable. He'd maybe had too much to drink last night and acted a bit roughly. It was her own fault for being so contrary, but still, maybe he should have been gentler with her. Her first time, too. Only it had been such a long time since he'd had a woman, he'd been nearly bursting for it.

'Get dressed, child!' Con said to his daughter. When she didn't seem to understand what he was saying, he gave her a quick shake. 'Get dressed, will ye?'

She shuddered and seemed suddenly to become aware of what was going on.

'We'll go home to your ma as soon as you're ready.'

But she didn't move till she'd repeated loudly and clearly, 'I'll not marry him, Da. Not for anything.'

'Oh, get dressed, you fool. Is this the time to talk of such things?' Con didn't even look at his friend because if he had, he'd have thumped him again and it was too late now to solve anything with violence.

In the shop Liza leaned against the counter as if her legs would no longer carry her. 'I'll – not – marry him,' she repeated in a thread of a voice.

Con snorted. 'You'll have to. You may be carrying his child already. I won't let him hurt you again, though.'

She could not hold back a sob. 'You couldn't stop him. You wouldn't be in the bedroom with us, would you?'

His voice softened. 'Did he hurt you very much, lass?'

She nodded and could not prevent another sob from escaping.

'I'm sorry for that.' Then he sighed and gave her a shove. 'Go inside and see your mother now. She'll know what to do. You'd better not go out till that face heals up, though. The bruises will have faded by the wedding, I dare say.'

She looked at him as if he were a stranger, this large untidy man with the mass of greying hair and the ruddy face, then stumbled through into the back room. But when her mother stepped forward, arms outstretched, Liza put up one hand to hold her at arm's length. 'Why didn't you come across the road to help me, Mam? You must have known what was going on.'

Mary's eyes filled with tears. 'I thought it was Con as had planned it. I didn't realise—'

'So it'd have been all right if Da had done it?'

'No. No, of course not. Only – you know what he's like for gettin' his own way.'

Liza looked at her scornfully, then shut herself in the scullery where she washed every inch of her body. Being clean made her feel a bit better, at least. She'd done enough crying now, though. Time to act. She went up to her bedroom to have a think.

Her mother's weeping echoed round the house for a while, and when Dermott and Niall came home that evening, there was a huge row with their father. Fists were raised, threats made and only Mary's intervention stopped a fight.

Her two brothers soon went out again, and Con left a short time later.

Her mother shouted up that tea was ready, but Liza refused to go downstairs so Nancy brought her up some bread and butter and a cracked cup brimming with strong tea.

Liza wouldn't talk about what had happened to her sister or anyone else, though, and could only force the food down by telling herself she needed to keep up her strength if she was to get away.

After that she lay in the bed she shared with her sister and little brother, her back to the room, pretending to be worse than she was. If Mrs P. didn't want her any more, she'd go into Manchester and try to find another place as maid. Or anything else that was offered. But one way or another, she was getting away from here and never, ever coming back.

Could Mr Marshall have been right about giving her a baby? No, he was just saying that to frighten her. She wouldn't think of him again – or what had happened. She'd just concentrate on getting away.

CHAPTER FOUR

When Benedict got home from the big house his family were all waiting for him, sitting round the kitchen table. He leaned against the door frame and announced baldly, 'Saul Ludlam wants me to go out to Australia with Josiah.'

His mother immediately burst into tears and his father started patting her on the back, avoiding his son's eyes.

Benedict moved round to stand in front of him. 'You knew what Ludlam wanted, Dad, didn't you? *Didn't you?*'

Jack shot an unhappy glance sideways at his wife. 'Yes. He told me yesterday, said he relied on me to persuade you it was the best thing to do – for all our sakes. Are you going to do as he wants?'

'I may, or there again I may not. I haven't decided yet whether I'll accept our kind patron's not-so-generous offer.' He watched in perverse satisfaction as fear crept across their faces.

'He *is* our landlord, son,' Jack said pleadingly.

'Well, he isn't God, not by a long chalk. And actually, I'm not one of his tenants. I just happen to work for you.' Such terror filled his father's eyes that for a moment Benedict felt guilty, as if he were the one who'd put it there. He wasn't, he reminded himself. It was Saul Ludlam who had done that, the arrogant old devil. He closed his eyes for a moment to shut out the sight of that fear, but his father's halting voice painted it just as graphically for him.

'If – if you don't do as he wants, he might not renew our lease.'

Benedict took a deep breath. 'Look, I haven't said I won't go, Dad, but I'll only do as he wants if he pays me enough to buy myself a piece of land out there, and so I told him.'

'You only care about yourself!' Martin muttered.

Benedict swung round towards his brother. 'And it's the

41

farm *you* care about, not what happens to me, *brother!*' Indeed, Martin acted as if Northbrook were his already – even though a Caine would never be able to own it, could only continue to lease it from the Ludlams.

The two men stared at one another in a silence heavy with the animosity that had lain between them all their lives, then Benedict let out a growl of anger and turned back to his father. 'I have to find out what I'll need to take out to Australia with me to set up a farm, Dad, so that I'll know what it's fair to ask from him. And since Ludlam wants my answer quickly, you'd better find another cowman because if we can't agree on terms, I'm leaving anyway. I've had enough of dancing to that man's bidding.'

His mother sobbed and pressed a handkerchief to her eyes – but she didn't come over to him.

His father stood motionless – and he didn't come near his son, either.

Benedict desperately wanted them to beg him to stay in England, to tell him that Mr Ludlam's wishes weren't as important to them as their youngest son – only they didn't do that, because he wasn't really important to them and never had been. Martin was the heir, the one who mattered most. It had been the same throughout his childhood. Nothing had changed. He'd be well out of it. 'I'll be going into Liverpool this afternoon. After that, I may go to Manchester – I don't know. I want to find people who really know about Australia and talk to them before I agree to this. I'm not taking Ludlam's word for anything. If I have to, I'll go down to London as well, and if *he* doesn't like me keeping him waiting, he can lump it.' He saw Martin open his mouth to protest and tossed at him in a tight, angry voice, 'And so can the rest of you.'

Which made his brother and the other members of his family treat him very stiffly for the rest of the morning as he made his preparations to leave. Well, he didn't care about that. He wouldn't *let* himself care.

In fact, Benedict had to go to all three cities before he could gather enough facts to be sure of his decision, and although he didn't enjoy travelling on them, he blessed the railways that made it possible for him to get around the country so quickly. Cheap, easy transport was slowly but surely freeing people like him from arrogant bastards like Ludlam. It was taking poorer people out into the broader world and showing them different ways of living, and even for those who didn't travel, the railways brought newspapers and information to towns and villages everywhere. His world was very different from the one his father had grown up in, and a good thing, too.

When he had finished his investigations, he sat on the train going back to Pendleworth, lost in thought. Why in heaven's name was Saul Ludlam insisting on their going to the western part of Australia? The Swan River Colony was a small place, by all accounts, not nearly as prosperous as Sydney or Melbourne. It had a tiny population compared with the other colonies, too – not even as many people as the town of Oldham, where his mother's family came from, though it was ten times the size of Britain. The men he'd spoken to had all advised him to go to the east coast of Australia instead – only he didn't have that choice.

Then he suddenly realised why Ludlam wanted to send Josiah to the quietest, most backward place he could find. The old man not only wanted to send his wayward youngest son as far away as possible, but to keep him hidden once he got there.

Benedict came back to a family who were still stiff and suspicious. Within the hour he grew so fed up of their long faces that he went round to see Grace Newton to talk things over with her. She was as welcoming and friendly as she'd always been and he relaxed in her company.

'You're a fine woman, Grace,' he told her as he drew her into his arms for the kiss she clearly welcomed. Take a wife with you, they'd said in London. There aren't many spare women out there. You'll end up marrying a maidservant if you don't – or worse – if you can find one that's not spoken for, that is.

'And you're a fine man, Benedict.' Grace twined her arms round his neck and pulled his head down for another kiss. She had loved him for years, turning down other fellows because the men just didn't match up to him, and she'd been starting to get worried when time passed and he'd said nothing. After all, she was twenty-seven, over a year older than he was.

But it was going to be all right now. She knew it. And she didn't care if she had to go out to Australia to be with him.

She'd have gone anywhere, done anything, to get Benedict Caine to marry her. Her expression was soft with love as she watched him stride away, such a good-looking fellow, so full of energy and purpose, and yet kind with it. No wonder he was popular round here. There was no one to touch him in her eyes.

The night after the attack Liza lay in bed and listened for the faint sounds of people in the nearby houses rising and starting their day. Quite a lot of folk had to get up before dawn and she was relying on them to alert her when it was time to leave. She'd lain awake most of the night, absolutely terrified of missing this opportunity. Once or twice she had fallen asleep briefly, waking with a start, terrified she'd overslept.

At last she heard the sound she'd been waiting for: people stirring in the house next door. Which meant it was nearly dawn.

She slid carefully out of bed, standing motionless as her sister muttered something. When Nancy settled down to sleep again, Liza picked up the pile of clothes she'd left ready on the floor and moved across the room with them clutched in her arms. She was shivering with cold, but she'd get dressed downstairs.

At the bedroom door she turned for a last look at her little brother and sister, only able to see dark silhouettes in the bed against the faintly lit window. She mouthed the word 'Goodbye!' with tears in her eyes and closed the door slowly and carefully.

The click of its latch sounded so loud in the darkness that she stood there for a minute with her heart pounding in fear, the bundle clutched to her chest. From the front bedroom she could hear her father snoring and there was no sound at all from her brothers' room. Well, they always slept like dead men and were hard to wake in the mornings. She hadn't really worried about them hearing her. As no one stirred, she risked moving again and began to tiptoe down the stairs.

In the kitchen she paused to drag on her clothes anyhow. When the cat twined itself round her legs, mewing, she pushed it away, not bothering to get anything to eat, wanting only to be on her way before someone heard her moving.

She crept into the shop and fumbled in the corner among the rags for her own clothes, stuffing them into an old pillowcase. There were so few of them left that she picked up the pile of clothes belonging to the dead Mrs Marshall and shoved them in as well. They fitted her quite well and were cleaner than most of the stuff in the shop. Besides, it served him right if she took them with her after what he'd done to her, and no one could say she'd stolen them because he'd given them to her.

Finally she opened the money drawer under the counter and took out the few coppers lying in it, hating to steal them, but she had to have something in her pocket.

'You'll need more than that!'

The voice was a mere whisper, but Liza, who hadn't heard anyone coming in, swung round with a gasp, blood roaring in her ears in panic. When she saw who it was, she sagged against the counter in relief and whispered, 'Mam! What are you doing up so early?'

'I haven't been sleeping well lately. I heard you creep downstairs so I came to see what you were doing. You're running away, aren't you?'

Liza looked at the shop door, wondering if she could turn the big iron key and make off down the street before her mother shouted to warn her father she was trying to escape.

Mary's face puckered and a tear rolled down her cheek. 'I'll not give you away, love. Here.' She fumbled in her pocket and held something out.

'What is it?'

'Money. I know where your father keeps his savings – not that there's much left now. When I guessed you were running away, I went and got some of it. Go on, take it. You have to get as far away from Pendleworth as possible. If Con catches you . . .'

Liza could feel tears welling up and when they spilled down her cheeks, she made no attempt to wipe them away. 'Oh, Mam!' she whispered brokenly. 'I don't want to leave you.'

Mary held out her arms. 'I know, love.' She buried her face in the strong young shoulder and sobbed desperately, the muffled sounds all the more anguished for her attempts to keep them quiet. 'I've not – not been strong enough to stand up to him. I'm sorry. Try not to think too badly of me.'

Liza hugged her convulsively, but knew if she stayed there much longer someone would overhear them, because walls were thin in these flimsy little houses. If Dermott or Niall chased after her, they'd catch her easily enough because they were strong – too strong for their own good sometimes when they got into brawls. There had been a couple of nasty incidents in the pub in the past year or two and after one of them, Mr Ludlam's rent collector had come to the house to warn the two young men to behave themselves in future or the whole family would be evicted.

Conscious that time was passing, she pulled out of the embrace, took the money, which was wrapped in a piece of rag, and stuffed it into her pocket. 'Thanks, Mam.'

'Where are you going, love?'

'I – I daren't tell you. But it's a long way away and I'll not be coming back.'

Mary smeared away another trail of tears and nodded. 'You're right, really. But if you ever can – one day – will you write and let me know how you are?'

Liza nodded, so close to breaking down she didn't dare try to speak again. She picked up her bundle and lifted the door bell carefully off its hook before opening the outer door. Taking a deep breath, not looking back, she slipped away into the chill greyness of a misty morning.

Mary went to close the door, leaning her forehead against the edge of it for a minute, praying fervently to the blessed Virgin to keep her daughter safe. Then she closed it quietly, leaving the bell off the spring, and tiptoed into the kitchen. When the others got up, she would have to pretend she didn't know Liza had gone and also pretend ignorance about the missing money. Her husband was going to be furious.

She sighed as she got the embers glowing. Sometimes she wished she could just go to sleep and not wake up. She spent a lot of time worrying about angering Con these days. He'd turned into a mean, violent man since they came to England. And yet they were lucky compared to the rest of her family, most of whom had died in the potato famine. She and Con had sold up before it all began, while there were still people with money to pay a fair price for their few bits and pieces of furniture. That had given them enough to start up this shop, and even if it wasn't doing as well as they'd once hoped, it kept the family more or less fed.

She gave a snort of grim laughter at that thought. Actually, the shop was doing as well as ever but Con was drinking up more of the profits lately and her two eldest sons were taking more than their fair share of what food there was in the house. The strange thing was, she never felt really hungry herself, but she knew Nancy and Kieran did, knew it and yet had done little to help them. Well, she was going to try harder from now on. She'd lost one daughter and she didn't want to lose the other. Nor would she let her youngest son, who had a gentle nature, become brutalised like his two brothers.

She swung the kettle over the flames then sat down at the table, not allowing herself to weep. When she heard Con's footsteps overhead, she put her head on her hands, pretending to be dozing, for she often got up early and came to sit quietly on her own down here.

She let her husband shake her awake and make her a cup of tea. This was the only time of day when he was at all like the old Con, the man she'd fallen in love with and married when she was a slip of a girl every bit as pretty as Liza. Once the day's work started, once his feet began to ache, Con became grumpy again.

'She awake yet?' he asked, jerking his head upwards.

'Liza?'

'Yes.'

'I haven't heard her.' Mary hesitated then added, 'You shouldn't be trying to force her to marry that Teddy Marshall, love. He's a nasty brute.'

'But a rich brute, compared to us. And once he's married her, he'll not let her family want.' Con sat down beside her and put his arm round her shoulders, staring into the leaping flames. 'We have to think what's best for all of us, not just Liza.'

Mary didn't try to argue. He would never change his mind once he'd made it up. So they sat in amicable silence for a while till Nancy came down to join them. 'Where's Liza?'

Con jumped to his feet. 'What do you mean, where's Liza? Is she not upstairs in her bed?'

'No, Da.'

Then all hell broke loose.

★   ★   ★

47

Benedict spent hours sitting at one end of the kitchen table making notes in pencil under headings like Farming Tools, Seeds and Plants, Household Goods and Chattels. Then he got out the inkpot, put a fresh steel nib in the pen and began to make proper lists in his best handwriting, two copies of each.

By the time he went back to see Mr Ludlam the following day, he had his figures sorted out and knew what he'd have to insist on if he went to Australia. He watched Saul Ludlam settle his pince-nez on his nose and run his finger down the lists. Containing his impatience, Benedict went over to stare out of the window, listening to the quiet shuffling of papers behind him.

At last Ludlam cleared his throat and when Benedict turned round, gestured to him to sit down again. 'You've been busy, Caine.'

'Yes, sir. I shouldn't like to go into such a big venture unprepared.'

'Can you make me another list, of the stuff Josiah will need to set up his farm? I gather it's better to take your own equipment out there with you.' Saul had hoped the man who ran the home farm would be able to do that for him, but the fool seemed incapable of doing anything outside his daily tasks and had only produced a scratchy, ill-written list, nothing like as thorough as Caine's well-penned notes. Saul stared down at the pieces of paper, feeling annoyed that a mere farm hand would write such an educated hand. Big black, slashing strokes formed the words; neat even figures sat in straight lines. There was too much educating the lower classes these days, by hell there was!

Benedict inclined his head. 'Yes, I can do that for you once we've agreed on my price for going. You'll have to tell me how much you want to spend on your son, though, and what sort of farming he's intending to get into.'

'I'll spend whatever it takes to set him up properly – but not generously. I've promised his mother to do that and I keep my word. What do I know about which sort of farming, though? You seem to have found out what's involved in settling there, so I'll leave it up to you.' Saul had promised his daughter-in-law only the previous evening that she would never want, so he intended to give Catherine some extra money for herself and tell her to hide it from Josiah, who had spendthrift ways. He did not want anything on his conscience.

After studying Caine's determined expression, he decided reluctantly that he would have to increase his offer. 'It's out of the question to let you have all you're asking for, but I'll give you a hundred pounds *and* provide half of the stuff on this list of yours. The rest you must find for yourself.' He started to push the papers back across the desk, as if the matter were settled.

Benedict reached out to stop the movement and met his gaze steadily. 'No. That's not nearly enough to persuade me, because I don't really want to go out to Australia – as you well know.'

Saul let the silence continue till it grew uncomfortable. 'Such a decision might affect the rest of your family adversely.'

'That would be your choice and on your conscience, not mine. I'm prepared to do as you wish if I can see some benefit in it to me, but since it'll mean turning my whole life upside down, it's only fair for you to make me adequate recompense – sir.' The last word was an effort every time he said it, but this was no time to anger Ludlam. Benedict took a deep breath and made a counter-offer. 'If I'm to make a life for myself out there, as well as for your son, I want three hundred pounds and all that's on the list – and I'll check the items off as they're crated, believe me.'

Ludlam gobbled with indignation. 'Impossible!'

Benedict shrugged and stood up.

'Where do you think you're going, Caine?'

'Home. Then I'm leaving Pendleworth to look for a small farm to rent.'

'Come back! I haven't finished with you.'

Benedict sat down again, arms folded, feeling a little more hopeful.

Saul settled down to the pleasure of a sharp bargaining session, during which the younger man twice stood up to leave and once Saul yelled at him to get out of his house, then, before he'd even reached the front door, yelled down the hallway for him to come back this minute.

Neither got all he wanted, but each felt satisfied with the

final bargain, for Saul believed Caine's solemn promise that he would stand by Josiah. His only regret now was that he would not be there to see his son sweating and straining to make a living. The very thought of that filled Saul with savage satisfaction.

That same day Dorothy Pringle got up as early as usual, even though she had worked until nearly midnight packing up her good china in straw and newspaper. It was Maggie's day off, so she went into the kitchen to make herself a cup of tea. When she opened the back door to let the fresh air in and banish the smells of last night's cooking, she cried out in shock as she saw the figure huddled on the step.

'Mercy me, child! What are you doing here at this hour?'

Liza pushed herself to her feet. 'I – I came to ask if you still want me to go to Australia with you, Mrs P.?'

Dorothy caught hold of the girl's chin, turning the bruised eye and cheek gently towards the light. 'What happened?'

'Da thumped me.' Liza had decided to say nothing about Marshall forcing himself on her. She was trying hard not even to think about that, because whenever she did, she felt like vomiting and weeping, both at the same time.

'Why?'

'Because I won't marry that horrible old man.'

As Dorothy glanced again at the livid bruises and puffy, reddened eyes, pity welled up in her. 'Come inside at once and let me put some ointment on that poor face of yours.'

But Liza didn't move. 'I'm sorry, but if you don't want me to go to Australia with you, I have to get away as quickly as I can.' She glanced down the lane as if afraid of someone following her.

Dorothy put one arm round the thin shoulders. 'Well, of course I want you! Didn't we agree that you'd think it over, then tell me your answer?'

Only then did Liza crumple and start to sob, allowing Dorothy Pringle to take her inside and cosset her.

When Andrew came down to join them, he exclaimed in shock at the sight of Liza's battered face, then declared himself quite happy to keep her presence a secret, because he hated cruelty in any form.

After a while Dorothy put down her teacup and said thoughtfully, 'If she stays here, Andrew, people will hear about her and her father will find out where she is and he'll have the right to take her away again. She'll have to go on ahead of us.'

Liza jerked upright. She'd hardly slept the previous two nights and was feeling so exhausted that the mere thought of moving on made her want to weep again.

Andrew nodded slowly. 'You're right. Kitty couldn't keep a secret to save her life and Maggie is an inveterate gossip. It's a good thing it's her day off. Do you have anywhere else you can go, Liza? We don't sail for another three weeks.'

'No. Nowhere.' She didn't tell them about the money her mam had given her, which she'd stopped to count on the way here. The thought of it made her feel much safer. You could live for a long time on five pounds.

'We'll have to find her somewhere to stay until we sail, then, somewhere she isn't known.' Dorothy frowned as she considered the problem. 'I have it, Andrew! Your old nurse. You were going to visit Phoebe anyway, to say goodbye, so neither Kitty nor Maggie will wonder at you going to see her today. You'll have to give her something for Liza's keep, though.' She glanced at the clock. 'If you leave now, you'll easily get back by nightfall.'

While he got ready, Dorothy prepared some food, explaining to Liza as she worked, 'Phoebe lives in a small village just outside Preston. When it's time to sail, you can catch a train quite easily from there to Liverpool.'

Liza, who had never even left the district before, let alone ridden on a train, nodded and gulped back her nervousness at the thought of doing such things alone.

As Dorothy tied up a bundle of food, she said abruptly, 'Don't let me down now, Liza. I'll really need your help in Australia.'

'I won't, Mrs P. I promise I'll work really hard. I'm that grateful to you.'

* * *

When Benedict left the grounds of Pendleworth Hall, he stopped and beamed round at the world, smacking one fist into the other. Even if it didn't work out, even if he didn't like it in Australia, he'd work hard enough to get out of this with enough money to come back and buy his own place in England one day.

'You're looking pleased with yourself.'

Benedict swung round. 'Oh, it's you.'

Josiah swept him a mocking bow. 'It is indeed. I've been waiting for you.' He hesitated, then grimaced and leaned back against a tree trunk. 'I wanted to talk to you, ask you to persuade the old man to send us to Sydney instead of the Swan River Colony.'

Benedict sat down on a fallen tree trunk and clasped his hands around one raised knee. 'I agree with you, but your father won't budge on that. I've already tried to persuade him, because I'd far rather have gone to the east coast myself. Near Melbourne would have been best. They say the place is booming since they discovered gold nearby. But your father's set his mind on your going somewhere quieter and there's no budging him from that.'

Josiah turned round and thumped his fist into the tree trunk, seeming oblivious to the pain and the blood on his grazed knuckles. 'Damn him!' he raged. 'Damn him to high hell! Why couldn't he have sent me to America? Why to that benighted spot?'

In spite of himself, Benedict felt sorry for his companion. 'He wants to bury you where no one will ever find you again. And me with you, it seems.'

Josiah stilled. 'You don't want to go, either?'

'Not really, no.'

There was silence, broken only by the wind teasing through the still-bare branches, then Josiah shivered. 'Well, I'm not spending the rest of my life there. We'll give it a few years, make a success of the venture, somehow, then we'll sell up – or at least, I will.'

'What you do is your own business, but before we can sell at a profit, we have to clear the land and that'll take some hard work. Backbreaking work, they tell me.'

Josiah's voice was scornful. 'I shall have enough money to hire labourers for that sort of thing.'

'If you can find them. I'm told they're scarce out there. So you're going to have to do some of the physical work yourself.'

'We'll see about that.' Josiah intended to create a gracious estate with a farm attached, a new Pendleworth. Cat's idea was the only consolation he'd found in this whole sorry mess. He was already considering what the house would be like. Brick, two storeys, with a basement and attics. A wide driveway. Lush gardens. A place of his own would be worth working hard for. And even if he never dared come back to England, there would be nothing to stop him going to live in America or somewhere more congenial if he didn't like Western Australia. His father wouldn't be able to trace him there. But at the moment, the money was only to be paid out bit by bit in Perth, so he had no choice but to go to the Swan River Colony.

Benedict shrugged. 'You can call your place what the hell you want, just so long as you understand that I'm not doing all the hard work while you sit on your arse playing the gentleman.'

'You've made your point.'

The two men fell silent again, then Benedict asked, 'What about Catherine? Surely she's too fragile to stand such a life? They tell me conditions are very harsh out there. Can you not leave her here and send for her later when you have a house built, at least?'

'She wants to come with me.' Josiah stared up at the graceful patterns of the branches, not really seeing anything but light and shadow. 'Strange as it may seem to you, she and I are good friends.'

Benedict ventured another piece of advice, 'I think you'd better get her a strong maidservant before you leave, then. They tell me you can't get servants for love or money out there. She'll need someone to do the heavy work.'

'She already has a maid. Penny is devoted to her and has agreed to come with us.'

'That Penny is a flibbertigibbet. You're going to need someone who can bake and clean and do the laundry, not someone who fiddles with hair and clothes.'

53

Josiah waved one hand impatiently. 'We can hire local women to do the rough work.'

'You mean the natives? I doubt they'll know enough. I'm told they're very primitive. Violent sometimes, too.'

Josiah reminded himself again that the other man was only trying to help. 'You can safely leave my wife's welfare in my hands, Caine. Believe me, I'll take very good care of her.'

Benedict wasn't at all sure of that, but as everyone on the estate knew, when a Ludlam got a certain look on his face and that chill tone in his voice, you might as well argue with the church tower as expect to change his mind. And for all his faults, Josiah was a Ludlam through and through, an arrogant devil like the rest of them.

Dismissing Josiah from his mind, Benedict went straight across to see Grace and ask her to marry him. He wouldn't take her out to Australia with him, but send for her to follow him once he'd got somewhere for her to live. She'd make a perfect wife for a busy farmer.

Catherine lay in bed, reluctant to get up. She often felt like that now, though in the past she'd loved going for walks in the early mornings in the grounds which were the only beautiful thing about this unhappy house. But if she stayed in bed much longer, her maid would start to fuss and worry, then Jos would come in to see what was wrong and before she knew it, they'd be calling in the doctor. And she didn't want to see a doctor. Definitely not. What was the point? No doctor could help her now.

So she dragged herself out of bed, forcing a smile to her face as Penny (who was sworn to secrecy about her mistress's illness) helped her dress and do her hair. Then she went down for the late breakfast the ladies usually took together two hours after Saul and his sons had left for the mill.

She paused by the dining-room door. Her mother-in-law was sitting in her usual place at the head of the table, eyes puffy and red. Still weeping over Josiah, no doubt. And the two sisters-in-law were bickering about something again. Stifling a sigh, Catherine walked across to fill her plate from the huge mahogany sideboard where candle burners under the silver dishes kept the food more or less warm. With a shudder at

54

the smell of the kidneys, she contented herself with a small piece of ham and a thin slice of bread.

'You're hardly eating anything lately,' Sophia worried. 'No wonder you're losing weight.'

'Oh, I'll have an apple afterwards.' Catherine forced herself to cut up the ham and placed a tiny piece in her mouth.

She became aware they were all staring at her. 'Sorry? Did you say something?'

Sophia patted her hand. 'I asked how you're feeling about going to Australia, my dear. It seems very unfair that you should be made to suffer because of Josiah.' She wiped away a tear.

Catherine concentrated on her food, though the smell of the ham nauseated her.

'We must make sure you've got everything you need to take out to Australia with you,' Sophia went on. 'We'll call in the dressmaker and get some new underwear made, as well as gowns. Plenty of gowns. Shoes, too. You'd better buy several pairs. And you'll need household linen, as well. You can't be sure of what you'll find to buy there.'

Suddenly nausea overwhelmed Catherine. 'Excuse me. I feel – a little faint.' She rushed upstairs to her room and vomited the small amount of food she'd eaten into the washing bowl.

There was a knock on the door. When she opened it, Sophia was waiting outside with a hopeful look on her face.

'My dear, you're not . . .'

Catherine was about to deny it, then remembered the story she'd spun to her father, the story which had obtained fifty golden sovereigns for her and a letter of recommendation to the Governor, whom James Rawley knew slightly, though she had kept that secret from Josiah, as she had the other money which Saul had given her as a personal gift. 'It's early days yet. I can't be sure.'

Sophia's plump face lit up and she gave her daughter-in-law a hug. 'I'm so glad for you.'

'Please don't say anything to the others. You know how I hate people to fuss over me.'

'But maybe if we tell Saul—'

'He won't change his mind about sending Josiah away, believe me.'

Sophia's face fell and she dabbed at some more facile tears. 'He's become very severe lately.'

When she had gone, Catherine lay down, filled with guilt for deceiving her gentle mother-in-law about her condition. She was worried about the long voyage to Australia, for all she'd tried to keep cheerful about it to Josiah. It was going to be a very difficult time for her, and she would miss the place where she'd grown up – had wanted very much to live out her life here.

Con Docherty scoured Pendleworth, knocking on every door in Underby Street, heedless of the gossip he was creating. He wanted his daughter back, wanted to make sure she was safe – even if she was the most stubborn female it'd ever been his misfortune to encounter. Why would she not marry Teddy Marshall? It'd make all their lives easier.

His moods ranged from anger to fear and back to anxiety again. Mary found it impossible to get a civil word from him. So did the boys.

Niall and Dermott had their own troubles. Marshall wanted his money back from Niall and kept saying he'd been cheated, but with two of them against one, he could do nothing except rage at them. He stormed across to the shop to demand his dead wife's clothes back as well, but when they looked, they found Liza had taken them with her.

'I'll have the law on her, the thieving little bitch!' he raged.

'Then I'll tell them how you forced yourself on her,' Con threw back at him. 'Besides, you gave those clothes to her. I heard you myself, and so I'll swear. On the Bible if necessary.'

So Teddy stormed back across the street and took out his anger on his sons and the woman who came in to clean for him.

CHAPTER FIVE

The group of emigrants from Pendleworth were not the only ones getting ready to leave for Australia. Agnes Fenton lay back in her large soft bed in the Liverpool hotel and stretched languorously. 'I shall miss this,' she told her husband. 'What do you suppose the beds will be like on the ship?'

'Narrow and hard. Come on, lazybones. You know we have to be on board by noon.'

She pulled a face, but got up. When he had gone out for a stroll, she summoned her maid to help her dress, then told Joan to finish packing and make her own way to the ship with the rest of the luggage. 'Take a cab. We have a few calls to make first.'

'Yes, Miss Agnes.' The maid, who was about fifty, looked shrewdly at the mistress whom she had known since girlhood. 'Regretting it now, aren't you?'

Agnes pulled a face. 'Yes, I am rather. But it's too late to change anything.'

'Well, if we can sail out there, we can sail back again.'

'I suppose so.' Agnes hugged her maid, then made her way down to the dining room, frowning. She hadn't told Joan but they would find it very difficult to return because Gerard's uncle was advancing them the money for this venture and would want paying back. She could not see her husband making an effective farmer, so it was to be hoped that they'd find other opportunities for his advancement in Western Australia. He had a few letters of recommendation and surely there would be some suitable government appointments for an ex-officer like him?

As she and Gerard ate breakfast, she set herself to make him laugh and succeeded – but she didn't succeed in banishing her own feelings of apprehension. She was at her best in company, loved going to the theatre and dancing, delighted in the latest gossip. What on earth would she find to do with herself in the colonies?

Only – she had helped Gerard spend most of his inheritance, not realising how little he had or how incompetent he was with money, so she supposed she must now help him mend his fortunes, and then take charge of them. She shook off her dark mood. She would do it, too, whatever it took.

Benedict did not get to bed until after midnight on his final night at home. Not only did he have to sit through a difficult final meal with his family, during which his mother never stopped weeping, but he'd also promised Grace a last visit.

He sighed. What a tangle it all was! He and Grace had married secretly by special licence a week ago. She had got away for two days on the pretence that she was visiting an old aunt, and he'd said he was buying supplies. He hadn't liked behaving dishonestly, but Grace had insisted that it'd be far easier for her if her parents didn't know. She was sure they'd try to stop her marrying him, even though she was more than old enough to know her own mind. They'd decided that she would stay here in England with her family until he sent for her, and only then would she reveal that she was married.

Why he'd agreed to this secrecy he couldn't work out now. Perhaps because his family would have fussed, too. Perhaps simply because Grace had wanted it that way.

And then yesterday she had shocked him by suddenly suggesting she come with him to Australia, had begged to come, in fact – and they'd had their first quarrel about that. As he walked along the quiet moonlit lane, he wished suddenly that he had not married her – not yet, anyway. It had complicated matters unnecessarily, and he would have enough on his plate making a new life for himself without worrying about her. He wanted to make up their quarrel, of course he did – only he hoped she would not start asking to come with him again. And what if she'd told her family? 'Eh, you're not cut out for telling lies, Benedict Caine,' he muttered as he turned into the lane that led to the Newtons' farm.

It was nine o'clock when he arrived, to find the house dark

and the family presumably in bed. What must Grace be thinking of him?

A dog began to bark furiously as he approached and while he was fending it off, another one sneaked up on him and bit his leg. He cursed and kicked it away, but by that time Tom Newton was standing at the door with his shotgun, demanding to know who the hell was out there.

Grace, still dressed, pushed forward. 'It's Benedict Caine and he's come to see me, Father – to say goodbye.'

'Oh, has he? Well, I don't remember him asking my permission to come a-courting you.'

She made a small, irritated sound. 'I'm seven and twenty, so I don't need anyone's permission.'

Benedict rubbed his leg and felt a stickiness on his hand as well as a hole in the material. 'You want to keep a savage brute like that chained up! Look what it's done to my leg!'

Grace made a tutting sound. 'Come into the kitchen and let me wash that wound for you, Ben.'

Her damned family sat round in their nightgear watching as he rolled up his trouser leg and she cleaned the blood away.

When she had finished, she smiled at him. 'I'll walk back down the lane with you, Ben.'

Mrs Newton laid a hand on her husband's arm and looked at him pleadingly.

Tom Newton glared at them both and snapped, 'You mind your behaviour, then, Caine!'

When they got outside, Grace stopped walking to look at him searchingly, her face gently lit by the moonlight. 'I'm going to miss you, Ben. Won't you change your mind and let me come with you? I could be packed by morning.'

'Eh, what's got into you, lass? You're usually more sensible.'

She sighed. 'Sometimes I think I'd rather be beautiful than sensible. Sometimes I'd like a man to be driven wild by my beauty, not by my dairying skills.'

Which made him feel guilty, so he kissed her, and that led to more of the familiarities which her father would have gone wild about.

When Benedict got back to Northbrook Farm all the windows were dark, so he lingered by the gate, glad of the full moon, studying the home he loved and trying to memorise every detail. Then he turned to lean on the closed gate and stare over the fields, savouring the peace and quiet. Moonlight was reflected from the duck pond, turning it briefly and erroneously into a thing of silvered beauty. A fitful breeze was rustling the branches of the big oak near the lane. He'd climbed that tree many times as a lad and had some of its acorns stowed in his luggage to see if he could grow a tree like it in Australia. He didn't want to go anywhere, didn't want to leave England at all. Damn Saul Ludlam! And damn Josiah, too!

The front door opened and someone walked slowly down the path to join him.

'Not going to bed tonight, son?'

'Dad! What are you doing still awake?'

'Waiting for you. I wanted to say thank you for what you're doing for us.'

Benedict stood very still. This was the last thing he'd expected, for his father had hardly spoken a word to him over the past few weeks.

Jack leaned on the gate beside his son. 'I know you think me weak, giving in to Mr Ludlam like this, but Benedict lad, I truly believe I'd die if I lost this farm. He may own it, but it's my life's blood as has gone into it. You'll see what I mean when you get your own land.'

Benedict pulled his father into his arms and gave him a big, cracking hug, surprised at how thin the old man had become. 'Well, you haven't lost it, have you?'

'Thanks to you.' Jack fumbled for his son's hand and put something in it, closing the work-roughened fingers round a soft leather pouch. 'So I thought – well, it seemed right that you should have part of your inheritance early, to give you something to fall back on if – if times are hard in Australia.'

'Dad, I don't—'

'It's only fifty pounds, but you may need it one day. And you've more than earned it. You're a good worker, son. You'll be sorely missed around the farm.'

Another crushing hug, a smothered sob in the darkness, then Jack Caine stumbled back towards the house.

Benedict swallowed hard, wiping tears away from his own face. This was the last thing he'd expected from his father and he didn't know whether this late recognition of what he'd done for his family hurt or pleased him. Or perhaps it did both.

Oh, hell, he didn't know anything tonight. And if he didn't get some sleep, he'd be good for nothing when he got to Liverpool.

When he arrived at the docks the next day, Benedict was still feeling angry and upset, so upset he hardly noticed the city streets he jolted through in the cab. He scowled at the ship, which looked old and tired. Why had Ludlam booked their passage on a sailing ship, for heaven's sake, when there were vessels with auxiliary engines plying the route now, even if they couldn't carry enough fuel to use their engines all the way to Australia? With this ship, they'd be at the mercy of the wind, and he'd read enough about the Doldrums to realise they could be becalmed there for days

When the steward showed him down into the single men's quarters, he stopped dead near the foot of the companionway, utterly horrified. He'd known Saul Ludlam had arranged for him to travel steerage, but the large cabin had bunks lining the walls and men lounging everywhere, and it reeked of unwashed humanity already. It was on the second deck down, so there were no portholes even, to bring fresh air. He shuddered and took an involuntary step backwards. It was one thing to read about the sleeping space allotted to passengers, another to see how narrow a six feet wide bunk meant for four people really was. How he would stand four months in this hell-hole, he could not think.

'This place is terrible!' He didn't realise he'd spoken aloud until someone cleared their throat behind him.

The steward was still hovering partway up the sloping wooden ladder that served for stairs. 'You look like you're used to something better, if I may say so, sir.'

'Aye,' said Benedict. 'By hell I am!' He wished now that he'd insisted on Ludlam paying for him to travel in a cabin, but he'd been more concerned with the tools and money. The old pinch-farthing!

'There are still a couple of bunks left in the deck cabins, if you want to pay a bit extra, sir.'

'How much extra?'

'Another ten pounds, sir.'

'And what sort of accommodation will that give me?'

'I'll show you, if you like.' He led the way up to a row of tiny cabins opening directly on to the deck. In each of these were two narrow bunks, one above the other, with about three feet of extra space at the rear for luggage and just enough room to stand up beside the bunks. The end cabin was unoccupied.

'What do folk from the deck cabins do about eating?'

'There's a dining space for them at the other end. It's not fancy, like that for the inside cabin passengers, but it's a damn' sight better than what steerage passengers get.'

'Can you arrange for me to change to one of these cabins?'

The man nodded and held out one hand.

Benedict dropped a silver coin into it. 'Will I need anything else, do you think?'

'I'd advise you to bring plenty of extra food supplies. Got some bottled lime juice?'

'Yes.'

'Pickles, dried fruit?'

'Some.'

'You should also buy yourself some decent ship's biscuits for later in the trip. The ones on board are not the best.' He winked at Benedict. 'I make a bit of extra money for myself selling stuff to them as has run out – dried fruit, ham and such. You might like to do the same. It's no skin off my nose because I never have as much as they want – well, there isn't the space for me to store it, is there? But you'd have room for some stuff in here.'

Another coin exchanged hands in expression of Benedict's gratitude.

Although steerage passengers were not allowed to leave once they had boarded the ship, by slipping a shilling into the hand of the sailor guarding the gangway that led on to the vessel, Benedict was allowed off with a warning not to take more than an hour or two. He found a provision merchant and purchased some extra supplies for his own use as well as food for resale, in an attempt to make up for the extra money he was having to lay out. On the advice of the man who served him, he bought two full hams.

As he was leaving the warehouse with his purchases on a little handcart pushed by one of the lads waiting by the door, he saw some pieces of wood on display, fine-grained and of many different colours and shades. He'd never seen anything quite like this and lingered to finger them.

The assistant came up to him again. 'We sell those for carving, sir. Some of the sailors make a bit extra on the side, them with a knack for that sort of thing. It helps pass the time on board ship.'

So Benedict added a bundle of pieces of wood, an extra couple of knives and some small chisels and gouging tools to his purchases. He hadn't done any carving for years because Martin had thrown his tools into the duck pond after one of their more violent disagreements, and most of them had been lost in the mud at the bottom for all his frantic searching. But he'd enjoyed carving when he was younger, and had learned a lot about woodwork generally from his grandfather and brother Paul. He only hoped he hadn't lost the knack, or he'd have wasted his money today.

The ship looked very small as he approached it, too small to carry over four hundred souls to the other side of the world. Four months on that thing! He'd go mad. And though it was an improvement on the steerage accommodation, he hated the cramped feel of his cabin, absolutely hated it. But it was too late to back out now.

'Damn the old bastard!' Benedict muttered under his breath as he arranged his possessions in the cabin. 'If it wasn't for Dad, I'd turn round and go straight back.'

On the day they were to leave Pendleworth, Catherine woke early and slipped out of bed to stand by the window staring out at the landscape she loved so well. She had said farewell to her family the day before, but the only one she really cared about was her younger brother Nick, whom she would never see again in this life. Tears came into her eyes, in spite of her resolve not to give way to her emotions, and she didn't even try to brush them away. It was going to be one of her bad days, too, she knew the signs by now.

The door to the dressing room opened. She would have recognised Jos's tread anywhere, so didn't turn her head when he stopped behind her.

'Saying farewell?' he asked in a voice that was huskier than usual.

She could not prevent herself from sagging against him and weeping helplessly.

'Oh, hell, Cat! Tell them we have no marriage – that should be easy enough to prove – and stay here in England. With your father's money you'll soon find another husband. There's no earthly reason for you to be exiled as well.'

But that stiffened her spine. 'I've never wanted to marry anyone but you, Jos, and I'm going with you.'

He closed his eyes for a moment and a sigh escaped him. 'I don't deserve you, my dear. But I'm glad you're coming.'

They stayed by the window until Penny, red-eyed, came to knock on the door and bring in her mistress's hot water.

By the time their train pulled into the station in Liverpool, Josiah had to help his wife off it, she was feeling so weak. He yelled for a porter to take their luggage, glad the trunks and other bigger things had already been sent to the ship. Poor Cat was as white as paper and looked about as substantial. Tossing a curt order over his shoulder to Penny to, 'Follow us with the luggage!' he swung Cat into his arms and carried her towards a waiting cab.

When the driver tipped his hat and opened the door for them, Josiah helped his wife inside and stood back to allow Penny to get in, but found she was no longer with them.

'What happened to our maid?' he demanded of the porter who was now passing their luggage to the cab driver to stow safely.

'That lass what got out of the train with you?'

'Yes, you fool, who else did you think I meant?'

'She give me this letter to pass to you and left. Took two of the bags with 'er.' Still annoyed at being spoken to so rudely, the porter added with relish, 'Fair run out of the station, she did.'

Josiah snatched the piece of paper and unfolded it, to read: *I'm sorry, Mrs Ludlam. I can't do it. Australia is just too far away. Sorry. Penny.*

He stood there, shocked rigid, then snapped, 'Wait a moment!' and rushed out of the station. If he could catch the girl, he could perhaps persuade or bribe her to go with them. But there was no sign of her. Oh, hell, what was Cat going to do without help?

Getting into the cab, he sat down beside his wife, who had her eyes closed and was huddled in one corner. 'My dear, I'm afraid Penny has run away.'

'*What!*'

'She left you this.'

Cat read the note, then stared at him in dismay. 'Can we find another maid, do you think? An agency, perhaps?'

He shook his head. 'We have to embark today by noon, so it's not possible. My dear, I can still send you home again.'

'No, Jos. I've told you before – I'm going with you.'

'I shouldn't let you. And Caine was right, damn him!'

'What about?'

'He said Penny was a flibbertigibbet and that I should get you a sensible maid instead.'

'Yes. But she knows – I mean, she *knew* my ways.' Catherine's face brightened suddenly. 'Maybe one of the steerage passengers would help me. Yes, there's bound to be someone on board who wants to earn extra money.' Relief flooded through her.

'Are you sure?'

'Yes.'

Jos's face looked like something carved out of granite as he leaned out of the window and told the driver to take them to the docks. Cat knew hers was white and drawn, had flinched from her reflection in the mirror that morning. Neither of them said a word on the way to the ship, or noticed much about the streets through which they were passing.

Liza travelled by train to Liverpool, where she was to meet her employers at the station. She sat on a hard wooden seat in a third-class compartment that soon filled with people, terrified that at any minute her father or brothers would find her, for Mr Pringle said Da had called at the house twice and was searching for her everywhere.

When the train arrived, she picked up her bag and followed the others out on to the platform and into the main area of the station, where she found a seat and waited, as instructed.

But every time a large man walked towards her, she could feel her heart start to pound. None of them looked remotely like Da or Mr Marshall, but still that didn't prevent terror at the thought of being hauled back to Underby Street from almost paralysing her.

At first the station was full of people hurrying to go somewhere. She clutched the shabby canvas bag which contained all her worldly belongings and looked round anxiously for the Pringles, wishing they would hurry up. Which was silly, because their train wasn't due in yet. She knew that, but still she kept looking for them.

An older woman with hard, cold eyes that made Liza shiver came over and sat down next to her, asking, 'All alone, dearie? Looking for a position?'

'I already have one and I'm waiting for my employers.' Liza got up and walked across to another bench, but noticed that the woman kept watching her, which made her feel uneasy.

When the time came, she went to stand near the platform where the train from Pendleworth would come in. She watched wide-eyed as ladies strolled along, their crinolines swaying, their voices quiet, their gloved hands slipped under the arms of top-hatted gentlemen, who tipped their hats to other ladies. How easy rich people's lives must be. They wouldn't have to run away from home.

At last she saw the Pringles coming down the platform behind a porter with a loaded trolley and groaned softly in relief.

'Ah, there you are, child!' Mrs P. smiled at her. 'No problems getting here?'

'No, ma'am, none at all.' But she was struggling not to weep with relief at seeing them.

The cab smelled of sweaty bodies and stale straw, and they were squashed together inside, even though the two ladies were not wearing crinolines. Liza was next to Miss Kitty, who pulled away from her as if she smelled bad and sat looking out with a sulky expression on her face. Mr Pringle had that silly smile on his face which meant he was dreaming again and Mrs P. wasn't even looking out of the cab window, just staring down at her hands and looking really sad.

The streets grew steadily shabbier as they approached the

docks, and when they arrived at the ship the *Louisa Jane* looked too small to carry so many people all the way to Australia. Mr Pringle had told Liza there would be nearly four hundred passengers on board. Well, they were going to be very crowded if they all had to fit into that ship!

She followed her employers across the dock to see the Medical Officer, who examined them one after the other to check that they weren't carrying an illness on board. It didn't take very long and he hardly touched the Pringles, but he made Liza take her bodice off, and poked at her chest, which embarrassed her greatly. When they went outside again, they had to weave their way through heaps of luggage of all descriptions from hat boxes to big cabin trunks, as well as tubs and barrels. How anyone ever made sense of all these untidy piles, Liza could not think.

As she went up the gangway, she glanced over her shoulder, seized by a sudden anxiety that someone would leap out from behind the piles of boxes to drag her off the ship. Near the top of the gangway, a tall man was leaning against the rail, staring at them so fixedly that she stopped walking for a moment, afraid he was looking for her. Miss Kitty's finger jabbed in her spine and she moved on again reluctantly.

Mr Pringle stopped at the top of the ramp, blocking the way, so they all had to wait. 'Benedict Caine!' he said in a pleased tone. 'So you're here already. Have you got all your things on board?'

Liza breathed a sigh of relief. The man wasn't a policeman or anything, then, just an acquaintance of Mr Pringle. And now she came to think of it, his face seemed vaguely familiar, as if she'd seen him in town or somewhere.

He moved forward to shake hands, his expression softening a little. 'Yes. I'm just about to go and take possession of my sleeping quarters.'

They had to make way for more people to board the ship, but Mr Pringle carried on talking to his friend, so Liza stood as far away from the ship's rail as she could, where no one down on the dock could see her. She could not help listening to the men's conversation and noticed that Miss Kitty was staring at Mr Caine with a daft expression on her face – but then, she stared at every unattached man like that. From the way she talked to her mother, all she seemed to care about in life was getting a husband. Well, she was welcome. If all men did to their wives what Mr Marshall had done to her, Liza was never going to get wed. Never, ever!

Mind you, she really liked the sound of this man's voice. It was quiet and calm-sounding, as if he never flew into a temper the way her father did. She liked the way he looked, too, with a fresh complexion and nice wavy brown hair.

'And this is Liza, our maid,' Mr Pringle said, pulling her forward, 'who has been brave enough to join us in our antipodean adventure.'

Benedict nodded at Liza, his eyes lingering on her for a moment. 'You're very young to leave your family.'

She wasn't having him treating her like a child. 'I'm over eighteen, sir. Old enough to know my own mind, thank you.' But that just made him smile and she could not help smiling back.

He wasn't thin and bony like Mr Pringle or burly like her brothers, but just right, somehow. You'd feel safe with a man like this if there were trouble, she decided as she stepped backwards again to let the family finish their conversation. Of course Miss Kitty was acting all fluttery and foolish, gushing out words to attract his attention. Why did she always behave like that? Surely gentlemen didn't like young ladies to be silly?

Mr Caine caught her smiling and winked, as if he understood exactly what she was thinking. Liza hoped he didn't. You weren't supposed to think of your employers and their families as silly. But Miss Kitty was – and nasty with it – and Mr Pringle wasn't at all sensible, either. Poor Mrs P. had a right old time with him. She'd heard them arguing more than once, usually about money. And although Mrs P. was putting a brave face on it, Liza knew her mistress was as unhappy as Miss Kitty about going to Australia.

A steward came along and urged them to move on and leave the way clear for other passengers coming on board, so Liza followed the Pringles along to the cabin all three of the family were to share during the voyage because she didn't know where she was supposed to go. She was astonished to find it a tiny place, smaller even than her attic bedroom had been in their former house. Were they really all three going to sleep here?

Miss Kitty burst into tears at the mere sight of it and once again begged her father to send her to her Aunt Nora's. When he shook his head, she went into full hysterics, throwing herself on the floor, screaming, 'I won't go! I won't!' and drumming her heels.

A lady poked her head out of the next cabin, pulled a sour face, clicked her tongue in disapproval, then vanished again.

Mrs P. dealt with her hysterical daughter by slapping her face – and very sensible, too, Liza thought – but had to repeat that action before Kitty would quieten down.

'We're here on board now, so you can just stop that, young lady.' She turned to her husband. 'Find a steward to take Liza down to the steerage section, will you Andrew, while I see to Kitty.'

He almost pushed Liza along the passageway in his haste to get away – he hated rows, Mr Pringle did – then handed her over to the first steward they met, muttering something about taking a breath of air.

The steward, a balding man who walked as if his feet hurt him, led the way across the crowded deck. 'Most of the other passengers are already on board now, so it's just the cabin passengers like your master to settle in. You were lucky not to have to go to the emigrant depot. Sleep over a hundred to a room there, they do, while they're waiting to board.'

He showed her to the top of a steep set of wooden stairs which he told her was called a companionway on board ship. 'The steerage section's down here. It's split into three parts, each with a separate entrance. Married quarters for families, single men's and single women's. Yours is down there. Single women's.' He shuffled away without another word.

Liza felt terrified as she stared around, swaying to keep her balance as the ship rocked gently. Was she really going to sail across the world in this creaking old thing?

Then she pulled herself together and started to climb down the steep wooden steps into the dimmer light below. She had no other choice, had she? Not now. And for the first time she thought about leaving Lancashire. She had been born there, unlike her elder brothers, and it was the only home she knew. Would she feel at home in Australia? Ma said that Da had never settled in England. He'd had no choice about moving, either.

★   ★   ★

In the cabin, Kitty was still sobbing. 'I can't share this – this rabbit hutch with you and Father. How will I get dressed and washed? And what if I want to,' she lowered her voice, 'use the chamber pot?'

'There's a water closet just outside the door, the steward showed it to us, so you won't have to use a pot at all.'

'But that's just a h-hole inside a cupboard, with people walking past.'

Dorothy looked at her sternly. 'Hole or not, it'll serve the purpose. Besides, who did you think was going to empty a chamber pot for us?'

'Well, Liza, of course.'

'Since her accommodation is separate from ours, she won't be able to help us as much as we'd like, not to mention what will happen to the contents of the pot if the ship rolls about in stormy weather.' Dorothy realised how very deeply distressed her daughter was and abandoned scolding to take her in her arms. 'Look, my darling, we must make the best of it now.'

Kitty pulled away. 'There is no best! It was a *stupid* decision of Father's! And unfair to us. If he wants to go to Australia, let him. Why does he insist on dragging us along with him? Why do you *let* him?'

Dorothy agreed totally about the stupidity of this venture, but was too loyal to say so.

'And how are we going to get dressed and undressed in here? I'll die of embarrassment if I have to undress in front of Father.'

'We'll work out some system for doing things decently. We can turn our backs to let the others get dressed.' Dorothy tried to speak calmly, though to tell the truth she was just as dismayed as her daughter, for she had not expected their cabin to be quite so small.

Lost in her own unhappiness, with her daughter weeping at intervals and complaining ceaselessly and her husband spending most of his time on deck, Dorothy did not think about Liza again that day. When a steward came to help her 'stow' things, she bent her mind to learning how to go on in this strange new world because somebody had to be practical. With his help, everything they had brought with them was tied or screwed down so that it would not fall about in stormy weather.

'The lamp especially,' he insisted, 'is not to be left standing around. Imagine what would happen if it tipped over and the ship caught fire when we were weeks away from land.'

Dorothy shivered at the thought – and shivered again at the prospect of being so far from land. She had not felt so low in spirits in her whole life and if anything else went wrong, was sure she would weep like her daughter.

Liza stood at the bottom of the companionway in the single women's quarters, staring round her in shock. There were two rows of bunks along each side of the room, one row on top of the other, and they all seemed to be full of women, sitting or lying, and staring at her. The bunks were divided into sections about six feet wide, with low planks separating one from another. Down the middle of the room was a table, fixed to the floor, with benches along each side of it, also fixed in place. There were bits of luggage everywhere and still more women were sitting on the benches gossiping.

A tall, stout woman in black with a sagging bosom and a severe expression marched forward from the dimness at the far end of the room. 'Who are you, girl?'

'Liza Dooley, ma'am.' They had decided it would be better if she changed her name, but it was hard to remember sometimes. 'I'm maid to Mrs Pringle, if you please.'

The woman's expression relaxed a little. 'That'll be why you're late boarding, then. I'm Mrs Hodsome, but you will address me as Matron. I'm in charge of the single women's quarters. In *complete* charge.' She narrowed her eyes and studied Liza. 'General maid or lady's maid?'

'G-general, Matron.'

'Hmm. Well, you look respectable enough. Please note that I insist on the highest standards of cleanliness from those in my care and will not tolerate moral laxity in any form.' She pointed to the upper bunk near the companionway. 'The others are full, so you'll have to sleep in the end one. It'll be colder there until we get further south, but you'll find it better once the weather grows hot. I daresay we won't get much water splashing down

71

the companionway in rough weather, because the hatches look very sound.'

Liza moved towards the bunk, followed by the woman's low monotone, explaining the situation as she must have done many times before.

'You're not allowed out of this cabin after ten o'clock at night, under any circumstances. People who want night service house their maids in their cabins.' She looked at Liza's shabby bag. 'Well, look lively! Take out what you need for the night, then stow your bag underneath the bunk.' She marched back to the far end of the room, from where she continued to stare at everyone.

A young woman poked her head out of the top bunk and winked at Liza. 'Hullo! I'm Molly, going out as general maid to Mrs Fenton. There's another woman to come yet in our bunk, but this is Joan Lomax, who's lady's maid to Mrs Fenton.'

An older woman lying at the far side of the bunk opened her eyes briefly to say, 'This is *not* what I'd expected! And not what I'm used to at all.' She closed her eyes again.

'The bunk looks very small for four people,' Liza ventured.

Molly shrugged. 'Well, it's all we have to call home for the next four months, so we may as well make the best of it. Do you kick in your sleep?'

'I – I don't think so.'

'You can lie next to me, then. I can't abide a kicker. Here, stick your bag underneath and then tell me about yourself. You can perch up here – you'll soon learn to climb in and out.'

Liza paused on the edge of the bunk, studying the striped ticking mattress. 'Aren't there any sheets?' Even at home they had sheets, however ragged they might be.

Joan gave a snort of disgust. 'None! I've complained, but *that woman* says they don't provide sheets, just throw away the dirty mattresses at the other end.' She closed her eyes again.

Liza decided to sit on the long wooden bench instead and when Molly followed her, she asked quickly, 'Where do you come from?' because she didn't want to talk about herself.

As her companion chatted quietly about having a married sister already out in Australia and hoping to find herself a husband there, Liza realised suddenly that for the first time in weeks, she felt safe. She closed her eyes as relief trickled through her. She had done it! Escaped from Da and Mr Marshall. And whatever Australia was like, she was never coming back.

'You all right, love?'

'What? Oh, yes.' Liza opened her eyes again and studied her surroundings as Molly chattered on. The single women were of all ages and appearances and from their clothing, some were very poor, while others were young and pretty, dressed in what looked like Sunday finery. Two who seemed younger than the others were weeping. 'What's wrong with them?' she asked in a whisper when Molly paused for breath.

'The poor things have been brought to sleep away from their families because they're over fourteen. They're not used to bein' on their own, but this Captain's got very strict rules. Unless they're cabin passengers, single women all have to sleep down here.'

'Over fourteen?'

'Yes. You're supposed to be a woman grown by then. But that one with red hair don't look grown up, does she, poor little thing?'

Having finished her tea, Matron stepped forward and clapped her hands to get everyone's attention. 'I wish to make a few things clear. For meals, you must form messes of eight with one person to fetch and cook the food for the others. The easiest way to do that is in pairs of bunks, upper and lower together.'

'Aren't they going to feed us today?' a voice asked, though it was hard to tell exactly who had spoken.

'Of course they're going to feed you. The Black Ball Line prides itself on its proper treatment of passengers, and the Captain insists on the highest standards being observed.' She broke off to point a finger at one of the sobbing, terrified girls. 'You there! Be quiet!'

The girl hiccuped to a halt.

'Now, where was I? Ah, yes, you will be served with bread and cheese today, and fruit cake for tea. There's no time for cooking as all the crew are needed to make ready. The stewards will be serving up soon, I dare say.'

Molly grinned at Liza. 'I volunteer for mess leader. I like cooking.' She turned to the people in the lower bunk. 'All right if I do the cooking for us lot at this end?'

73

A short time later she went to collect their group's food, coming back with four loaves, a big fruit cake and a chunk of hard cheese, as well as a pail of water and some tin mugs. 'This is to last for the rest of the day. We don't even get a cup of tea and just look at how hard this cheese is!' she said in disgust. 'They've left it standing uncovered. But at least there's one bit of good news. The steward says the other maid as was to share our bunk has run off, so there'll just be the three of us up above.'

And that, thought Liza, looking at Joan's ample form, would be bad enough. It was one thing to sleep with your family, quite another to sleep with complete strangers.

That night in the stuffy steerage area she could not help weeping and once started could not stop, though she tried to hide her misery from her companions. She could hear others weeping around her, as well, soft sounds of muffled anguish in the darkness.

After a time she grew angry with herself. She had *wanted* to leave Lancashire, hadn't she? If she'd stayed she'd have had to marry Mr Marshall. No, this was the only thing for her to do and she must make the best of it, try to stay cheerful.

But the tears kept slipping down her cheeks as she thought of her mother, Nancy and Kieran. What were they doing now? Were they missing her? Would she ever see any of them again?

Of the Docherty family, it was Niall who persevered longest in the search for Liza, because he was furious at being tricked by her. A few weeks after she'd left, he found a woman who remembered seeing a lass of her description hurrying out of town early one morning, weeping. And she had been going towards Ashleigh, so it could only have been the Pringles to whom she was fleeing, whatever they'd told his father about not seeing her.

The following morning, he made his way to the tiny hamlet where the sods lived, sure he'd find Liza there. But the house was unoccupied.

'They've all gone to Australia,' an old man working in a nearby garden told him. 'Went last week, they did. They'll be at sea by now.'

'Did they have a girl with them?'

''Course they did.'

'Aaah.'

'Their daughter.'

Niall could have shaken him. 'Anyone else go with them? A young maid, perhaps?'

'No. That maid of theirs is an old biddy and she told me herself she wasn't going to Australia. I don't blame her. I wouldn't go there, neither.'

Niall walked slowly back into town. He was sure Liza had run away to the Pringles, and if that sour-faced elderly maid had refused to go with them, what was more likely than that they'd taken his sister instead? He said nothing to his father, taking pleasure in keeping the information from him.

If he ever got the chance, though, he'd pay that stupid little bitch back. Make a fool of him with Teddy Marshall, would she? Just let her show her face in Pendleworth again. And he was still going to ask around a bit, till he found out exactly where the Pringles had gone.

CHAPTER SIX

In the morning, Josiah woke up and cursed to find himself in a narrow cot hardly wide enough to contain his large frame. He'd tossed and turned all night, trying and failing to get comfortable, and felt stiff from having to sleep in such a cramped position. He stood up, yawning and stretching, then quietly opened the door that led into the slightly larger cabin where his wife was housed. Relieved to see her sleeping soundly, he decided to dress and go up on deck to watch the departure.

Did ships always roll you about like this? he wondered a few minutes later as he staggered along the alleyway between the two rows of inner cabins and climbed the stairs to the poop deck.

'Going to be nice and brisk today, sir,' said a passing steward.

'Rough, do you mean?'

The man grinned. 'That depends on how strong a stomach you have, sir.'

'Oh, hell! That's all we need.' Josiah made his way to the rail, thrown off course a little by the movement of the ship. As he clung to it, he looked round to see what was causing so much noise and discovered ropes creaking, sails flapping and sometimes making sounds like gun shots, not to mention men calling, that damned ship's bell, and even this early children rushing round on the lower deck, shrieking at one another.

When he saw two passengers standing by the rail on the upper deck, talking, he was surprised to realise one of them was Caine. 'Didn't expect to see you up here,' he offered as a greeting.

Benedict grimaced. 'I took one look at the accommodation below and got mine changed. Mind you, the deck cabins are not the most luxurious places in the world, either, but at least I have a bunk to myself.' He grinned. 'But don't worry. You won't have to put up with me all the time. Us second-rate passengers have a separate dining room from you nobs, though they do allow us to use the poop deck in your august company.'

Josiah could not think what to say to that. Caine was treating him as an equal, something he was not sure he liked.

'I'm lucky,' Benedict went on. 'I've got a cabin to myself, even if it is the end one and the wind does howl under the door. Oh, and by the way, this is Gerard Fenton, Captain. He's a cabin passenger like yourself, but not too top-lofty to speak to me.'

'Military Captain not naval, but I've left the regiment now,' the other man amplified with a smile, holding one hand out to Josiah. 'Pleased to meet you, sir.'

Silence fell as they studied the ocean and the busy traffic of smaller ships and boats of all shapes and sizes.

Pringle joined them and again it was Benedict who made the introductions.

'Isn't it all exciting?' Andrew beamed at them. 'The steward tells me the pilot's taking us out, but he'll be leaving us once we get to the light-ship. Then, unless we're very lucky, we have to wait for a favourable wind. Sometimes that can take days.'

Josiah listened to their conversation with half an ear as he watched the docks receding, seeing the individual buildings blur into vague shapes, then clump together to form the city outline. He hated to see England vanishing into the distance and blinked his eyes to clear away the tears. Pringle – clearly the sort who had to talk your ear off all the time – was commenting excitedly on everything that happened, whether it was worth commenting on or not. Benedict was watching the emigrants crowded on the lower deck with apparent interest and amusement, so Josiah turned to look at them, too, but they seemed a very ordinary lot, as unremarkable as a market day crowd in Pendleworth.

The children, unaware that this was a momentous occasion in their lives, were running to and fro, getting in everyone's way. He could see some of the adults below him weeping openly, husbands holding wives, older children clutching their parents' or each other's hands. The older people seemed the most unhappy. For them there would be little if any hope of returning for a visit. He could understand how they felt. By hell, he could! Even if he managed one day to return to England, he could never go back to Pendleworth. And that thought hurt like hell.

'It's a sad moment, isn't it?' he murmured, betrayed into a confidence by the strength of his feelings.

'Sad and yet hopeful, surely?' Andrew replied. His expression became dreamy. 'They say it's a fine, healthy life out there, and that if you work hard you can make your fortune.'

Josiah wanted to shake the fool and tell him that anyone who left England by choice was a lunatic, but held back the hot flow of words. 'It's my father's idea that I go out to Australia. Personally, I remain to be convinced it's a good thing.'

A pretty woman with a rather sharp face came across to join them and Fenton put one arm possessively round her shoulders. His wife, presumably. Well, he was welcome to her!

Pringle's wife and daughter arrived. The wife was rather solid-fleshed, but had a kindly face beneath her greying hair. The girl was pretty enough in a sharp-featured way, with soft brown hair and a fine pair of eyes, but she had a sulky expression. Josiah saw her brighten at the sight of Benedict and thought: You're not old enough to interest a man like him yet, girl.

When Andrew put his arm around the older lady's shoulders, she gave him a bitter look, as if angry about something, but he didn't seem to notice, too busy introducing her to the Fentons.

As conversation flagged, Josiah seized the opportunity to approach Mrs Pringle. 'I wonder – could I solicit your help for my wife, ma'am? She's not well and her maid ran away at the railway station, so we're without help at the moment. We're hoping to find someone suitable among the steerage passengers.'

'Oh, the poor dear! Yes, of course. Why don't you show me to your cabin now?'

He was surprised. 'Don't you wish to catch a last glimpse of England?' She cast a suddenly anguished glance towards the shore and he realised that she, too, was an unwilling emigrant.

'No, not really. It'll only make me feel sad to stay here. Andrew, keep an eye on Kitty, will you?'

Josiah led the way down to the alleyway that ran below the poop deck. 'We have two cabins, actually. This one is my wife's.' He knocked on the door, peeped inside and gestured to the visitor to enter.

Catherine pressed a handkerchief to her mouth. 'I'm pleased

to meet you, Mrs Pringle, but I'm afraid the motion of the ship is – is upsetting me.'

Dorothy touched Josiah's arm. 'Perhaps you'd like to go back on deck, Mr Ludlam, and I'll stay with your wife for a while?'

Relieved, he went back on the poop deck, finding himself a place where he could stand alone and take a last look at the country he loved, the country he did not want to leave.

Later that day Benedict braced himself against the movement of the ship and watched with great interest as the pilot, having guided them out to the light-ship, took his leave. As the man moved towards the rail to climb down into his boat, steerage passengers who had been on board for a while rushed up to give him their last letters to post to their families at home.

'We're at sea now,' someone said nearby and everyone started to cheer.

Benedict saw Josiah watching them do this with a scornful expression on his face. Andrew was cheering with the rest, but Kitty had tears in her eyes. Mrs Fenton had gone below, but Fenton was still there, exchanging excited comments with Andrew. Neither of them was conspicuous for intelligence, in Benedict's opinion, though Fenton was good-looking in a beefy sort of way.

He caught sight of the Pringles' young maid, standing at the rail on the lower deck, her face alight with hope, and for some reason his own spirits lifted at the sight of her. She had a piquant face and that mass of dark hair was beautiful. There was something about her that lingered in your mind so that you kept remembering her: the way she smiled, her bright eyes and alert expression. What a contrast she was to Kitty Pringle.

He forced himself to look away. No more eyeing pretty young women, he told himself firmly. You've got Grace now.

He soon forgot the lass as England faded into the distance and could not help sighing to see the last of it. He didn't really want to leave, of course he didn't. But he was young and strong, so if anyone could succeed in Australia, he could, surely?

★   ★   ★

As she stood by the rail, hemmed in by the other passengers, watching the land fade away into a grey blur, Liza breathed deeply, enjoying the salty tang of the fresh air. One of the sailors said they'd been fortunate to catch a favourable wind straight away. She felt lucky, too – lucky to have escaped. The movement of the ship filled her with exhilaration and she was enjoying the bustle of departure.

A short time later people started to turn pale and make their way down below. Others stayed to vomit over the rail, some being foolish enough not to take account of the wind direction when doing so. Within an hour of the pilot's leaving them, the crowd on deck had thinned and many people were lying sick and helpless in their bunks. Liza went down and helped tend others in the single women's quarters, but the smell grew steadily worse and she decided she'd do better on deck if she was not to be ill herself. Grabbing a hunk of bread and forgetting Matron's order to venture out only in groups, she climbed up the companionway, marvelling that already it seemed quite natural to use the steep ladder-like steps.

There were far fewer people on deck now, though they, like her, seemed to be enjoying the brisk air. She looked up towards the poop deck where only the cabin passengers were allowed, but could not see Mrs P. or Kitty. Mr Pringle was there, though, and made his way down to join her for a few minutes.

'Feeling all right, Liza?'

'I'm feeling fine, sir.'

'Good, good.'

'Is there anything I can do for Mrs P?'

'I'm not sure. Yes, perhaps there is. Kitty is feeling ill and has taken to her bed, though I told her she'd be better staying on deck. My wife also confessed to some nausea and poor Mrs Ludlam is really suffering. Perhaps you could come and see if the ladies need help?'

Within minutes Liza was clearing up after Miss Kitty, who hadn't even bothered to find a bucket but had vomited all over the floor. She helped Mrs Pringle, who had been more careful, then she found a bowl and stuck it beside Miss Kitty's bed. 'If you use that next time, Miss, it'll make it easier to clear up.'

Kitty raised her head enough to snap, 'Don't you speak to me like that!'

In the bunk opposite, Dorothy said wearily, 'Liza is quite right, and I shall have something to say myself if you don't take more care next time. Of course, if you want your clothes to smell of vomit . . .' She let the words trail away.

'*She* can wash them, can't she? What else do we pay her for?'

Liza gasped in outrage at this remark.

Dorothy turned to the maid. 'Liza, you should perhaps remember that I am the one who is paying you and that I don't expect you to serve anyone who speaks to you so rudely.' She stared across at her daughter, who sobbed and turned her back. Suddenly Dorothy remembered Josiah's wife. 'If you have time and are feeling well enough, could you look in on Mrs Ludlam, please, Liza? She's in the last cabin on this side, the big one at the end of the passage – and she's quite ill. Not just with seasickness, either.'

No one answered Liza's knock, so after a moment's hesitation she opened the door and peeped inside. Mr Ludlam was kneeling beside the bed, but by the colour of his face, he, too, was feeling unwell.

'Who the hell are you?' he snarled as he turned his head.

'I'm Mrs Pringle's maid, sir. She sent me to see if I could help.'

He closed his eyes and sighed in relief. 'Sorry. I didn't mean to – to—' He pressed one hand against his mouth and rushed out of the cabin.

Liza turned to the lady on the bed, who was so white she looked like one of the marble statues in the churchyard. Wringing out the cloth in a bowl of water that was slopping about with the ship's movement, she wiped the pale face.

The lady opened her eyes and tried to smile. 'Thank you.'

'I'm happy to be able to help, Mrs Ludlam.' As the lady pressed her hand to her mouth, Liza held out the bucket, but very little came up.

'It – hurts.'

'The steward told me we're in for a blow. But at least that means we don't have to wait around for a wind.'

Catherine groaned.

'Shall I change your nightgown, ma'am?'

'Please. There's a clean one in the cabin trunk – bottom drawer.'

As Liza was removing the stinking, sodden garment, she saw the evidence of more than seasickness and froze. The two stared at one another, not maid and mistress but two women drawn together by impending tragedy.

Catherine said quietly, 'Don't tell my husband. Please.'

'Of course not.' Liza put on the clean nightgown. It was like helping her young brother dress, so flat and thin was Mrs Ludlam, except for the lump. But at least she said 'thank you' and 'please', unlike Miss Kitty. 'I'll just go and empty this, then I'll come back and see if there's anything else I can do for you.'

When she returned, Mrs Ludlam seemed to be sleeping so Liza sat down for a minute by the bedside.

The door to the other cabin opened and the husband looked in. 'How is she?' he mouthed.

Liza tiptoed across to whisper, 'A bit better, I think.'

He looked round at the tidied cabin. 'Thank you for your help. Sorry I shouted at you. I was feeling sick myself.'

'Would you like me to set your cabin to rights as well, sir?'

He leaned against the door, still feeling dizzy. 'Please.'

'Perhaps you should lie down till you get used to it?'

Josiah did as she bade him, surprised at how capable she seemed for such a young girl. Within minutes she had his cabin set to rights then disappeared to ask the steward for more drinking water, returning with the man in tow.

'I've got to go and check on my mistress now, but I'll come back and see to your wife again later, if you like, Mr Ludlam?'

Josiah nodded, then lay back and closed his eyes.

'Good little sailor, isn't she, sir?' the steward said admiringly.

'Lucky bitch!' Josiah growled, feeling the nausea rising again.

The rough weather cleared up the following day and the ship became a lively centre of activity. Unless they had duties to attend to, the single women were only allowed up on deck under Matron's supervision. She forbade them to speak to any man who was not a relative, and the steward told Liza that Matron was famous for her strictness and so was the Captain.

'You want to warn your friend,' he ended, nodding towards Molly. 'She's got an eye for the men, that one has, and our Captain will make a big fuss if he catches anyone out in immorality. Locked one poor young woman up in the storeroom for a week on the last trip, they did, to punish her.'

But Molly just tossed her head when Liza passed this information on. 'I've enough sense not to get caught, thank you very much. Why do you think I volunteered to do the cooking? What the eye doesn't see . . .' She winked.

As the days passed everyone settled down into the ship's routine.

'I shall be surprised if poor Mrs Ludlam lasts the journey,' Dorothy said to her maid one day as they both stood by the rail on the poop deck. 'You don't mind helping her, do you, Liza dear?'

'I like to. She's very polite and grateful, and Mr Ludlam isn't bad once you get to know him, either. He growls a lot, but he really cares about her.'

Dorothy studied her. 'You're looking well. In fact, I don't know when I've ever seen you look so well.'

'I'm enjoying myself. I like sailing. And there's always plenty to eat.'

'Ship's food?' Dorothy shuddered.

Liza chuckled. 'When you've known what it's like to be really hungry, you're glad of anything. I'm not the only one down in steerage to feel like that.'

Later, when Catherine saw her eyeing the leftovers on her tray and told her to finish them off, Liza accepted with alacrity. But since the poor lady wasn't eating enough to keep a sparrow alive, she took it upon herself to coax a few more mouthfuls of each meal down, and felt pleased with herself when she succeeded.

After a few days' respite the weather turned stormy again, and the Bible classes, reading groups, choir and other organised activities stopped as people took to their bunks.

'You're lucky, you are,' Molly grumbled to Liza. 'Don't you *ever* feel seasick?'

'Just a bit sometimes when I get up in the mornings, but that soon passes.' It was saying it aloud that made Liza realise and she froze where she stood. Sick in the mornings? Oh, no, she hadn't had a monthly since – not since *that time*! And after helping her mother through a couple of pregnancies, she knew exactly what that might mean. It couldn't, it just couldn't. Oh, surely not?

She went up to see to her mistress, but on the way there stopped for a moment to stare into the water and worry about her condition.

'You're up early, young Liza.'

She looked up to find Mr Caine behind her, sitting carving. 'Oh, I didn't see you down here, sir.'

'It's more sheltered on the lower deck today.'

She went over to look at what he was doing, carving a delicate flower. 'That's lovely!'

He smiled down at it. 'I've never had the time to do really fancy stuff before. I've made a couple of mistakes in this one, but I think I've hidden them well enough.'

'What's it for?'

'Just practice. When I get my house in Australia, I intend to make all my own furniture.'

'Your wife will love that.'

He stiffened. 'What made you say that?'

She looked at him in surprise. 'I just thought you'd be getting married one day. Most of the gentry do, don't they?'

'I'm not gentry!' His voice was harsh. 'Nor do I want to be. I just want to own my own land and farm it properly.' He saw she was looking upset. 'I'm sorry. I didn't mean to shout. And I do intend to have a family one day—' But he wasn't going to tell anyone about his marriage until he had to. He didn't want Josiah sneering at him, nor did he want word getting back to Lancashire until he and Grace were ready to announce that they were married.

Liza's face clouded over. 'I don't ever want to marry.'

'Nonsense! A young woman like you is bound to fall in love one day.'

'Not me, sir. I've seen what it leads to for women.' The

84

words reminded her of her new worries and she turned away abruptly, going to the cabins to see how her ladies were faring. Being late with her monthlies was probably just caused by the journey and the strangeness of everything. She'd get them in a few days, of course she would.

As the stormy weather continued, Liza was kept busy ministering to the Pringles and the Ludlams, for even Andrew was suffering during this prolonged patch of bad weather. When Mr Caine realised how hard she was working, he came to help her with the gentlemen, which was very nice of him, considering how grumpy Mr Ludlam could be.

At a quarter to ten each night a bell was rung to warn the steerage passengers to go below, and a short time later the steward came into the cabin to remind Liza, 'The bell's gone. You'd better make your way below, young lady. Matron doesn't take it kindly if her charges don't get back to quarters in time.'

Liza cast a worried look at Mrs Ludlam and whispered, 'I don't like to leave her. She's been really bad today.'

'Well, don't say you haven't been warned.' He glanced over her shoulder. Anyone could see the lady was suffering from more than seasickness. They got them on ships sometimes, sick folk who hoped a sea voyage would cure them. It didn't usually, though.

Liza decided to spend the night with Catherine.

At eleven o'clock, however, Matron erupted into the cabin. 'So there you are, Liza Dooley!' she hissed, with one eye on the lady in the bed. 'What do you think you're doing, staying up here at night? Get back down to your bunk at once and don't you dare go missing on me again! And you can think yourself lucky I haven't caught you with a man, or I'd have you confined below for the rest of the voyage. The rules are made to preserve decency and I make very sure they're not disobeyed.'

Liza didn't move. 'Mrs Ludlam needs me.'

Catherine struggled into a sitting position. 'Liza has been here with me for several hours, Matron. There's nothing indecent about that.'

'I'm sorry, ma'am, but it's against the rules for her to stay the night, and the Captain's very particular about that sort of thing. She's not your personal maid, after all. And if you don't

85

mind my saying so, girls of her age need careful watching or they take advantage.'

Liza followed Matron down to her bunk, enduring a scolding all the way there and feeling angry that anyone should even think such things about her.

The next day she was summoned along to Matron's little cubicle.

'Have you anything to tell me, young lady?'

Liza blinked in bewilderment. 'I – I don't understand.'

'I've been questioning your bunkmates and they tell me you haven't had your monthlies, though we've been at sea for three weeks now.'

Liza flushed. 'I'm sometimes late.'

'When did you last have a monthly?'

'That's no one's concern but my own.'

'Don't you dare speak to me like that! Answer my question at once.'

'Just – just before we came on board.'

'Then you'd better pray you get another soon. I've got my eye on you and if I find you're carrying the fruits of immorality, you'll be confined to these quarters for the rest of the voyage, then handed over to the authorities when we reach Fremantle. That is all. You may go.'

Back at the bunk, Molly nudged Liza and whispered, 'I didn't tell her about you feeling sick in the mornings, but what are you going to tell her when nothing happens?'

'What do you mean?'

Molly tapped her nose. 'I wasn't born yesterday. Who's the father?'

'No one. I mean – there's nothing wrong with me.'

But as the days passed, Liza could feel Matron's eyes on her, could see the woman looking at her belly and she still felt sick in the mornings. She'd now missed two of her monthlies and what's more her breasts were starting to feel tender. What else could that mean but a baby? And it wouldn't be long before everyone knew it.

What was she going to do? She didn't want a baby – and certainly not Teddy Marshall's baby. She didn't want anything but a quiet, busy life as the Pringles' maid. It wasn't fair!

CHAPTER SEVEN

Catherine looked at the young maid's unhappy face and asked softly, 'What's wrong, dear?'

Panic set Liza's heart thumping. Had Mrs Ludlam guessed? Did something show? 'I – I don't know what you mean, ma'am.'

'You've lost all your sparkle. And I can tell there's something amiss, so don't deny it.'

'It's the stormy weather, that's all. It's making me feel a bit down.'

'Nonsense. You're an excellent sailor and you love it here on the ship – or you did until recently.' Catherine hated it. Being confined to this small cabin was a terrible way to fritter away her precious remaining days. Even in calmer weather she found it hard to summon up the strength to go up on deck – though she forced herself to do that occasionally so that Jos would not suspect how bad things were. She took the girl's hand. 'Tell me what's troubling you. I may be able to help.'

'I – I—' And suddenly it was all too much. Liza burst into tears, buried her face in the covers and blurted out everything. How Mr Marshall had forced himself on her, how she'd run away to avoid marrying him and how she thought she was having a baby – and Matron was going to keep her shut up in the storeroom for the rest of the journey if she found out.

Catherine listened to the confused tale, asking gentle questions from time to time and stroking the thick, wavy hair that had fallen out of its ribbon again. 'Shh, now. Shh. No one's going to lock you up. Let me look at you first. Some women show early, and some don't. Stand up!'

Liza struggled to her feet, blinking in surprise.

Catherine studied the slender body, which did not show any sign of pregnancy yet. 'You couldn't be mistaken, could you?'

'I've missed twice now. And – and I feel a bit sickly in the mornings. Matron's noticed that I haven't had my monthlies. She notices everything, she does.'

'Sit down. No, here on the bed, next to me.' Catherine took hold of the hot damp hand, thinking how unfair life could be. She believed every word the girl had told her, because that vivid face with its beautiful dark-fringed blue eyes did not, could not, belong to a liar. Sadness nearly overwhelmed her for a moment. What would she not give to have a child, to be able to leave something of herself behind?

And at that moment the idea was born which was to dominate and brighten her final days – only she didn't tell anyone about it. Not yet. Not till she had thought it through and convinced Jos of its practicality. 'How would you like to become my personal maid, Liza? If you came to live in my cabin, no one would know anything about your condition for quite a while.'

Liza gaped at her. 'But what about Mrs P?'

'I'm afraid Dorothy will be the loser, for she'll have to give up her maid. Leave her to me. The main thing is: do you want to work for me?'

'Oh, Mrs Ludlam!' Liza burst into tears again. 'Oh, I'd love to be your maid and stay up here. You won't regret it, I promise you. Not for a minute.'

'Then stop crying and go and find Mrs Pringle. Ask her if she'll come and speak to me, then go and get some fresh air till I send for you again.'

Catherine felt a lot better herself at the prospect of helping the young maid. She wasn't frightened of death, for she was too tired to care most of the time, and she sincerely believed there would be a better life waiting for her thereafter, but she hated the thought of wasting her final days on earth. And possibly, just possibly, what she was considering would help Jos cope – afterwards.

When she had passed on the message, Liza went to join Molly, who was clutching the rail and scowling out across the sea.

'It gives me the pip, all that water does. I wish I'd never come. An' we've only just started.' Molly grinned at Liza. 'I'm that fed up I'm even thinking of going to Reverend Beeton's Bible Class. There, what do you think of that?'

Liza chuckled. 'You must be desperate.'

'Why don't you come as well? We might have a bit of fun.'

'I can't. I'm helping Mrs Ludlam.'

'That pale lady?'

'Yes.'

'What's she like?'

'Nice. Kind.'

'You're lucky to have something to do. Lucky you don't get seasick.' She grimaced. 'I think I'd better go and lie down again. It's getting rougher.'

Liza went to stand by the rail. There weren't many other people on deck, and those who were had occupied the more sheltered spots. At the other side the children were in the reading class that one of the fathers had started. A woman from Sheffield had started a choir which met in the afternoons and was to put on a concert later. There was a reading group where one person read to the others, sharing in turn the books they had brought with them. Liza would have joined that if she'd had the time. She loved to listen to stories.

She marvelled that there was nothing in sight but water and more water. She hadn't realised how big the oceans were. The sailors said they were making good time, though. She looked up at the billowing sails, enjoying the shadows patterning them like writhing grey snakes. These came from what the sailors called sheets, halyards and standing rigging, but what she still thought of as ropes. Turning her face into the wind, she let it cool her flushed cheeks.

Benedict noticed the reddened eyes and wondered what had upset her. She was a nice lass and everyone enjoyed her cheerful nature, but she had been looking unhappy lately. Acting on impulse, he walked down to the lower deck to join her at the rail.

Before he could speak, she turned to him, her face alight with excitement, her cheeks rosy and her dark hair streaming behind her. 'It's wonderful, isn't it? I'm so glad I don't get seasick.'

Something twisted in his heart, some response to her joy

and the sparkle in her eyes. Whatever had upset her must have been sorted out, he decided, for she looked like her old self again. For a moment he could not speak, only stare at her. She was only a girl still, years younger than he was, and he had no right to touch that soft skin or run his fingers through that mass of lovely hair – but he wanted to, he definitely wanted to.

'How are the animals?' she asked.

'Unhappy. You can't blame them, really.' The smaller creatures were travelling on deck, penned in wooden cages, and the larger animals were shut up below. He went down several times a day to tend them, for the poor things were miserable in the fetid darkness and seemed to derive comfort from his presence. He hoped that most would survive the journey, for he had spent good money on them and they were carefully chosen as a basis for his breeding stock.

'I'd hate to be shut up in the dark,' Liza said softly.

'Me, too.'

They stood together in silence for a while, then she said thoughtfully, 'Mrs P's embroidery is a bit like your carving – almost alive. She's been trying to teach me, but I'll never be as good as she is. She does flowers that seem real, with such beautiful colours you feel you could almost pick them. She's brought piles of silks with her, because she says you don't know what you'll find to buy out there.'

'A lot of us have brought things along to pass the time. What did you bring?'

Liza flushed. 'I didn't – I couldn't—' She looked at his steady quiet face and knew she had nothing to fear from this man, so told him the simple truth. 'I ran away from home, you see, and I couldn't bring much with me.'

'Why did you run away?'

She bent her head, the sigh so quiet that only he could hear it, then told him about her da wanting her to marry Mr Marshall. When she had finished, she didn't look up, not wanting to see scorn on his face. For some reason, it mattered greatly what he thought of her. 'Please don't tell anyone else about that, Mr Caine.'

Without thinking, he reached for her hand, a gesture instinctive to him when offering comfort. 'Of course not. I'd never betray a confidence.'

She let him hold her for a moment, finding the warmth of his larger hand comforting. Then, as a child cannoned into her and nearly knocked her over, he grabbed hold of her shoulders and held her steady until she had got her balance.

Safe in his arms, Liza looked up at him, laughing. 'They're little devils, some of them, aren't they? It's a wonder they don't fall overboard.'

When Dorothy Pringle summoned her back to Catherine, Benedict did no carving for quite some time because he simply couldn't get the memory of Liza's laughing face out of his mind. She was like a young filly, too slender, but graceful with a child's unconscious gait, and she was going to be lovely when she grew into full womanhood – if life didn't brutalise her first. But whatever she became was none of his business and why he'd even gone to speak to her, he couldn't think, except that life on board ship seemed to be breaking down some of the barriers society had set up. With everyone but Josiah, that was.

He turned to study the other man, who was standing on the upper deck staring across the water as he often did, the hunch of his shoulders not inviting people to join him.

Benedict sighed. You couldn't go on hating someone as unhappy as that – even if your own future had been forcibly joined to his.

Josiah stared at his wife in surprise. 'How on earth did you persuade the Pringle woman to let you have her maid?'

Catherine chose her words carefully, still hoping not to have to tell him the whole truth. 'I explained how helpless I felt, how seasick I've been – and she understood how great my need was.'

'I don't like you asking for her pity.'

'It's not just that. There was another reason. But promise me you'll not tell anyone this, Jos?'

His dark brows drew together at that and he looked at her through narrowed eyes. 'Not tell them what?'

'Promise me first.' She knew he always kept his word.

'Oh, very well.'

'Liza is expecting a baby.'

He reared backwards. 'Then she's no fit maid for you and I'll not—'

'Jos, dear, let me tell you the whole story before you jump to any conclusions.'

His voice was heavy with sarcasm. 'You mean the story she spun you?'

'The story Dorothy has confirmed, for she knows the family and saw Liza afterwards – saw her bruises.' She saw him gradually relent as she related the sad tale.

He remained unconvinced by her proposal though. 'Well, I'm sorry for the girl, but haven't you enough on your plate without taking on someone else's troubles?'

'Jos, dear, I shall *enjoy* helping her.' But he was still frowning and muttering about it not being right, so she took a deep breath and said quietly, 'And anyway I shall need more help as the weeks pass, I'm afraid.'

He became very still. 'Are you not – feeling any better?'

'No, dear.'

He stared at her, sheer terror in his eyes.

'I don't think I'll get any better, Jos. I have a lump in my breast and it's growing larger.'

There was a long, fraught moment of silence before he commanded harshly, 'Show me.'

She hated to reveal her wasted body, but it seemed the only way to convince him.

He stared down at her in horror. 'Oh, God, Cat, why didn't you tell me about this before? You must be in such pain!'

'I didn't want to trouble you.'

'You should have stayed in England, let them look after you properly.'

'No.' Her voice was very firm. 'I've realised now that I was meant to come on this voyage, so that I could help Liza.'

Her eyes were glowing with a certainty he didn't share, but he didn't contradict her.

'I can teach her so much, as well as helping her. Then, later on, she'll help me. Oh, Jos, how wonderful not to die useless and alone! I'll have both you *and* Liza.'

He could hold back his emotions no longer but buried his head in her lap, kneeling in almost the same spot as Liza had earlier and weeping harsh, bitter tears. For Cat was his only real friend and he didn't know how he would cope without her.

Again she found herself stroking someone's head, making

shushing noises, giving comfort, and as she stared blindly across the cabin, the other idea that had come to her grew stronger, more certain, and she nodded. It would be the right thing to do – all she could do for him now.

Matron stared at Liza with hostility in every line of her face. 'I don't know how you got round that kind lady or why she wants someone like you for a maid.' Her voice was very scornful. 'But don't think I haven't noticed that you still haven't started your monthlies, and before you try to leave here, I'm going to see Mr Ludlam and tell him what I suspect, then we shall refer the matter to the Captain.'

Everyone in the single women's cabin had fallen silent and was listening, staring at the two of them. Liza stood frozen in horror and humiliation.

Before she could move, Matron took her by the shoulders and pushed her into the dark storeroom at the rear.

When the door banged shut, Liza sank to the ground in the stuffy darkness, too shocked for tears. She'd been feeling so happy as she came below to pack her things. Now she was terrified. Would the Captain lock her up here for the rest of the journey? She knew by now how much power such a man had at sea. Feeling as if she could not breathe, she drew her knees close to her chest, clasping her arms round them, so lost in despair she did not even notice when a rat ran over her foot.

What seemed like a long time later she heard some muffled sounds outside and a man's voice shouting. Was that the Captain coming? She shuddered and shrank into an even tighter ball as the voices drew nearer. She could make out Matron's flat harsh tones now, and a babble of shrill cries and sounds, but couldn't make out what anyone was saying.

When the door opened, she couldn't move, just looked up, numb with terror.

Josiah stared down at the girl's tear-stained face, feeling a sudden surge of pity for her. But mostly he was concerned for Cat. How dare this damned fool of a Matron try to stop her getting the service she wanted? *Needed!* He was glad of the anger, glad to vent his rage at what was happening to his wife on someone else. 'Get up, Liza, and collect your things. You'll not be coming back down here—' he had to swallow hard before he could complete his sentence '—whatever happens.'

She did not move, so he reached out to pull her to her feet.

Only then did Liza realise she was being released. She brushed away her tears and followed him quickly out of the darkness, edging past a scowling Matron, then rushing along to her bunk, terrified the woman might still try to stop her. As she crammed things into her bag, Molly winked at her, but Joan turned her head aside with a sniff of disapproval.

When she had packed everything, Liza turned to the man standing impatiently beside her. 'I'm ready, Mr Ludlam.'

Josiah looked at the half-empty canvas bag. 'Is that all you've got?'

'Yes, sir.'

'Come along, then. My wife's waiting for you.' He turned to Matron, who had followed them across the cabin and was standing between them and the companionway. 'Get out of my way, woman! Go and find some more children to bully!'

'You have no right to take that girl away. I shall speak to the Captain about this.'

'So shall I!'

Canvas bag clutched to her bosom, Liza followed him to the bottom of the steep wooden steps, confused for a moment when he stood back to let her go first, as if she were a lady.

At the door to his wife's cabin, she tugged at his sleeve. 'Sir.'

'What?'

'I just wanted to say – you'll never regret helping me, sir. I'll look after her really carefully, I promise.'

Pleased and surprised by her speech, he nodded and opened the door. 'Well, Cat, here she is. That damned interfering harpy had her locked in a cupboard.'

Catherine looked across at him with her luminous smile. 'Thank you, Jos, dear!'

He tried to smile back, but couldn't. She looked so thin, so ill! 'The steward's going to bring us a mattress for the girl.'

'Her name's Liza, Jos.'

He grunted and looked round at the maid again, still waiting next to him. 'Yes, well, for Liza, then. I'll go and complain to the Captain immediately because I don't want that old harridan interfering again.'

Catherine looked at the girl's tear-stained face. 'They didn't hurt you, did they, Liza?'

'No. I was just – she shut me in the storeroom and I – I thought they might stop me coming to help you.' Her voice wobbled as she spoke.

'I wouldn't have let them do that. Nor would Jos.'

Liza gave her a tearful smile, then looked round the cabin with a proprietorial air. 'I'll start by tidying this place up first, shall I? It's a right old mess in here, isn't it?'

Within a few minutes she was humming as she worked.

Catherine fell asleep to that soft, happy sound.

As the days passed she began to feel a little better, for daily life was now less of a struggle. She enjoyed her new maid's cheerful company but watched the girl more carefully than was apparent, for before she put her plan into action she must be sure it was right for Jos.

As the days passed, Liza couldn't see the purpose of half her 'lessons', as she came to think of them, but if Mrs Catherine wanted her to learn something, then learn it she would. She was aware that the other woman was dying, but by unspoken consent both of them avoided talking about that.

The first thing Catherine did was replace Liza's ugly clothes, because she couldn't bear to see her in such lumpy, ill-fitting garments. She had more clothes than she knew what to do with and would soon have no need of any of them. She gave a stunned Liza a simple dress or two, and helped her to alter them, also equipping the girl with everything from underclothes to a warm cloak of fine blue wool, which had hardly been used.

'But Mrs Ludlam – it doesn't seem right,' Liza protested, overwhelmed by this generosity but betraying her feelings by stroking the fabric with a tender fingertip.

'Of course it's right. I want my maid to do me credit and I'm enjoying dressing you properly. Besides, you couldn't keep wearing that woollen dress.'

The weather was getting very hot now, making everyone on board listless, and they were making slow progress through the Doldrums. Some people grumbled, but Liza enjoyed the heat. How wonderful to wear only the lightest of clothing and yet be comfortable, day and night!

However, she didn't let her happiness with her new possessions deter her from looking after her mistress. One day she waylaid Josiah to ask him if he could carry his wife up to the poop deck.

He gave her one of his superior, long-suffering looks. 'I asked her earlier if she wanted to go up, but she said not.'

'I know. But if you *persuade* her, sir, I'm sure she'll be much more comfortable up there. Please! It's so stuffy in that cabin and she's that uncomfortable.'

'Hmm.' He went in to see his wife and had to agree about the stifling heat in the cabin, so said firmly, 'I'm going to carry you up on deck, Cat. It's much more pleasant there – though it ain't really cool anywhere, of course.' He didn't wait for an answer but called out, 'Liza! Find one of those damned stewards and ask him to prepare somewhere for my wife to lie on deck.'

'Yes, sir.' She darted out with her usual speed and enthusiasm.

Looking after her, Jos grinned. 'She's perked up, anyway.'

Cat smiled. 'Yes. The young are very resilient.'

He stared down at her. 'Is she doing all you wish?'

'More than I'd hoped for. She's a very intelligent young woman, given the chance. Having her around cheers me up.'

'She's a hungry young woman, too. Don't give her *all* your food, Cat.'

She hadn't realised he'd noticed but didn't deny it, just laid her hand against his chest to steady herself as he walked. 'I'm eating better than I was, I promise you. Liza won't touch my left-overs until I've eaten a certain amount, which she decides on.'

He threw back his head and laughed for the first time in days. 'She *is* a clever little minx.' Then he grew serious again. 'But you're definitely looking better since she came to you.'

'I'm feeling better, too. But, Jos – I don't think it'll change matters, so don't let that raise any false hopes.'

His expression became bleak.

On deck the Pringles were gathered around a wooden chaise-longue which the steward had pulled across. Dorothy helped Liza to arrange the feather mattress and pillow, but Kitty stood glowering at everyone impartially, as usual making no offer to help.

From another patch of precious shade Benedict watched them. He'd found you needed to follow the shadows round the deck in the heat of the day to keep cool – well, as cool as you could, anyway. As the sun continued to move across the sky and he drew nearer the group of women under the canvas awning, he laid down his carving, tired of it now, feeling a sudden desperate longing to go for a long walk through the cool, shady woods at home.

'Can I please see what you're doing, Benedict?' Catherine called.

He carried his piece of wood across the two yards of holystoned deck that now separated them.

'Why, it's lovely!' She was treating him as she had in their childhood, like a big brother. She turned to her husband, who was standing by the rail, near the group but not part of it. 'Come and look at this, Jos!'

He came across, fingered the piece, then picked it up to study it more carefully, looking surprised. 'Didn't know you were an artist, Caine.'

'Not an artist, a craftsman.'

Josiah ran one fingertip across the pattern of English leaves and flowers. 'You're damned good.'

'Thank you. I appreciate that coming from you.' Josiah was known to have some artistic leanings, a facility for sketching and painting in water colours, though it was also known on the estate that Saul Ludlam did not like his son wasting time in such unprofitable pursuits. 'I'd have thought you'd be doing some painting to while away the time? You brought some things with you, didn't you?'

Josiah shrugged. 'I'm not in the mood.'

Over the next few days, Liza persuaded her mistress to let herself be carried up on deck every day. And for all her weakness, it was Catherine who drew the group together – at first because it was the sort of thing she did quite naturally, but later because it had occurred to her that in Australia they would do better together than alone – especially her Jos.

'Why do you not take up some land close to my husband and Benedict?' she asked the Pringles one day. 'Surely it would make things easier if you had some familiar faces nearby?' She smiled as she added, 'Lancashire faces.'

Andrew said instantly, 'I'd be glad to do that. I know far too little about farming and Benedict here knows a great deal, but I can't think what I'd have to contribute to such a scheme.'

Catherine smiled at him. 'Not only a familiar face, but someone who will act as a good neighbour. That's important, too.'

Later that afternoon, noticing how tired her mistress was looking and unable to find Mr Ludlam, Liza approached Benedict. 'Do you think you could carry Mrs Ludlam down to her cabin for me, sir?'

'Of course.'

When he picked Catherine up, he was shocked at how light she was, for her bones felt as fragile as those of a bird and were barely covered in flesh. He was afraid he'd let his shock show, but she didn't say anything and her smile didn't falter, so perhaps he hadn't betrayed his feelings, after all.

Liza led the way, chatting cheerfully as they went. Did she realise how ill her mistress was? Benedict wondered. Then he noticed how watchful she was beneath the chatter. Of course she did and was bravely pretending that everything was all right. She was a good lass.

'Everyone is so kind to me,' Catherine murmured sleepily as he laid her down on the bed.

Benedict walked out, feeling desperately sad.

Not until her mistress's eyes closed did Liza let her own smile fade. Mrs Ludlam was now taking laudanum at night to enable her to sleep and they both knew it could only be a matter of a few weeks at most.

Tears filled her eyes suddenly at the thought of losing this woman whom she had grown to love dearly, even in such a short time, but she blinked them away resolutely. It upset Mrs Ludlam if people showed distress over her condition, so Liza was not going to show her feelings – not until it wouldn't matter, anyway.

In the tiny cabin next door, Josiah covered his eyes with

his forearm and didn't even try to stop the unmanly tears. Cat had looked so bloody frail today that it had brought everything home to him. And yet she had talked cheerfully of the others' needs in Australia. She was so brave, but that wouldn't stop her dying – and in pain, probably. And he'd have to watch it helplessly.

Afterwards he'd be alone, and what the hell was he going to do without her? A dozen times a day he turned to her. He *needed* her, dammit! He was seriously considering throwing himself overboard after she died, because what was the point of going on? He was losing everything that mattered to him – first Pendleworth, now Cat. What else did he have to live for? There would be nothing for a man like him in Australia, he felt certain.

The day came when Catherine decided it was time to share her idea with Jos. She sent Liza for a walk on deck, then asked him to sit with her. 'I'm much weaker now—'

'Oh, God, Cat! Don't go yet!' It was a cry of pure anguish.

'I think I'll have a few more weeks left, but I've been taking something for the pain at night and now I have to take it in the daytime, too. It makes me sleepy so – so I want to have a little talk with you while my mind is still clear.' She took his hand and summoned up all her powers of persuasion. 'You see, I have an idea.'

He clasped both his hands around hers. 'What about? If there's anything I can do – anything at all – you have only to ask.'

'I've been worrying about what you'll do without me, Jos.'

He gave a harsh caw of laughter. 'Me? What the hell do I matter?'

'You matter very much to me. You always have done. I love you. I wish – wish things could have been different between us, that you might have had children to comfort you, at least.' She paused for a moment then went on steadily, 'But I've thought of a way to make things easier for you.'

At that he let go of her to clasp his head in his hands, saying in a muffled voice, 'You're too good for this world,

99

Cat, but you've no need to worry about me. I'll manage all right.'

She took a deep breath, sure he would reject her idea violently at first. 'I think the best thing for you would be another wife – and – and you should remarry fairly soon after I d— after I leave you.'

'*What?* Hell, Cat, another wife is the last thing I need! What use am I to a woman!'

She continued as if he had not spoken, 'I thought Liza might be suitable.'

Josiah was so shocked by this that for a moment he could not utter a single word.

'She's going to need someone to protect her, you see, and—'

He stiffened. She *did* mean this seriously. 'Cat, don't!'

'Hear me out, Jos!'

'But—'

'You did say you'd do anything for me, after all. I'm only asking you to listen to my suggestion.'

He groaned, but held his tongue.

'Liza would make you a good wife, given the circumstances.'

'How can you say that? She's a servant and, whatever else I am, I'm still a gentleman.'

'I know. I wouldn't suggest this in England, but in Australia things are going to be different, you know they are. There you're going to need a working wife, not a hothouse plant like me. Liza's strong and healthy. She won't sulk or expect to be waited on. And she'll look after you.'

He made a scoffing noise in his throat, but didn't speak.

'She'll need you, too. With a child born out of wedlock, she'd have a hard time – so she'd be grateful to you.'

'Oh, yes! I'm *sure* she would. Very grateful. How has she persuaded you into this?'

Catherine frowned at him. 'Jos, you're not even considering what I'm saying and Liza doesn't know what I'm suggesting. I'm explaining it to you first.'

'But, Cat—'

'We could tell everyone it's your child, you see, that she used to be your mistress. Benedict wouldn't contradict you on that. I intend to speak to Reverend Beeton myself – tell him it's what I want – ask him to perform the marriage ceremony. Afterwards.' She could see her husband pulling away and clutched his hand, saying desperately, 'It'll work, I *know* it will.'

'No.'

'Jos, *please*! Just think about it.'

'*No!* Not even for you.' He stood up and walked into his own cabin, slamming the door behind him. He stayed there, separated from her only by a flimsy wooden wall, but a long way away mentally. How could she ask him to do such a thing?

When half an hour had passed and he hadn't rejoined her, she eased herself out of the bed and stumbled across to the door that connected their cabins. 'Jos!'

There was no reply.

'Jos, come back and talk to me.'

She knocked on the door again, then groaned as the room whirled round her and sank to the floor in a faint.

Jos heard her fall, but heaven help him, he could not face her, so ran up to the deck and grabbed Liza's arm. 'Your mistress needs you!'

Then he went and stood by the rail, staring out blindly over the water, by turns indignant and horrified at what Cat had suggested, wondering if the maid really was cunning enough to have put this foolish idea into his wife's head.

In the cabin Liza found her mistress lying on the floor just coming round from a swoon. She rushed across to help her sit up, then said, 'I'll go and get Mr Ludlam to carry you back to bed.'

Catherine grabbed her arm. 'No. I'll be – all right. Give me – a minute.'

'But Mr Ludlam—'

'Is angry with me. Best to leave him alone for a while.'

She allowed Liza to help her to the bunk and lay there with her eyes closed, one arm shielding her face. She knew Jos. He needed time to think through what she had suggested. He'd come round eventually, because he simply could not manage alone – and because she wanted it.

Kitty looked at the pile of dirty clothes and scowled at her mother. 'It's Liza who should be washing these. She's deserted you, after all you've done for her.'

'She's helping Mrs Ludlam who is dying. *You* can wash your own things. Catherine can't.'

Kitty pressed her lips together. She hated to think of death so looked the other way when Mrs Ludlam was nearby, using her anger at Liza to divert her attention from that dreadful wasted body and skull-like face.

Dorothy tried to sound cheerful. 'We shan't have any help in Australia, so we shall have to learn to do everything ourselves.'

'It's going to be horrible. I wish I were *dead*!'

Dorothy pulled her into her arms and rocked her to and fro, making shushing noises. At first Kitty tried to draw away, then she suddenly collapsed against her mother and began to sob.

After a while she stood up, wiped her eyes and said in a hard, tight voice, 'I hate Father. *He's* done this to us. He can't manage money at all, can he?'

Dorothy shrugged, not feeling it right to criticise a father to his child.

'Well, I'm going to learn how to manage money – and how to make it, too. I'm not going to stay in Australia for the rest of my life.' Kitty gave her mother a long, level glance. '*You* can put up with it, *you* can make the best of things. I'm going to find a way to escape one day, believe me.'

Dorothy reached out to smooth Kitty's soft brown hair back from her brow. 'If that's what you want, I hope you'll succeed, darling.'

'I'll make sure of it. Whatever it takes. Now,' Kitty glared at the pile of dirty clothes, 'come and show me how to wash these.'

'I think Liza had better show us both.'

An angry snort was the only answer.

'She hasn't done this on purpose, you know. Why are you so angry with her?'

And Kitty couldn't tell her that it was jealousy of Liza's bright happy face, jealousy too of the way Benedict Caine, yes, and even her own father, smiled when they were with Liza. Only Josiah Ludlam seemed immune to the maid's attractions, but then, he had eyes only for his wife. There was no one at all who cared for Kitty, no one to whom she could really talk among the other cabin passengers.

And whatever the cost, she *would* go back to England one day! She would lie, steal, do whatever was necessary. She knew she was going to hate Australia, just knew it!

CHAPTER EIGHT

As she went to bed that night Catherine thought of another argument to persuade Jos to do as she wished and smiled as she realised it would probably tip the scales.

In the morning, when she had eaten what she could from her breakfast tray, she told Liza to come and sit down.

'But I haven't tidied up the cabin yet, Mrs Ludlam.'

'Do it later. I need to talk to you. Here! Come and sit on the bed next to me.' She took a deep breath. This was not going to be easy. 'Liza, after I die—'

'Don't say that!'

'I must. Because there's something I want you to do for me – afterwards.'

Liza could only nod, because her throat felt full of tears at the prospect of being alone again.

'After I die, I want you to marry Jos.'

Sure she must have misheard, Liza did not at first reply, just stared at her and frowned.

Catherine took hold of the girl's forearm and gave it a little shake. 'Did you hear what I said?'

'I'm – not sure.'

'Then I'll say it again. I want you to marry Jos after I die.'

Liza's mouth dropped open. She had heard it right the first time. *'You can't mean that!'*

'I do. I'm very serious about it. He's going to need someone to look after him. He's not as – as strong as he appears. And *you* will need a home for yourself and the baby.'

Liza blinked at her in bewilderment. 'But why would he want to *marry* me? I can be his housekeeper and still look after him, can't I?'

'No. It'll cause a scandal and then people won't think well of him.' And the last thing Jos needed was any hint of scandal.

Besides, if Liza were only his servant, he could dismiss her and go his own way – and that way might lead him into trouble.

As it began to sink in that her mistress was perfectly serious, Liza blurted out, 'I don't want to marry anyone, Mrs Ludlam. Not ever.'

'You *need* to marry someone.' This time the girl's shudder was very marked and Catherine suddenly realised what it meant. 'Did he hurt you very much, that man?'

Liza could only nod, her throat closing with tears.

'Well, that's another reason for marrying Jos.' Catherine lowered her voice. 'You must never, ever tell anyone this, but my husband is – well, he's different from other men. He doesn't like doing that sort of thing to women. He's never touched me and he wouldn't touch you either.' She pointed to the connecting door. 'As you can see, he doesn't even share this cabin with me.'

'I thought that was because you were ill.'

'No.' Cat sighed and could not continue for a moment. 'What Jos needs is someone to look after him and, above all, to keep him cheerful. He gets very downhearted at times, you see. And there's another thing. His father has promised to give him five hundred pounds when his first child is born.'

Liza clutched her stomach, thoroughly bewildered now. 'But this isn't his child.'

'No one in Pendleworth need be told that. Jos's father is a horrible man, a bully. Have you seen him in town?'

Liza nodded. Everyone had seen old Mr Ludlam driving past with his nose in the air. It was whispered that no young woman was safe with him, and they certainly had trouble getting maids to stay at the Hall. Even she knew that, because she had heard Mrs P. talking about it to Maggie.

'He was *mocking* Jos when he offered him that money, not expecting to have to pay it. And although Mr Ludlam is rich, he hasn't really been very generous with us in this venture. He wants Jos to experience hardship. So for the first time in my life, I'm quite prepared to cheat someone.' A tear slid down her cheek and Cat brushed it away impatiently. 'Finding him another wife is the last thing I can do for Jos.' Her breast heaved as she tried to keep calm, but a sob escaped her. 'Then I can die in peace. Oh, please do as I ask. *Please!*'

'But I'm your *maid* – are you sure he wants to marry me? He could find someone who—'

'He doesn't want to marry anyone. This is all my idea, because I fear he may try to take his life if he's left on his own – afterwards.'

Liza looked at her wonderingly. 'You must love him very much.'

'Yes.' But although she continued to speak persuasively, all Catherine could win from Liza was a promise that if Mr Ludlam thought it right, she would consider it. In the end she gave up the attempt for the time being and lay back on the pillows, feeling exhausted. 'Go and bring Jos to me, please. He'll be up on deck.'

'Yes, ma'am.' But when she got on deck, Liza was so embarrassed she could not look him in the eye and stared at her feet all the time she was delivering her message.

Then, as she watched him walk away, looking so fine and gentlemanly, she decided that the laudanum must have turned Mrs Catherine's brain. That was the only explanation she could think of. Why on earth would a gentleman like him want to marry a girl like her? A girl from a poor family. A girl carrying some other man's baby in her belly. And even if he did, she could not even begin to imagine how they would get on living together.

Down in the cabin Josiah said angrily, 'You've told her, haven't you? Without even waiting to see whether I'd agree or not?'

'Yes.' Catherine listened quietly as he spoke at length of the reasons why it would not be wise to marry the girl. His voice was very loud and he waved his arms about a lot. He reminded her of a small boy shouting and blustering.

'Have you thought,' she said softly and persuasively when he ran out of words, 'that if you marry Liza, you'll be able to claim the child as yours – and then your father will be forced to pay you five hundred pounds more?'

'Have you been listening to a word I've said?'

'Not really, Jos. I'm too tired. I just need to know you'll be safe when I'm gone.'

'And you think an uneducated child like Liza will keep me safe?' He threw back his head and laughed.

She listened to the bitter echo behind his laughter, looked at the despair in his eyes, the lines of strain on his face, and begged, 'Please, Jos, *please* do this for me! I know it will work. Consider it my last request, if you like. Or do it only for the money. Just do it.'

'Cat—'

She threw his hand off her arm and played a final card. 'I know you're thinking of killing yourself. You have to have something to *live* for, Jos – and some way to get back at your father.'

Then she burst into tears, weeping so wildly he was afraid for her, but when he took her in his arms and tried to calm her, she kept begging him to do this for her and her weeping grew more hysterical.

In the end he held her at arm's length and said, 'Very well.' But he had to repeat this before it sank in.

There was silence for a long time, then she whispered, 'Promise me.'

'I promise I'll do as you ask and marry Liza if – afterwards.'

Cat sagged back against the pillows, her face as white as the fine linen and lace that surrounded it and her voice a husky whisper. 'Oh, Jos, you'll not regret it, I promise you. You know you like children. Well, now you'll have one of your own to raise.'

It was his sense of the ridiculous that saved the day. 'I'm very sure I shall regret it, Cat.'

'Then live to curse me, but *live*, Jos!'

It was he who lay awake that night. How the hell was he going to live with an uneducated creature like Liza? What would they talk about? Marrying someone like her would be a ridiculous thing to do even if he had needed a wife's body – which he never would, for the thought of touching a woman in that way made him shudder. But Cat knew, damn her, that he never broke his word to her. And he would not do it this time either.

On deck that day Benedict could see Liza wearing a deeply

troubled expression again. He glanced quickly sideways. Dorothy was involved in another argument with her daughter and Andrew was staring dreamily across the sea. No help for the poor girl there. He could not just leave her on her own, looking so unhappy. Cursing himself for every sort of fool, he went across to her. 'Is something wrong?'

Liza nodded, too upset to pretend otherwise.

'Would you like to tell me about it?'

She considered this, head on one side, but Mrs Ludlam had said not to tell anyone. 'I'd better not.'

'If you ever do need to talk to someone . . .'

She smiled at him. 'I'll come to you, Mr Caine.'

'Promise?'

'Yes.' He was a kind man. She always felt comfortable with him, enjoyed talking to him, but this was definitely not the sort of problem she could discuss with him. Or with anyone else.

Benedict left Liza to her thoughts and went back to his carving, though he sat for a long time with his knife in his hand, doing nothing. He didn't like to see her looking racked with worry. Normally she had such a capacity for joy that it made everyone around her feel more cheerful. Even Catherine had been looking better since the young maid had gone to work for her. He'd begun to hope that Josiah's wife would manage to live until they reached Australia, help him to settle in. He'd need help. He had such unrealistic ideas of how you made money from farming. He was in for a few shocks, one way or another.

He saw Josiah come up on deck, hesitate and scowl in Liza's direction. Then he walked across and offered her his arm, something he would not normally do to his wife's maid. As the two of them began to stroll up and down the deck, both looking stiff and uncomfortable, Benedict watched in puzzlement. What the hell was going on here?

'My wife has told you what she wishes us to do,' Josiah began, and felt the arm that lay trembling on his jerk then go rigid, fingers digging into his coat sleeve.

Liza stopped walking to stare up at him. 'Yes.'

'And you've agreed to do it?'

108

'I said I would think about it if you considered it right.'

They started moving again, pacing slowly along the deck.

'I didn't know what to say to her, sir. I was surprised and – and it didn't seem like a very sensible thing to do – only she got so upset and – and she's right about one thing, at least: I shall need help afterwards, for the baby's sake.' Liza looked down at her still-flat belly and then up at him. 'Sometimes I can't believe it's happening to me. I haven't even started to show yet.'

Josiah ignored that, for he found the processes of procreation distasteful. 'I was not attracted to the idea, either. But my wife got very upset with me when I refused her.'

Liza stood still, pulling her arm away. 'Then you don't want to do it?'

Her voice rang with such relief he was a little piqued. 'I don't want to marry anyone. Especially so soon after . . .' His voice trailed away. 'I still can't believe Cat's dying. Can't believe I'll lose her.'

'She's in a lot of pain, now, sir. I – I think when it gets worse, it'll be a merciful release.'

'Not for me! Never for me.' Another long silence then he said harshly, 'But I have given her my word to do as she wishes.' He stared Liza in the eye as he said slowly and clearly, 'And I always keep my word.'

She stared up at him in shock. He had agreed to marry her? *A Ludlam?*

'Well, you needn't look as if someone had threatened to hang you at dawn!' Josiah said irritably. 'Most girls of your station would jump at the offer.'

Liza scowled at that. 'Well, I'm not "most girls" and I don't want to marry anyone.' She remembered her manners and added quickly, 'Thank you all the same, but I don't think marriage will suit me. Now, if you've done with me, sir, I'll go back down and see if Mrs Ludlam needs anything.'

He kept tight hold of her arm. 'I haven't finished discussing this yet, young woman.'

'You won't change my mind, sir.'

'Cat says – and quite correctly – that I shall need a housekeeper.'

'I could be your housekeeper without marrying you.'

His hand tightened on her arm. 'Shush, you little fool! Keep your voice down!'

She lowered her voice and the pressure on her arm relaxed a little. 'Well, I could.'

'And have everyone thinking you were my mistress? No, thank you.'

'If I don't care about that, I'm sure you needn't either.'

He found he did care. And was surprised by that. He was determined to make a success of life in Australia, become a respected member of the community – if only to show his father. 'There is also the question of the money. Five hundred pounds would mean a great deal to me and would help me to build a decent house – or – or something of that nature.'

Liza didn't like Mr Ludlam's tone. He was talking to her as if she was stupid. 'And what would happen to me and the baby *after* you got the money?'

'If I married you, nothing would happen. You would stay with me "until death do us part" as they say in the marriage ceremony, for then you'd be a Ludlam. You could bring up your child in relative comfort, though I tell you now that I would not allow you to betray me with another man or to run away.'

Liza stopped walking, really worried now. 'But I don't want to marry anyone!' she repeated in a despairing whisper. Again she tried to pull her hand away, but he still would not let go.

They took another turn about the deck in complete silence then Josiah said, 'You do not have just yourself to consider. There is also the child.'

Her feet stopped moving as she closed her eyes. 'Yes.'

He stared down at her, realising for the first time that most people would call her pretty; that if she were properly dressed she might not look too bad. 'My wife wishes very much for us to marry. It's important to me that Cat have everything she wants before she – she leaves us.'

'Yes.'

'So I would be greatly obliged if you would give the matter further serious consideration, Liza.' Josiah released her arm, bowed and walked away.

She stood and watched him, thinking that even his walk was arrogant and he was more like his father than he realised. She was not surprised when he went to stand at his usual vantage point by the rail, his expression so forbidding that everyone left him alone. One or two of the cabin passengers were whispering and looking at her, probably talking about the way he had given his arm to a mere maid when he could barely manage a polite greeting to the rest of the ladies.

What would those same ladies think if they knew he had just offered to marry her? A faint smile crossed Liza's face. They'd be horrified, that's what. The smile faded. What *was* she going to do, though? She didn't want to marry him, definitely not. Only there didn't seem anything else she could do to keep herself and the child safe. Mrs Ludlam would soon be dead and you couldn't get a job as a maid when you had a baby to look after. And Liza wasn't going to let anyone take her child away from her, like they did in the poor house. Oh, no!

She drew in a long, shuddering breath and turned to go back to her mistress.

Benedict was the only one to notice Liza stop partway down the steps that led to the cabins below the deck. As she pressed her hands to her flushed cheeks, her face was full of something that was surely panic. Then she squared her shoulders and continued walking, expression set and determined. Whatever it was, she had come to some decision. He wished she'd confided in him, though.

He grew angry with himself for thinking about her yet again and turned back determinedly to his carving.

'That looks so lovely, Mr Caine.'

He looked up to see Kitty hovering nearby. Here was another unhappy young lady. He didn't have the heart to repulse her, though he'd rather have been left alone, but when she tried to flirt with him yet again, he set down his tools and said frankly, 'I don't like it when you flirt, Kitty.'

Tears filled her eyes and she ran away, clattering down the steps to the cabins. Which made people stare at him accusingly. Oh, hell, would this voyage never end?

Catherine Ludlam died exactly two weeks later, passing away gently in her sleep, so that when Liza woke up on her pallet bed nearby, she did not at first notice anything wrong. Finally realising how still her mistress was, she scrambled out of bed –

but it was too late. There was nothing anyone could do now to help the poor lady.

Liza stroked the pale cheek. 'I won't let you down,' she whispered. 'I'll remember my promise.' Then she flung on some clothes and went to rouse Mr Ludlam.

Funerals at sea were disgusting, Josiah decided, holding on to his anger to keep from disgracing himself. And the thought of his Cat being consigned to the ocean, falling down, down, down through the clear blue water to lie on the bottom like a piece of discarded rubbish, was hardly to be borne.

The only way he could face the funeral service was by floating himself through it on a cloud of brandy. He listened to Reverend Beeton mouth the usual phrases, glad that at least Cat had a proper clergyman to pray over her, if not a proper coffin.

Her body, in a weighted canvas shroud, had been placed on a long plank with one end on the bulwark and the other held by two seamen. A Red Ensign was draped over the body and held by the bosun.

The Captain spoke softly: 'Commit her to the deep. We pray she will now be with God.'

The sailors tilted the plank and the mortal remains of Catherine Ludlam slid from under the flag to be claimed by the ocean.

Josiah groaned and took an involuntary step forward, greatly tempted to throw himself into the water after her, promise or not. Someone grasped his arm and it took him a minute to realise that it was Benedict.

'You all right, Josiah?'

He nodded.

Benedict kept hold of the arm and turned to Liza, standing quietly behind them with tears running down her cheeks. 'Has he been drinking?' he whispered.

She nodded.

'How much?'

'A lot. Brandy.'

'I see.'

But Josiah was a Ludlam and all the Ludlam men could hold

their liquor. 'You don't need to hold me up,' he said loudly. 'I've not had enough to make me fall about.'

He saw the cabin passengers, who had gathered around them, draw back. When he looked towards the lower deck, he saw the emigrants muttering and some women weeping, as people always did at funerals, even though they had not known the dead woman. Children were fidgeting and soon life would start flowing again – for everyone except Cat.

The Captain came up to him. 'My sincere condolences on your great loss, Mr Ludlam.'

Josiah nodded and held himself still as one by one the other passengers came up to make similar remarks. He was beyond speech, because if he had opened his mouth he'd have bawled like a damned baby. So he nodded acceptance of their trite phrases and waited for it all to end, distantly aware that Benedict was hovering near him, standing guard; not even noticing Liza or the Pringles, who were also standing behind him in a protective half-circle.

As soon as he possibly could, he turned and went down the steps, stumbling once, but righting himself without help from Benedict, who was still dogging his footsteps like a damned watchdog.

Liza was wondering what to do next when she saw that Mr Ludlam was struggling with Benedict at the bottom of the steps. Without thinking, she rushed to join them.

'Sir, what are you doing?'

'I'm worried he might throw himself overboard,' Benedict whispered.

'No need to damn' well whisper!' Josiah roared. '*She* can't hear us now. And anyway, it's none of your bloody business, Caine. But I'm not going to throw myself overboard. *She* saw to that, didn't she, girl?'

'Sir, please! Come and lie down now.' Liza tugged at his coat sleeve.

Swaying slightly, he stared down at her, then inclined his head and allowed her to tug him into the narrow passage between the cabins. But he went into his wife's cabin instead of his own, groaning aloud to see it so empty.

Liza tiptoed inside after him.

Benedict watched them from the corridor, uncertain what

113

to do. Then, as the door closed, he turned and went to sit on the bottom of the outside stairs – just in case she needed help.

Inside the cabin Josiah made his way unsteadily towards Catherine's bed. After standing for a minute looking down at it, he suddenly collapsed on it, sitting with his head in his hands. 'She's gone,' he muttered. 'She really is gone now.'

Suddenly he was racked by sobs, sounds so harsh that Liza felt tears of sympathy come into her own eyes. Bent over, his hands covering his face, he rocked to and fro in an agony of grief. She could not bear to see anyone in such pain and rushed across to comfort him. Without knowing how it happened, she found herself sitting on the bed with her arms round him, stroking his hair and making the sorts of noises that had always soothed her little brother and sister when they were upset.

It was a long time before he stopped weeping.

When at last he drew away, she remained where she was, eyes lowered, not sure what to do.

He stretched out one hand and turned her face round towards him, wiping away one of her tears with his fingertip. 'I couldn't have borne it if you hadn't wept, too.'

It seemed a strange remark. 'Mrs Ludlam was very easy to love.'

'I don't even have a handkerchief,' he muttered and seized a corner of the sheet, using it to mop his face.

'Shall I clear up the cabin?' Liza asked as the silence dragged on.

Josiah waved his hand. 'You can do what you want. This is all yours now.'

She was shocked into absolute stillness.

His voice was slow and heavy. 'We both promised her that we'd marry. You're not going to go back on that promise, are you?'

Liza swallowed hard and shook her head.

'A week, she told me. Wait a week, then get married. She made me promise to do that. Because of the baby.' He laughed. 'She even provided a ring.'

'But, sir . . .'

He refused to answer and stared into the distance for a

long time, 'It's all I can do for her now. So find yourself a wedding dress from among her things. We'll get married next Monday.'

Then he went out and left Liza sitting motionless, feeling as trapped as any rabbit in a snare. She was terrified of marrying him – but equally terrified of not doing so.

CHAPTER NINE

Within an hour of the burial the Captain, alerted by a vindictive Matron, had summoned the Senior Steward. 'What's happening about Mrs Ludlam's maid now?'

'I've received no orders of any kind, sir.'

'Then give Mr Ludlam my compliments and request him to attend me in my cabin. The girl can't stay with him.'

'Yes, sir.'

Josiah declined in the crudest of terms to visit anyone that day and cursed the steward for disturbing him.

'Really, sir, I think you'd better go and see the Captain. He wants the maid moved back to the single women's quarters. Very big on morals, our Captain is.'

Damned interfering prig! Josiah thought. With a groan, he swung his feet off his bed, brushed his hair and straightened his clothing before following the steward.

Reginald Harrow did not mince his words. 'Sad as this day is for you, sir, I'm afraid that in the interest of maintaining this ship's high moral standards you must tell your wife's maid to move back to the single women's quarters at once. She cannot stay with you.' He cleared his throat uneasily. 'Besides Matron tells me she is – um – with child. So it is essential to keep her under strict supervision now that she has no mistress to do that. Do you – ahem – have any idea who the father of the child is? Is the female very promiscuous? If so, I can promise you she will be strictly dealt with.'

Until then, Josiah hadn't thought much about Liza's position, beyond feeling vaguely that Cat had been exaggerating. Now, he suddenly realised that the vultures were about to descend on the poor little bitch who had been so devoted to his wife, and that only he stood between her and a lot of unpleasantness. *Strictly dealt with*, indeed! Well, he'd had a bit of experience with smug, self-satisfied moralists himself and he wasn't going to toss poor little Liza to their most untender mercies.

'I know exactly who the father is,' he drawled, leaning back in his chair and deliberately allowing the silence to continue until the Captain was fidgeting, before adding, 'myself. And since Liza has only been with one man in her life, I wouldn't exactly call her promiscuous, would you?'

Harrow goggled at him and burst out, 'Then I say shame on you, sir, for taking advantage of the girl. And with your wife dying, too! What's more, you needn't think such a liaison is going to continue on my ship.'

'Oh, it didn't happen on board your precious ship. It happened before we left England. My wife had been ill for some time, you see.' Even to speak of Cat made a lump come into Josiah's throat. 'Since we were coming to Australia, we both felt we could not leave Liza to fend for herself, so we asked the Pringles to bring her with them as a maid. We were unable to have children ourselves, and had thought to adopt the infant.'

The Captain's face was now red and he was making little puffing noises. 'Well, that does not change my mind. And I cannot believe a gently born lady like your wife would have colluded in such plans.'

Josiah found himself taking a savage enjoyment in goading the pompous idiot. 'You need not fear for your high moral standards. I have every intention of marrying Liza and giving my child a name. I thought next Monday might be a suitable day. What do you think?' He watched in satisfaction as the Captain turned even redder. 'Reverend Beeton will be able to perform the ceremony for us. He is a clergyman, after all.'

'Sir, I take leave to tell you that you are despicable to speak so with your wife barely cold. I shall interview the girl and see what she says about this.'

Josiah stood up. 'Not without me being present, you won't. And I take leave to tell you that you're poking your nose in where it's not needed. I'm a passenger, not a member of your crew.' He saw this was only making the Captain look more furious and bit off further angry words. 'What's more, if you talk to Reverend Beeton he will confirm that my wife was anxious for me to marry Liza after her death – for the child's sake – and spoke to him about it before she died. Now,' Josiah was suddenly weary of this game, 'if you have any compassion, let me grieve in peace.'

He left without waiting for a response, rage coursing through him. Was he never to be free of mealy-mouthed puritans poking their noses into his affairs?

Without thinking he slammed open the door of the main cabin to find Liza in her shift, changing from the good clothes she had worn for the funeral into her working ones. With a squeak, she snatched a sheet off the bed and held it in front of her.

He turned his back on her, saying curtly, 'Get dressed again as quickly as you can. And put your good things on. It's my guess we're about to have visitors.'

She scrambled back into them. 'I – I'm ready, sir. Who is it who's coming?'

'That officious nincompoop of a Captain.'

'Oh.'

Josiah inspected her critically. 'Get out that cream shawl of my wife's.' He watched her pull it out of a drawer in the cabin trunk and smooth its soft fabric for a minute, then drape it round her. It was not necessary in the heat, but it did lend her more dignity. 'Yes, that looks better. And don't let them browbeat you when they come.' He went across and smoothed back her hair with a light, impersonal touch. 'Can't you fix this more tidily?'

Liza's hands were trembling as she tried to rearrange it, tying it back with a ribbon. 'Wh-what did the Captain want?'

'To accuse us of immorality. To send you back to the single women's quarters. To let that hag bully you again.' He saw the terror in her face and lifted her chin. 'As my wife, you'll have to learn not to show fear to people like that, Liza.'

'But, sir—'

'Josiah.'

She gulped. 'Josiah, then—'

There were footsteps outside. He pushed her to sit on the bed. 'Look down your nose at them! It's all they deserve.'

There was a knock on the door. When Liza tried to jump up and answer it, he grabbed her skirt and pulled her back, then positioned himself beside her with one hand on her shoulder.

'You're not a servant now. Let them open the blasted door themselves. They're not exactly welcome guests in my quarters after all.' He raised his voice and called, 'Come.'

Reginald Harrow marched into the room, followed by the clergyman, who was looking ill at ease. The Captain waited until the door was closed before saying, 'Reverend Beeton has confirmed that your wife did indeed wish you to marry this young woman.'

'For the – the child's sake,' Reverend Beeton stammered. 'A most Christian, forgiving lady. She will be sadly missed.'

Josiah dug his nails into the palms of his hands and said nothing. Damned if he was going to make it easy for them.

The Captain glared across at them. 'I still cannot condone an unmarried woman staying here. Until you are married, this – this female must move back to the single women's quarters. And if she were not with child by you, I would refuse to allow such a hasty and improvident marriage to take place at all on my ship.' He snapped his fingers and pointed to the door. 'You, girl, go with Reverend Beeton, and see that you behave yourself!'

Liza tried to get up but Josiah pushed her down again. 'She's not going down into that hell-hole again, nor will I have her bullied by that sour-faced old biddy.'

She tugged at his sleeve. 'Josiah, I can—'

'Quiet, my dear. Let me handle this.'

The Captain folded his arms. 'No unmarried female is staying in a cabin with a man to whom she is neither related nor married, not on my ship.'

Josiah realised there was only one way out of this, feigned a weary sigh and turned to Liza. 'What do you say, my dear? Shall we be wed today or do you wish to spend a week down below with the dragon?'

Liza looked at him in horror. 'Today? But Mrs Ludlam was only just buried. It would seem so – so disrespectful.'

'No, not disrespectful to Cat,' he corrected gently. 'You know it's what she wanted – it's just happening a little more quickly than we had anticipated.' He raised his voice. 'And I am doing it now only because I don't wish the mother of my child to be ill-treated by interfering busybodies.'

Liza looked up to find kindness on his face, something she had only seen there before when he was talking to his wife, and that made her feel better about marrying him. Perhaps if he were kind to her, things would not be too bad. 'I'll do whatever you think right, Josiah – though I'd rather have waited.'

He nodded and turned back to Reverend Beeton. 'I wish to protest at this, sir, and assure you that the hastiness of this marriage is none of my doing. But I will not have Liza bullied.'

The clergyman turned to the Captain. 'Perhaps—'

Furious at the way Ludlam had spoken to him, Reginald Harrow snapped, 'The wedding will take place in an hour's time in the dining room. You, girl, will remain here with Reverend Beeton until I can send someone to chaperone you.'

As he changed his clothes, for he refused to be married in a shirt that had been worn for two days, Josiah realised that Cat had already achieved part of her purpose. He no longer felt like throwing himself overboard, but more like throwing the Captain over the side. He grimaced into the shaving mirror. 'Never been a saviour of the oppressed before,' he told it. 'Not sure I'll be good at it either.'

And there would be a child. He liked children, had greatly enjoyed the company of his little nieces and nephews, and to his surprise the idea of being a father appealed to him. He hoped the baby would be a boy, but whatever happened, he would not treat it as his father had treated him.

When Dorothy Pringle came into the cabin Reverend Beeton left in relief, muttering something under his breath about 'never heard anything like it'.

'The Captain has told me what's happening,' she said briskly, 'and anyway, Catherine explained what she wanted a while back.' It had surprised her at the time but she supposed it did make sense in a strange sort of way because she too had seen how low in spirits Josiah became sometimes. She worried about Liza, though. Would he treat her well? Be kind to her?

Liza got out the white silk gown Catherine had selected for her as suitable to marry in and put it on. When she tried to fasten it up, however, her hands were shaking too much to manage the small carved ivory buttons.

'Let me help you with that, my dear.'

'Oh, Mrs P., I don't know whether I'm coming or going.'

'Do you really want to marry him? If not, you're welcome to come back to us, you know.'

Liza stood motionless for a moment, her eyes unfocused. 'I don't want to marry anyone, if truth be told. I don't want a baby, either. But I haven't much choice now, have I? And anyway, I promised Mrs Ludlam I'd do it.'

'But surely you could wait a few days? It seems wrong to do it today of all days.'

'That's the Captain's fault, not ours.' Liza stared at herself in the mirror, wishing she didn't look so pale. 'I don't want to go back to the single women's quarters, not even for an hour. Matron would make my life a misery.'

'Very well, then. Let me do your hair. We want to make sure you look your best. And you'd better call me Dorothy from now on, dear.'

When they got there, the dining room was empty of all save Benedict Caine, who was looking very grim and determined. 'Let me talk to Liza alone for a minute, will you, Dorothy?'

She nodded and went to stand outside the door.

He came and took Liza's hands, looking earnestly into her eyes. 'Are you *sure* this is what you want, lass?'

'I don't have much choice. I'm expecting a baby.'

'And we both know it's not *his* baby, whatever he's telling people. Could the real father not have married you?'

He was still holding her hands and she let herself cling to them for a minute, realising she would not feel nearly as bad if she were marrying this man. 'The father wanted to marry me, but he'd have beaten me, made my life a misery.'

'Then why—' He broke off. He had no right to ask this.

'Why did I lie with him?' She laughed, but it was a thin, mirthless sound. 'Because he forced me. Because my own brother dragged me into his house for money.'

Benedict stared at her in horror.

She pulled her hands away and took a step backwards. 'I have a baby in my belly and I need a husband. No one else is offering to marry me – unless *you* would care to?' She saw him flinch and laughed again. 'No. Who would want a woman like me for a real wife?'

He could not move or speak for a minute because he wished

121

– oh, hell, he didn't know what he wished. 'I hadn't realised the circumstances. Oh, Liza, Liza! What have they done to you?'

Her mouth was pressed into a tight line, her eyes hard and angry. 'Josiah has saved me, that's what he's done. And so has Mrs Ludlam. I'm grateful to them both.'

There was a tap on the door and Dorothy returned. 'The Captain's on his way down.'

Liza moved to stand near her, staring out of the porthole at the endless expanse of water, wishing she were anywhere but trapped on this ship.

Andrew Pringle came in first, beaming at everyone as if this were a happy occasion, followed by Reverend Beeton, very tight-lipped, then finally the Captain, stiff and disapproving.

Last of all the groom sauntered in, immaculately clad but wearing a chill, arrogant expression. 'I take leave to tell you again, sir, that I resent this officious insistence of yours on our marrying today,' he told Reginald Harrow. 'And I wish to make that plain to everyone here.'

The Captain did not reply but took a step backwards, as if dissociating himself from the proceedings. 'Get on with it, Beeton.'

So they stumbled through a mockery of a marriage ceremony, with Liza whispering her responses in a voice that hardly carried to the witnesses and Josiah snapping out his almost before the clergyman had told him what to say.

When Reverend Beeton declared them man and wife, Josiah stood and stared down at Liza as if he had never seen her before. So Benedict gave him a nudge and he took a deep breath before kissing the air above his new wife's cheek.

Andrew came forward to salute the bride with a smacking kiss on both cheeks, then Benedict realised people were expecting him to do the same. Liza was staring down at her hands, blushing furiously.

Pity filled him and as he stepped forward to take her in his arms, he whispered, 'Chin up, lass. And don't let anyone look down their nose at you.' Then, because tears were trembling in her eyes and she looked young and frightened, he pulled her close and kissed her gently on each cheek.

The bridegroom held out an arm to his new wife, and when she laid her hand on it, led her over to sit at the long dining table fixed to the floor. Ignoring the Captain, he yelled, 'Steward! Where's that wine? I intend to drink my new wife's health.'

'You must hold me excused. I do not consider this to be an occasion for celebration.' Reginald Harrow made a stiff bow to the company and walked away to enter the marriage into his log.

The clergyman stood looking from one to the other, uncertain what to do. His wife had refused point blank to attend the wedding and said any decent woman would shun the new Mrs Ludlam. But the bride was looking terrified and he knew how tenderly she'd looked after her mistress. He decided that if Christ could forgive sinners and drink wine at a wedding, so could he.

When the glasses were full there was a moment's awkward silence then Andrew stepped into the breach and proposed a toast to the bride.

After that Josiah raised his voice. 'I propose another toast. To Catherine!'

'Oh, yes!' Liza raised her glass to clink it with that of her new husband. 'To Mrs Ludlam!' she echoed, adding very softly, 'I've done as you asked.'

Benedict was the only one close enough to hear her last words. He shook his head. Even though he knew why Josiah was doing this, it would cause a scandal that would not be easy to live down. He wondered if gentle Catherine had realised the difficult position she was placing Liza in, but even if she had, it would probably not have stopped her because her thoughts had been all for Josiah, and had been ever since her girlhood. Though their marriage had been an abomination, she had made no attempt to get out of it. And now, here was another abomination being perpetrated, with poor Liza the victim this time.

Josiah set down his empty glass and stood up, again offering his arm to his wife. 'I believe we should go for a promenade on deck now, my dear.'

'Oh, no!' Liza protested involuntarily, then whispered to him, 'They'll all stare at us. Can't I just go back to the cabin?'

He took her limp hand and threaded it through his arm, noting for the first time that she was a little taller than Catherine and more sturdily built. 'No. You must learn to outface gossips, my dear. It's the only way to deal with them.'

But even he felt uncomfortable as the other ladies turned away and ignored his greetings, behaving as if his new wife were invisible. Which did not stop him from taking two turns around the small upper deck and greeting each person by name both times he passed by. He also noticed that the steerage passengers were staring at them from the lower deck, whispering to one another and pointing. Who the hell had told them about it?

As they walked near the edge of the upper deck one of a cluster of young women waved and called out, 'I wish you happy, Liza!'

She stopped dead in her tracks, tears coming into her eyes, and managed to nod back.

'Thank her, then!' Josiah hissed, and after Liza had done so, nodded his head to the young female below and continued the leisurely stroll. After the second turn around the deck, however, he took pity on his white-faced wife and escorted her below.

Now that the excitement of besting the Captain had passed, Josiah was feeling very low again. He saw Liza into the cabin and said abruptly, 'We'll need to face them again later at dinner, I'm afraid. Be ready at six.' Then he went into his own cabin and shut the door on her.

Sitting alone, she tried not to weep. Her thoughts were in turmoil and she looked down several times at the wedding ring, amazed to see it still there. Was she really Mrs Josiah Ludlam? A married lady? She didn't feel like it and when she looked round, she half expected the former Mrs Ludlam to come back from an outing on deck.

'How am I going to bear it?' she whispered, pressing one hand against her mouth to stop herself from weeping.

As the minutes passed so did the urge to weep, and she began to think more calmly about her future. She laid one hand on her belly, an action which made her feel less alone. The skirt beneath her hand was silk. She had been transformed from maidservant into gentleman's wife at a dying woman's whim. Indeed, she had not really had much say in anything that had happened to her for the past few months. But as she sat alone in the cabin that was now hers, stroking the soft white silk of her skirt absentmindedly, determination began to grow in her and she looked down at the ring on her hand, given to her by her former mistress, saying in a low voice, 'I don't know whether you've been kind to me or cruel, Catherine Ludlam. I don't know anything very much, really, except I'm alive and you're not, and I'm going to have a baby to care for.'

It was almost as if the shade of her former mistress rustled past her, nodding in sympathy, and that eased something inside her.

When it was time to get ready for dinner, Liza looked down at her wedding dress and decided to change. It seemed better not to flaunt herself in her late mistress's best finery. And she'd have to call her predecessor Catherine, too. She said it aloud for practice. 'Catherine.' Then she added apologetically, 'I hope you don't mind.'

She chose a simple blue gown that she and her former mistress had altered together, sewing it one hot day as the ship lay becalmed in the Doldrums waiting for wind. When she put the dress on, Liza nodded at herself in the oval mirror. That was better, more like her.

Then she frowned at her hair, which had come loose again and was flowing down her back. Married ladies didn't wear their hair like this, only unmarried younger ladies like Kitty. She pulled the mass of thick, springy hair back, wondering how to confine it, and went to search in the drawers of the cabin trunk. These things were hers now and Catherine herself had said she was to use them, but still she felt guilty rummaging through them. There was a whole drawer containing lace collars and cuffs, ribbons of all colours, lengths of braid and crocheted silk hairnets. Yes, that was it, a hairnet! She pulled one out and bundled her hair into a low chignon, then added one of the bits of lace and ribbon that Catherine had worn to dinner when she was well enough to join the others. Studying herself in the mirror, Liza nodded. That looked better. Definitely less childish.

When Josiah knocked on the door that led to his smaller cabin, she called, 'Come in!' He stood in the doorway staring at her until she began to feel uncomfortable. 'Is something wrong, Josiah?'

He shook his head and moved forward to sit on the edge of the bed. 'No. I just wanted to check that you were ready to face them, child.'

'Yes. And I'm not a child. I'm eighteen. How old are you?' She didn't even know that about him.

'Twenty-eight. Ten years older than you.'

He remembered suddenly how bewildered he had been at eighteen, not understanding his own nature, terrified sometimes that he was going mad. Liza didn't look bewildered, as she had earlier, but determined.

'I want to thank you for marrying me and giving the baby a name,' she went on. 'And I was wondering. Do you – would you rather move into this cabin now? It's bigger than yours.'

'No. It would remind me too much of Cat.'

Silence fell and each sought desperately for some topic of conversation, but found nothing to say. It was a relief when the bell rang to summon them to the dining room, even though they both knew the meal would be another ordeal.

'If you don't know which knives and forks to use, watch the others,' he said as they left the cabin.

She smiled. She'd set tables for the Pringles enough times to know what each piece of cutlery was used for, and eating in the cabin with Catherine had given her practice in using utensils properly. It was the people she was afraid of, not the cutlery.

She was relieved to find herself placed in the middle of their own group, with Andrew on one side, Josiah on the other, Dorothy and Kitty opposite them. Although this protected her to some extent, the other passengers stared down their noses and no one addressed a single remark to her, which made Liza feel uncomfortable.

When the Captain said grace, he made some pointed comments about sinners, during which Josiah yawned loudly and Andrew was overcome by a fit of coughing.

After the meal all the passengers went on deck and promenaded up and down, because it was still very warm. Liza turned towards her cabin, but Josiah took hold of her arm and muttered, 'Not yet.' Then he walked her up and down a couple of times before letting her go below.

Afterwards he leaned against the rail in his favourite position and stared out across the water, wishing this damned voyage would end. He stayed there until everyone else had gone to their beds and when a steward touched his arm, jerked in shock.

'Are you all right, sir? It's getting late.'

'I'm as right as I'll ever be.'

'Can I fetch you something?'

'No. No, thank you. I suppose I'd better go below.' He hesitated outside Liza's door, but could not face her again tonight. Besides, there was no light showing. She was probably sound asleep by now.

Liza wasn't asleep. She had dozed a little, but woken with a start when people began to make their way to one of the other cabins. There were little bursts of noise and activity as people used the two water closets, then settled down for the night.

Things had been quiet for a long time before she heard Josiah come down. It was their wedding night. Would he come to her? Insist on doing it? Or had Catherine been telling the truth? Did he really not like touching women in that way? Liza lay there tensely until she heard him settle down. He coughed a couple of times, blew his nose, then like the others settled into sleep.

She was exhausted but still wide awake. It would not be easy being Mrs Ludlam. Josiah had been kind to her today, but she'd seen him, even with Catherine, turn suddenly spiteful, or glum, or bitter. She wished suddenly that she could see her mother, just for a few minutes, wished she had someone to put their arms round her and care about her. But she had no one. Tears came into her eyes and she had to muffle her sobs in her pillow. She wept for a long time.

CHAPTER TEN

Time seemed to pass very slowly after the wedding, because Liza had so much less to do with only herself to look after. And Josiah, of course, when he would allow her to do anything for him, which was not often.

The other ladies on the upper deck continued to ignore her, though Mrs Fenton stared at her a lot and did not seem quite as hostile as the others. Liza felt very lonely, for she could not expect Dorothy Pringle always to sit with her, and although Josiah spent time with her every day in public, he was not exactly talkative and after their strolls round the deck she always felt downhearted at the prospect of a lifetime of such cold, impersonal remarks and long silences.

The ship was following a 'composite circle' route, which the First Mate said was quicker than going via Cape Town. The Captain was hoping to arrive at Fremantle within seventy days of leaving Liverpool. Unfortunately, this meant they wouldn't be stopping anywhere on the way and would go far enough south to encounter icebergs.

As the weather grew rougher and colder, several of the cabin passengers took to their beds again with seasickness and the stewards were kept busy looking after them. The hatches that led below were occasionally fastened shut and those in steerage left to fend for themselves. At these times even the cabin passengers were told not to come up on deck, though they were not actually locked in and could sit in the dining room if they wished. Such days dragged badly for Liza. If she had been a better reader she would have read Catherine's books, but by the time she had spelled her way laboriously through a single page, she had lost all sense of a story.

She found it chilly and guessed that Benedict Caine's deck cabin must be even colder on stormy days. He made no complaint, though sometimes he looked pinched and grey, or bleary-eyed, as if he, too, had not slept well. She found her eyes turning to him whenever he was on deck. She enjoyed watching him. He and her husband were both tall men but Benedict radiated energy whereas Josiah seemed to radiate unhappiness. Benedict attracted people to him and was often surrounded by a lively group who would stand watching him work on his carving while they discussed all sorts of things. Liza wished she dared join them, but if she approached the group, people drifted away as if they wanted nothing to do with her, and only he would speak to her.

One night the tossing and pitching grew so bad she was sure the ship was going to founder, for it seemed to pause on the crest of each huge wave, shuddering and creaking as if about to break into pieces. She lay in bed, growing more and more fearful, then at a particularly violent roll she panicked and flew across the cabin to hammer on Josiah's door.

He flung it open so quickly he could not have been asleep either. 'What is it? What's wrong?'

Liza burst into tears. 'The ship's going to sink, I know it is, an' please, Josiah, I don't want to die alone.'

He stared at her in surprise then let out a bray of scornful laughter. 'It's just a storm, you silly child.' He removed her hand from his arm and added more gently, 'I don't think we're likely to founder. Our Captain may be a bigot, but he seems to know what he's doing. Go back to bed, there's a good girl.'

But she clung to his arm in the darkness. 'Will you come and sit with me, just for a bit? Oh, please! I don't want to be alone.'

He let out an exasperated grunt. 'For a short time only. I'm tired, even if you aren't.'

So he lit the wall lamp and they sat there without saying a word. After a while he began yawning. 'Why don't you read a book when you can't sleep?'

She could feel herself going red and wriggled uncomfortably, not knowing what to say.

'Liza?' There was silence, then, 'You can read, can't you?'

'A bit. Not – not well enough to read them hard books of Catherine's, though.' Tears of shame slipped down her cheeks and she could not look at him as she tried to explain. 'Da used to keep me home from school to help in the shop so I didn't get much chance to learn the big words. I'd like to read better, though.'

When Josiah spoke again, his voice was no warmer in tone, but at least it was not scornful. 'We'd better practise your reading, then. I can't have an illiterate wife.'

She didn't even know what illiterate meant, but she looked up eagerly. 'Will you really learn me to read better?'

He winced. 'I'll *teach* you to read better, Liza. *You* will do the learning.'

She considered this, head on one side, and nodded as she saw the difference. 'I'll enjoy that.' With him there, she wasn't as frightened of the storm, somehow, so she snuggled down under the bedclothes. 'Can we start the reading tomorrow, please?'

'Well, as soon as the weather grows calmer. I doubt either of us could concentrate with the ship rolling about like this.'

'Promise.'

'I promise.'

When she beamed at him, he found himself smiling back, then sat and watched her fall sleep. But he didn't return to his own cabin for quite some time because he, too, was relieved not to be alone. Only towards dawn, when the ship's movements became less violent, did he return to his bed, still thoughtful.

For all her eagerness to learn, Liza spent most of that first lesson in tears, because the book was full of long words and Josiah could not hide his scorn at how few of them she knew. Well, no one in her family used such words, so she didn't even know how to say them, let alone read them.

In the end he snapped, 'I can't take any more today. Practise that page. Go over it until you know it.' Then he slammed out of the cabin.

Liza was terrified he would stop teaching her, so she dried her eyes and picked up the book with hands that shook a little. She wished she could use one of the easy books the steerage children had for the lessons that were held each morning. But if she asked to borrow one, it'd show people how ignorant she was and they'd laugh at her, then Josiah would get even angrier.

Slowly and laboriously she spelled her way down the page.

Several times she could not work out a word at all and tears rolled down her cheeks, so desperate was she to do better and win praise from him.

The following morning Josiah raised one dark eyebrow in that way he had and asked, 'Another lesson?'

'Please, Josiah.'

He escorted her to the cabin, sat down beside her at the small table and opened the book.

Liza stumbled through the same page, her voice getting fainter and more hesitant as he listened in silence, correcting her when she made a mistake. When she got to the bottom, she looked at him fearfully.

'You've remembered more than I'd expected.' He tapped the book. 'We'll do that page again, then we'll go on to the next.'

She began again in a voice that still wavered with nervousness.

He slapped one hand across the page, stopping her in mid-sentence. 'Why are you so afraid of me? What do you think I'm going to do, you silly girl? Beat you?'

'I d–don't know. You might. You look ever so angry.'

Josiah paused, staring at her as if he had not seen her before. 'Were you beaten often?'

'Da used to hit me sometimes. And – and my big brothers hit us little 'uns quite a lot. But Mam didn't hit any of us.' She could not speak for a moment, because she suddenly had a picture of her mother sitting by the kitchen table and it upset her.

This brief glimpse into Liza's life touched his heart. 'I see. Well, I promise not to hit you whatever you do. Go on. Begin the page again.'

He kept her at it for another half-hour, then leaned back and yawned. 'That's enough philanthropy for one day.'

She didn't understand what that word meant, either, and had to ask Benedict later.

Liza remained an incurable early riser and if the weather was fine, she was often the only cabin passenger on the upper deck. She enjoyed standing by the rail as the ship plunged up and down. The wind and movement filled her with energy and the ship seemed almost to fly through the water some days. She would watch the sailors washing the decks and laugh at the antics of the single men, who usually came up from steerage first to wash themselves. There were canvas screens round the half barrels filled with fresh sea water in the washing area, but the men did not always bother to hide behind them, and sometimes they messed around, throwing water over one another. She knew she shouldn't be watching them, but she enjoyed their high spirits.

Gradually the lower deck would fill with steerage passengers, so many of them crowded together there and just herself and one or two others on the upper deck. It didn't seem fair.

Benedict sometimes came out of his tiny cabin quite early as well, but he did not join her and Liza knew why. If he spoke to her when she was alone, it would cause more gossip. She seemed to live her whole life as a watcher these days. She would watch the fires lit in the galley on the main deck before five o'clock. From about six or seven o'clock, mess leaders were busy there, helping the cooks prepare stirabout or plain porridge or boiled rice with treacle, and then carrying it below to their groups.

When the weather was rough there were mishaps, with some unfortunate people spilling the food they had just finished cooking as a sudden movement of the ship sent them sprawling across the deck or made them fall down the companionways. Then she would not be able to help smiling tolerantly as she watched the poorer children rush to pick up what they could, wolfing down the spoiled food before anyone could take it away from them. Some of them seemed to have grown quite a bit during the voyage. Well, she had herself, and not just because of the baby. She had never eaten so well in her whole life, not even at the Pringles'.

A little later she would watch some of the better-off steerage families come up to the galley with extra provisions to be cooked. Benedict sold them ham by the slice and she had overheard some of the cabin passengers sneering at him for his money-grubbing ways, but she didn't blame him. For the first time in her life Liza had money of her own and it felt good. Catherine had given her a purse full of coins before she died and ordered her not to tell Josiah about it. Liza had counted out the money one day and been awed to find over a hundred pounds.

Whenever it rained, she would watch enviously as the steerage passengers rushed up on deck to catch the pure water in any kind of container they had to hand. She would have done the same, but when none of the other cabin passengers made any move, she sighed and went back to stand in the passage between the two rows of cabins, watching from there. The Chief Steward set a canvas awning to catch the run-off on the upper deck, and the cook put out a couple of buckets, but they could have got far more fresh water if they'd tried. By now the ship's water tasted foul, even when flavoured with lime juice.

One dreadful day there was an accident which upset everyone. The breeze was blowing stiffly and the vessel was sailing close-hauled with sails and rigging taut from the force of the wind. Liza was on deck when the mains'l sheet parted and the unsecured clew of the sail flapped madly in the wind. It struck a young woman standing by the rail and knocked her overboard into the foaming sea. The poor thing's shriek of terror could be heard all over the ship.

A sailor on deck instinctively threw a long, weighted heaving line in her direction as she thrashed around in the water, rapidly sinking under the weight of her wet clothes. It was a futile gesture and as the vessel swept quickly away from her, it was obvious she could never be rescued.

The traditional call of 'man overboard' brought the Captain rushing to the poop deck and he stood alongside the helmsman, eyes raking the ocean, then called up to the men working in the rigging, 'Any sign?'

Liza found herself praying they would say yes.

'No sign at all, sir.'

'Take a good look. We have to be sure.'

'No, sir, nothing. She went under very quickly.'

The Captain paused for a few moments, shaking his head sadly, then turned to the man on the wheel. 'Still nothing? Right, then, maintain course. How are we headed?'

'Sou' sou'east, sir.'

There had been dead silence on the deck while the sailors were calling to one another, then a woman screamed and there was a babble of cries.

The distraught mother, who had had to be held back from throwing herself overboard, was taken below in hysterics by a group of women, while the father remained by the rail, weeping openly.

Sobbing herself, Liza turned to find Benedict beside her, offering a handkerchief. As she took it from him, she muttered, 'It all happened so quickly. One minute she was alive and next – she was gone.' She dried her eyes and handed the handkerchief back. 'That girl was the same age as me, you know. I used to talk to her sometimes in the single women's quarters when I first came on board ship.' Only the girl had acted young, was the spoiled darling of her parents, and Liza had always felt much older than her.

His face was sombre. 'Aye, well, life's like that. Just make sure you keep hold of the lifelines in rough weather, if you have to come up on deck. Or better still, stay below.'

Liza glanced sideways. For all his heartless words, he looked upset, too.

As he caught her eyes, he asked softly, 'How are things going? Is he kind to you?'

She didn't need to ask who *he* was. 'Things are fine.' They weren't fine, but she supposed they were as well as could be expected. She changed the subject. 'How's that new carving going, then?'

Josiah suddenly appeared beside her, putting his arm round her shoulders, as if to show everyone she belonged to him, and speaking to Benedict with a funny edge to his voice.

Liza tried to move away, but Josiah held her still, so she stood and listened, wondering yet again why the two men were never quite at ease with one another.

But she noticed that Benedict did no more carving that day. That even Mrs Beeton looked upset. That Dorothy Pringle mopped her eyes a couple of times for no obvious reason. That Josiah kept closing his eyes and shaking his head, as if upset. She noticed a lot more than they realised.

The following morning a memorial service was held on the lower deck for the dead woman and everyone attended, even the cabin passengers going to stand at the edge of the poop deck to join in the prayers as a sign of respect.

Before it began, the Captain addressed them all. 'I hear that some passengers have been saying we should have turned back yesterday. I'm afraid that would have been no use and I stand by my decision to continue. It would have been both difficult and dangerous to wear the vessel round in such a strong wind, even more dangerous to try to let down a workboat. And even if we had turned back, we could not have been sure of going back to the same spot. No instruments are that accurate.' He nodded to Reverend Beeton to begin, then stepped back, his expression solemn.

After the service, Liza turned away without looking where she was going and bumped into Mrs Beeton, who pushed her aside, hissing, 'Get out of my way, you!'

That gratuitous insult was the final straw. The clergyman's wife went out of her way to be nasty and had several times made insulting remarks that were meant to be overheard. Liza moved to block the other woman's path, setting her hands on her hips and demanding, 'Why do you always speak to me like that?'

'Because you're a harlot!'

'If you knew what had happened, you'd know I'm not! And anyway, even if I was, it says in the Bible that you should forgive sinners.' But the woman's expression did not soften, so Liza moved aside to let her flounce past, nearly bumping into Mrs Fenton who had been standing behind her.

The following day was cold and stormy again and Liza was so cold and fed up of being alone in her cabin that she decided to go along to the dining cabin, which the ladies used as a sitting room when it was not needed for meals. She knew they wouldn't talk to her, but at least she could listen to them. Besides, it was always warmer in there. Outside the door she hesitated, then told herself not to be a coward and pushed it open.

Mrs Beeton looked up, stared at her in shock and snapped, 'You're not wanted here. Go below and sit with the other servants. They're more your sort.'

Liza drew herself up. 'I'm a cabin passenger and have as much right as you to be here.'

'Insolence!' Mrs Beeton turned red.

'Just the truth. And I may have been a servant before my marriage, but at least I have more compassion for others than you do, for all you're a clergyman's wife.' But Liza could not bear to stay after that. Better to huddle on her bunk wrapped in a blanket than endure more insults.

In the evening, during the nightly ordeal of dinner, Mrs

Fenton looked down the table, caught Liza's eye and said, 'An excellent soup this, is it not, Mrs Ludlam?'

Everyone at the table fell silent in surprise.

Liza gaped for a moment, then Josiah nudged her and she managed to stammer her agreement.

Mrs Beeton sniffed audibly.

Gradually the conversation resumed.

After dinner Mrs Fenton came across the deck, again watched by everyone, stopped in front of Liza and said loudly, 'I think we've been guilty of rudeness towards you, Mrs Ludlam, and I'm sorry for it. I'm Agnes Fenton.' She held out her hand.

Liza shook it and managed to say, 'I'm pleased to meet you, Mrs Fenton.'

'Agnes. And you're Liza, are you not? Shall we take a turn about the deck together? It seems a lot calmer now.'

'Y-yes. That would be . . .' she remembered a word Catherine had used a lot '. . . delightful.'

Arm in arm the two of them promenaded up and down, still the focus of all eyes, some of them hostile. As they reached the far end, Liza blurted out, 'Why are you doing this?'

'After seeing that poor young woman drowned, I decided life is too precarious to be unkind to people who've done me no harm. And also, I will admit, because I'm very bored and would be glad of some new company. Mrs Beeton's mind does tend to run on death and illness. I thought it might be interesting to talk to you sometimes. You're bound to have a different view of the world.' Agnes glanced sideways with a quizzical smile. 'I hope my frankness doesn't offend you?'

'No. I prefer people to be honest. That girl's death upset me, too.' Liza's hand went to her belly instinctively. 'How unhappy her mother must feel.'

'When is your baby due?'

'December.'

'Do you want a boy or girl?'

Liza smiled. 'I can't decide. I just hope it'll be healthy and have a happier life than me, and that I can look after it properly.'

Her words touched Agnes. 'I feel the same about my own baby.'

'Oh. It – it doesn't show. Is this your first child?'

A shadow crossed Agnes's face. 'No. I lost one a year ago. She only lived two days.'

'I'm sorry. My mother lost three babies. She always said it was God's will and at least she'd not have the trouble of feeding another mouth.' Liza flushed. She had not meant to reveal so much about her background.

'Your family is quite poor, then?'

'They manage without anyone's charity. My father has a second-hand clothes shop. My mother is – she's not well.' Tears came into Liza's eyes. 'I don't know how she'll be managing without me. I wish—' She broke off.

Agnes frowned at her. 'You didn't want to come to Australia?'

'Not really. But I had to.' Again she could not stop herself from glancing down at her belly.

'Ah, yes. Well, at least Mr Ludlam recognised his responsibility towards you.'

From then on Agnes Fenton spoke to Liza sometimes and even lent her a book, which Josiah had to read to her so that she could talk about it. It was a funny story, all about ladies wanting to find the richest husbands they could, but Josiah taught Liza what to say when she discussed it and Mrs Fenton nodded agreement at her parroted comments in public, then quizzed her in private about what she really thought, gurgling with laughter at her replies.

The other ladies nodded a greeting at Liza sometimes now, but that was all. None of them really talked to her.

And Mrs Beeton continued to ignore her ostentatiously. Which suited Liza just fine.

CHAPTER ELEVEN

When the storm abated, the Captain announced, 'I expect to sight Western Australia within a day or two, so I shall have the trunks brought up on deck tomorrow morning for the final time. We haven't made quite such good progress as I'd hoped, but we haven't done too badly.'

There was an immediate hubbub of voices and every face round the long dining table brightened.

The following morning all was hustle and bustle as first the cabin passengers' trunks, then the motley collection of trunks, wicker baskets and bundles belonging to the steerage passengers, were brought up on deck so that people could get out a change of clothing. After everything had been taken below again, the decks remained crowded with people longing for a first sight of land, but they were to be disappointed that day.

The next morning, however, Benedict sniffed the air and declared, 'You can smell it.'

'Smell what?' asked Kitty.

'Land.'

Liza watched him close his eyes and inhale, longing written clearly on his face. She closed her own eyes and imitated him, but wasn't sure whether she really could smell anything or whether it was just her imagination.

It wasn't until noon that a cry of 'Land ho!' from the crow's nest made everyone rush to the rail again, but of course they could see nothing yet from down on deck. This made people restless, and they moved to and fro all afternoon, talking and gesticulating. Liza wished she was on the lower deck, because up here people were more restrained and she, too, wanted to jig around with excitement and found it hard to sit still or walk sedately.

Then Gerard Fenton, who had a pair of binoculars to his eyes, suddenly called out, 'There! Isn't that something?'

They all peered in that direction of his pointing finger and it seemed to Liza as if someone had smeared a dirty thumb mark along the horizon. 'There's not much to see.'

Benedict glanced down at her, grinning. 'Disappointed?'

'Yes. I thought – you know – there'd be cliffs and mountains and things.'

She gasped suddenly and clutched her belly. 'Oh, it moved! My baby kicked me. Oh, Josiah, isn't that exciting? It's happy to reach Australia, too.'

But her husband looked at her with disgust then strode away across the deck.

Liza stared down, trying desperately to blink away the tears before anyone noticed.

Benedict laid one hand on her arm, saying gently, 'I think any child is a wonder, Liza. Don't let him spoil it for you.'

'I'll try not to. But it's difficult sometimes.' She sighed and continued to stare at the horizon until she had calmed down again. She didn't know why she got so upset at the way Josiah behaved. It wasn't as if they'd married for love, after all. But it hurt her when he looked disgusted.

Benedict stood quietly beside her, also staring out at the horizon. He wished he could be the one to help her and share the joys of this whole adventure with her, for she had a great capacity for enjoying life. But he did not have the right and his own future was mapped out quite differently.

Two important things were within his reach, however, and by hell, he meant to achieve them: he was going to get a piece of his own land, and he wasn't going to be subservient to anyone from now on.

As they approached the Swan River Colony, Benedict pointed to a large island. 'It's called Rottnest. The sailors tell me it's used to incarcerate the natives who've committed crimes.'

'Poor things,' said Liza softly. 'It's cruel to take them away from their homes and yet keep them within sight of their land.'

'They're not the only ones to be taken away from their homes,' Josiah said sourly.

Which caused another awkward silence.

As they drew closer to the island, the sailors fired two guns and two rockets to ask for a pilot but none came out, so the ship dropped anchor to wait until morning, because the coast was treacherous with many reefs just off shore.

Liza got up as soon as it was daylight, feeling excited. She had company even on the upper deck that morning and plenty to watch. Signals were fluttering to ask for a pilot and again a gun was fired.

Just before ten a small boat brought the pilot out to them and he was immediately surrounded by people asking questions about the colony so that the sailors had to make a way through the crowd for him. He took the wheel and guided the *Louisa Jane* across the few miles of sea to Fremantle.

There was silence as they approached the harbour because it was not what anyone had expected.

'This place is just a damned village!' Josiah's voice was thick with anger.

'This is only Fremantle. Perth will surely be larger,' Benedict offered, though he, too, was disappointed.

'Perth is definitely larger than Fremantle, but still not large,' commented a passing officer. 'If you're expecting a city, you'll be disappointed, I'm afraid. Perth is only a small town by English standards, for all it's the capital of Western Australia.'

He left a silent group of passengers behind him.

Individual houses, painted white and surrounded by gardens, were dotted haphazardly up a gentle slope – you couldn't even call it a hill. And though they weren't hovels, most of them were not large by the gentry's standards, just cottages really.

'Well, we'll have to make the most of it, won't we?' Liza said to Josiah, taking his arm without thinking. He stared down at her as if he hated her, as if he hated the whole world, and she took an involuntary step backwards, letting go of him.

'There is no best.' His words were throbbing with pain. 'How can you talk like that? Are you completely insensitive?'

'I'd better finish my packing.' She hurried away.

'You'd no need to make her cry just because you're unhappy!' Benedict snapped and moved further along the rail, turning his back.

Guilt flooded through Josiah and he knew Cat would scold

him for his unkindness. But the reality of Fremantle had made him feel raw with anger all over again at what his father had done to him. His only hope of happiness was to make enough money to leave this place and move somewhere more civilised – somewhere out of his father's reach. France, perhaps. Then he could visit England occasionally. Even America was too far away from Pendleworth.

Only now he had Liza to look after and the child she was carrying. Why had he agreed to marry her? Cat had been wrong to insist on it. He did not follow his unwanted second wife down to the cabin, did not even want to see her just then.

The cabin passengers disembarked first, to jeers and catcalls from the steerage passengers who were waiting in frustration to be released from the crowded ship. Liza had trouble walking on land, so unused was she to a surface which stayed still beneath her feet, and would have fallen but for Josiah's arm, though he was staggering a little, too.

They waited near a jetty on a rough sandy surface for the paddle steamer *Lady Stirling* to ferry them to Perth,

Liza enjoyed the sail up the river, but the colours of the landscape seemed wrong to eyes accustomed to the English countryside. The greens here looked dirty and faded, and the trees were different in shape, with sparser foliage.

'This is July,' Benedict said suddenly. 'Mid-winter. And most of those trees still have leaves. Strange, isn't it?'

Andrew beamed around. 'Won't it be wonderful not to have snow and ice?'

'This is a dreadful place!' Kitty exclaimed.

Dorothy didn't say anything. She, too, had found the first sight of their new country bitterly disappointing and was hoping desperately for better things from Perth.

But to their disappointment it looked very similar to Fremantle, if slightly larger. Two long jetties had been built for the boats to pull up at. Behind them the scene seemed very rural, with only the occasional larger building. One of the steamer's crew pointed out the Colonial Hospital, a square building two storeys high, with verandahs, and also Perth Boys'

School, which looked more like a small church. But there was nothing at all grand about this capital city.

When they'd tied up at the jetty, Benedict hired two lads from those hovering nearby with handcarts to take them and their luggage to a hotel, but even this displeased Josiah, who looked down at his feet clad in well-polished leather half boots and then at the unpaved road and asked, 'Is there nothing but damned sand here?'

The hotels were mostly full, but they found a small one which had two rooms free, though they had to share these, with the three women sleeping in one, the three men in the other. When a cockroach ran out from under the wardrobe, Kitty shrieked and jumped up on one of the beds, so Liza stamped on the insect and pushed the pieces of it back underneath with her toe.

'Is that how you did the housework?' sneered Kitty, climbing down again.

Liza set her hands on her hips. 'If you're not more polite to me, I'll let the next one run over your toes. Maybe it'll even crawl up your leg.' She smiled as Kitty squealed in terror. 'It's only a blackbeetle. Benedict says you get lots of them in a hot country.'

'They won't harm you,' Dorothy said quietly. 'Don't be so silly.'

Kitty burst into tears and flung herself face down on the bed. The other two exchanged long-suffering glances and continued to unpack, ignoring her.

When the men knocked on the door and suggested taking a walk, the three women agreed in relief, but even that was not reassuring, for although the central streets of Perth were quite busy, they soon petered out into mere sandy tracks.

It was a silent group who dined that night on very plain food, badly cooked and presented.

For the next few days Benedict travelled between Perth and Fremantle on the little steamer, arranging for the disembarkation and temporary agistment of his and Josiah's animals, most of which had survived the voyage but were not in good condition.

He and the other men also started to make inquiries about purchasing land. When they heard of somewhere, they would hire horses and ride out to inspect the place, which left the three women with little to do but stroll around the town or along by the river.

But each time the men came back looking disappointed.

'The soil round here is poor and sandy,' Benedict said gloomily. 'I can't think why your father sent us to this part of Australia, Josiah. And if the summers are as dry as people say, then we're going to need running water on our land – only that fellow told us today that some of the rivers and streams don't run in the summer.'

'But surely we can collect rainwater?' Liza said.

'Apparently it hardly rains in the summer. You can go five months without a drop falling.'

She could not even imagine that. In Pendleworth it rained every day or two, whatever the season. And it had rained a few times since their arrival here, sudden heavy showers that sent folk rushing for cover and sheltering beneath verandahs.

While the men were looking at land, the three women tried to find a house to rent temporarily, because it was expensive staying in a hotel and Dorothy had admitted that the Pringles could ill afford the cost. However, there was a shortage of accommodation in Perth and those immigrants who couldn't afford to stay in a hotel or take lodgings were housed by the government in crowded conditions in the old Courthouse, which was now the Immigration Depot. Dorothy was worrying that Andrew might soon have to apply for accommodation there for them, humiliating as that would be.

The hotel was not a pleasant place to live and the food was poor. Liza would rather have eaten bread and cheese than the tough roasted lamb they got most nights, it had been made plain that if they did not purchase meals here their rooms would be given to people who would. What was going to happen to them? Had they come all this way for nothing?

She was secretly relieved, however, not to be sharing a room with Josiah. She'd have to do so one day – and then she could only pray that Catherine had been telling the truth and he wouldn't want to touch her.

The following day she went for a brisk walk on her own, tired of Kitty's complaints and feeling full of pent-up energy. She was standing looking down the slope towards the river when she saw a young woman stumble and fall to her knees. When Liza ran to help, she found the stranger very pregnant under her voluminous shawl and looking exhausted.

The woman leaned against her, gasping. 'I'm sorry. I just – I felt faint. It's been a long day. And – and I still feel dizzy. I'm supposed to be – to be meeting my husband here.'

There was a shout and a man came running towards them. 'Breda, what's wrong?' He put an arm round the woman.

Liza began to pick up the scattered shopping, waiting with the various parcels until they were ready to move on.

The woman made an effort to pull herself together, but when she tried to walk, clutched her husband again. 'I'm sorry, David. I don't think I can walk to the cart yet. I feel so dizzy. Did you – did you find somewhere for me to stay?'

'No. There's no one will take you in and help with the baby, and the sheep prices are down as well so I doubt we could afford to pay for help anyway.'

They stared at one another in dismay, then realised they were ignoring their companion. 'I do apologise. We haven't introduced ourselves or thanked you for your help. I'm David Lowrey and this is my wife, Breda.'

'I'm Liza Ludlam. We've just arrived on the *Louisa Jane*. My husband is out looking for some land to buy or lease.'

'Ha! He'll have to be rich to buy anything near Perth.' David turned again to his wife. 'I'm sorry, my dear. We'll just have to go home and – and try to manage.'

Tears came into Breda's eyes and one rolled down her cheek. 'We *must* find some help, David.'

She looked so white and tired that Liza stepped forward. 'Why don't you leave your wife with me, Mr Lowrey, and fetch the cart? She's in no state to walk.'

He looked at her in patent relief. 'Do you mind?'

'Of course not. I've nothing better to do. We're staying at a hotel until we can find a place of our own.' She grimaced. 'And to tell the truth, I'm bored and fed up. I'm used to keeping busy.'

When he had fetched the cart and helped his wife into it, David Lowrey hesitated then said, 'Please excuse me for

144

intruding on your affairs, but if you're looking for somewhere to live while you're deciding where to settle, well, we have a brand new barn that's never been used for animals. It isn't grand, but it's sound enough and it'd be a lot cheaper than a hotel.' He exchanged glances with his wife, who nodded to him to continue. 'You see, Breda desperately needs a woman to help her when the baby is born. You – you wouldn't know anything about birthing, would you?'

'Well, I'm no midwife, but I helped Mam with our Kieran, and I helped Mrs Roberts next door with two of hers. I seem to have been looking after babies ever since I was big enough to hold them.'

His face lit up. 'What about your husband? Does he know anything about farming?'

'I'm afraid not – not yet anyway. Josiah is a gentleman settler. But he has a partner who's a farmer and we're with friends who're hoping to farm. There are six of us, three families, and we want to stay together.'

'Well, my offer still stands. It's a good big barn and could hold you all easily. From where we live you could look at land further south, where it's cheaper. Though you'd have to clear your blocks yourselves, probably, if you took up new land.' David saw she didn't understand and added, 'Clear the trees to give you open fields, I mean. A lot of the land is forested.'

'Oh, I see.' Liza had taken a liking to him and his fresh-faced wife. 'Why don't you come back to the hotel and talk to the others about your offer? It might be just the thing for us.'

They found everyone sitting on the hotel verandah looking dejected. Liza hurried towards them, words tumbling over one another in her excitement.

'I think I've found somewhere for us to live!' She turned and gestured to her new friends to join her. 'This is Mr and Mrs Lowrey.'

Hands were shaken, then David explained about his offer before saying, 'Perhaps Breda and I should go and sit in the cart to give you a chance to discuss things.'

'Isn't it exciting?' Liza burst out when they'd left.

Even Josiah was smiling at his wife's excitement as he said, 'We can discuss this better sitting down, don't you think.'

'But it is exciting, isn't it?' she repeated, flopping down beside him.

'It's a bit of a risk,' Andrew worried.

'Coming here was a risk,' Dorothy said pointedly.

But Liza noticed that everyone, even her husband, looked at Benedict to see what he thought before they made a decision.

'I vote we accept Lowrey's offer,' he said. 'We'll not only save money, we'll be able to learn about local farming methods from him, which is just as important.'

'Go and live in a *barn!*' Kitty exclaimed in a shrill voice. 'Mother, no!'

'Shh, love.'

'I liked the look of Lowrey,' Benedict said thoughtfully. 'He has an honest face. And I hate to waste my money here.'

'We should accept, then,' Josiah decided, his lips twisted into a half-sneer, half-smile. 'After all, I've never experienced the delights of living in a barn before.'

Transport was a problem and in the end Benedict shared the purchase of a covered cart and two draft horses with Josiah, finding a vehicle for sale cheaply which needed a little work but was basically sound. The animals that drew it would have to double as plough horses and riding animals. Josiah turned up his nose at them and purchased another horse purely for himself to ride, a neat bay mare. Andrew purchased a smaller cart and one horse.

It took them most of the day to reach the Lowreys' farm, which was quite a way south of Fremantle. Sometimes when the rain eased and the going was suitable, Liza would walk beside the cart and Josiah occasionally got off his horse to walk beside her.

At one stage they came to a small wayside inn, where they were able to buy a drink of beer for the men and a pot of tea for the women. The owners questioned them eagerly about England and the woman at least seemed very wistful about it.

'Have you ever seen the Queen?' she asked.

Liza laughed. 'Goodness, no.'

'I have. Once, in London. When we went to see the Great

Exhibition just before we left. She's Queen of Australia, too, you know. That always comforts me.'

The only thing that comforted Liza was that she was a long way away from Mr Marshall and her two elder brothers. If Dermott and Niall knew she'd married a Ludlam, they'd be trying to take advantage of the situation, thinking all the Ludlams must be rich.

At last they came to a roughly made signpost with the words *Luska Farm* burned on it and turned left along the narrow track. As it petered out they came to a tiny cottage surrounded by trees.

'Is this it?' Josiah muttered. 'It's only fit for a damned labourer!'

Breda came out to wait for them on the small verandah, smiling, and David came striding out of the trees behind the house, waving a greeting. 'You found us, then.' He didn't miss Josiah's scornful expression. 'The house is small, I know, but two rooms are all I've been able to build for the moment. It keeps the rain out, at least. There are more important things to do when you're clearing land. Breda and I lived under a piece of canvas for the first two months. Come on. I'll show you the barn.'

Although it was about twice as big as their two rooms at the hotel combined, it had a dirt floor and little else except a pile of hay.

'You can use the hay for temporary beds, but you'll have to make partitions if you want privacy,' David said as he left them to unload.

'It's not – not very comfortable,' Dorothy faltered once they were alone.

'It's soundly built and will save us a lot of money,' Benedict insisted, studying the ceiling. 'We can't do anything about fixing up partitions tonight, so I think we'll just have to sleep on the hay wrapped in blankets.'

Kitty moaned.

Josiah closed his eyes and breathed deeply.

'Well, we'd better get some blankets out, then,' Liza said briskly. And it was she who organised the other women, while Benedict supervised the unloading of what they would need from the carts. At one stage they looked at each other across the barn and he grinned at her, rolling his eyes at Kitty's complaints. She hid a smile and continued spreading blankets for herself and a scowling Josiah.

In the days that followed, Liza enjoyed Breda's company and the lessons her hostess was giving them about cooking over an open fire and managing without so many things she had taken for granted in England. It was wonderful having another young woman to talk to and since Breda had also been a maid before her marriage, they had a lot in common. Like many maids in the colonies Liza's friend had married what was considered 'above herself' but she and David seemed very happy together.

Then the birth started. The colony was short of doctors and they did not come out merely to birth a child, even if they could be summoned in time, so Liza took charge of the bedroom, and to her relief the baby – a boy – was born with a minimum of fuss.

Afterwards she left David gazing adoringly at his son and went outside to join Dorothy, who was cooking the evening meal in the small kitchen built separate from the main house for fear of fire, and which actually had only two walls to protect it against the prevailing winds, though it was sheltered by a roof.

'How are they?' Dorothy asked.

Liza sat down with a tired smile. 'They're both fine. You know, I didn't realise births could be so easy. My mother always has such trouble. It went on for two days with our Kieran.'

Dorothy eyed her shrewdly, realising she must have been worrying about this. 'Breda's young and healthy – and so are you.'

'Yes.' But what if she were like her mother? How would she manage then? What if there was no woman to help her? Would Josiah be any use? Why, he rarely even touched her and she could not imagine him performing the intimate tasks necessary to help her give birth.

Liza went to sit on the edge of the verandah, exhausted, wanting only to rest. The sky was clouding over and it was going to rain again, but it was not really cold. If this was the coldest part of the winter, what would the summers be like?

She hoped they would soon find somewhere to settle, and that she would at least have a house in which to bear her child. Beyond that, she didn't know what she hoped for. The future seemed a puzzle to her. She was just trying to live from day to day, and to keep as cheerful as she could.

CHAPTER TWELVE

In England yet another row erupted in the Docherty household. Con ended it by threatening his two eldest sons with the beating of a lifetime if they did not mend their ways.

'No Docherty has ever been involved in thieving!' he roared. 'If I find you accepting any more stolen goods in my shop, I'll call in the constable myself to take you away, I will so.'

For a minute it hung in the balance as to whether they would challenge him, then Dermott's eyes fell and he muttered, 'Yes, Da. Sorry, Da.'

Seeing that he was now standing alone against his father, who was still stronger than either of them individually, Niall gritted his teeth and made a suitable apology.

When he and his brother got outside, he waited till they'd turned the corner then slammed one fist into Dermott's guts so that he doubled up and fell, to lie squirming and groaning on the road. Niall kicked him twice deliberately. 'If you don't back me up next time, you bastard, I'll make you *really* sorry.'

'You'd no need,' Dermott wheezed, finding it hard to breathe, 'no need at all – to do that.'

'I'd every need. One day me an' Da are going to have a set-to and I want you on my side, not his.'

'But he's our father!'

'An' he's a stupid old sod who could be making ten times as much money as he does if he only looked around a bit.'

Uneasily aware that Niall was talking about buying and selling stolen property, Dermott said nothing. He knew his brother was determined to make money and didn't much care how he did it. He liked to think that he, too, might find a richer future than their parents, but he didn't want to attack Da and he particularly didn't want to upset Ma, who was sad enough about Liza's disappearance as it was. Niall didn't care about Mam – well, he didn't care about anyone, really, except perhaps his brother – but Dermott remembered Mam's many kindnesses when he was little and occasionally slipped her a shilling or two extra.

Niall flung one arm round his brother's shoulders, his anger subsiding as quickly as it had boiled up. 'Ah, come on, will you? I'm sorry I thumped you and I'll buy you a pot of ale to prove that.'

But they both knew he was not really sorry and that he would expect more support from Dermott in the future. And get it. He was the leader and always had been.

The stock was brought south to Luska and safely penned, so that the poor creatures could recover completely from their sea voyage. Benedict and Josiah decided to hunt further south for land, in an area they'd heard about from some bullock drivers they'd met on the road. Mandurah was a small town built on a very large inlet about thirty miles long and several miles wide, and the area apparently was full of wild game, with fish swarming in the estuary. There were two rivers, each of which had tributaries of brooks and creeks.

The two men left, expecting to spend five or six days away, a week at most, but twelve days passed before they returned, by which time everyone was worried about their safety.

When they turned up one sunny afternoon, they were both in an excellent humour.

'We've found it,' Benedict announced, beaming at everyone. 'There's good land near Mandurah with permanent running water, and we're going up to Perth tomorrow to see if we can buy it.'

Josiah grimaced. 'It's more expensive than we'd expected – ten shillings an acre the Government is asking just now – but people say if we buy the parts with water and lease the nearby land, we can purchase that later.'

Andrew's face fell. 'That's too expensive for us.'

'But this place is worth it.' Benedict hesitated, then asked gently, 'Have you nothing you can sell, to give you the chance to buy a smallholding at least?'

Andrew glanced sideways at Dorothy, then pursed his lips. 'I'll have to think about it.'

It was she who approached Benedict later to ask, 'Are you sure this is the best land we can get?'

'Yes. Very sure.' His eyes were filled with compassion. 'I know Andrew's not always practical, but if you settle nearby, I can help you.'

Tears came into her eyes. 'We have no call on your kindness.'

'If a man can't help a friend, what is he worth? Besides, it'll suit me to know my neighbours.'

Dorothy sighed. 'Very well, then. I have a gold locket, a bracelet and a diamond ring which were my mother's. I've been keeping them for an emergency. Would *you* sell them for me?'

'But surely Andrew . . . ?'

'No. Definitely not. He doesn't know how to drive a bargain. I'd trust you to do that and to give me all the money you get, but he'd find something to spend it on before he even got back.'

'Won't he mind my selling them for you?'

'Yes, but he won't say anything because the jewellery is mine.' It was the only part of her inheritance she had managed to hang on to, apart from the small annuity.

'He's a hard worker, you know.' Indeed, Andrew seemed to love working outdoors, which was more than could be said for Josiah.

'Yes. He should have been a farm labourer, shouldn't he? Not a gentleman, and certainly not in charge of money. And, Benedict, I want you to pretend you get less for them than you really do and give me the rest of the money without telling him.' She saw his surprise. 'I must have enough left to get back to England – just in case. I would hate to throw myself on my sister's mercy, but if we lost everything, I'd have to.'

Liza approached Josiah after supper. 'Would you come out for a walk with me? It's a fine evening.'

He looked at her in surprise. 'Very well.'

When he offered her his arm, she took it for a short time,

allowing him to guide her along the track that led to the farm. Then she grew impatient of this dawdling pace and pulled her arm away to walk more briskly by his side

As they walked on she heard him sigh and said quietly, 'You hate it here, don't you, Josiah?'

'Yes. Don't you miss Lancashire?'

She bent her head to one side, considering. 'In some ways, yes. Da calls himself Irish, but he used to call me his "Lancashire lass" before . . .' she hesitated, then added defiantly, 'before he took to the drink.'

'But wouldn't you still prefer to be back there?'

She shook her head firmly. 'No. I didn't have a very good life in Pendleworth, so maybe – maybe I don't expect as much as you do. I just want to be able to look after my child.'

'You're hardly more than a child yourself.'

She looked at him, a sad expression on her face. 'I haven't felt like a child for a long time. Kitty's still a child, but I'm a woman.'

They walked on again.

'Who was the father?' he asked abruptly.

She shuddered. 'I don't want to talk about that.'

'I won't ask again, but I have a right to know if I'm to act as father to the child.'

So she told him, her voice shaking as she relived that dreadful night and her brother's betrayal.

Josiah didn't say anything until they were nearly back at the farm, then: 'We need not mention that again, but thank you for telling me.'

Liza didn't know what to think. She rarely did with him.

After the formalities of purchasing the land had been completed, they hired some large wagons drawn by bullocks to transport their things down to the blocks.

They made slow but steady progress, able to rest and water the horses regularly because the bullocks did not move quickly even at their best pace. The road was merely a track which had been cleared by cutting down smaller trees, going round larger ones and making rough crossings over brooks and streams. One of the drivers told them that most of these streams dried right up in summer, but now, after the winter rains, they were at their fullest.

Once or twice they came to a tree which had fallen across the track recently, then the men had to shift it before they could continue.

'Good timber round here,' commented Benedict as he walked along beside the wagon. 'We'll be able to build our houses from our own trees as soon as we set up a saw pit.' He grinned up at Josiah, who was now driving. 'Had any experience of saw pits, have you, lad?'

'I've seen them used.'

'Well, if you prove handy, we can save a great deal of money by making our own planks.'

Josiah's lip curled in disgust. 'I shall buy some dressed wood, dammit, and pay someone to build my house. I certainly don't intend to wait months to get a roof over my – over our heads. I'm not having my wife and the baby living rough for a day longer than they have to.'

Liza stopped walking for a moment to stare at him in surprise. This was the second time he had spoken about the child as if it really were his. 'I don't mind living rough. I want to help you, not be a burden.'

'Well, *I'd* mind.'

A little later, they passed yet another place where wild flowers grew in rich profusion and Liza got down to walk among them, sometimes bending to caress the delicate blossoms. The driver of the nearest wagon told her some of their names: kangaroo paws, tiny orchids and everlastings. Once there was a creeper which had overrun a half-burnt tree and she stopped to sigh at the beauty of its deep blue flowers. 'I'd love a dress that colour,' she said dreamily.

'It would suit you,' Dorothy agreed.

'Isn't it beautiful here?' Liza flung out her arms and danced along for a few steps until her body reminded her that it was carrying extra weight. 'Oh, I'm so glad we're going to our own land now, aren't you?'

Even Josiah smiled at the picture of youthful happiness his wife presented, but Kitty muttered something about 'showing off'.

One of the bullock drivers grinned down at Liza as his team

clomped past and called, 'You keep that attitude, lass. The ones as succeed here are the ones as keep cheerful.'

'And work hard,' said his co-driver. 'It's hard work, clearing land is. You'll soon stop wasting your time a-dancing.'

'Don't ever stop dancing and being happy!' Benedict said later in a low voice, offering a hand to help her over a small stream. 'We all enjoy your cheerfulness.'

Perched on the log that helped those on foot cross the stream dry-shod, she hesitated, looking at him uncertainly. 'I don't want to seem childish. Only I forget sometimes.'

'Forget what? To be prim.' He grinned. 'You'd never succeed even if you tried. Besides, you have a right to be young.'

They camped the first night on cleared land near the tiny wooden house of some complete strangers, who were very apologetic at not being able to offer them shelter indoors, but who did offer them cooking facilities and fresh water. The house was made of rough-sawn timber and the roof was covered in huge pieces of bark, weighted down by ropes with big rocks tied to the ends of them.

Afterwards the three women slept underneath one of the big wagons, the three men under another, and the bullock drivers under the third. During the night it began to rain, so they had to climb out and wedge themselves on the wagons as best they could, pulling the canvas covers over themselves.

Liza woke up at dawn to hear parrots squawking in the trees nearby. They were black with white tails and were making so much noise she could hardly hear herself think. She watched them in delight.

The owners of the house came out with a bucket full of hot tea. The drivers dipped up tin mugs of it and gulped them down with noisy relish, then went off to capture the bullocks from the rough paddock their hosts had allowed them to use.

Rain suddenly began to fall in torrents again and the women took shelter beneath the verandah while the men finished loading the carts and harnessing the horses.

'Ready to leave!' called the chief driver.

'We'll follow you shortly!' Benedict shouted back.

They caught up with the big wagons sooner than they had expected, however, because one was bogged down. It took three hours to get it out of the muddy patch and involved unharnessing bullocks from the other wagons until there were a dozen beasts straining at their harness and six men shoving from behind and calling out encouragement.

When the cart rocked, lurched and moved a little, Liza held her breath, then when it rocked some more and suddenly began moving, she cheered and danced up and down alongside it. Benedict grinned at her, Josiah gave her one of his tight half-smiles and Andrew chuckled openly, but Kitty turned away and Dorothy just closed her eyes and sat quietly on the seat of the cart, looking absolutely exhausted.

After three days on the road they came to a rough signpost that Benedict had made and nailed to a tree and turned left along an even narrower track, heading inland instead of south towards Mandurah and the estuary.

'I wanted to see the town,' Kitty complained.

'It's not really a town, love,' her father told her. 'In England we'd have called it a village, and a small one at that.'

Branches brushed against the carts, shedding moisture on to the canvas hoods, but beneath them the sandy soil mostly drained well, so they did not get bogged down again.

'How far is it now?' Liza asked as the afternoon wore on.

'A couple of miles,' Josiah said, scowling around him in distaste.

'Will we get there before nightfall?'

'I'm hoping so. Though there will be nothing different to see, even so. It's just trees and woodland like this – and our very own swamp, too.'

'But it'll be our home, won't it? That'll make it special for us.'

'Home!' His voice was harsh and so loud everyone could hear it. 'I'll never feel at home in a place like this! Home is Pendleworth and . . .' He broke off, realising the others had turned round to look at him. 'Oh, God,' he said in a savage undertone. 'Will I never have any privacy?'

Liza could hear the pain in his voice and laid one hand tentatively on his arm, but he shook her off and turned his back, so she left him to himself.

When they got to another marker, Benedict called, 'This is where my land begins.'

Since the Pringles' land was on the other side of Josiah's, it had been arranged that they would all go to Josiah's block and camp there, working together to clear some land on which each family could build a house.

As the horses began to move forward again, following in the tracks left by the bullocks, Josiah said quietly, 'I'm sorry, Liza. None of this is your fault. I shouldn't take out my anger on you.'

'A lot of things haven't been my fault this past year, Jos. But I'm not going to let them get me down.'

He grew angry again, in spite of his best resolve. 'What have you lost?' he jeered. 'A precarious existence with not enough to eat? A father who beat you?'

But Liza was growing weary of his moods. 'Oh, you're a right old misery, Josiah Ludlam.' She had the satisfaction of seeing she'd rendered him speechless. Good! She wasn't going to creep round and act as if he was a god, even if he was a gentleman.

Benedict called out just then, 'Liza, this is where your land begins.'

'So we've arrived at Pendleworth at last,' she said softly, unable to stay angry.

Josiah echoed the word. 'Pendleworth.' But he closed his eyes and his expression was full of pain.

It was at that moment she realised how very deeply this exile had hurt him, would go on hurting him – and how right Catherine had been to find him a wife, even an ignorant girl like herself. On impulse she risked further rejection by linking her arm in his, saying nothing. This time he didn't shake her off.

In England, Grace Newton was fretting. It seemed she could do nothing right for her parents these days. She wished she had persuaded Benedict to take her out to Australia with him. It would have made things so much easier. But she did not complain, just set herself to endure.

If he doesn't send for me quickly, I'll go out to join him anyway, she vowed, as she continued to perform her duties

157

about the farm with her customary efficiency. She spent the evenings sewing, making as many things as she could think of for the house she would one day run for Benedict in Australia. And if her eyes sometimes grew dreamy, no one said anything.

When she told them, her family were not best pleased with the situation, and said openly that she had thrown herself away when she could have wed Michael Norwick five years ago and been mistress of a well-run farm by now.

She didn't care. She had only ever wanted Benedict Caine.

CHAPTER THIRTEEN

Four weeks later Josiah paused during the manual labours he detested to wipe the sweat from his brow and scowl down at his rough, scarred hands — no longer the hands of a gentleman. He and Liza were both sleeping on the cart underneath a big piece of canvas slung over a rope tied to two huge trees, and although they were warm enough, rain blew in on them sometimes and mosquitoes plagued them, especially at nightfall.

As he stared around, he decided suddenly that he'd had enough of living rough and strode across to the cooking area. 'Liza, I've changed my mind. I'm going into Mandurah now to see if I can buy some wood and arrange to have a house built. I'm damned if I'll continue living like this, however much money it saves. Will you be all right here on your own?'

'Don't you think you should — well, discuss it with Benedict?'

'No, I should *not* discuss it with him. He'd only try to persuade me to wait. I'm sick and tired of living like a peasant and I mean to change that.' Josiah went to catch his riding horse from the rough enclosure he and Benedict had fenced for their stock, then changed his dirt-stained working clothes, scrubbing fiercely at his dirty hands.

She shook her head as she watched him go, thinking yet again that he was not cut out for a life like this.

When he returned from Mandurah that evening, he wore a triumphant expression. 'I bought a load of dressed timber and hired two men to build the hut for me. They're coming here in a day or two. I've said you'll cook for them while they're building.'

Liza nodded. She was getting quite good at cooking over an open fire now — and at holding her tongue. Josiah, however, was not good at persevering with tasks he disliked. She knew Benedict had had several arguments with her husband already and from what she'd heard, Benedict was in the right. But Josiah would not listen to her so she didn't waste her breath, just left him to it.

Unlike him, she loved this place, especially the huge trees, and would stroll beneath them sometimes, simply enjoying her own company and the sun-dappled peace of this land, for even in winter there were days of cloudless skies and sunshine gilding everything. She felt she could make it into her home but was beginning to wonder if her husband would ever be satisfied here, whatever they did. She had always thought the gentry must be happy, since they had so much money and plenty to eat, but Josiah was one of the unhappiest people she had ever met.

When Benedict saw two men drive along the track from Mandurah with the first load of timber, he followed them to the property everyone now called Pendleworth to find out what was going on. 'You're a fool,' he told Josiah bluntly. 'I could have got that wood far more cheaply for you. As soon as they hear you speak, people double their prices.'

Josiah ignored that, but looked at him thoughtfully. 'How much would you charge me to supervise and work with them, to make sure they do a good job?' Already he was bored with the details of the work.

'You're hiring me?'

'Didn't I say so? How much?'

'Ten pounds. I'll earn it, believe me.' He was not surprised when Josiah didn't attempt to bargain about this.

The two men showed Benedict how bush cottages were erected, and with him keeping an eye on their work and also helping out, not to mention Josiah's own inexpert assistance, the small house was constructed very quickly. It even had a plank floor inside because Josiah refused point blank to live on a dirt one. The planks were rough, but Benedict promised to sand them down, then stain and polish them later.

There would not be proper windows, however, until they could bring some glass down from Perth, but Benedict made wooden frames with shutters and at Liza's suggestion, they attached muslin from Catherine's big trunk of materials to them, so that in the evenings the moths would not flutter inside to dash themselves against the lamp. She hated to see that. They had a muslin-covered inner door, too, as well as a solid wood outer door for security. Josiah had suggested the muslin door, having read somewhere of how buildings were kept cool in India. If they threw pannikins of cold water on the muslin in the hot weather, then the air blowing into the house would be cooled, it seemed.

Liza didn't say anything, but she was looking forward to the hot weather. She had enjoyed it on the ship and didn't see why she wouldn't enjoy it here, too.

It was a big occasion when the Ludlams moved in, even though they had only straw-filled mattresses on the floor to sleep on. When they had unpacked the piano, the fine walnut table and the six chairs that went with it, the parlour looked 'almost civilised' as Josiah put it.

'Shall we invite the others over for a meal to celebrate?' Liza asked hesitantly when they were alone in the house.

'Not yet. First I want to enjoy some peace and privacy.'

Which meant he didn't talk to her, just sat and read by the light of the lamp. So Liza got out her reading book and spelled her way through the first few pages again, happy to find that she had not forgotten the words. But she'd rather have had some company, and although he saw her fiddling with the book, he did not offer to help her with her reading.

Later on, he uncorked a bottle of port and drank it all — which made him snore during the night and scowl at the world the next day.

Was this to be the pattern of her life from now on? Liza wondered miserably. She might as well not exist unless he needed something. But she would not let herself weep.

One morning, Benedict and Josiah went off to explore more carefully the swamp through which the stream ran. It was rank-smelling marshy ground, dried out at the edges now and thick with the droppings of the many animals which drank there each evening.

'If we can dig out a deeper part during the dry season,' Benedict said, pacing the area out, 'we could dam it to form a small lake. That way we would never lack water.' For he was worried by how much the swamp had dried out already now that the weather was mostly dry.

'A lake?' Josiah nodded approvingly. 'Yes, that would provide a fine vista from the house.'

'The water is more important than the bloody vista!' Benedict snapped, but Josiah wasn't listening to him, just standing back and eyeing the ground, muttering about perspectives. Benedict sighed. Would anything ever turn this arrogant, restless man into a practical farmer? However, to his relief, even though the days continued dry and sunny, the stream still ran, though at a much reduced rate.

'We ought to give that damned trickle of water a name,' Josiah said idly one day when the two men were taking a short rest from clearing more ground.

'Why not call it after your wife?' Benedict replied.

'Catherine Brook?'

'No. Your present wife, the one who's going to live here.'

Josiah shrugged. 'I can't see the point.'

'You're unfair to her, you know. Liza does well by you, works hard without complaint. It'd be a way of saying thank you. And I shall call it Lizabrook from now on.'

The two men's gazes locked for a moment, then Josiah said in a sneering tone, 'You're getting too interested in Liza's welfare. Let me remind you, Caine, that she is *my* wife.'

'In name only.'

Silence hung between them, thick with sudden animosity, then Benedict turned and strode away, calling over his shoulder, 'I'll be back this evening to start digging out the swamp.'

He went home and flung himself down on the wooden bench he had erected outside his tent, reaching for the canvas water bag hanging from a tree to keep its contents cool by gradual evaporation. After gulping some down, he leaned back and looked around. His camp was trim, but he would have to make himself a proper shelter once winter came again. He was spending too much time advising others and helping Josiah. He kept trying to tell himself to get on with his own land clearing, but then he'd see Liza's ungainly body bent over some patch of ground and find himself helping out with yet another small project which would make life easier for her.

The trouble was, he continued to enjoy her company and

she always greeted him with a sort of suppressed relief, chatting as if starved of talk. He'd bet Josiah hardly spoke a word to her most evenings. Dorothy was too tired to go visiting by the end of the day and Kitty, who was nearly Liza's age and could have been a friend, remained openly hostile.

'Oh, Liza, why didn't I meet you before I spoke to Grace?' he groaned, burying his head in his hands. After a while he stood up and decided to make a start on his own cottage to keep his mind off things best not put into words.

'Pendleworth!' he muttered at one stage as he levelled a patch of ground. 'It's a bloody stupid name for a place in Australia.'

Andrew was the only one who seemed truly happy to be here, but even he looked grey and tired sometimes, as if he were not well, and Benedict knew the Pringles had very little money left. Would any of their group ever find their way through this maze of gruelling hard work to a happy and decent life? Well, he was going to try. This was his own land, at least, and that knowledge was a great comfort. He'd have to send for Grace, didn't really know why he was putting that off when he needed a wife to work beside him.

But he could not prevent himself from dreaming of Liza again. And he didn't write to tell Grace to join him. Not yet.

When Benedict left, Josiah stayed by the marsh, picturing a small lake. There should be rolling lawns running down from the house to the water, with children playing on them – he paused at that thought, then smiled. Well, one child at least. He frowned as he wondered if he'd ever have the money to do what he wanted here. This was not rich farming land, though they'd chosen the best that was being offered. He would have to find some other way to make money and that wasn't going to be easy.

Suddenly Liza appeared beside him, proffering a tin mug of lukewarm water and smiling.

'Thank you.' Josiah gulped it down thirstily. 'How can you look so cheerful?' he asked as he handed the mug back to her.

'Because the sun in shining, my washing is dry already, and

I'm going to spend the afternoon clearing more ground for growing vegetables.'

He rubbed his stiff back. 'I thought women were supposed to get tired when they were carrying a child? Why are you so different? Where do you get all that damned energy from?'

'From the good food we eat.'

'Kangaroo meat!'

She shrugged. 'It tastes all right to me. Why are you so often in a bad mood?'

'Because I am.' He turned his back on her and went back to clearing the ground.

Liza returned to her outdoor kitchen and reached for her stewpan, then stiffened. Something had moved behind her in the woods, something large. She swung round, pan in hand, and saw a native woman leaning against a tree, as if exhausted. Before either of them could speak, the woman's eyes rolled up and she crumpled to the ground.

Liza dropped the pan and ran across to her. The woman was unconscious, and looked thin and ill. On her arm was a wound that had festered, the flesh hot and angry around it.

'Where the hell did she come from?'

Liza turned to see Josiah standing beside her, spade raised like a weapon. 'Put that down! She's not dangerous, she's just fainted.'

'Come away from her!'

She shook her head. They'd seen natives several times, but Josiah hadn't tried to make friends with them as Andrew and Benedict had – and as Liza would have liked to do. 'She's ill, Jos. Help me carry her back to the house, will you?'

'Leave her where she is. Let her own people tend her.'

His wife confronted him then, hands on hips, belly jutting out aggressively. 'I'm *not* leaving her here to die. So either you help me or I'll drag her back on a blanket.'

Josiah put down the spade and moved forward reluctantly. 'She's no responsibility of ours, you know.' But he picked the woman up and carried her back to their clearing, laying her on a blanket Liza spread quickly in the shade of a tree. As they stood watching, the woman stirred and opened her eyes, but at the sight of Josiah she gasped and cringed back, throwing one hand across her face as if she feared he would strike her.

'She's terrified,' Liza said, her heart going out to the stranger. 'And look at the bruises on her face. Someone's been hitting her.' She went to get a mug of water, then helped the woman to sit up and sip from it. Her eyes spoke her gratitude, but soon afterwards they closed again. Liza laid her down and sat back on her heels, frowning.

'Where does she come from, do you think, Jos?'

'How the hell should I know? Ask her when she wakes up. I have work to do.' He got himself another drink of water, then stalked off through the woods.

The woman slept for the whole of the afternoon. As dusk crept across the clearing, she began to stir. At the same time there was the sound of footsteps crashing through the bush and men's voices calling to one another. Not Josiah's voice or Benedict's. Liza stiffened, listening. There was an angry tone to them that reminded her of her brothers or Da when they were in a bad mood.

Glancing sideways, she saw that the woman was awake and had a look of terror on her face again. She struggled to get to her feet, but was too weak to stand up, let alone run away. Were they chasing her? Well, they weren't going to get her and ill-treat her. Putting one finger to her lips, Liza took hold of the stranger's hand and helped her into the house. There, she helped her companion into the bedroom and pushed her down on the bed, covering her with blankets and fluffing up the feather mattress around her to hide the slight body. Then she lay down herself so that she hid the other woman. Closing her eyes, she pretended to be asleep.

The voices came closer and she was dismayed when two absolute strangers tramped into the house, flung the bedroom door open and walked inside. Sitting upright as if she had just been woken up, Liza pretended to be shocked, letting out a scream. 'Josiah! Help, Josiah!'

But there was no answering call so she cowered back in the bed, feeling the warmth of the woman's body underneath hers; feeling, too, that it was trembling.

The men stared at her. 'Who the hell are you?' one of them demanded. 'I didn't know anyone had settled round here.'

As he approached the bed, Liza let out another piercing

scream and this time, to her enormous relief, there was an answering shout in the distance.

The second man came to stand beside the first and kicked the bed. 'Stop your caterwauling, you stupid bitch! We've not touched you.'

But his eyes were roaming across her body, and she was sure she saw disappointment in them at the sight of her enormous belly. The other man turned round to look at their possessions, his eyes narrowed as if estimating their worth.

'We're hunting for a native woman. She lives with us, but she's run away.'

'Your maid, you mean?' Liza asked, pretending to be stupid.

'Yeah, well, she does help out around the house as well as – er – working for us.'

They both guffawed.

They were clad in decent clothing, but their skin and clothes were dirty and they gave off a ripe smell that made Liza feel sick. What worried her most was the guns they were carrying. Both Josiah and Benedict owned weapons, but unless they were hunting for kangaroo they kept the pieces in the house, saying you could not be too careful with guns, and forbidding her to touch them. But it was absolutely terrifying, she discovered, to have one pointed at you. Suddenly she wished she had a weapon of her own and knew how to fire it, so that she could counter threat with threat.

'When's it due, then?' one of them asked, gesturing towards her belly with his gun.

'Don't point that thing at my baby!' she cried, but made no move to get up off the bed.

He leaned forward, scowling. 'I asked you a question, you stupid bitch. Answer it.'

'My baby's due in December.'

'Who are you living with, then? You're no lady from the way you talk. You could do better for yourself than this place, once you've dropped the brat. There's not enough white women to go round in the towns, you know, and some folk have to make do with black ones.'

They both chuckled, but broke off as a voice behind them snapped, 'This lady is my wife and I'll thank you to speak to

166

her politely from now on – *if* you ever have need to speak to her again, which I sincerely hope you won't.'

Liza could not hold back a sob of relief. Even dressed in rough working gear, her husband was every inch a gentleman. Something about the way he held himself announced it even before he spoke in his deep cultured voice.

The two men exchanged glances, then slowly lowered their rifles. One moved forward towards Josiah, hand outstretched. 'I'm Pete Greenby. Living in Pinjarra at the moment, when I'm not out after sandalwood in the hills.'

The hand was ignored and he let it drop again, scowling as he gestured to his companion. 'This is Ralph O'Mara, mate of mine. We're looking for a native woman who's run off. She's, er—' he glanced towards Liza and snickered as he finished '—our maid.'

If anything Josiah's scornful expression deepened. 'Well, as you can see, there's only my wife here, so I suggest you get on your way.'

'Wouldn't have a cup of tea going spare, would you?' the one called Pete asked.

'No, I wouldn't.' Josiah was puzzled as to why Liza was lying in bed, since she never normally rested during the daytime unless he forced her to. It worried him that she might be feeling unwell. 'You can have a drink of water, then I'll ask you to leave. My wife's in no condition to wait on anyone, as you can see.'

As they stared back at him, Liza could have sworn she saw the rifles twitch. Her heart began to pound. Were they going to shoot her and Josiah, and rob them?

Then another voice spoke from behind the men and she shuddered in relief.

'Aren't you going to do as my friend asks?'

Benedict stepped into the room, his own gun at the ready. For some reason he looked far more menacing than Josiah, and the men clearly thought so, too, because they began to edge towards the door.

'Just going,' said one.

Liza put one hand to her forehead, announcing, 'I feel faint.'

Benedict and Josiah moved towards the front door, shepherding the men before them. Not until she saw them walking away did Liza lift the blanket and help the native woman to sit up.

Josiah returned to the house just then. 'Oh, hell, I was hoping she'd moved on.'

'She can't. She's ill.' As Liza eased herself carefully to the edge of the bed, it was Benedict who came to help her while Josiah remained where he was. Liza had noticed that the larger she became, the less her husband seemed to want to touch or even look at her.

'Your friend had better stay inside the house for a while, in case they come back,' Benedict said.

The woman looked at Liza. 'Thank you. I couldn't run any more.'

'Why are they chasing you?'

'They took me from my people.' Tears filled her dark eyes suddenly. 'They tied me to the bed and took turns. I ran away but didn't know where to go.'

Memories of Teddy Marshall made Liza's eyes fill in sympathy. 'Well, we won't let them take you back. You can stay here with us.'

Josiah stepped forward. 'Just until you're well enough to travel.'

'You speak good English,' Benedict said.

A faint smile came over the woman's face. 'My father was Irish.' Then she sighed and lay back, looking at the end of her strength.

Liza went to fetch some hot water from the kettle hanging near the low fire and washed the wound carefully. The woman watched her, but her eyelids were drooping and as soon as Liza stopped work, she lay back with a sigh and was asleep within seconds.

'We'll need to get her out of your bed,' Josiah said.

'Not yet,' said Liza easily. 'I'll make her up a bed on the floor if you'll get me some hay to stuff another mattress. And starting tomorrow, I want you to teach me how to load and fire a gun. I've never felt afraid here on my own before, but I did today. I need to be able to defend myself.'

One hand placed on her stomach showed she was thinking of defending the baby as well.

'She's right,' Benedict said. 'We should teach all the women to shoot.'

Josiah gave a snort of laughter. 'Pringle hasn't even got a gun. He leaves it to us to bag the kangaroos. All he's good for is growing vegetables, grubbing up trees and going fishing in the estuary.'

'Well, you don't mind eating his vegetables and the fish, do you?' Liza wished Josiah wouldn't always sneer at people.

He ignored her remark and looked at Benedict. 'Want a drink of port? I think we've earned it.'

'No, thanks. I'll get the hay for the mattress.'

Josiah made no attempt to help, just poured a glass and threw himself down on one of the chairs.

'There's time to get some more work in before dusk,' Benedict said pointedly when he returned to leave the hay on the verandah.

Josiah laughed and raised the glass to admire the colour against the sunlight streaming through one of their muslin-covered windows. 'I've had enough of that sort of work for today.'

As Liza walked outside to start cooking the evening meal, Benedict came over and whispered, 'Is he drinking much?'

She nodded.

'That's all we need! Will you be all right?'

'Yes, of course.'

'You can send her to me if Josiah won't let her stay.'

'Oh, I'll make sure she stays.' Liza watched him go, sighed and got on with her work, waking the woman a little later and persuading her to eat and drink some more water.

Liza watched her husband pick at a meal, then slump in his chair and pour himself another glass of wine. She could see he would not be fit to talk to, so decided to go to bed early. Outside a breeze rustled the branches and an owl called – at least it sounded like an owl. When she looked through the doorway into her bedroom and saw the double bed, she did not bother to make up the new mattress for the invalid, but simply shared her bed with her guest.

It felt good not to sleep alone, but it also made her wonder how Nancy and Kieran were, and that brought tears to her eyes. Until she came to Australia, the only time she had had a bed to herself was at the Pringles – and even then she had been able to hear Maggie snoring on the other side of the thin attic wall.

Josiah wouldn't even touch her, let alone share a bed with her. You needed people to touch you sometimes, she had found, but the bigger she got, the more he stayed away from her. Without thinking, she snuggled against her companion and drew comfort from the warmth of another human body.

Liza could have been happy here in Australia because she didn't mind working hard and helping to build up a farm – but her husband's scornful attitude really hurt sometimes, and the loneliness was beginning to get her down. Perhaps things would be better once she'd had the baby. She hoped so because she couldn't go on like this.

CHAPTER FOURTEEN

In the morning, Liza woke to find the native woman lying on one elbow staring at her. 'Are you all right?' she asked.

'Better.' The woman hesitated then said, 'You shared a bed with me.'

'Well, there was plenty of room.'

'But I'm – I'm black.'

Liza stared down at their two hands, lying so close on the covers, and smiled. 'Not really black. Not much darker than me, actually.' Then she saw the tears in her companion's eyes. 'What's wrong?'

'No one's treated me like a normal person for a long time.'

'We're both women, aren't we? But I don't know your name. I never thought to ask you last night.'

'My mother called me Dinny. It means "little kangaroo" in our language.' She hesitated then added, 'But my father called me Davnat, which is Irish.'

'Which name do you prefer?'

'Dinny.'

'All right. I'll call you that, then. And I'm Liza.'

'Don't I call you missus?'

Liza let out a snort of laughter. 'I don't feel like a missus. We're about the same age, aren't we?'

'I'm twenty-two.'

'I'm not yet nineteen. But you'd better call my husband Mr Ludlam. He'd definitely prefer that.'

Since Liza was incapable of standing on ceremony, Dinny soon found herself responding in a similar way. Within days the two of them were firm friends and had exchanged stories.

Dinny's Irish father had died when she was eighteen. Since she and her mother had moved to this district with him from much further south, they had no relatives nearby when they were left alone, something which had preyed on her mother's mind. But she had been too weak to travel south again.

'I'm as much a "foreigner" to my people here as I am to the whites,' Dinny said sadly one day. 'I don't fit in anywhere.'

Liza squeezed her hand in quick sympathy. She'd felt like that herself sometimes during the long evenings sitting with Josiah, trying to occupy herself with embroidery or reading the same old pages of a book while he mostly ignored her. 'How did you come to be with those men who were chasing you?'

'When my mother died last year, I found it hard to get work and I had to live rough. They captured me one day and then . . .' Her voice faded away.

Liza took her hand and gave it a sympathetic squeeze. 'Did no one try to help you?'

'There was no one to know or care. They kept me in their camp and tied me up when they went into town.'

Liza approached Josiah the next day, first making sure he was in a good mood by cooking his favourite meal. 'I want Dinny to stay here because I'm going to need some help with the baby.'

'You want to hire her as a servant, you mean?'

Liza frowned, then realised this was the only way he would accept the situation. 'Yes. And if those men try to capture her again, would you go to a magistrate and tell him she's our maid? She'd be safe, then, because he'd listen to you.'

Josiah looked at her thoughtfully. 'Well, I'd rather have had a white maid, but you're going to need another woman with you when have the child, so why not?' He certainly didn't want to be involved in the birth.

'And can we pay her?'

He raised one eyebrow. 'I'm not in the habit of cheating my servants, Liza.'

'No, of course not.'

By early December, Liza was moving more slowly, though she still insisted on keeping active, to Josiah's disapproval.

'Ladies usually take to their beds at this stage,' he said one day, 'or at least keep to their rooms.'

'What do they do there?'

'How should I know what they do? Rest, I suppose. Keep out of sight.'

Liza set her hands on her hips and glared at him. 'Well, you may not like looking at this,' she patted her belly and stuck it out as far as she could out of sheer perversity, 'but I'm not going to hide in my room. I'd go mad sitting around with nothing to do.'

'Oh, do as you please. You always do anyway.'

'I do not! I spend half my life trying to please you only I never seem to succeed.'

'Kindly keep your voice down. You sound like a fishwife.' He turned his back on her and went out to tend the animals.

Liza blinked away the tears that were threatening. 'Well, I'm not hiding!' she muttered defiantly.

As the days passed, she was even more glad of Dinny's companionship because Josiah avoided her, not even looking at her if he could help it.

He'd been working hard with Benedict to clear more land, but one day seemed in a dark mood from the moment he got up, finding fault with Liza's cooking, pushing his breakfast aside with a comment about the food he was forced to eat in this benighted hell-hole, and slouching off to the fields. He came back to the house earlier than usual in the afternoon, washed himself with his usual fastidiousness, then got out one of his precious bottles of brandy. Liza rolled her eyes at Dinny and kept out of his way.

He took the bottle outside, sat down on one of the sawn-off pieces of log which they used as stools, and leaned back against a tree, staring into space in between sipping brandy from a fine crystal glass. Once he covered his face with his arm for a long time.

She kept peering out of the window, worried because she had never seen him so down-spirited before.

'He's a very unhappy man,' Dinny said softly, coming to stand beside her.

'Yes. I've never really seen him look happy.'

'He never will be. He has a darkness hanging over him.'

Liza glanced sideways, saw her friend staring into space as if she could see things beyond the shadows, and shivered suddenly.

The air around them seemed dark and full of menace. To take her mind off it, Liza gave the house a thorough cleaning, even though she felt more tired than usual that day.

And all the time Josiah stayed outside, not moving, not looking towards the house. He refused food and had consumed most of the brandy by the time dusk fell.

Before she went to bed, Liza went to stand in the doorway and call, 'Goodnight, Josiah.' He did not turn his head or reply but continued to stare into the darkness as if he could see something no one else could beyond the circle of lamplight that shone through their muslin-covered door and windows. Liza shivered and went into her bedroom.

She couldn't seem to settle, though she was normally a sound sleeper. She wished Dinny were still sharing her bed, because it was comforting to have a warm body with you at night, but Josiah had refused to countenance his wife sleeping with a maid so Dinny now slept in a corner of the living room, rolling up her bedding during the day.

Suddenly Liza gasped in shock as her whole belly grew rigid. When she spread her hands across it, the normally soft flesh felt as hard as a board. It wasn't a pain, not exactly, but it was an uncomfortable feeling and she knew what it meant: the baby was coming. At last! As her stomach muscles relaxed again, she let out a long sigh of relief and patted the bump that seemed to have been there for ever. 'We'll do all right, love,' she whispered. 'Just you and me.'

She knew it could take a while to have the baby so she began to get her things ready but didn't call Dinny in to help. However, the spasms grew stronger more quickly than she had expected. When a particularly sharp pain stabbed through her, she could not help moaning and calling, 'Dinny!' But there was no answer.

She went to look for her friend but Dinny's bed was empty. The other woman sometimes went out at night to walk through the forest and Liza had envied her that freedom. Josiah would have had a fit if she'd tried it.

Suddenly she felt afraid. What if she were like her mother? What if she *died* trying to have the baby? She peeped into Josiah's room, but he wasn't there either and she had to bite back a sob. She needed help. Where was everyone?

When she looked outside, she saw him sprawled on the ground under the tree where he'd been drinking earlier. She waited till another of the pains had passed, then shook him. 'Jos, I'm having the baby. Will you please go and fetch Dorothy?'

But he didn't move, just lay there by his overturned stool, breathing so loudly it was almost one continuous rumbling snore.

Liza shook him again, but that only changed the pattern of his snoring for a moment. As another pain stabbed through her she leaned against the tree, unable to hold back a moan of terror. There was no one to help her. She was going to die here all alone.

She turned towards the house but stumbled and fell to her knees, sobbing now. Then someone slipped an arm round her and when she saw Dinny beside her, she sobbed aloud in sheer relief and clutched her friend's arm. 'My baby's coming!'

After helping her to bed, Dinny lifted Liza's skirt and examined her lower body, seeming to know exactly what she was doing. She smiled. 'It's coming quickly, too. You're lucky.'

'Lucky? Oooh!' When the next pain had passed, Liza lay there, one arm across her eyes, and suddenly she knew who she needed. 'Please, Dinny, will you go and fetch Benedict?'

'You want a *man* here?'

Liza burst into tears. 'I want Benedict. I need him. *Please!*'

Shaking her head in disapproval, Dinny slipped out of the small house into the warm, still night, skirting Josiah's unconscious body with a scornful look and then running easily through the moon-dappled forest.

Left on her own, Liza panicked as another pain hit her, and in between sobs begged the baby to wait until Benedict was there. She had no doubt he would come to help her, none whatsoever. But would he be in time?

When two more pains had ripped through her she stopped weeping and lay watching a large moth beat to and fro outside the muslin-covered window frame. The gentle sounds of the night sifted into the house, making her feel calmer.

Another pain took her by surprise, but this time she clamped her mouth shut and tried to endure it, only moaning a little as it built up then subsided.

The spasms seemed to be coming quite quickly now; in

fact everything was happening far more quickly than it had ever done with her mother. With difficulty, she took off her normal nightdress and donned the shorter one she had prepared for the birth, but the effort left her panting.

The long slow minutes passed and one pain after another seized her. Then she heard someone running towards the house and looked up to see Benedict standing panting in the doorway, with Dinny behind him. She held out her arms to him, so filled with relief she kept saying his name, over and over.

He rushed across the room to hold her close and stroke back the damp hair from her forehead. 'How bad is it, love?'

At those words, Dinny looked sharply from one to the other though neither of them noticed. When Liza moaned, Dinny pushed him gently away to make another examination.

'I saw Josiah outside. Dinny said he's drunk.' Benedict's voice was thick with scorn.

'He didn't know about the baby. He passed out before my pains started,' Liza gasped as another pain pulsated through her, different this time.

Dinny nudged him. 'She needs to sit up now.'

He looked at her. 'You do know what to do?'

'Oh, yes. My mother used to help women have babies. She taught me so I'd have some work to do.'

But he was still worried, not knowing how much he could trust her. He turned to Liza. 'Will you let me stay with you and help? It can't be all that different from the animals and I've plenty of experience with them.'

'I want you to stay. Need you. Do you mind?'

For a moment they stared at one another, all barriers gone between them.

'I'd do anything for you,' he said gently. 'You know that, don't you?'

'Yes.' Liza rode out another pain with Benedict holding her hand and joy singing through her. He did feel for her – as she felt for him. For the moment that was enough. It gave her courage and hope. Suddenly she was fiercely glad that Josiah was not there with them.

Then she lost herself in a desperate need to bear down. As the contractions took her over, she let her body guide her, crouching as Dinny urged her, clutching Benedict's hand sometimes, blind to everything but the need to bring her baby into the world.

When the pain eased suddenly, she blinked and opened her eyes for the first time in a while and Dinny helped her on to the bed. Benedict was hovering over her, holding something wrapped in a towel, something which squirmed and wailed. 'You have a daughter, Liza.'

For a moment, they both stared at the tiny baby, then tears of joy began to trickle down Liza's cheeks. 'Is she all right?'

His voice was husky with emotion. 'She's perfect.'

The room seemed filled with wonder as Liza stared down into a crumpled face topped by swirls of dark hair. She could hear the infant's faint, snuffling breaths and when she touched the perfect little hand, the fingers clenched around her index finger and love wound itself tightly round her heart. 'A daughter,' she said in a tone of awe. 'I have a daughter.'

'She's beautiful,' whispered Benedict, unaware that tears were rolling down his cheeks as well. 'Oh, Liza, she's so beautiful.'

Their eyes met across the downy top of the child's skull and for a moment it felt as if they were a family, he the father, she the mother, and this their baby. Then reality took hold and Liza drew in a deep, shaky breath, forcing herself to say, 'I do hope Josiah likes her.'

She saw Benedict draw back a little at her words and she knew that the moment of rapport had passed. She was not married to this man and, although she loved him, could do nothing about that. But she had her daughter now, at least. Through her tears, she smiled down at the child and whispered, 'Catherine. I'm going to call her Catherine Mary.'

'I'll leave Dinny to help you.' Benedict went outside, but at the sight of Liza's so-called husband, lying there breathing stertorously – the person who had promised to look after her and then left her to manage on her own – rage filled him and overflowed in a desperate need to do something. He shook the other man violently, shouting, 'Wake up! Damn you, wake up!' But Josiah only groaned and turned away, so Benedict let the slack body fall back on the ground. 'She needed you!' he said, the words throbbing with anger. 'Dammit, she doesn't ask for much but you let her down even in this.' Then he left Josiah lying there and walked slowly back through the moonlit woods to his own tiny hut.

The place had never seemed so lonely. All he could think about was how much he loved Liza. He had not realised quite how much before this night. She might be another man's wife and he might be tied to Grace, but that made no difference to the depth of his feelings. Tears trickled down his cheeks and when he brushed them away one lingered on his finger, glinting in the moonlight for a moment. 'Oh, Liza, Liza, what a mess this all is!' he muttered, his voice breaking on the words. 'Why did I rush into a loveless marriage?'

He lay on the bed, but could not sleep. As soon as it grew light, he walked across to tell Dorothy that Liza had given birth and to his relief she promised to go and visit.

'It's ridiculous how you all fuss over her!' Kitty snapped. 'Women of her class have babies very easily, you know.'

Benedict's disgust at her unkind words must have shown because she flushed and walked outside to the kitchen, her expression as unhappy and brooding as Josiah's had been.

Dorothy accompanied him to the front door. 'Don't worry. I'll go over there straight after breakfast.'

'She only has that maid of hers,' Benedict worried. 'Josiah might just as well not be there.'

'Well, Dinny seems a very capable young woman to me. She and Liza have grown very close.'

He sighed. 'I know she's capable. I just worry about Liza. Especially now.'

'There's nothing you can do. She has a husband.'

When Dorothy patted his cheek in a motherly gesture, Benedict realised he had betrayed his feelings. 'I know I have no right.'

'All friends have a right to help one another.'

He forced a smile. 'I'll get back home, then.'

He decided to clear more land, working till his hands were raw and bleeding, till his back felt ready to break, till his muscles screamed for rest. But nothing he did made any difference because everywhere he turned he saw Liza's face full of joy, saw the tiny baby lying in her arms, so beautiful and delicate, and he wanted to weep, to sob aloud with the pain that he could not be the one to look after them.

* * *

Josiah woke to a head that was pounding and aching and a mouth that tasted foul. Groaning, he lifted his head. As he looked down at his crumpled clothes and smelled the sour sweat on his body, disgust surged through him. What had got into him to drink so heavily? To lie outside all night like a sot? What would Catherine think of him? He winced. Why did he always think of her first? It was Liza now, not Catherine. He was married to a stupid, ignorant little maidservant who could hardly read, not to a lady of breeding.

Well, at least he felt purged of his bitterness and longing – for the moment, anyway. There was no sign of Liza so he got to his feet, knocking over a spade leaning against a tree and cursing as he tripped over it.

Dinny came to the door of the cottage. 'The baby's come.'

He stopped short, unable to believe what he'd heard. 'What? What did you say, girl?'

She looked at him disapprovingly. 'The baby was born during the night.'

'And Liza?' Had she died? Oh, heavens, please not! Josiah was surprised to realise that he would not now like to be without her, for all her imperfections. He could not move for a moment, only ask again, more urgently, 'Is she – is Liza all right? Tell me, damn you!'

Dinny nodded. 'Of course. She's young and strong. The baby's all right, too.'

Relief flooded through him and he stumbled across to the cottage on stiff legs, shoving her aside. As he stood in the bedroom doorway, a shaft of sunlight through the window gave the place a feeling of church and sanctuary, a feeling intensified by the sight of Liza, sleeping peacefully in her bed, quiet for once, not bustling about, humming and chatting. Beside her on the floor was a drawer with a bundle tucked into it.

The bundle stirred and he tiptoed across to stand beside the bed. As he stared down at the child, the breath caught in his throat – so tiny and pink, its head smaller than his hand. It was sleeping and when he bent over it he could hear the faintest of breaths, see the little chest rising and falling. Wonder surged through him. He didn't know whether it was a boy or a girl, but it didn't matter because whichever it was he could claim it as his. He had never expected the privilege of becoming a father, never realised how much he would like the idea.

Josiah reached for the baby, picking it up with infinite care and cradling it against his chest, supporting its head as he had seen women do. It woke and began at once to snuffle and search for something to suck, then blinked its eyes and stared up at him. Dorothy had told him that new-born babies could not see properly for several weeks, but to him it seemed as if the child was looking straight at him, looking into his heart and taking hold of it.

'She's beautiful, isn't she?'

Liza's voice made him turn round and smile. 'Very beautiful indeed. A girl, eh?'

'Yes.'

He took a step forward. 'Liza, I'm sorry I let you down. I'm deeply ashamed of my behaviour last night.'

'I had Dinny – and Benedict.'

Josiah's voice was sharp again. 'Caine was there? At the birth?'

'Yes. Dinny fetched him for me.'

Jealousy speared through him. 'Could she not have gone for Dorothy?'

'Dorothy doesn't know anything about birthing.'

'And he does?'

'He's a farmer – he deals with it in animals all the time. And he was a great comfort to me.'

'Damn him!'

'Why do you say that?'

'Because—' he saw the shocked expression on her face and could not say what he wanted to, so compromised on, '—because I wish it had been me.'

'Oh. But you didn't like . . .' She shaped a mound in the air over her flat stomach.

He flushed, knowing she was right.

Liza didn't see any point in dwelling on their problems, so forced a smile. 'Anyway, it's all over now, and I was lucky – it happened very quickly and I had no trouble.'

'Good.'

The baby began to cry, breaking the tension and proving

immediately that there was nothing whatsoever wrong with her lungs.

'Give her to me.' Liza began to unbutton her nightgown, then flushed as she saw Josiah staring at her because they usually avoided undressing in front of one another. Well, no use trying to hide what she was doing. She took the baby from him, putting it to her breast and smiling at how quickly the feeding instinct worked. She forgot him, forgot everything in the wonder of feeling her child suckle, closing her eyes with the sheer ecstasy of it.

He stood entranced, watching, for this tiny new life seemed the most precious thing he had ever seen.

After a while, Liza looked up and told him quietly, 'She's called Catherine.'

'A perfect name. Catherine. Though we'll call her Cathie, shall we?' Not Cat, never Cat. 'And perhaps Sophia as well, for my mother?'

Liza shook her head, determined on one thing. 'No. Catherine Mary. For *my* mother.' Suddenly she could not hold back a sob.

'What's wrong?' Josiah's voice was gentle.

'I was just wishing I could tell her she has a granddaughter. Even if I write, she'll never see Cathie, will she?' Liza looked down. 'And I can't help wondering what life will bring to my baby. I do hope she has a happier life than me.'

He felt unusually protective. 'Your life has only just begun, Liza. Eighteen seems very young to me. And I'm sure things will get better – for both of us.'

'I'm nineteen now.'

'You didn't tell me when it was your birthday.'

'Would you have cared?' She was thinking aloud, only half aware of him. 'Nineteen isn't old, not really, but I feel sometimes as if I've lived a thousand years. As if life has picked me up, squeezed me till I hurt all over and then thrown me aside.' Sudden misery overwhelmed her, not only for herself but for the absence of Benedict. She wanted *him* to be here, not Josiah.

Her husband touched her hand gently. 'Things will get better.' He gestured around him, his expression scornful, then looked down at the child and the scorn faded, to be replaced by an expression of hope and wonder, rare for him. 'One day I'll make enough money for you to live more easily, with servants to do the hard work. It won't always be like this, I promise you. And we'll make sure Cathie does have a happier life than either of us.'

'I don't need servants and money to be happy, Josiah. I need affection and – and company.' Tears filled Liza's eyes. He didn't touch her to offer comfort as anyone else would have done, just threw words at her.

'This is just weariness after the birth. Both my sisters-in-law became very miserable for a time, then they recovered. I'm sure you will, too.' He had listened to her humming and singing as she worked, seen how lacking in shadows she was while he always felt full of darkness. He had not fitted in back in England and he did not fit in here either. Nor could he in truth see himself making a success of this life as he had hoped and moving somewhere more congenial. All that lay ahead was hard work and a primitive lifestyle. His father's punishment was biting deep.

He glanced out of the stupid muslin window, reminding himself that he really must get some proper glass, though it wouldn't grow cold again till the following winter. Outside he could see only trees. In every direction they overshadowed things, cutting him off from sun and life, breeding gloom and despair. Only on the cleared land did he feel a little better, with the open sky above him.

He was relieved to hear someone arriving. He and Liza were tied to one another for life, but he could not talk about his feelings to her or even feel comfortable for long in her company.

Dorothy bustled into the house. 'You should have sent for me last night.' She beamed down at the baby. 'Oh, isn't she lovely?'

'I had Dinny. She was wonderful. She knew exactly what to do.'

When Cathie had finished feeding, Liza let Dorothy take the baby and change her. She felt tired, and as the first few days passed also riven with emotion – one minute happy, the next weeping helplessly into her pillow. Dinny said this was quite normal and called it 'baby tears'.

Liza didn't feel at all normal. Her life was in a dreadful mess, but she could only go forward now along the path on which Catherine had thrust her. Affection of the sort husbands and wives usually shared was not for her and Josiah, and she could not turn to Benedict for it either. But at least she could still see him, speak to him, be near him. That would be a comfort. As would her little daughter.

When she looked down at the now sleeping infant, Liza shed a few more tears then fell asleep herself.

'She has babies easily,' Dinny told Dorothy. 'I think she'll have a lot of them.'

Dorothy didn't share her optimism, not with a husband like Josiah. 'I'm glad things went well. The rest of her life isn't easy at all.'

CHAPTER FIFTEEN

Josiah could not bring himself to write to his father until several months after Cathie's birth. He wanted to claim the money, of course he did, but he hated the thought of any contact with the tyrant who had cost him everything he loved, and who had made Catherine's last weeks so miserable. However, in April 1858, he strolled across to see Benedict one evening.

'I didn't tell you before, but my father offered me five hundred pounds when my first child was born.'

Benedict stared at him, then said quietly, 'But you don't have a child.'

'I consider Cathie mine – and so does the world – only *he* won't take my word for it that she exists, so will you write a letter supporting my claim?'

'Telling lies, you mean?'

'You can call it that if you like.' Josiah waited a moment, before adding, with a sneering sideways glance, 'It'll make a big difference to Liza's life and future, that money will.'

Benedict stared at him, wondering how much Josiah had guessed about his feelings for Liza. 'I'll think about it.'

And with that Josiah had to be content, though he grew so irritable over the next few days that Liza and Dinny avoided him as much as they could.

Benedict went across to see the Ludlams one morning five days later. He found Liza there, humming softly to herself and scrubbing the outdoor bench on which she prepared food for cooking.

'You sound happy,' he said.

She turned, smiling at him. 'I am. Though I think Cathie is teething, she's been so restless lately, and look at her poor little cheek.'

He went to study the child, who was lying in a makeshift

184

cradle near her mother. Since he had seen her being born, he'd felt a special link to her. 'Poor little thing.' He looked up at the mother, also smiling down into the cradle. 'Is she keeping you awake?'

Liza shrugged. 'A bit. I don't mind, really. Her gums must be painful. But the disturbed nights are making Josiah really grumpy.'

'Does he get grumpy often?'

She nodded. 'Oh, yes. He doesn't show it as much when other people are around, but some evenings he hardly says a word.' She wrung out her cloth and surveyed the results of her labours with every sign of satisfaction, then said thoughtfully, 'But it's bound to get him down living like this, isn't it, and I know he hasn't got a lot of money left. I wish—' she broke off and shrugged. 'What's the use of wishing? You just have to make the best of what you've got.'

'Where is he?'

'He's ridden into Mandurah to buy some supplies and won't be back till evening.' And he would be carrying more bottles of rum in his saddlebags.

'I'll come across later to see him, then.' And would agree to what Josiah wanted for Liza's sake. And the child's.

That evening Josiah greeted him stiffly.

'I'll do it,' Benedict told him.

'That's good news. I've written my own damned letter.'

'You'd better show it to me. I don't want to put anything in mine that'll contradict what you say.'

Josiah produced a single sheet of paper and handed it to him with a mock flourish. 'My very first epistle to my father since I came here and I wish to hell it could be my last.'

After studying the letter, Benedict looked up at Josiah in puzzlement. 'Shouldn't you have told him about Catherine's death?'

'Why?'

'Well, her family have a right to know, surely?'

Josiah's smile became a sneer. 'They'll be happier if they think she's still alive – and beside, my father's more likely to pay the money if he thinks it'll benefit Cat.'

Benedict frowned and studied the letter again. 'I don't like this – this extra deceit.'

'You don't have to like it!'

Liza, who had been sitting quietly by the fire, said, 'I think you should tell her family, Josiah. It's not fair to them to let them think she's still alive!'

He turned on her. 'Well, I don't agree and I happen to know them all far better than you do. Old Rawley is a nasty sod, almost as much of a tyrant as my own dear father. Rawley was quite happy to let his only daughter be sent to Australia, you know, because it's the son who counts for him. Cat asked him to persuade my father not to send us so far, but he refused, said it'd be the making of me. Unmaking, more like. And do you think they'll be pleased to hear that I've married a *servant*? After Cat? Do you think my father will cough up that much money for a servant's brat? I'm damned sure he won't.'

'Don't speak to Liza like that!' Benedict snapped, hating to see that hurt look in her eyes.

Josiah turned on him, seeming almost manic in his rage. 'I'll speak to her how I like. She's *my* wife, not yours, and it's I who have given her brat a name. She owes me absolute loyalty and gratitude, and I don't see that she has anything to complain about.'

Liza bent her head over her mending.

Benedict could see her hands shaking, but knew better than to try to offer her any comfort. Unable to sit still, he stood up and began to walk to and fro. It was Liza's unhappy expression that decided him to continue with this. She'd be the one who had to bear the brunt of Josiah's moods if he refused. And what did it matter, after all, if Saul Ludlam was cheated? A man like him did nothing to earn the love of his children. He'd probably never find out.

Benedict had settled down here in Australia, was even growing to love the land he was wresting from the forest, but like Josiah he missed Lancashire greatly at times and bitterly resented having been sent out here at an arrogant man's whim. Sometimes as he listened to Liza talking, homesickness would overwhelm him, because her accent and her little sayings reminded him of the Lancashire he had known, not the polite, hypocritical world of the Ludlams and Rawleys. And although the way she spoke was changing under Josiah's influence, her voice would probably always carry the echo of Lancashire in it,

just as her nature seemed to him to embody the sturdy determination of Lancashire folk to make something of themselves.

'All right,' he said curtly. 'I'll write to your father. But
I'm not telling any direct lies. I'll bring the letter across
tomorrow.'

Josiah smiled at him. 'Thank you.' He didn't even turn to
look at Liza, let alone apologise to her for his rudeness.

When Benedict had gone, she set her sewing aside. 'I'm
tired. I think I'll go to bed now.'

'Don't you want to see what I've written?' he asked
mockingly.

'No.'

So he was left with only a bottle of the new rum to share
his pleasure.

In September 1858, over a year after he had sent Josiah away,
Saul Ludlam put down his knife and fork to glance at the
envelopes on the silver platter beside him. He stilled and pressed
his lips tightly together as he saw a letter from his youngest son.
He would recognise that handwriting anywhere, overlarge and
very rounded. Childish, to his mind. This was the first letter
they had received from Josiah since his departure for Australia,
and he was not at all sure he wanted to open it.

Muttering in annoyance, he told the maid to take the letters
to his study and went on with his breakfast, finishing the food
on his plate and not speaking to his sons, who always shared
this early meal with him.

When their father had left the room, Matthew asked, 'What
brought the thunderclouds down this time?'

Isaac glanced over his shoulder, not wanting his father to
overhear them. 'There was a letter from Jos. I'd recognise his
writing anywhere.'

Matthew gave an angry snort. 'Well, let's hope it isn't
bad news.'

'I'm glad Mother wasn't here to see it. I daresay Father will
check there's nothing – well, upsetting in it before he shows
it to her.'

'She's missing Jos, still cries for him.'

They both resented the fact that he was their mother's

favourite, that she had never stopped hoping to hear from him, even though a year and a half had passed since his departure.

Isaac hesitated then murmured, 'I hope Jos is all right, though.'

'He will be. He always manages to look after himself, that sod does.'

In his study Saul opened the envelope reluctantly. Halfway through the letter he gasped in shock and scowled around the room before continuing. He was not so gullible as to believe a creature like Josiah had fathered a child. 'Catherine Mary! A name doesn't make it a child. It takes a man to do that and he's no man. Well, he's not getting five hundred pounds out of me so easily.'

But there was another, smaller note enclosed, this time from Benedict Caine, brief and to the point:

> To Mr Saul Ludlam:
> This is to confirm that Mrs Ludlam gave birth to a child a few weeks ago, a little girl, whom they have named Catherine Mary.
>   Conditions here are much harsher than we had expected, but your son is working hard to clear his land and no one could fault his efforts.
>   I swear this to be true.
> B. Caine
> (Psalm 85, Verse 10)

Saul stared at the letter in disbelief. 'How did he get Caine to write this?' he asked, shaking it angrily. He couldn't believe Caine would be party to a lie, for the fellow was more likely to toss the truth in your face. Then, of course, he had to get out his Bible and find the reference.

'"Mercy and truth are met together."' Saul read aloud, swore again and thumped his desk. 'How can I believe him?'

Not until later in the morning did he pick up his son's missive and stalk into the parlour where his wife was sitting staring out of the window. Her expression was so sad that he knew she was thinking of Josiah again.

'I have word from our son.' He tossed the letter into her lap. 'And it's taken him long enough to write.'

Sophia stared at him for a moment in sheer disbelief, eyes filling with tears even as he watched.

'Josiah?' she asked faintly.

'Which other son would need to write to us? Did you not share a meal with Matthew and Isaac last night?'

She picked up the piece of paper with a hand that trembled. Blind with tears, she held it out to him, saying, 'Please, Saul, read it to me. Please!' before beginning to sob quietly into her handkerchief.

He took it from her reluctantly and read it aloud.

'A child!' she whispered when he had finished. 'Josiah has a daughter.'

'Yes.'

'Catherine told me before they left that she thought she was with child.'

He stiffened. *'What?'*

'I found her being sick one morning, so I guessed.'

'You're sure of that?'

'Of course I am. I thought she must have lost the child or they'd have written to tell us about it before now. She looked so ill. But then some women do when they're in a delicate condition. I dare say the voyage did her good. They say sea air is very beneficial, do they not? Oh, Saul, Saul, can he not come home again now? Must I be punished as well as him?'

She clutched his sleeve and he peeled her fingers from it gently, holding the hand in both his for a moment and patting it absent-mindedly. He had sworn to himself that he'd never tell her what her youngest son was like and had made the rest of the family promise the same when he realised that they had long since guessed. He did not know how he could have been so blind and that only added to his anger.

'He's better where he is, Sophia. The hard physical life of a settler will make a man of him.'

'He'll never be like you and the other boys, Saul. He's cast in a gentler mould. Why can you not accept that?'

'Because a man must learn to work and fend for himself.'

His wife was weeping again, soft helpless tears. 'But I'll never even see this grandchild. Ah, Saul, Saul, you're so hard on that poor boy. And he must have been very unhappy not to have written. You know he can get very low in spirit sometimes.'

One of his daughters-in-law came in, hesitated and looked to him for guidance on whether to stay.

'You'd better help her.' He gestured to his wife. 'We've heard from Josiah. He's become a father, it appears.'

Then he went back to his study to write a letter to his bankers and ask them to send a draft for five hundred pounds to his youngest son. If Catherine herself had told Sophia she was with child before they left, then it must be true. He would keep his word about the money, though it went against the grain to give Josiah anything more.

That same ship brought a letter from Benedict to his family, enclosing one for Grace. In it he told them about the land he had bought and what things were like in Western Australia.

Benedict's mother wept just as bitterly as Sophia had, and his father did too when no one was near – but Martin only sneered at the news. 'He'll be lucky to make a go of it in such dry conditions. I don't envy him.' He was glad his younger brother had left – hoped Benedict would never return.

'He asks that we give this letter to Grace ourselves, so that her father won't read it first,' Jack Caine worried to his wife. 'I don't like to deceive a neighbour, I really don't.'

She turned it round in her hands. 'He must be thinking of wedding her, then, if he's writing to her. Well, she'll make a good wife for a farmer, Grace will. I haven't seen much of her lately, though, have you?'

'No. Come to think of it, I haven't heard whether she's back from her aunt's. She was ill a while back, I did hear.'

'Perhaps I'd better go over to visit,' Sally suggested.

But when she drove the gig over to the Newtons' farm, Grace's mother said she was still at her aunt's. Sally could see no alternative but to leave the letter there and went away wondering how she had offended her neighbour, who had been very stiff with her.

It was two days before Grace received the letter, which had been opened and read by her father first. This infuriated her and was the final straw that made her take a decision contrary to Benedict's wishes.

★　　★　　★

After much deliberation, Liza had also written a letter which Josiah had sent off to England for her. She had sent it to the Dochertys' priest, begging him to pass on the enclosed note to her mother secretly. She was fairly sure she could trust him to do that because Father Michael was a kindly man. In the letter to the priest she explained that she didn't want her two elder brothers finding out where she was and following her out to Australia, so had not given an address. She could not actually imagine any of her noisy family arriving in the quiet bushland, with the tall whispering trees she was growing to love and the brightly coloured parrots flying around, shrieking and squabbling – but still, wanted to make very sure Niall and Dermott could never trace her. She didn't trust them.

The letter arrived in Pendleworth on a cool day in September. The priest read and re-read it, pleased that little Liza had found a safe haven and a husband to care for her. He raised his eyebrows when he saw who that husband was and whistled softly, finding it hard to believe that a Ludlam would marry a Docherty, whatever the circumstances.

The next day he went to visit Mary Docherty, reading her the letter several times, then praying with her and chatting quietly till she had calmed down from her storm of weeping. After a final reading, he left the crumpled piece of paper with her. She could not read, but to see her touching her daughter's letter, kissing it and stroking the paper, was very moving. The poor woman had not long to live but this message had undoubtedly brightened her last months on earth. The Lord moved in mysterious ways sometimes, but in this his heavenly master had acted kindly, he had indeed.

Father Michael went about his work and gave the letter no more thought.

Mary Docherty gave it much thought, remembering what it said word for word, smiling sometimes at the idea of a little grand-daughter called after her. She did not show it to her husband and decided she would destroy it as she drew nearer death, for she had no illusions about her condition. But just for a little while she would keep it and touch it sometimes. That seemed to bring her favourite child closer, for she still missed Liza dreadfully, though Nancy was turning into a good girl nowadays and her Kieran had grown into a kind-natured, loving lad, totally unlike his brothers.

Their second hot season in Australia began in November, not a busy season for farmers and too hot for a sane man to work at clearing land. Feeling desperate for a change of scenery, Josiah decided to go up to Perth for a few days. He'd had more than enough of domesticity, especially in such a small house, and although he loved little Cathie, he wanted – needed! – to be among civilised people again, people of his own class. Liza did her best to learn and improve, he would grant her that, but it wasn't enough. She could read fairly well now and pick out a few tunes on the piano, for she seemed to have an ear for music, but she could not converse of literature or the broader world, and would never be his social equal.

And the baby was teething again, her crying nearly driving him mad. Usually he enjoyed playing with her and would carry her outside sometimes to see the small herd of cows and the flock of sheep that Benedict cared for so well. He could talk to her as he could talk to no one else, calling her 'Cat' when he forgot and describing his plans for Pendleworth Homestead. He could see in his mind the gracious house that would one day stand here and the thought of it brought him some comfort. Not that the child understood what he said yet, but one day she would, and in the meantime she laughed and gurgled at him when he spoke to her.

In Perth he ran into Gerard Fenton and found him good company after over a year of secluded, bucolic life. The two of them went back to the Fentons' house, a small place by English standards but a hell of a lot bigger than Josiah's three-roomed shack in the bush. They had consumed a bottle of rather fine claret by the time Agnes came home from visiting a friend and were about to open another, which she laughingly demanded to share with them once she had gone to check how her little son was.

Josiah studied her in approval. She was clad in a crinoline, its pale blue folds swaying around her as she walked. Her hands were soft and white, and she gestured gracefully as she talked, making them laugh at her comical descriptions of shopping in

Perth, where if the shopkeeper had run out of something it would likely be many months before it could be obtained. The child was in the care of a nursemaid, which Josiah knew Liza would not have wanted even had they been able to afford one. He was sick of seeing her carting Cathie round on her hip, like poor women did, sick of all her attention being focused on the child. She might be a good mother, but she was also a gentleman's wife and should learn to behave like one.

Agnes insisted Josiah leave the hotel and stay with them for a few days. 'I've been moped to tears since Harry was born. How did Liza go – did the child live?'

Josiah nodded. 'Yes, indeed. It's a little girl whom we've named Catherine – Cathie for short.'

There was a pause, then Agnes gave him a cheeky smile. 'Very appropriate. Are mother and child both well?'

'Very well. I think Liza actually enjoys life in the country.'

Agnes raised one eyebrow. 'As you do not?'

'No. As I do not.'

'Why did you come out here as a settler then, Mr Ludlam?'

He chose to tell them some of the truth. 'My father decided it'd be best for me, and since he held the purse strings, I didn't have much choice. It was he who insisted on my buying a farm, too. In fact, I was not able to spend the money he gave me on anything else. He wasn't – er – pleased about Liza's condition. Her family are tenants of ours.' He watched their reactions, pleased to see them swallowing this tale. 'But if I could find something to do other than farm work, I might settle down more happily here, I think.' He left it at that. They would understand his unspoken plea for help. Talking to his social equals had made him realise how wrong he had been to bury himself in the bush. People such as this could be very helpful to one of their own kind and, as Gerard had said, they must stick together and maintain standards.

The evening passed so pleasantly that Josiah could feel his misery peeling away, layer by layer.

He spent the next few days making one or two new acquaintances with Gerard's help, speaking to the Governor's aide and presenting the letter of introduction Catherine's father had given him. He hoped it would help him find some sort of official position which would supplement the meagre income to be expected from a newly cleared farm. If the region near Mandurah hadn't been so rich in fish and wildlife – yes, and Andrew Pringle so skilled with his gardening, so that they could eat well at very little cost – Josiah didn't know how they'd have managed without dipping into their small capital. He could only pray his father would keep his word and send the five hundred pounds he'd promised on the birth of the first child. That would make a big difference to their lives.

When he reluctantly decided that he must return home, they had a quiet farewell dinner, then Agnes went to bed and Gerard Fenton lingered over the bottle of fine port Josiah had bought for the occasion.

'This port's travelled well, hasn't it? Um – might be worth your coming back to Perth in a month or two.' Gerard held the glass up against the lamp, admiring the rich ruby colour.

Josiah raised one eyebrow. 'Oh?'

'I hear there are going to be a few government posts going – nothing special, the odd magistrate's position or supervisor of road gangs – but there might be one that's suitable for you. From what you say, I gather that would be helpful?'

'Yes. Very.'

'Agnes is giving a party for my birthday in January. Join us for it. It'll be hot as hell, but we intend to celebrate anyway. We shan't be able to put you up here, I'm afraid, because her cousin's coming down from York, but we shall be able to introduce you to some, shall we say *useful* people? And in the meantime, I'll keep my eyes open on your behalf and nudge the Governor's aide if something crops up.'

CHAPTER SIXTEEN

Cathie Ludlam was not officially christened until she was several months old, though Liza had been brought up enough of a Catholic to christen her unofficially with ordinary water the day after she was born. When Josiah eventually announced that he had managed to arrange for a christening ceremony to be performed by a visiting clergyman in Pinjarra, Liza was delighted. They hardly ever went to services because there was no proper church in Mandurah and it was nearly two hours' drive to the one in Pinjarra. Even that was a rather tumbledown place built by the settlers from local materials, thatched any old how and whitewashed. Josiah said it was a disgrace.

The christening took place just before the service, so of course they had to stay on for that. Cathie, who had slept most of the way there, howled loudly when the water touched her forehead and Liza could not quieten her for some time. When Josiah moved a step or two backwards, his face tight with disapproval, she turned her back on him and received a sympathetic smile from a woman nearby. Liza was enjoying the outing. It was wonderful to see other people and she hoped to stay and meet some of them afterwards.

But although the rest of the congregation lingered outside the church to chat, Josiah insisted that he and his wife must leave straight away.

'Why could we not have stayed?' Liza complained as they drove slowly home. 'I haven't seen another woman for months, except for Dorothy and Dinny.' She didn't count Kitty, for the two of them ignored one another as much as possible.

'Farmers, shopkeepers and persons of the labouring classes are *not* our social equals and I do not intend to seek out their company.'

'Well, they're my social equals!' Liza muttered. 'More than.'

'They may have been once but no longer, and I will thank you to act in public as befits Mrs Josiah Ludlam!'

Liza sat slumped on the driving bench, her enjoyment of the outing spoiled. As she stared down at her lap she thought about his words and scornful attitude. When she turned her head, she could see her daughter sleeping peacefully in the back of the cart, lying in a bed made from a large box. The sun was shining and the world ought to have been a happy place, but it wasn't because Josiah wouldn't let it be.

'When you treat me as your wife,' she said at last, 'then perhaps it will be easier for me to behave like one.'

He turned his head quickly. 'What the hell do you mean by that?'

She gestured to the baby in the back. 'It'd be nice to have another child or two, don't you think?'

Disgust etched itself on his face. 'I had thought you accepted the circumstances of our arrangement? That sort of thing is out of the question between us.'

'But it only took one night with – with *him*. Surely, you could manage it, just for a night or two?'

'No, I could not.'

'But Josiah . . .'

His voice was thick with loathing. 'Cat assured me that you understood the conditions of our marriage quite clearly.'

'Yes, but—'

'Such an activity is not, and never will be, possible between us. Get that through your stupid head now and don't ever raise this topic again.'

As they trundled along in silence Liza tried to dry the tears from her eyes without his seeing, but he glanced sideways. 'I've got some grit in my eye,' she said quickly.

He spoke more gently, but still coolly. 'You're crying, Liza, and I'm sorry for it, but it will make no difference.' He could not touch a woman in that way. Not under any circumstances. And if he hadn't been able to do it with Cat, how much less likely was it that he could manage it with Liza?

They were very stiff with one another for several days afterwards and she was relieved when he went to visit his friends in Perth again. She'd have liked to go with him and see Breda, had even thought of asking him to take her, but

196

who would look after her house and the newly hatched chicks if she went? And how would Cathie cope with the travelling? No, this was not the time to go away. It might be lonely here, but Josiah had begun to brood again and she'd be glad to have some peace for a while.

Smoke from Pendleworth drifted across the cleared land towards Benedict's farm, to which no name had been given because he could not settle on one which pleased him or which he felt suited the land. He frowned at the smoke. It seemed a great shame to burn so much good wood, and he had begun to wonder if there might not be a market in Perth for his carvings or even for furniture made from this beautiful jarrah wood. He hadn't trained as a cabinet maker but he had picked up a lot from his maternal grandfather and brother, and loved the work. He could not persuade Josiah to help him in the sawpit, however, for his neighbour increasingly refused to do any physical labour. And Andrew hadn't got the time to spare – or the muscles. In fact, he had been looking very tired and grey lately, much older than his fifty years, and though he insisted he was feeling fine, it seemed obvious to the others that clearing the land was too much for him.

Benedict looked round, brow wrinkled in thought. His plans would mean employing someone, a ticket-of-leave man, perhaps, if he was to progress beyond subsistence farming. But could he find someone with the requisite skills – or at least the capacity to learn them? That was always the difficulty here, it seemed, finding capable workers.

He went once more to look at his latest carving, a design he had recently perfected, using some native plants. Could he afford to employ someone now? He was already spending money at a faster rate than he had anticipated. Staple food supplies like flour and tea and sugar were so expensive. He looked at the cows grazing outside, meat animals only at the moment because he had no one to manage a dairy for him. There wouldn't be anywhere to sell butter, which didn't keep all that well in the heat anyway, but you might make cheeses if you built a cellar to keep things cool and . . . No. He shook his head. Not yet.

He smiled wryly. There was clearly no way to get rich

quickly here, as Josiah had hoped, however hard they worked. There was only a future filled with the steady years of labour needed to build up a thriving farm or business. And even then, Benedict still had to buy the rest of his land. This sort of future could be enough if you loved the land, as he did – as his neighbour never would – though life would be far more satisfying if you had a wife you loved to share it all with. He cut off that thought sharply. For him, now, that was not possible.

He had written to tell Grace not to try to join him yet, but he ought not to have done that. Only how could he face her with his thoughts so full of Liza? Young, joyful Liza, with the sparkling eyes and the furious energy and enthusiasm. Loving, gentle Liza, rocking her baby and singing her to sleep in a soft, husky voice. Unhappy Liza, whose eyes sometimes looked haunted.

And what sort of life had he to offer to Grace? Benedict stared round the single room with its bare earth floor, beaten hard now by his comings and goings. He had promised himself proper glass windows instead of shutters before next winter and he really should start building on another room, because one day Grace would have to join him here – but it all seemed too much trouble at the moment, and anyway it was the land that counted most when you were getting a start.

Josiah was making grandiose plans to obtain bricks and build himself 'a proper house' once his father's money for the baby came through. The two of them had argued about that only the previous day. Benedict intended to build only as he could afford it, and to use mostly timber he had cut down and left to mature himself. For all his lack of patronage and friends in high places, he suspected he might wind up in a more secure position than Josiah in the end, if he played his cards right.

He nodded as he came to one decision, at least. From now on, he would not burn any more of the large felled trees which might be turned into planks and later made into furniture.

He didn't hanker after riches, but if he couldn't have his heart's desire, he might as well concentrate on making money. And for that, farming alone would not be enough.

When Josiah returned from another visit to Perth on a hot,

dusty day he was in high spirits. 'Well, wife! You see before you the new magistrate for the Brookley district which is to be developed in this area. The Governor is planning to have a town site marked out and to encourage more families to settle nearby. The surveyor will be coming down to do that in a week or two.' He waited and when Liza said nothing, added, 'Are you not going to congratulate me on my appointment?'

She was puzzled by his joviality. 'Well, if it's what you want. I thought you just wanted to settle the land, make a big homestead called Pendleworth?'

With one of his sudden changes of mood, Josiah turned spiteful. 'No, it isn't want I want. What I actually want is to go home to the real Pendleworth, and well you know it. But my father has made sure I can never do that. At least the magistracy will pay me a stipend, so that we shall have some money coming in – and I shall be doing something more suited to my station than grubbing in the earth.' He scowled down at his hands, callused now from the work he could not avoid. 'I intend to hire men to do that sort of thing for me from now on and pay Caine to supervise them.'

He had taken her so much by surprise Liza could not think what to say except, 'I'm glad you're pleased, then.'

'What's more, I'm to be in charge of some road gangs, as well, and we are to build a magistrate's office and accommo-dation for the convicts here, which the Government will help with by providing materials and labour. We shall have a more suitable house for our station then.'

Liza heard the mockery lacing his words. Would he never be truly satisfied with anything? She did not need to live in a mansion to be happy. She could be quite happy in their small house if it were not for his moods.

'The first road they are going to make,' Josiah said, not even looking at her, 'will link us to the one that leads from Pinjarra to Perth and Fremantle – at whatever point the surveyor they're sending sees fit. Then at least we shall not be totally isolated. Why, I daresay it will not take us more than two days in dry weather to get a cart of produce through to Perth. That should help Pringle, eh? He can plant whole acres of cabbages then.'

He drained the cup of tea Liza had made for him and went outside to pace out the cleared land, muttering to himself, trying to work out where to put the new building. After a while he came back to take her outside and share his decision with her. 'We'll build it over there, I think, at right angles to the house, joined by a verandah but as a separate building. And I shall have a bedroom there, a large room with space for a writing desk as well as a bed, not a monk's cell like the room I inhabit now.' Catching sight of Dinny, who was standing in the shadow of a tree – for she always stayed in the background when he was around – he said, 'Can you send that woman over to fetch Benedict?'

'She's called Dinny. And you could perfectly well ask her yourself.'

But her friend had already slipped away to do as Josiah wished and he wasn't listening, just muttering to himself and pacing out the ground.

By the time Benedict arrived, Liza had the evening meal ready and invited him to join them. The three of them sat inside the house to eat it at the big table, with a white cloth and napkins, which Josiah always insisted on, though it made for a lot of extra washing. He did not allow Dinny to eat with them and tonight she waited on them, exchanging half-smiles with Liza as Josiah ordered her to fetch this and take away that.

Afterwards the two men went outside and talked for a long time, walking up and down gesturing and, at one stage, arguing quite fiercely.

Dinny stood beside Liza on the verandah, watching them, and when it became clear where Josiah was intending to build, she shook her head. 'It's bad ground there. That's not a good place to build. Tell him to build at the other side of the house.'

'Me? I can't stop him once he sets his mind on something. When does he ever listen to me, anyway? I'm more like a servant than a wife.'

Dinny stood very still, closing her eyes for a moment or two, then said in a strange, slow voice, very unlike her usual gentle speech, 'My people's voices cry out from that place. Something terrible happened there. And will again.'

Liza looked at her in shock. As she turned back to watch her husband, she admitted to herself that she shared Dinny's dislike of that particular spot, which was covered with ash, fragments of charred wood and the remains of a large tree which Josiah said must have been struck by lightning.

When the men came inside again, Liza tried to suggest building the new house at the other side of the present one, but Josiah told her sharply that she didn't know what she was talking about. She did not join in the conversation again, except to say farewell to their guest.

Benedict walked back to his lonely home, cheered by his new prospects, even though he thought Josiah was being stupidly extravagant. The payment he was to receive for superintending the building works would enable him to employ a man, and together they would make better progress in clearing his land, draining the swamp and laying up supplies of timber.

As he got ready for bed, his thoughts turned to Liza, which they often did and a smile softened his face as he pictured her playing with her baby. Then it faded. She deserved a proper family life. He had noticed how curtly Josiah spoke to her sometimes and how she tried to hide her hurt at this. But if Benedict had said anything in her defence, it would only have made matters worse. Josiah might not want her himself, but she was his wife and he was as possessive of her as all Ludlams were of their property.

Two weeks later one of the Assistant Surveyors for Western Australia, George Palter, arrived at Pendleworth accompanied by two convicts. They were to set up camp near the homestead while marking out the new road.

Palter was very officious about his duties and spoke curtly with the two convicts, but dealt courteously enough with Liza. The first thing he did was ride up and down the various nearby tracks with Josiah, looking for a suitable town site and the best route to mark out for a proper road leading to it. The convicts, men of about Josiah's age, were very quiet when their supervisor was around, but their eyes lingered on both Liza and Dinny when he was not there – not impertinently, but as if they were simply enjoying the sight of a woman.

Their first task was to build themselves a hut behind the Ludlams' home.

'Will they be all right working here unsupervised?' Josiah

worried. 'I'm thinking about my wife and child's safety, as you will realise.'

Mr Palter was smugly confident. 'Oh, yes. These two are up for their tickets of leave soon and they won't want to blot their copybooks, believe me. That would mean they'd have to go back to Fremantle Jail. Besides, your manager has agreed to keep an eye on them.'

'Who?'

'Caine, isn't he called? He seems a very capable fellow.'

'Oh, yes.' Josiah refrained from saying that Benedict was an independent landowner like himself and only occasionally worked for him.

'You're lucky to have him, you know. Good farm managers are as scarce as cocks' eggs out here.' Palter sniggered at his own joke.

Josiah tried to smile with him, failed and changed the subject. 'How shall you make the road?'

'I'm afraid we wouldn't even call it a road in England. We shall simply remove some of the smaller trees to allow a clear passage for wagons, though we'll have to go round the bigger trees, which are more trouble than they're worth to uproot. The main thing is to avoid boggy ground and to make sure we have suitable crossings for the winter streams. We're very rough and ready about roads here, I'm afraid, but they serve their purpose. Once you put a road in, settlers usually follow.'

'And the town site? Where is that to be?'

'To the south of your property, Mr Ludlam. Actually, the best place would be on the Pringles' land. I've spoken to them, and I'm sure we can come to some agreement about that. They say they're happy to sell part of it back to the Government. Though it won't be what you'd call a town, just a small settlement, with an inn, perhaps, and a few decent-sized sites, so that men can practise their trades and yet still have enough land to grow most of their food, keep a cow and some hens. The Governor intends to have a small house built there for a constable, who will be answerable directly to you, and I believe you are to build on a room here where you can sit as magistrate.'

Josiah nodded, but he was still frowning. 'Will one constable be enough once we have more settlers and convicts working on the roads?'

'Oh, yes. We don't need to station soldiers in this district nowadays because the natives have settled down a lot. It was quite bad earlier on, though.' Palter hesitated and glanced sideways. 'I – er – see you've got a native girl acting as your maid. I should keep an eye on her, if I were you. You can never trust them.'

'Oh, Dinny is harmless enough.'

'She may be harmless, but she'll wander off and leave you for no reason just when you need her most. They have no sense of responsibility, none at all. You'd be better getting a white maid to help your wife, if you could find one.'

Josiah stifled a sigh. Palter's fussy ways were already irritating him and he could not help worrying about the two convicts they were leaving behind.

His companion seemed to read his mind. 'If you're still worrying about those fellows, don't. They're political prisoners, a much better class of person. The surly one was a gentleman and quite well educated, though you wouldn't think it to look at him at the moment. No one will want to deal with him socially, of course, after he's released, but he'll probably keep his nose clean. They'll work hard enough today, because if they don't build themselves a hut, they won't have any shelter at night.'

'They're not carpenters, then?'

'No, but they've built huts before and they know that I'm aware of exactly how much work can be done in a day. You'll need to keep an eye on them when I'm gone, of course, if we get them assigned to you for a while as we discussed. And above all, you'll need to keep them away from the drink.'

When Palter repeated his warning about the native woman to Liza the next day, she fired up immediately. 'Dinny is my friend, Mr Palter, and I trust her absolutely.'

'Well, on your own head be it, Mrs Ludlam. But don't let her take that child out of your sight.'

Liza was glad when he left, much preferring the company of the two convicts to his. She'd given them a drink of tea after he and Josiah had gone and stayed to chat to them, enjoying their company for they'd been nothing but polite to her and to Dinny. One of them said he had left behind a baby very much Catherine's age, a little boy who would be six years old now. He'd looked so sad when he said it that Liza's heart was touched.

Josiah could not prevent her from talking to them like equals as she served them with their meals, which she insisted on cooking instead of giving them the food rations to deal with as they pleased.

'They're supposed to fend for themselves,' he objected.

'They don't have time to cook the meat till it's tender after they've finished work, and what difference does it make to me to toss a few more bits and pieces into the pot?' For they ate a lot of stew, it being the easiest thing to cook in her primitive outdoor kitchen. Not that she minded eating it, but Josiah did and when he got one of his dark moods on could wax very scornful about 'poor men's fare'.

Once Liza became so angry about this that she simply tipped his plate of stew all over the table and stormed out. He followed her to yell and shout, but for once she shouted right back.

She and Dinny had chuckled about it later after she'd calmed down, because he had looked so shocked.

After that, he did not criticise the food she served him — though he did not praise it, either, however hard she tried to vary what they ate.

By the time the long hot summer was over and April had arrived, bringing the first winter rains, the road was finished and the two convicts had left. Their rough hut stood ready to house other convicts who might be sent to work in the district under Josiah's supervision and the Ludlams were now more appropriately housed in a new building, which put Josiah in a better mood for a while.

It stood at right angles to the old one, with a verandah and walkway connecting the two. This meant that when he retired to his room, as he often did in the evenings, Liza was left in the old part of the house, with Dinny and her daughter for company. She tried to tell herself that was just fine, but it made her feel even more unwanted than before. *Out of sight, out of mind*, she thought bleakly.

It amazed Liza to think that it was two years since they had left England, but when she said so to Josiah he snapped at her, then grew downcast, sighing a lot and complaining how slow progress was in this benighted country.

When the convict Fergal Riordan gained his ticket of leave, he came back to work for Benedict, as the two men had agreed.

'We can build you a lean-to at the back of my house, if you like, so that you have a room of your own,' Benedict offered.

Fergal glanced at him. 'I wonder, would you allow me to build myself a tiny shack a little way into those woods of yours?' His look pleaded for understanding. 'I've had years of being crowded together in cramped conditions with unwashed humanity and must confess to a desperate craving for silence and privacy.'

'It must have been bad,' Benedict said quietly.

'Aye, it was. And still is, for I'm not free to return to my family, am I? And even if I did, they wouldn't want me. My father-in-law came to see me in prison before I left Ireland. He said he'd look after them all – but on the strict condition that I never tried to return. Teresa hasn't written to me, not once, so I don't even know how the children are. You'd think she'd let me know that, at least, now wouldn't you?'

Benedict reached out and squeezed his companion's shoulder gently. 'Choose a spot that pleases you, Fergal lad, and I'll help you build a place of your own. As long as we use the wood from my block, it makes no difference to me. I'll even knock you up a table and chair, not to mention a magnificent rope bed.'

'Thanks.' Fergal swallowed hard, then gave that crooked smile that was so much a part of him, teeth gleaming white against his tanned skin. With his cropped black hair, he looked tough and somehow threatening – until he smiled and then you realised how gentle a person he really was. 'You'll not regret it, Mr Caine.'

'I'm sure I won't. And it's Benedict. I don't stand on ceremony nor do I care about your past, so long as you work hard with me here.' He hesitated for a moment then added, 'If you'll stick with me, I'll make sure you get a piece of land of your own later – and opportunities to mend your fortune, too.'

Fergal stared at him. 'Do you mean that?' At Benedict's nod, he turned away for a moment, fighting tears. After the past few years, hope was very hard to cope with.

Benedict said nothing, just busied himself with the cooking.

From then on, the two of them worked well together. After they had cared for the animals, a lot of their time was spent sawing wood and setting it out in weighted piles to season. Fergal discovered that he shared Benedict's love of carpentry, even laughing at the tribulations of working in a saw pit and coming out covered in sawdust which clung to every inch of sweaty skin.

The changes in land ownership to accommodate the small township had helped the Pringles who had received a small amount of money in compensation, as well as another piece of uncleared land, but they were still struggling to make a living. Andrew went from one enthusiasm to another about what he did with his land, though he always returned to his beloved gardening, and Benedict felt desperately sorry for Dorothy, who was looking tired and dispirited.

One day he came up with the idea that the Pringles should build on some extra rooms and turn their house into an inn, just a small place with one of the cheaper wayside licences. He would invest a little money in it, and help them with the building. It would mean they could earn a little money by selling meals and maybe even fresh vegetables, too. He also suggested they plant vines and dry the fruit. You couldn't get most fresh produce to Perth in time to sell it, but you might find a market for sultanas or raisins.

This suggestion appealed to Andrew and once more he dived into a new enthusiasm, neglecting many of his duties around the house as he learned about vines and found someone to give him cuttings.

Benedict persuaded Josiah to help them in the application for a liquor licence, and he agreed on condition they called the place the Pendle Arms. If he pleaded the Pringles' lack of money and his own need for somewhere to house people who were attending his magistrate's court, it was likely the licence fee would be waived completely. Everyone knew the Governor found it easier to do things which did not involve the actual expenditure of money, for the Government in England did not fund the colonies lavishly.

'Run a common inn!' Kitty exclaimed. 'I can't believe you'd do this to me, Father.'

'There is no shame in honest work,' Andrew said mildly.

'Well, I find it shameful that our house should be turned into an inn. And I won't serve in it, whatever you say. I'd rather die first.'

'If you don't help with the work, there will be no food or clothes for you,' Dorothy said grimly.

'Mother, you can't mean that!'

'I most certainly do.' She hesitated then admitted, 'Do you think I like the thought of it any better than you do, Kitty? Of course I don't.' She scowled across at her husband and he cleared his throat noisily then walked out, as he usually did if she tried to complain or argue with him. She turned back to her daughter with a sigh. 'We need to eat, love. And at least if we run an inn, I'll be the one who deals with whatever money we earn. I'll make sure you get a little for yourself. Your father is growing very vague about such things these days and he's happier working in his garden.'

'He's brought us right down in the world, hasn't he? We're almost paupers now.' Kitty dashed away a tear.

'Yes. But I promise you, darling, that if you help me whole-heartedly, I'll find a way to send you back to your aunt in England one day.'

'By then it'll be too late. I'll be too old to find myself a husband.'

'You might even find one here.'

'I won't stay in Australia!' She cast a look black with hatred around them. 'This is not living, it's just – just *existing*.'

Afterwards Dorothy grew very thoughtful. Although she was resigned now to spending the rest of her life here, she was not resigned to her seventeen-year-old daughter's suffering the same fate. From that conversation was born a determination to make something of the inn and save enough money to send Kitty back. Well, Dorothy actually had enough money to do that now, but she could not bear to leave herself without any reserves. No one knew about her money but herself and Benedict, and that was the way she wanted to keep it. 'Josiah tells me some other settlers are coming to the townsite—'

'I'll believe that when I see it!'

'—and if we have an inn plus a small store, maybe we can save enough to pay your fare to England.'

'Father won't let me go.'

'I'll make sure you do go – if we can get the money together – with or without his permission.'

The two women stared at one another for a few pregnant moments, then Kitty asked in a voice thick with tears, 'Do you mean that?'

'Of course I do.'

'If I thought there was some hope of escaping, I'd work my fingers to the bone.' She brushed away a tear. 'You know what will happen, though. You'll make some money, then Father will take it and spend it on some stupid idea that fails.'

'Only if he knows about it. And I promise you he won't this time. I've hidden it very carefully in two places.' For once Dorothy felt close to her daughter. For once Kitty did not speak sharply but sat lost in thought, her face looking alternately young and vulnerable, then drawn and unhappy.

Andrew had a lot to answer for, bringing them to this place, and Dorothy would never forgive him for it. She looked in the mirror sometimes and saw a woman ageing rapidly, with lines of unhappiness graven upon her face. Her hands were too rough for the fine embroidery at which she excelled. Well, she would not let her daughter be buried here, whatever it cost to get Kitty away. And the first step towards that would be to learn about innkeeping.

Part Two

CHAPTER SEVENTEEN

1860

By the time Cathie Ludlam was two, the small settlement at Brookley had several more families living there, struggling settlers who relied on the inn for basic supplies like flour, sugar, tobacco and rum. Dorothy hated the smell of the rum, but people came regularly to have their bottles or jugs filled so she kept a good stock of it. Some folk were also glad to buy fresh fruit and vegetables from Andrew, who had stopped trying to clear land now and just pottered around his garden plot, leaving most of the daily work to his wife and daughter.

Strangers occasionally passed through Brookley as well, taking a detour on the way to Pinjarra or the hills where they might be searching for sandalwood to sell or else coming to see Josiah in his position as local magistrate. Even these few brought in small sums of much-needed money to the Pringles.

However, one day Dorothy came back from visiting Liza to find that her main savings from the inn takings had gone. She rushed out to her husband who was working in the field. 'Have there been any strangers passing through today?'

Andrew stood up and eased his aching back. 'No. No one.'

'But someone's taken my money.'

His smile faded. 'My dear, it was very wrong of you to keep that money from me. I am still the head of this household and it is for me to deal with our finances. If I find you doing such a thing again, I shall be extremely angry.'

She stared at him. 'But – that was my money. I earned it through hard work. I have a right to it.'

'You have no right to any money! That is a husband's right – in law as well as by tradition.'

She burst into tears and when he turned his back on her, threw herself at him, beating him with her hands and screaming at him.

Kitty came running and helped calm her mother down, but when she found out what had happened, she too turned on her father, screeching at him that he had turned them into drudges and if he didn't even allow them to keep the money they earned, she wasn't working in the inn any more.

It did no good. When had reason ever prevailed with Andrew? He did not return the money but informed them that he had invested it with Jem Davies, the local carter. One day, he promised them serenely, they would see a good return on that money.

Jem Davies refused to return it, said he had spent it on buying some new horses, but he did agree to sign a written statement acknowledging the debt, something Andrew had neglected to obtain.

When Dorothy had recovered from this setback, she gave her daughter a grim-faced assurance that she would find a better hiding place next time. 'I do have a little money left,' she admitted in a whisper. 'But I dare not spend that on fares to England.'

'You mean, you've had enough money all the time and never told me?'

'I need the security of a fare to England for myself as well, in case something happens to your father.'

'You're as bad as him. I could be in England by now, living with my Aunt Nora.' Kitty burst into tears and refused to lift a finger for the rest of the day.

It took her a long time to recover from this destruction of her hopes and Dorothy began to worry that the girl was only a shadow of her old self. Her face grew thin and miserable, her hair lank, her clothes not washed as regularly as they should have been. It was as if she'd given up hope when her father took the money.

'See what you've done to us!' Dorothy told Andrew in the privacy of their bedroom.

He turned his back on her, declining to answer.

*　　*　　*

The Ludlams now had by far the largest house in the district, with spacious verandahs joining the two parts of the building, where people could sit on rough benches and wait their turn to see the magistrate.

One evening, as Liza sat out on the old verandah and watched Josiah play with Cathie, the longing she had been trying to suppress burst forth again. 'I wish we had a son as well, Josiah. It won't be good for Cathie to grow up an only child. Already you're spoiling her. You even let her sleep in your room last night.'

'She fell asleep on the sofa there. I saw no need to disturb her.'

'You enjoyed having her there. Confess it.' Liza looked sideways at him. 'You'd like another child, too, wouldn't you?'

Without even turning to look at her, he said in icy tones, 'Yes, I'd like one. But that is simply not possible, so I'd recommend you to stop fretting for what cannot be.'

But Liza was doing more than fretting; she was planning to take action. That night she washed herself carefully, so that nothing about her could give offence to Josiah's fastidiousness, put on a clean nightdress and waited until he had retired to his room. Giving him a few minutes to get settled, she listened for the bed to creak and then waited a little longer. Maybe if he were drowsy, he'd be easier to persuade.

Heart thudding, she crept across to his door. Beneath it she saw a line of light from a candle and heard someone shifting around to get comfortable. Only when the candle had been extinguished did she take a deep breath, open the door and creep inside.

He sat bolt upright. 'Who's that?'

'It's only me, Josiah.'

'Is something wrong?'

She reached the bed and tugged the covers back. 'Yes. Very wrong. I want another baby. Need one. Oh, Josiah, can't we . . .' She reached out to touch him and he flinched backwards.

'Get away!'

'Surely you can make the effort to get one baby? I won't

213

ask you again.' She tried to take hold of his arm, but he threw her aside.

His voice was burred with disgust. 'Don't *touch* me!'

'Please. Oh, please, can't we try!'

His laughter had a hysterical edge to it. 'If I couldn't do it with Cat, do you think I could do it with a common slut like you? I'd as soon make love to a cow in a byre as touch you!'

'*Josiah!*'

He shoved her away from him so violently she fell off the edge of the bed, crying out as she landed on the floor. But that wasn't enough for him and he rushed round and grabbed her by the front of her nightdress, hauling her to her feet, shouting, 'Take your revolting body out of here and don't *ever* come near my bedroom again! You hear me? *Don't – ever – come here – again!*' With each phrase, he shook her and half-lifted her another step or two backwards. When he got to the open door, he threw her outside and slammed it shut.

She lay on the verandah, her whole body shaking with sobs. Was that how he really thought of her? Common slut, he'd said. Revolting body!

After lying weeping for a few moments she stumbled to her feet and turned towards her own room. But suddenly it was all too much for her: this strange marriage, his constant scorn of her, her own confused longings for more. She could bear it no longer and fled to the one person she could trust, leaving the front door open behind her and running through the night in her flimsy house slippers, sobbing aloud.

The moon mocked her with its cool silvery light. The trees rustled and branches tore at her hair. She hardly noticed them. There was only one thought in her mind. Benedict! She had to get to him, had to be with someone who didn't find her disgusting, who would hold her as she needed to be held.

Back at the house, Dinny stood by the open front door, sighing, then closed it and went to lie on the bed in Liza's room, staring at the smaller bed beside it, relieved the child had not wakened. She did not know what had happened between Liza and her husband, but whatever it was, her friend had been hurt badly. Mr Ludlam was a strange man who talked to Dinny as if she were half deaf, sneered at nearly everyone he met – and occasionally drank himself into a stupor. He had a darkness inside him that seemed to be eating him up. Sometimes she felt sorry for him but mostly she disliked him, hating what he was doing to her friend.

'Stay with Benedict tonight, Liza,' she murmured. 'He will heal you, make you a woman.' She had seen how the two of them looked at one another, seen and envied them. She wished she had someone who cared about her, but what man would want a woman of mixed blood except to use and hurt? She was an outsider who did not belong to the native people of this region and if she went to Ireland, her father's country, she was sure she'd be even more out of place.

Only Liza seemed to accept her, be fond of her, treat her as an equal – and need her. And this piece of land also seemed to welcome her. Dinny felt safe here, more at home than she had ever felt before. Which was almost enough. If she only had someone to love and be loved by, she'd be rich indeed. Liza was not the only one who needed a man, but she was far more likely to find one than Dinny.

Benedict was woken by someone thumping on his front door. He slipped out of bed, instantly alert. 'Who is it?'

'L-Liza.'

Terrified there might be some disaster, he flung back the wooden catch and opened the door to find her pressed against the rough wooden wall, head buried in her arms, sobbing hysterically. She was wearing only a nightdress and her feet were bare.

He gathered her in his arms instinctively. 'What is it? Have you been attacked?' He stared round but could see no one else. What the hell had happened?

Sobbing even more loudly, she flung her arms round his neck, pressing herself against him. 'Hold me, Benedict. Please just h-hold me!'

'Shh, now!' Without letting go of her, he drew her inside, pushed the door closed with one heel, then nudged the catch into place with his elbow. For lack of anywhere else they could both sit he carried her across to the bed. 'Is it Cathie? Has something happened to her? Tell me, Liza!'

She managed to stop sobbing for long enough to say, 'N-not Cathie. Me.' Then she broke down again.

So he held her close and was unable to resist pressing a kiss against the hot damp skin of her temple. As he did so, she murmured and raised her face to his, and it seemed the most natural thing on earth to kiss her and go on kissing her.

As desire shivered through him, however, he forced himself to stop. He had no right to touch her and had promised himself to do nothing to hurt her. She was quieter now, but her body was still shaken from time to time by echoes of those agonised sobs. And not only did she fit into his arms as if she had been made to lie there, she had not tried to pull away.

'Oh, Liza, my little love,' he whispered against her hair. 'What's upset you so? Tell me. If there's anything I can do to help you, you know I will.'

'It's Josiah. He – I—' She faltered to a stop. Josiah had considered what she had done disgusting. Would Benedict think the same?

'There's nothing you cannot tell me,' he said quietly. 'You know I love you. I don't have the right, but I can't help it.'

The moon gave them enough light to see each other's faces. As she looked up at him, she said simply and directly, 'I love you, too. Oh, Benedict, I love you so much! I've tried to be a good wife to Josiah, but he doesn't want a wife! He – he—' And she could not help weeping again, though more quietly now, a soft despairing sound that tore at his heart.

'What did he do to you, love?'

'I – I went to him – I wanted another child to love. But he – he threw me out of his room – and he said such dreadful things.'

Benedict was silent, then kissed her again and held her close, stroking her hair. 'I don't understand a man like him, not at all, but I don't think he can help how he is. And – I don't think he is capable of getting a child on you – or any other woman.'

'Then there'll just be me and Cathie.' She looked at him again. 'I'd leave him in a minute if you wanted me, Benedict. It's not enough, what he can give me. It's only money and – and I can't face his scorn for the rest of my life. He says cruel things to me sometimes. How am I to bear it? How am I to bring my daughter up in such an atmosphere?' She had sworn to herself that her child should be happy, loved, cherished, but Josiah had made her fear that he would teach Cathie to despise her – as he did. Already some of his remarks to the child had an edge to them that was unflattering to the mother.

Pain flooded through Benedict. 'I can't ask you to come to me, Liza, you know I can't. It would destroy your reputation utterly. People wouldn't talk to you. It'd just mean going from one unhappy situation to another.'

'I wouldn't care about that if I had someone who really loved me. What does it matter if people despise me? And as for talking to me – who do I talk to now?' she laughed harshly. 'Certainly not Josiah. He treats me like a housekeeper and he always will. Anything he does for me is so that people will not scorn him for marrying so far beneath him. I've never met his friends in Perth. He won't even let me stay to chat after church or take me to visit Breda.'

'Oh, Liza. Darling Liza, you know I'm . . .' he hesitated then said '. . . promised to Grace. She's waited for me for years. I can't just throw her off. If I'd known – if I'd met you before – but I didn't and I can't just abandon her. She doesn't deserve that.' He knew himself to be a coward, but could not spoil this moment by telling Liza the full truth, that he and Grace were married.

She sagged against him. 'No one really wants me,' she said dully. 'No one in the whole world.'

He could not help kissing her forehead gently at that and murmuring, 'I do want you. You know I do.' Then as she turned up her face, he kissed her soft quivering lips. 'Oh, Liza! What a sad tangle this all is?'

He made no conscious decision to make love to her, but something seemed to drive him on, some need to do more than hold her – and it was as much her need as his.

When he began to touch her, she accepted his caresses like a plant desperate for water, making soft sounds of pleasure.

Each time he touched her, Liza experienced a sense of healing, a feeling that she was not repulsive, not unlovable. One man had abused her, another had scorned her, but in Benedict's arms she felt truly loved. It was so natural to caress him in return that she did it, shyly, hesitantly, but with her love showing in even the lightest touch.

When he groaned in his throat and tried to draw back, she whispered, 'Don't stop. Oh, Benedict, let me have something to remember. Let some man love me truly for none has done that yet.'

He held her at arm's length. 'Are you sure?'

Her expression was radiant. 'Very sure.'

Moonlight flooding through the window added a gentle glow to the scene as, with the greatest love and reverence, he took off her clothes and allowed her to help him shed his own. She was beautiful, soft and willing – but most of all she was Liza, the woman he dreamed about, the woman he loved. Murmuring the words of affection so long pent up inside him, he began to show her how it could be between two people who did most truly love one another.

It was the first time he had performed this act in love himself, and it was as much of a revelation to him as to her. Soft murmurs and gentle caresses led slowly to fulfilment so ecstatic that they both cried out together, and then sank into the great warmth and joy that comes after being as close as two humans ever can.

They did not sleep, did not even say much, just lay nestled against one another, flesh to warm flesh, neither wanting to break the spell. But he knew that from then onwards no woman would ever satisfy him but her.

And she in her turn knew that she had experienced something few women ever found, knew that she was deeply and truly loved by this man. At that moment she determined to persuade him to run away with her, make a new life. She was sorry for the other woman who was waiting to marry him, of course she was, but he would not make this Grace person happy if he loved someone else. She knew that with utter certainty, for she was trapped in a loveless marriage herself – and it grew worse, not better as the years passed.

Only as dawn began to slip gilded fingers through the cracks in the walls and the shapes of gum trees came into focus through the dusty window panes did Benedict stir. 'My little love, you must go back now.'

'Not yet.' Liza pulled his head towards hers and kissed him with all the passion he had roused in her, so that they made love once again – hurriedly, urgently, in the soft pink light of early morning.

Afterwards, he found her nightdress and they laughed together as his fingers fumbled to pull it over her head. He threw on his own clothes anyhow, then walked with her through the sleepy murmur of a forest just awakening to day, his arm round her shoulders.

At the edge of the clearing, he stopped and watched, his heart aching with sudden loss as she left his embrace and moved quietly across to Josiah Ludlam's house.

At the door she paused, reluctant to go inside, turning to gaze hungrily back at him. For a moment all was still, then she waved once and disappeared from his sight.

Benedict drew back into the woods, but did not leave. He had not said anything of his worries to her but he intended to make sure Josiah wasn't waiting for her, wasn't going to punish her for seeking elsewhere the love her own husband was incapable of offering. He waited for a long time, till the sun began to warm his shoulder blades, standing there in patient vigil. But there was no sound from inside the house.

Later, when Dinny opened the front door and began to sweep the verandah, he could see Liza inside playing with her child. The sight filled him with bitter regret that she could not be *his* wife, could not share such pleasures with him, and he had to close his eyes to hold in that pain.

A little later he saw Josiah walk along the verandah, scowling as usual, and he tensed. Would Jos say something? Did he know where his wife had been? But he entered the living room and sat down at the table to eat his breakfast without showing any signs of anger, though he did not seem to be talking to his wife, just accepting his food from her and eating it in silence.

With a sigh of relief Benedict turned back towards his own home. Liza was safe.

The hut seemed smaller and dustier, echoing with loneliness without her, though it had been a place of radiance and joy the previous night. He ran his fingertips across the rumpled bed, breathing in the faint scent of their lovemaking, then forced himself to go outside and begin his day's work. No one must know that anything unusual had happened, not even Fergal.

But unknown to them both, Josiah had been awake when Liza returned, and he had seen her and Benedict through the window. The way they'd stood had betrayed their intimacy and he had smiled bitterly on a sudden hope that their union would bear fruit – fruit which he could harvest and pick. He would be a willing cuckold this one time, for no one would know. But after that, his wife must live a life above reproach.

Liza had touched a need in him last night. He, too, wanted a son – and he also wanted the money another child would bring from his damned father. And he didn't know which he wanted most.

Liza went to Benedict regularly from then onwards. Not every night, but every week at least. They did not talk of the future, did not make plans, just lived in the present, stealing a little happiness, lost in the glowing brightness of their love.

In his arms she found more happiness than she had ever thought possible, and it was not just the love-making but the feelings they had for one another which made even lying chatting a pleasure. Of course they still met in company as well, but when there were other people around, she tried not to look at him too often and knew he was being similarly careful.

Dinny knew Liza's secret and kept an eye on little Cathie for her on the nights she was away from the house, though the child still sometimes slept on her father's sofa when she fell asleep playing in his room – indeed, Cathie considered this a great treat.

Liza didn't think Josiah had guessed what was happening, though, for he was drinking heavily again, so she waited for the nights when he emptied a whole bottle of rum. After her husband had staggered along to his bedroom, she would listen for the snoring to start, then know it was safe to leave.

Three months later she began to suspect she was pregnant and was filled with great joy at the thought of carrying Benedict's child, even though it was early days yet. She was also filled with great determination. She would not allow this child to be brought up by Josiah Ludlam. He was not only spoiling Cathie, but constantly saying things to her that mocked Liza. He seemed to delight in finding ways of hurting her lately.

She thought things over for a week before she told Benedict about the coming child, trying to gather arguments that would persuade him to run away with her. They could go to Sydney or Melbourne, change their names and earn a living there. No one need ever know they weren't married. They'd take Cathie with them, of course, because Liza couldn't bear the thought of losing her small daughter. And if dearest Dinny wanted to go, they'd take her, too.

Liza would sit staring into space with a half-smile on her face as she spun these dreams and wove her plans. They had to be practical, do things properly. Benedict would have to go up to Fremantle and find out about ships. They could take refuge with David and Breda while they waited for a vessel to leave – she was sure her friends wouldn't turn her away, for she and Breda corresponded regularly, though the couple's small children, two now, and Josiah's lack of co-operation prevented meetings being arranged.

She had heard that there were far more people in the eastern part of Australia, so surely she and Benedict would be able to hide over there?

And they need not lose everything. David and Breda would sell Benedict's block of land and then one day there would be money from that to help them buy another. In the meantime she had enough money for them to live on, thanks to Catherine, and anyway Benedict would easily find a job. He was so clever, could do so many things.

Then one morning Josiah caught her vomiting. He stood watching her.

Liza wiped her mouth and said, calmly she hoped, 'I must have eaten something that disagreed with me.'

He threw back his head and laughed, cruel sneering laughter, then stared at her belly. 'Did you think I didn't know what you were doing, you and Caine? I not only knew – I *allowed* it because I wanted you to get with child. You were right about that. A son would fit in very well here. But now you're in whelp, you won't need to go chasing after your lover again.'

His crude words made her wince. 'You can't stop me going to him!'

'Oh, I can, believe me. I'll make very sure you don't spend any more time with him now that it's not necessary. No one knows what's been happening and no one's going to know.'

She stared at him in horror. His tone was harsh and a vein was beating in his forehead with the force of his anger.

Josiah continued to stare at her for a moment, his head on one side. 'I'll put a lock on your bedroom door, I think, the window too. Make sure you're shut safely in as soon as it grows dark. We don't want you wandering in your sleep like a bitch on heat, do we?'

She could not think what to say.

He looked at Dinny, who was hovering nearby. 'And if I find you helping my wife to go to him, I'll accuse you of theft and make sure you're thrown into jail. Do you understand that? Answer me! *Do you understand?*'

Dinny stared back at him mutinously, but he had all the power, especially over her, so she waited until he looked ready to explode at her lack of an answer, then nodded slowly.

'And you're not to speak of this to anyone – anyone at all – even *him*.'

She nodded again.

Liza suddenly found her courage. 'I'll run away! You can't watch me every minute of the day.'

Josiah shrugged, 'If you do, I'll take Cathie away from you – and the law will be on my side. I can't have my daughter growing up with an immoral mother, can I? And just to make sure of things, I'll accuse Caine of theft. It'd kill a man like him to be shut up in prison.' He nodded thoughtfully as shock drained the colour from Liza's cheeks. 'In fact, now I come to think of it, I doubt we'll even need the lock on your bedroom door. You'd do anything for him, wouldn't you? Especially to keep him out of jail.'

Liza sagged against the wall. 'You're a cruel man, Josiah Ludlam, exactly like your father. You don't want me yourself, but you won't let me be happy with someone who does.'

'But I do want respectability here in the colonies, want it very much,' he responded, 'and you're the answer to that. You and our dear children.'

While he was hearing a couple of cases in the public room that separated his bedroom from the old house, Liza looked at Dinny. 'What am I going to do?'

'I don't know.'

The two women sat together, not saying anything else, just offering one another the comfort of their companionship, the occasional touch of hand upon hand. Liza felt rebellious, angry and horrified at the thought of spending the rest of her life with Josiah Ludlam. She did not even feel like his wife any more. There had to be some way to escape. Surely someone as enterprising as Benedict would find it? They would find it together.

The following week, when Josiah was again holding a hearing and she was working in her garden, she heard a rustling sound and turned to see Benedict crouching behind a bush. She worked her way to the end of the row, then, when she too was hidden from the house, flung herself into his arms.

He held her close, breathing in the scent of her hair, which she rinsed in water in which gum leaves had been steeped to perfume it. 'I've missed you, my little love.'

'Yes.' Her voice was thick with tears. 'And I've missed you.'

'Jos came to see me, told me he knew about us and warned me not to see you again. He says you're carrying my child.' Benedict held her at arm's length to look her in the eyes. 'Is that true?'

She nodded.

'Why did you tell him and not me?'

'I didn't tell him – he found out.'

'Ah! That's not what he implied.'

'Oh, Benedict, he says if I try to run away with you, he'll accuse you of theft and – and if Dinny helps me, he'll do the same to her, see she's put in prison. And,' Liza gulped loudly, 'he says he can keep Cathie from me.'

He groaned and pulled her close again. 'Unfortunately, he can do all those things.' And once again, a Ludlam had the power to interfere in Benedict's life. 'Damn him!' he muttered in her ear. 'Damn all Ludlams.'

'Benedict, you're not going to let him keep us apart, are you? If we plan things carefully, surely we can still find a way to escape?'

He knew he'd been living in a fool's paradise and cursed his own cowardice. 'Liza – I should have told you – I was wrong not to – but I – I already have a wife. I didn't just promise to marry Grace, I actually married her before I left England.'

'What?' She stared at him in horror.

'So there's not just you and me involved, you see, there's her to think of as well.'

Anger filled Liza and spilled out painfully. 'So you were just *using* me! All this talk of love . . . It wasn't love you felt for me, but lust!'

'No, never that! Liza, no!'

But she shoved him away from her and ran into the house, trying not to sob aloud.

Benedict started to move after her, then stopped and shook his head. No, best to let her go. Best for her if she hated him. Not only had he Grace to think of, but if he tried to run away with Liza and things went wrong, she would be in a far worse position than she was now. He knew how much her child meant to her, and he knew how ruthless the Ludlams could be.

Another thought made him stop walking and suck in a gasp of sheer agony. The coming child – *his* child – he'd never be able to acknowledge it. How could he bear living so close, watching it grow, without being able to show his love? He wanted children – what normal man didn't? – but not like this!

They had been living in a foolish dream for the past few weeks, he and Liza, though it had been the happiest time of his whole life. Now reality had clamped down on them, as it always did, and even here Josiah still had the power of wealth and privilege. His sort had rallied round to make him a magistrate and the same clique in Perth would no doubt find him other lucrative posts as time went on. As long as he obeyed their rules. As long as there was no scandal.

If he had had anything to offer Liza, Benedict might still have been tempted to try to take her away, but most of his money was sunk in his farm and he had very little cash left – no, painful as it would be, better to leave her where she was, in a respectable, comfortable home.

That night he sat and stared at a bottle of cheap rum, took one swig and wondered whether to seek a few hours' oblivion. Then he shook his head. No, nothing would wipe out the image of Liza from his mind and heart. She was his sunlight, his dearest love, and always would be.

He would do his duty by his poor unsuspecting wife

and work so hard that he fell asleep at night out of sheer exhaustion. You paid for your pleasures, paid very dearly sometimes.

Oh, dear God, how was he to bear it?

CHAPTER EIGHTEEN

───❖───

Liza was furious with Benedict and stayed furious for days, banging and slamming round the house, glaring at the world, speaking curtly to those who came to see Josiah and refusing to discuss the reason for her rage with either her husband or Dinny.

Josiah watched her thoughtfully and when she made excuses to avoid even being in the same room as Benedict, didn't fool himself that she was doing this in obedience to his wishes. There was something else causing this intense anger and he intended to find out what.

He confronted her one day, insisting in his languid but inexorable way on knowing what had happened between her and Benedict.

Liza froze. 'What do you mean? Nothing has happened.'

Josiah's voice was silky smooth and very certain. 'Oh, yes, it has. It's he who's causing this anger and I want to know why.'

She tried to hold them back, but the words burst out of her like acid. 'Because he's already *married* that's why! And he never said. I'd not have gone to him if I'd known that.'

'What difference does that make? You're married as well.'

She stilled for a moment, then looked at him sadly. 'I don't feel married, Josiah. And you don't act like a married man, so – so what I've done can't hurt you.'

He breathed in deeply. That hurt his pride. Very much. But he didn't intend to reveal his weakness to her. 'To whom is Caine married? It must be someone in England? He surely hasn't met any eligible women here.'

'What does it matter who he's married to? He's married and that's that!'

When she tried to leave, he grabbed her arm. 'Tell me who

226

it is, Liza!' He saw refusal in her face and added quickly, 'You're not leaving this room until you do.'

For a moment more she resisted, then tossed at him, 'She's called Grace. That's all I know. And – and she comes of farming stock, so will make a good wife for a farmer.'

'Grace?' Josiah murmured the name several times, but it meant nothing to him. He had not been involved in the running of his father's estate, nor had he bothered to get to know the people who lived nearby. 'Is that all he said about her?'

'Isn't it enough? He was just – just using me.' Liza's voice rose in pitch. 'You're *all* using me and I'm sick of it.'

'Well, you've been using me as well?' He raised one eyebrow at her startled expression. 'You used me to give your first baby a name and you'll continue to use that name for the second child.'

As his words sank in she flushed, knowing he was right. But it sounded so heartless and she had not meant it like that, had only been young, alone and desperate to provide for her child. And Catherine had used her, too, should not have pushed her into this marriage.

'I presume you'll be staying with me more willingly now?'

She nodded, closing her eyes to blot out her husband's triumphant expression. What else could she do but stay? She would have two children to look after now.

'Good. We'll make a fine family, shall we not? But Liza—'

When the silence lasted too long, she looked up. 'What?'

'It's not to happen again. I shall be quite happy with two children. I should be very *un*happy if word got out that my wife had betrayed me.'

'Ha! That won't happen again. Never! I'm done with men. All of them. I'd be done with you, too, if I could.' Hands on hips, she scowled at him.

Josiah smiled. 'That's settled then. But don't go. We need to talk about a few other things.'

Liza flung herself into a chair, expecting another lecture. He was always telling her how to act. Don't do this! Don't do that! Even in the privacy of their own home he wanted her to behave as if a hundred people were watching her.

He sat opposite her, hands clasped, the two index fingers raised and tapping against one another as if they had a life of their own. 'I've been tidying up my business affairs. For Cathie's – for *both* children's – sake, so it's best you know how things stand.'

She looked at him in puzzlement.

'I'm about to make my will and I intend to leave all I own to my,' he grinned and corrected that, 'to *our* children. But only on the condition that you and they are still living with me.'

There was absolute silence. She glared at him. 'And what about me?'

'Oh, I'm sure your children will love their mother enough to see that she's properly looked after. And I don't intend to die soon, believe me.' He felt himself to be settling down here now, coming to terms with life in an Australian colony. It was not the sort of life he'd have chosen but it was better than he had at first expected it to be – or it would be once he was better established. Maybe when he was more financially secure, he'd be able to buy himself a house in Perth and spend most of his time there – leaving Liza and the children at the farm, of course.

She sat and thought this over, then shook her head. 'That isn't fair.'

'What do you mean, "isn't fair"? How dare you question my decision?'

'I'm the one who's working hard here, not the children. If you don't intend to look after me in your will, then I don't see why I should even stay with you.' After all, she still had Catherine's money.

Josiah chose to be indulgent. 'I'm not exactly in my dotage, you know. It's just as likely that you'll die before I do.'

'Accidents do happen.' Liza folded her arms across her breast. 'So I want things leaving to me, Josiah. That's my price for staying and for being a good wife to you.'

He was outraged. Leave everything to a common trollop like her? 'Never!' With the children he'd at least have a chance to mould their characters as they grew up. *She* would always betray her origins.

Liza shrugged. 'Then I'll go away and make a new life of my own.'

'You will not.' He read defiance in her expression. 'If you even try, I'll not only keep Cathie but the new baby as well. The law will support me in that.'

Desperation made her risk everything. 'Oh, will it? Well, if you ever try to take my children away from me – *ever!* – I'll make the biggest scandal the colony has ever seen. I'll reveal everything about you. And we'll see who gets the children then! You'll enjoy people knowing that you're not able to be a proper husband, I'm sure. They put men like you in prison, don't they?' Benedict had told her that, for her own protection, and she felt a surge of satisfaction at the sudden fury on her husband's face and wondered for a moment if she glimpsed something else behind it. A hint of fear, perhaps.

He sucked in his breath. 'You can prove nothing, you little gutter bitch!'

Liza patted her still flat stomach. 'I can prove who fathered this child.' Anger crackled in her voice as she added, 'And what good does name-calling do? I'm not – never have been – what you say.' She broke off for a moment then continued, desperate to make him understand her side of things. 'I'm only trying to look after myself, Josiah, surely you can see that? Besides, if you're sure you're going to live for a long time, what can it matter who you leave things to?'

He watched her fiddling with her wedding ring, twisting it round and round. She had pretty hands, even reddened with work as they were. Small but very capable. And she was not a gutter bitch. Look at the way she had cared for Cat. He felt some of the anger drain from him. 'I'm sorry. I shouldn't have called you that, Liza.'

She stared at him, trying to read his expression. She thought his apology sincere, but who could tell what he really meant behind that nose-in-the-air expression of his? 'I've done a lot for you, Josiah. Given you the children you could never have had, worked hard here,' she waved one hand in an encompassing gesture, 'very hard – and I'll go on doing it. But I want to be named in the will and I'll insist on seeing it, too. I'm not – not feeling very trusting about anyone these days.'

His smile was a mere baring of the teeth. 'Well, well, Caine *has* upset you, hasn't he?' He was glad of that. Anger would make her easier to manage.

'You've all upset me. So when you go up to Perth to consult a lawyer, I want to come with you. It's time I went there again. I have things to buy and I need a change of scene.' She raised her eyes to meet his, not flinching away but holding his gaze in a way she had never done before. She looked older suddenly and very determined indeed.

'Well, why not?' It would be good to get her away from Caine just now and he could always change the damned will later. He'd indulge her this time. In fact, it would probably be good tactics to do so. But he'd definitely change the will later.

Josiah refused yet again to go to Perth via Luska. 'Breda is not a suitable friend for my wife,' he said coolly.

'But—'

'We shall dine with the Fentons. Agnes was friendly towards you on the boat. I'd prefer you to pursue that acquaintance instead. If you're wise you'll make every effort to get her on your side because she's a rather clever woman and has some useful connections, both here and in England.'

And he also knew that, like most of the wives of those he now called his friends, Agnes was lonely and intermittently homesick. This made them more ready to consort with those whom they would have despised back in England, and would despise again if they ever returned there. Though they did not, under any circumstances, associate with the families of ex-convicts, the ladies would sometimes accept a woman like Liza if she fitted into their behaviour patterns – and he would see that Liza did that.

'Take some elegant clothes with you,' he ordered. 'I'll help you choose from Cat's things. You'll need to look as much the lady as is possible for someone like you.'

Speechless with indignation at this final gratuitous insult, she watched him walk out then began to pace up and down the kitchen. He didn't even notice when he was insulting her because he only thought of what he wanted. Would she ever be able to live up to his expectations? Liza paused to stare sadly out of the window. She had no choice but to try, for her children's sake.

Perth seemed larger than Liza had remembered, or perhaps that was only in comparison to the lonely bush tracks and small settlements of Mandurah and Pinjarra, which was all she'd seen for over two years.

She visited the shops in the capital city on Josiah's arm, not buying much but being seen, which he said was important. On the surface he was an attentive and loving husband, but his whispers were instructions as to how Liza was to behave towards his acquaintances or reprimands when she had said something of which he didn't approve. She got no praise for her efforts. It surprised her, though, how many of the gentry stopped to speak to Josiah and be introduced to his wife. She had not expected him to be so popular.

When Liza took tea with Agnes Fenton, she dressed as elegantly as she could and gained a nod of approval from her husband before she set off. She found the other woman as sympathetic as she had been on the ship, and soon confided that she was expecting another child. 'That's why Josiah brought me up to town – to give me a treat before I grow too big to travel.' She added – casually, she hoped – 'And he's going to make his will, I believe, while we're here.'

Agnes wasn't fooled about the importance of this. 'Be sure he makes it in your favour, then.'

'Oh, I shall! I've already insisted on that.'

'You've changed a lot, grown up since the voyage out.' Agnes leaned back in her armchair and studied Liza thoughtfully.

'I've had to, haven't I? Besides, that's nearly three years ago now.' A lifetime, it felt. The other Liza, the one who had lived with Mam and Da, seemed like a totally different person.

'Are you happy here in Australia?'

'Sometimes. I enjoy the warmer weather, and I like the country. I didn't have much choice about coming here, but I've tried to make the best of it.'

'Have you ever regretted marrying Josiah?'

A long silence, then Liza looked at Agnes's face and saw sympathy, not hostility, so risked the truth. 'Sometimes.'

Her hostess threw her head back and laughed. 'Don't we all have our regrets! I'm glad you admitted that. Now we can stop pretending all's perfect with our lives.' At that moment she decided to take an interest in the little Ludlam, who looked

231

sad underneath those fine, if somewhat outdated clothes. 'Come and visit some of my friends with me tomorrow.'

Until Josiah explained it to her later, Liza did not understand how much of an honour this was. But he was very pleased with her and showed it, calling her 'my dear' as they dined with some of his other friends, and speaking of 'our little daughter' fondly to all and sundry, as well as delicately mentioning his hopes for a son 'this time'.

None of that prevented Liza from going to the lawyer's with him to see the will signed or from insisting that Mr Gotting's clerk read it through to her and explain exactly what each phrase meant.

Josiah watched her thoughtfully, deciding she wasn't as stupid as she had at first seemed. Perhaps he'd be able to bring her up to scratch if he made more effort to train her.

That night he stayed up drinking with one of his Perth acquaintances and since it was rather late by the time he got dressed the following morning, and his head was thumping, decided not to go back and instruct Gotting to draw up a new will. He'd do that next time he came to Perth on his own.

He had some money behind him now and would have more once the new baby was born, for his father would never go back on his word. He was just glad Liza didn't show her condition yet. He loathed the sight of her with a swollen body and did not wish to be seen with her in public when she looked like that.

As they approached Pendleworth again, Liza felt anticipation building in her and realised in surprise that it really did feel like home now. She jumped down from the cart and rushed to cover her daughter's face with kisses, relieved to see how well the child looked, and then gave Dinny a big hug, too. Which made Josiah angry again. Well, let him be angry. She was sick and tired of trying to please him.

A month later Josiah received a letter from his mother, only the second one his father had allowed her to write. He took it away to read and Liza thought he looked deeply saddened when he returned.

'How are your family?' she ventured.

'Well enough. Both my brothers' wives have whelped

232

again.' Josiah's mother had written as lovingly as ever, telling him how greatly she missed him still, and all his homesickness had surged back in a great dark tide as he read her carefully penned words.

He tried to control his feelings, telling himself again and again that he was making a pretty decent life here, and that things would only get better as time passed. But as dusk fell each day he found himself seeking the oblivion of the bottle, longing for it. Mostly he drank rum, which was cheap and readily available, and mocked himself for doing so. How he had scorned the local spirit when he first arrived! Well, he didn't scorn it now. It was the best medicine of all for those in exile. He did not even care nowadays whether Liza found him still sprawled snoring in his office when she got up in the morning.

During his drunken slumbers he dreamed again and again of the cool green hills near Pendleworth – the real Pendleworth, not this shabby imitation. He knew he was being curt and irritable with Liza and could not help that, but he continued to enjoy Cathie's company, seeing the child as a phoenix rising from the ashes of his life. He might not have sired her, but by God he would mould her into the sort of daughter any gentleman could be proud of.

He insisted she be moved out into a bedroom of her own, the small room next to his, since only poor people shared their bedrooms with their children as Liza had been doing. And he made plans to hire a governess soon to educate Cathie properly.

Liza protested about the move but was overruled in a short, bitter quarrel.

She missed her daughter's presence beside her at night. Her back ached and she felt sickly in the mornings, often sleeping later than usual. She was not carrying this child as easily as she had carried the first, and even though it did not show yet, she could feel its presence in her mind as well as her body. It was a boy, she was sure of that. He'd look just like Benedict, then they would all be in trouble. Josiah would disown her, send her away, take Cathie from her. These worries built up into mountains during the dark, sleepless hours and didn't go away entirely during the daytime, either.

One chill winter's night her thoughts got into a worse tangle than usual, so after tossing and turning for hours she threw on some clothes, wrapped a cloak round herself and went out for a walk. She saw a lamp still burning in Josiah's room and tiptoed carefully along the verandah in the other direction.

It was a strange thing to do, going for a walk in the moonlight, but she felt strange tonight. It had been fine during the past few days, fine but cold, and she was glad of the warm cloak.

The world seemed different in the gentle silver light and when a voice called softly from behind her, she turned and smiled at Dinny. 'It's a beautiful night, isn't it?'

'Very. It's going to rain again later, though, so you shouldn't go too far.'

'Oh, let's enjoy the dry spell while we can,' Liza laughed. 'I know you go out walking at night sometimes.'

'Well, the sun can get too hot, but the moon always seems like a friend.'

They strolled a little further together, not filling the silence with conversation, just enjoying the crisp air and the shadow-patterned brightness of the night. Then Dinny stopped and frowned. 'Isn't that – can you smell smoke, Liza?'

They were both instantly alert. Like all settlers, Liza had heard tales of the danger of bush fires and Dinny had experienced them before.

'Where's it coming from?' Liza sniffed the air.

They both said at once, 'It's coming from the house!' and set off running, not wasting their breath on more words, but pounding back along the sandy track.

Without stopping Liza grabbed Dinny's arm and gasped, 'Go and fetch Benedict! If the house is on fire, we'll need help!' She didn't even consider the bad feeling between the two of them, because she knew he would come at once if she ever needed him.

Dinny turned and ran along a narrow path that cut through the woods.

Liza ran on alone, terrified of what she might find. When she was still quite a way from the house, she saw the red glow of flames and words began to pound inside her head in time to her steps: 'No, no! Don't let her be hurt. Don't let my Cathie be hurt!'

In the house Josiah stirred and groaned as movement made his head hurt. Then he drew in a lungful of smoke and began to cough, which woke him properly. He dragged himself to a sitting position, but was still too fuddled to think straight, for he'd consumed a whole bottle of rum during the evening.

Suddenly he noticed the lurid light flickering in the corner of his bedroom where his desk stood and where he had left a lighted lamp near an open window. There were noises which at first he didn't recognise: sharp, crackling, hungry sounds. Then he realised what had happened and stumbled from the bed, feeling dizzy and coughing again as smoke swirled round the room.

Outside he called, 'Liza! Liza! The house is on fire. Get the child out!'

But there was no answer.

'Dinny! Where are you? Wake your mistress!'

But she didn't answer either.

He rushed into the old part of the house but found no one there. Had the stupid bitch gone out to her lover again after all her protestations? If she was lying with Caine again, he'd make her sorry.

He stood in the cleared area in front of the house, still finding it hard to think clearly but moving away from the fire by instinct. When he heard the sound of a child crying, he grunted in dismay and stood still. Cathie! Where was she?

The crying was replaced by the sound of coughing and choking, then the thin wailing started up once more. He realised it was coming from the small room next to his.

'No!' he groaned. The child's new room lay next to the fire – and *he* had put her there.

Flames were now licking up the walls and showing through the wooden shingles on the roof. It seemed impossible that something as solid as a house could burn so quickly. Cursing under his breath, he started back, the main thought in his mind to get the child out.

The smoke was far worse now, boiling out of the doors and windows in dark clouds shot by lurid flashes of flame. He had not realised fire could spread so quickly, or sound so loud and menacing. Covering his mouth and face with one arm, Josiah began to run along the verandah.

When he burst into Cathie's room, he found it filled with smoke and although he could see flames leaping along the wooden wall, could not see anything else very clearly. He knew where the bed lay and made his way across the room in that direction, sobbing aloud in relief as his hands found first the wooden bedposts, then the figure of the little girl lying there, still untouched by the flames. But she wasn't moving! Terror slammed through him and he shook her hard as he snatched her up.

Cathie coughed and choked, beginning to sob weakly.

She was alive!

He grabbed a blanket to wrap round her and protect her with before turning to fumble his way out again. The smoke was growing thicker by the minute and he couldn't even see the door. 'Shhh, now,' he muttered, as he tried to get his bearings. 'Shhh.' But the child kept crying. His eyes were stinging, and his throat was hurting with the acrid smoke. It took him a minute or two even to find the door, and by then he was coughing and wheezing too.

As he bumped into the half-open door, he muttered, 'Thank God!' Only a few seconds now and he would be safe.

But there was another loud crackle of flame and without warning a burning beam from the roof crashed down on his back. Josiah screamed with the pain of it, but somehow managed to jerk it off and keep hold of the child. Blinded by the smoke, his shirt smouldering, he staggered forward. As he came out of the door, there was another roaring sound and a wall of flame seemed to surround him, setting light to his hair.

He felt totally disoriented and when he heard a great cracking sound overhead, paused for a second to try to work out what was happening, which was the best way to go. Before he could start moving again, more pieces of burning wood showered down on to him.

Liza arrived back in time to see a figure whose clothing was alight stumble along the verandah and fall beneath a shower of burning shingles. Even as the person began to get up again, a larger flaming mass crashed down. Something rolled forward from the figure's arms, a bundle which was also alight. As a loud wailing sound came from it, she realised it was her child and rushed towards it, screaming, 'Get up, Josiah! Get up!'

She beat out the flames on her daughter's clothing with her hands, not noticing the pain. Pausing only to check that Cathie was still alive, she ran to put her down at the other side of the clearing, before turning back towards the figure near the verandah.

Liza's heart began to thump in terror. *Josiah hadn't moved at all!*

Benedict, Fergal and Dinny arrived as she was trying to lever the flaming wood from her husband's body with a chunk of firewood from the nearby pile, oblivious to the sparks whirling around her and landing on her own clothing and skin.

Shielding their faces with their arms, the two men went to her aid and Dinny went to check the child.

A voice ordered, 'Liza, take his arms and pull him out when we lever the beam off him.' Dropping her piece of wood, she grabbed the prone figure's arms, sobbing under her breath.

The nearby flames were so hot it was agony to stay there. A wind had risen, whirling more sparks and embers around them. To their left another big beam crashed down, making them all jerk back in shock for a moment. Then they bent to their task again, and the men somehow managed to lever the mass of glowing wood off Josiah's back.

At once Liza began pulling him away, but he was heavy and was making no move to help himself, so she didn't get far.

Fergal held the burning beam up while Benedict pushed Liza aside and took over, saying. 'Move back! I'll deal with him.'

Just then thunder cracked overhead and lightning zipped across the sky.

They all glanced up, praying for rain, but none fell, even though the thunder and lightning seemed quite close.

Benedict and Fergal carried Josiah across the clearing away from the worst of the heat. Cradling the weakly sobbing child in her arms, Liza watched helplessly as flames started to spread from the new wing along the roof of the verandah that joined it to the original dwelling. Dinny had one arm around her.

As she cuddled Cathie to her breast, Liza could smell scorched clothing and for the first time felt the pain in her own hands, but she took heart from the vigour of her daughter's cries. That was all that mattered: Cathie was alive.

'Is the child badly burnt?' Benedict called as he bent over Josiah again.

'I don't think so.'

'Thank God!' He stared down at the charred clothing and blackened skin on Josiah's back, feeling sickened.

Dinny left Liza and went across to the still figure. She bent over for a moment, then straightened up and touched Benedict's hand. 'There's nothing you can do.'

'What? Is he . . . ?'

'Dead,' she said simply. 'Look at his head!'

Lightning obliged to show them that one of the beams had crushed Josiah's skull as it fell on him and the dark patch was not hair but burnt flesh.

'Better he died quickly than slowly with those burns,' Dinny said in her soft, deep voice.

'He's dead?' gasped Liza. 'Dead? Josiah?' She swayed on her feet, feeling as if the world had swung upside down.

Thinking she was going to faint, Benedict scrambled forward to take her and the child into the shelter and comfort of his arms.

'I'm all right,' she managed after a moment. 'You can let go of me.'

But he didn't and she hadn't the strength to push him away. She felt distant and dizzy, and her eyes kept going back to the still body on the ground nearby. *Dead!* How could Josiah be dead? How was that possible?

They heard voices calling from the direction of Brookley and this time when Liza pushed Benedict away he moved, but not far, and she could still feel his eyes on her.

Andrew burst into the clearing, to stop aghast at the sight of the burning building. Then he rushed round to the group, clearly illuminated by the flames. 'Is everyone all right?'

'Josiah's dead,' Benedict said in a low voice.

Liza bent over her daughter, rocking her in her arms, covering her face with kisses, seeming unable to think what to do, hearing fragments of explanation.

'Burning beam – fell right on top of him – crushed his skull – must have died instantly.'

The words seemed to echo inside her head and make no sense.

More lightning flashed, heightening the sense of nightmare and unreality, but the rain still held off. She looked up at the sky. Why did it not rain?

Andrew tugged at Benedict's arm. 'Isn't there anything we can do to save the rest of the house?'

Benedict realised that shock had stopped him thinking clearly and bent his mind to the task of saving what he could for Liza. 'We can try to break down the end part of the verandah. Maybe that'll stop it spreading to the other building.'

'Let's do it, then.'

Just at that moment there was a roaring sound as a strong wind blew up from nowhere to buffet them. Only then did rain began to fall, big heavy drops, which soon turned into a wall of water.

'It's too late,' Liza sobbed, not moving as the rain pounded down on her head. 'It's too late. He's dead.' She began weeping wildly.

'Bring the child and come home with me,' Dorothy said gently, putting an arm round her.

Liza didn't move. 'Josiah saved Cathie's life. I saw him carrying her, sheltering her with his body. If he hadn't gone back for her, he'd still be alive. And she – she'd be dead instead.'

'Liza—'

Dinny spoke from behind them, so quietly that only the women and Fergal heard her. 'He was redeeming his soul, making up for the bad things he had done.'

Fergal looked sideways at her. 'Why do you say that?'

She shrugged. 'Redemption is what you white people believe in, isn't it?' Her father had tried to teach her to worship his god, but she didn't know what she felt about it all. However, some ideas had stayed with her, and the idea of paying for your sins seemed only reasonable. Her mother had told her stories, too, of her own people who had angered the gods and paid for it.

'Was Ludlam so bad that he needed redeeming?' Fergal wondered aloud.

'He wasn't a good man. He didn't make Liza happy and he'd have made her even more unhappy as the years passed if he'd lived.' Dinny stared across at her friend. 'She's a good woman.

She deserves happiness herself, because she gives it to others in full measure. No one else would help me, but she did. And she'll help a lot of other people in the future.' She was quite sure of that.

The moment of prescience passed and Dinny fell silent. The spirits or gods or whatever they were had spoken in her heart, and now they had moved on to speak to someone else. Her father had had these same 'foretellings', as he had called them, just once in a while. He'd said it was his Celtic ancestry. Her mother said it was spirits who took possession of you. Whatever caused it, it happened to Dinny sometimes and then she could not help speaking of what was to come. But whether that was from her father's side or from her mother's people she didn't know or care. She just wished she was not cursed with the gift, because sometimes people blamed you when the things you spoke of actually happened.

Benedict called out and Fergal joined the other men in making sure that the rain really had put out all the flames, while Dorothy led Liza, carrying a still-wailing Cathie, along the track to the inn. Dinny hesitated, then stayed behind. She would not be welcome in Brookley.

Even Kitty, silent witness to the horrors of that night, did not speak as the three women walked back through the downpour to their home. But she felt a sneaking satisfaction that Liza had lost her rich protector and probably her home. She'd not be able to look down her nose at people now.

When they met some more neighbours coming to find out what was happening, it was Kitty who stopped to tell them. Then she walked slowly after the other women who had moved ahead. For once, she did not feel nervous of the quietness of the bush. It was a harsh country, too hot in summer, wet and windy in winter. She hated it and was not going to let it kill her as it had done Josiah. She'd waited long enough. Whatever it took, she'd find a way to go home.

CHAPTER NINETEEN

Liza found that there were endless formalities to go through when one of the gentry died so suddenly. The next day Benedict rode into Pinjarra to inform the magistrate, who came to view the body and question them all about the fire.

She was glad to have Dorothy by her side as she answered the questions and avoided looking at her husband's body, the mere thought of which made her feel sick. The odour of burning seemed to linger everywhere: on her body and in her clothing, not just in the charred ruins. Cathie had hardly let go of her since the fire, and Liza found the warmth of the small body in her arms comforting.

However, the magistrate seemed far more concerned with what Benedict and Andrew had seen than with what Liza had to tell him, and treated her as if she had only half her wits.

At first she just answered the magistrate's questions, feeling frozen and unable to think clearly, her eyes going back again and again to the canvas-covered body on the ground. Could that really be all that was left of Josiah? Against all reason she kept expecting to hear his voice or see him coming round the corner with a disapproving frown on his face. She had hardly slept the previous night – nor had her daughter, who was fretful, disinterested in food and still coughing a lot after her ordeal.

'How will the widow manage?' the magistrate asked the men in a low voice. 'Is there a will? Money?'

That made Liza straighten up and interrupt him. 'My husband had a will drawn up last time we went to Perth and he left everything to me. So, yes, there is money.'

'She'll have to go up to Perth, then, to sort all that out,' the magistrate told Benedict, as if she had not spoken. 'Perhaps later, when she's recovered?'

'We'll see that she gets there,' Benedict promised.

Liza bounced to her feet and set her hands on her hips, welcoming the anger which made her feel fully alive again. She glared at them both because Benedict at least should have known better than to speak about her like that. 'I'm perfectly capable of arranging a trip to Perth myself, thank you very much!'

The magistrate turned to her at last. 'But what about your stock and house? You're not thinking clearly, Mrs Ludlam. You can't just abandon things here to go to Perth. You'll need the help of your friends to run this farm. And besides, you're very young for all this responsibility.'

'I'm twenty-one.' She hadn't even bothered to remind Josiah of her last birthday, and it had passed unnoticed.

The magistrate clicked his tongue and sighed, as if there were something wrong with that. 'You're legally able to take charge of your children, then.'

'Fergal can come over to look after the farm,' Benedict offered, 'while I escort Mrs Ludlam up to Perth.'

'A ticket-of-leave man in charge?' The magistrate looked down his nose.

'I've found him very willing and reliable. He was a political prisoner, not a criminal.'

'Political misdemeanours are as much crimes as robberies. As an educated man, he should have known better.'

Liza cleared her throat to gain their attention. 'Thank you for your offer, Mr Caine, but that will be neither necessary nor proper.'

The magistrate nodded approval of that.

'I'm sure Mrs Pringle will come with me and we can hire someone to drive us to Perth.' Liza looked questioningly at Dorothy, who had been a wonderful comfort to her, and received a nod of assent.

'You'll take Fergal with you and the Pringles' cart, then,' Benedict stated in a flat voice, daring her to contradict him. 'You won't want to trust yourself to strangers, surely, Mrs Ludlam?'

Their eyes met, locked for a moment, then she nodded, but only because it was the sensible thing to do. As long as *he* was not coming with her, she would manage. 'Is the rest of the house safe enough to live in? Because if so I'll move back here.' The Pringles' small house felt crowded, and as Kitty had refused point blank to share a bedroom with Liza, she was sleeping in the small parlour. To add to the annoyance, those who patronised the inn sat and stared at her as if she had suddenly grown horns.

As she gazed across at the still form of her husband, Liza's eyes were suddenly blinded by tears. For all his faults, Josiah had not deserved to die like that. 'We'll have to arrange a burial.'

'I'll do that,' Benedict said.

The Mandurah magistrate studied him thoughtfully, then looked at Liza equally thoughtfully. 'I'm afraid there is no clergyman to hold a service. And it would not be advisable,' he cleared his throat and looked embarrassed, 'to wait too long.'

Liza nodded. Did he think she didn't understand that dead bodies decayed?

'I think you should stay on with us, though, my dear,' Dorothy protested. 'You could come over and help Dinny clear up here during the daytime, perhaps.'

But Liza had no intention of becoming dependent upon anyone again – or of spending any more time than she could help with Kitty Pringle, who had smiled at her this morning and asked in sweetly acid tones, 'How will you manage now, Liza Docherty, with no man to lean on? I bet someone as ignorant as you will soon lose everything. And it'll serve you right, too!'

But Liza did not intend to lose anything.

After the magistrate had left, Andrew asked her where she wanted them to bury Josiah. When she suggested near the lake, they all walked down to the part of the swamp that had been reclaimed and turned into open water and together chose a spot on the bank. She addressed all her remarks to Andrew.

The following day Benedict caught Liza alone. When she would have turned away, he stopped her. 'I need to know. Will you be all right?'

'Yes, of course I will. I'll have Dinny. We'll be fine. And I'd prefer you to stay away from me from now on, if you please.'

His eyes seemed to be burning into her, as if they were saying a hundred things his lips dared not, so she bent over her daughter and began talking to the child in a quiet, soothing tone. After a moment, she heard him walk away, and glanced up to see Fergal following him.

When the two men had disappeared down the track, Liza let out a long, quivering sigh of relief and walked back to the lake. Standing next to the new mound of earth over which they had all prayed together, she found more tears slipping down her cheeks. Josiah had lost his life saving that of the child to whom he had given his name. Liza had never really understood him, had resented the way he treated her most of the time, but she was grateful to him for saving Cathie and would be for the rest of her life.

Hearing the quiet tread behind her, she turned to hold out her free hand to her friend. 'You will stay with me, won't you?'

Dinny clasped her hand and nodded.

'It's strange, but I can't seem to think what to do.'

'What Mr Caine said: hire someone to manage the farm and wait for the new child to be born. And it's about time we baked some bread, isn't it? We've nearly run out. We'll do that tomorrow. It's a good thing the kitchen wasn't burned down.'

Torn between laughter and tears, Liza hugged her, leaned against her for a minute, then stood back resolutely. 'Yes. We'll bake some bread.' It seemed as good a sign as any that life could now move on.

It was several days before the two women were ready to set off for Perth. Dorothy had found some black garments among Catherine's possessions and insisted on helping Liza to alter them. 'You must *look* right,' she insisted. 'Your husband's friends will not respect you if you don't wear mourning.'

So Liza let her do as she pleased, but insisted Dorothy take one of Catherine's many dresses in return for her help, and also that a dress be altered for Dinny as well, now that Josiah was not there to complain about that indulgence. Realising how their roles had been reversed, she watched Dorothy hesitate and urged, 'Please take it. I can never use so many clothes. They're already out of fashion, Agnes tells me.'

Dorothy made a helpless gesture with her hands, then picked up a dress and stroked the fine fabric with roughened fingertips. 'Thank you.' It had been a long time since she'd had something as elegant as this to wear.

'Do you think Kitty would take one from me as well?'

'I don't know.'

'Choose one for her, then, and persuade her. I don't know

244

why Catherine thought she would need all these clothes.' She watched Dorothy finger the other garments. 'The blue would suit her.'

'All right.'

And Kitty did not send the dress back.

They set off the next day, a chill winter's morning with mist lingering in the hollows and making the world seem a little unreal. As the cart rumbled along, with Fergal driving, Liza sat thinking about the future. She turned to her friend. 'I suppose I'd better write to Josiah's family and tell them what's happened. Will you help me with the letter, Dorothy? I don't want to sound too – too uneducated.'

'Benedict has already written to them. We thought – it seemed better to—' Dorothy's voice trailed away for a moment, then she added, 'Benedict doesn't think Josiah told them about Catherine's death, so that they wouldn't quibble about the money.'

'Oh.' Liza knew there had been no chance to take the letter into Mandurah or give it to anyone going to Perth to post. 'Do you have it with you?'

'Well, yes.'

'Then give it to me. I'd better add a line or two explaining who I am.' And she wanted to see what he had written, as well.

With a worried expression on her face, Dorothy fumbled through her carpet bag. 'Here.'

Liza hesitated, staring at the sealed and folded piece of paper, then lifting the wax carefully with her fingernail.

Sir

It is with deep regret that I have to tell you that your son Josiah has been killed. He died a hero, saving his daughter's life when the house caught fire. He has left everything to his widow, who has friends to assist her, and who is expecting another child.

B. Caine
15th June 1860

It seemed a very curt way to inform a family that they had lost a son and Liza didn't see why her own existence should be ignored. 'I'll add a note later. We won't send it quite yet.' She put the letter away among her own things and Dorothy did not protest.

In Perth, Liza called first on Agnes Fenton, who would, she felt, be of more use than Dorothy in dealing with legal matters, even though her friend's presence lent her the necessary respectability.

When she had got over the shock of hearing about Josiah's death, Agnes came with them to see Josiah's lawyer. Mr Gotting produced the will and offered to deal with the legal formalities.

Liza frowned. 'I'll let you know later. Could you please give me the will now, Mr Gotting? Josiah's copy was destroyed in the fire.'

'It'd be better if I held it here for you, Mrs Ludlam.'

'I believe it's my right to take it.' She held out her hand and with a frown he handed over the papers.

She stared at it, reading slowly, but even before the end of the first page, she stopped. 'This isn't the will my husband signed in April.'

Herbert Gotting hesitated. Knowing how his friend Josiah had really felt about leaving everything to a wife like this, and assuming she was illiterate and too stupid to understand what was happening, since she'd had to ask the clerk to read the will to her before signing it, he had substituted the previous will, which still looked after her but appointed Gotting himself to manage the Ludlams' affairs until the daughter, the main beneficiary, was twenty-five.

Agnes came to peer over Liza's shoulder. 'This will is dated last year, Mr Gotting. I know Josiah made a will more recently because he told me so himself.'

Herbert snatched the papers from Liza's hand and pretended to study them. 'Oh, dear! My most sincere apologies, Mrs Ludlam. My clerk must have made a mistake.' He left the room and two minutes later brought back another document, which both Liza and Agnes checked carefully

'This is the one. I'll take it with me.' Liza began to fold it up.

'Surely it'll be safer here?' he protested.

She stared him in the eye. 'I'd be afraid of someone mixing them up again.'

There was a pregnant silence, then he said, 'At least let me have a copy made first. How can I administer it if—'

246

'I haven't decided yet who is to—' Liza began.

Agnes stepped in smoothly before her friend could make more of an enemy of him than she had done already. 'We'll keep it very safe, I promise you.'

'I don't trust that man,' Liza muttered as they left the building. 'Agnes, where can I find myself another lawyer? I don't *have* to deal with that Mr Gotting, do I?'

Agnes pursed her lips. 'No, of course not. Look, I'll introduce you to my own lawyer. His office is just round the corner.'

Ronald Munson was a Scot of indeterminate age with a face that was open and honest. To Liza's relief, he didn't treat her like a fool either.

'I can see no difficulties with administering this will, Mrs Ludlam. It's quite straightforward actually.' He hesitated then added, 'I don't wish to interfere, but would you like me to apprise your late husband's family of his death and – well, about the child you're carrying? After all, it is their grandchild. These things often come better from a lawyer.'

Liza stared at him, then looked down at her hands, clasped tidily in her lap. If she said no, if she didn't tell Josiah's family about the child, people here would find it strange. And yet his father had known of Josiah's true nature so might have doubts about who had fathered the baby – and she wasn't having her child branded a bastard. What should she do for the best?

'Mrs Ludlam? Are you all right?'

'What? Oh. I'm sorry, Mr Munson. Yes, I would appreciate it if you could let them know. To tell the truth Josiah didn't get on very well with his father. And – and I also have a letter for the Ludlams from my neighbour, Mr Benedict Caine, who lived on their estate in England and who came out to Australia with my husband. I've never met them, you see I'm not sure he'd even told them about his first wife's death, so – so perhaps you could do that for me? You could send Mr Caine's letter with yours.' Which would avoid the necessity of her writing at all, for she was self-conscious about her handwriting, which was very childish and unformed, as Josiah had often pointed out.

'Very well, Mrs Ludlam.'

Liza signed the papers he presented then left the office in a very thoughtful mood, grateful when the other two women insisted she retire to her room to 'rest'. She had a lot to think about, her whole future to plan. Only she couldn't think what to do.

When she returned to the farm, Liza tried to keep matters on a purely business footing between herself and Benedict, but as he was running the farm for her, she could not avoid him completely. His presence still disturbed her, made her feel as if there was not enough air to breathe – and made her long for what she had lost. The looks he gave her said he had not forgotten their relationship either but she kept reminding herself that he already had a wife, that he had not even told her he was married, and that thought was usually enough to stoke up her anger. Well, most of the time, anyway.

The ruins had been cleared away and all the rooms in the original house made habitable once again, though a faint smell of smoke still seemed to linger in the air.

'We can get some more timber and rebuild the other rooms, if you like?' Benedict offered. 'Though I can't do it for you at the moment. I'm a bit busy running two places. I'll need to take on another man.' He saw her scowling at that pre-empting of her rights and hastily amended it to, 'We, I mean! We'll need to do that if we continue to run the two farms as one.'

Liza didn't even need to think about it. 'I don't want that place rebuilding, but perhaps when you have time you could make a lean-to bedroom for Dinny. Cathie can sleep with me again. Since the fire, she wakes up crying sometimes. And – and if you're going to continue managing the farm, I insist on paying you for your work.'

Benedict's voice was a low growl. 'I don't need paying to help you. You know that, Liza.'

She kept her gaze slightly to one side of his face. 'Well, I prefer to pay you, and if you won't allow me to do so, I'll find someone else to help me instead.'

'You've grown very sharp lately.'

'Is it any wonder?' She was not surprised when he spun round and strode away.

At the edge of the clearing he paused to call, 'Do what

you want about money, but I'm still going to look after things for you.'

As the weeks passed the weather grew slightly warmer with less rain and the sunny days and crisp nights that heralded the approach of spring. Liza was sleeping badly still and on several nights had gone outside to sit on the verandah, just staring at the moonlight and shadows. Somehow she never felt afraid here and loved the bush. Loved everything about Australia, in fact. The grey streets and huddled terraces of Pendleworth seemed like a bad dream now, though she still thought about her mother occasionally and wished she could see her again. She hoped the letter she'd sent had set her mother's worries about her at rest, if nothing else.

If only England were not so far away! She hadn't realised how big the world was until the long voyage out to Australia. When the baby was born, she would write to her mother again. Josiah wouldn't be here to prevent her and she would ask Father Michael to write back this time to let her know how her family were doing.

On these sleepless nights Dinny would sometimes come out to join her and sit there quietly, sharing the rustling silence of a moonlit night without the need for conversation. One Liza gave in to temptation and asked, 'Will you keep an eye on Cathie for me? I want to go for a walk.'

She took the same path as on the night of the fire. When she got to the place where she and Dinny had stopped before, she found herself glancing behind, half expecting to see a glow in the sky, but the world remained peaceful and that soothed something inside her.

She took the path that led along the cleared land, stopping to lean against the split-pole fence and resting her head on her clasped hands for a minute. She felt bewildered and insecure, for she had lost Benedict as well as Josiah and that loss grieved her more. Tears trickled down her cheeks and she brushed them away impatiently.

When she heard footsteps she swung round and gasped. There was Benedict standing a little way apart, looking at her as a man would gaze at a lost dream.

His voice was deep, yet soft. 'You're weeping, Liza.'

She could only shrug, turning half away from him, wondering whether she should simply walk on and ignore him. But she couldn't move, couldn't deny herself a few minutes of his company, here where no one could see them.

'I wish—' He leaned against the fence a few feet away from her, covering his eyes with one hand so that his voice came out muffled '—I wish desperately that I had the right to be with you and help you.'

'Yes, well, you don't.' She turned too quickly and caught her heel in the cloak, crying out as she felt herself begin to fall. But he was there, catching her and then muttering a curse as he drew her to him.

'Liza, what are we going to do?' he groaned into her hair. 'I can't sleep either, can't stop thinking about you. Did you believe I'd stopped loving you? Was that why you were weeping? I'd never do that! You're the love of my life and you always will be.'

She clutched him with both hands. 'Oh, Benedict, I miss you so much.'

They kissed, but although the passion was there, always there simmering beneath the surface, this was a gentle kiss, tasting of sadness, salty tears and loss.

'I never thought it possible to love anyone as I love you,' he said solemnly, his eyes holding hers.

She stretched out her right hand and caressed his cheek. 'Nor I. I didn't believe such love existed. When I read about it in Catherine's books, I thought how silly the people were – only I'm just as silly for it's you I think of day and night, you I long to be with.' She shoved him away with a sudden return to anger. 'Only I can't! You're married! And I'm a fool to care for you still.'

He could not let her go with harsh words between them. 'Heaven help me, but Grace is nothing to me. And you – you're everything, Liza.'

Moonlight caressed their faces as they stared at one another, painting a clear bright picture of their love, for it showed in every line, every feature.

He groaned and pulled her to him. 'I can't live without you, my lass.' Then he held her close and whispered the shameful words he'd been wanting to say ever since Josiah's death, 'Would you – would you still run away with me? Trust yourself to me? Make a new life with me?' The odds against them seemed almost insurmountable, and he would be breaking his solemn vows to his wife, but heaven help him, he could not bear to lose this woman. 'I don't have much money, don't know if I can sell this farm for anything like what it's worth, but I'll work hard and – and I'll always treat you as my true wife.'

Liza's face was full of wonder. 'You'd leave Grace for me?'

'Yes.' He touched her belly gently. 'And for the child. He's mine and I want him to know he's mine right from the moment he's born.'

'And Cathie? She's not your daughter.'

'Did I not help you bear her? She feels like mine and she'll never know from me that she isn't, I promise you.'

For a moment longer Liza hesitated, staring at him, then she sobbed and threw her arms round his neck. 'Oh, Benedict, I've been so lost. I don't care about money, just about us being together.' Then she pulled back a little, still holding him, her face brightening. 'But it's all right because I have plenty of money. Josiah had quite a bit left in the bank from the five hundred pounds his father sent him after Catherine was born, and—'

Benedict stiffened. 'I don't want his money.'

'It'll make a big difference to us.'

He stepped back. 'No, I won't touch it.' He couldn't bear the thought of using it.

'Benedict, I'll work beside you and bear you children, but I'm not going to throw away good money. I know what it's like to be poor, to run away from home with only a few shillings in my purse, terrified out of my wits, then to be totally dependent on others. I didn't want to marry Josiah, but it seemed like the only thing I could do. Catherine was a kind lady, but it was Josiah she loved, him she was thinking about when she made him marry me. She didn't care about my future or my happiness at all. So I feel I've *earned* the money he left! I did my best to be a good wife to him, even if I could never meet his standards, and I'm *not* throwing it away.'

'I will not take it!' Benedict's voice had a hard edge to it.

'You've got as much stupid pride as he had! Well, I'm not giving up my security as well as my respectability.' Liza spat the words at him and walked away. He did not try to stop her, so she continued walking. Not weeping, just filled with anger and pain – and that great emptiness of this further loss echoing sadly inside her after the short moments of hoping they might find a future together after all.

Three days went past. Liza tended her house and garden, spending time with her daughter and the woman who had become as close to her as a sister. Dinny seemed to sense that she didn't want to talk about whatever was bothering her so held her peace, working alongside Liza, just being there.

Fergal came across every day to do the necessary jobs and tend the animals. He brought no word from Benedict and at first he, too, worked in silence.

On the second day, however, when Dinny carried some food out to him at noon, she saw that he'd cut his hand quite badly and was trying in vain to stanch the flow of blood. Setting the food down, she quickly slipped off her apron, binding it round the cut.

He gave her a shamefaced smile. 'Stupid of me. I wasn't thinking what I was doing. I ought to know how to handle an axe by now.'

'You were feeling sad.' She could sense it in him, always there beneath his gentle smiles and friendly words.

He nodded.

'I've noticed that before in you.'

'Then you notice more than most people.' His voice rang with the bitterness so long pent-up inside him. 'They don't think ex-convicts have feelings or the right to decent lives of their own, even after they've served their time.'

'They don't think people like me have feelings either,' Dinny murmured.

'What do you mean, "people like me"?'

'Black people,' she flung at him defiantly.

'Are you so different from me?' He took hold of her hand with his uninjured one, fingers warm and soft on hers. 'You have the same number of hands and feet as I do, and your hair is no darker than mine.'

'My skin is darker, though.' She studied her hand as it lay in his, making no attempt to pull away.

'Does that matter?'

'To most people it does.'

'Well, it doesn't matter one jot to me.' Fergal moved his wounded hand incautiously and winced as more blood seeped out. 'Damn! That's going to stop me working properly for a few days.'

'You'd better come to the house. It's a deep cut. We'll wash it and find some proper bandages there.'

He looked down at her blood-stained apron. 'Sorry about this.'

Dinny smiled, that wide serene smile that was peculiarly hers. 'It will wash.'

At the house, Liza tutted over the cut and decided it needed to be sewn together. 'I think we ought to send for Dorothy. She knows how to do such things better than I do.'

Fergal pulled a face. 'Is it really necessary?'

'I think so. The cut will come apart and bleed every time you move it. And you won't be able to work with it like that.'

'Oh, very well, then. Wrap it up in the apron again, and I'll walk over to her house.'

As Liza was doing that she turned to her friend. 'Dinny, will you go with him? He's lost a lot of blood and he's looking a bit pale. We don't want him collapsing on the way.'

'All right.'

So the two of them set out, walking through the golden afternoon, silent at first. Then Fergal turned and smiled at her. 'This isn't necessary, you know. I'm all right, apart from the cut.'

'I enjoy being outside, and there was nothing pressing to do.' She stole another glance at him and caught him gazing at her.

'You're a fine-looking woman, Dinny.'

She stopped walking for a moment and risked saying, 'Am I? But I still have no man.'

'Well, I'm sure you'll meet someone one day.'

'I meet many men who flinch from the colour of my skin

and yet want to use my body. There are not many who want me, would stand beside me openly.'

Fergal cradled his arm against his body. 'If I weren't in this state, I'd be happy to prove how little it matters to me what colour your skin is, lass.'

She gave him another of those long thoughtful looks. 'You have a wife back in Ireland, haven't you?'

'Yes. Whom I haven't seen since I was convicted and who has never even written to me. Her father says she doesn't want to see or hear from me again. Ever. So she's not really a wife. And yet,' he sighed, 'I'm still tied to her in the eyes of the law.'

'My father was Irish. He was called Cullen Fitzgerald.'

'A good Irish name.'

'I would be happy to have a man in my bed again,' Dinny said with simple honesty, her expression leaving him in no doubt of her meaning.

He groaned. 'Dinny, I can't do that to you! I've nothing to offer you.'

'If you don't want me—'

'It's not that. Of course I want you. A man would have to be blind not to want you.' Her soft, plump body had been haunting his dreams for a while now, but he knew Liza would be angry with anyone who treated her friend badly. 'It's just that – well, it wouldn't be fair to you.'

'I think it would be fair if it were what I wanted too.'

'There might be consequences. We might make children,' he said hoarsely. 'I seem to get children rather easily.'

She laughed softly, her teeth white and even, dark eyes glowing with sudden amusement. 'You make too much fuss about marriage, Fergal Riordan. I'm of an age when a woman longs for children. I don't think Liza would throw me off the farm even if I did bear you a child.'

He closed his eyes, then looked down ruefully at the throbbing arm. 'Now is not the time to do anything. And perhaps that's for the best. You should think about it before – before we do anything rash. Talk to Liza, perhaps.'

'You think about it, too.' Then Dinny started walking again, with that free stride that spoke of a body at ease with itself.

He thought her far more attractive than his wife who had brought a good dowry but had hated the marital act and been a selfish creature. It would not be fair to Dinny but he knew he would not be able to resist her invitation to share a bed if she offered again. Now that he was no longer locked away in a stinking prison, now that he was eating well and living a healthy life, his body was crying out for a woman – and the thought of this particular woman pleased him greatly.

CHAPTER TWENTY

Benedict tossed and turned, unable to sleep for the second night running. He kept seeing the hurt expression on Liza's face, kept seeing her walk away from him, not looking back, her whole body stiff with anger. Why had he not called out to her? The damned money, that was why! And his damned pride, too. He could not bear the thought of being dependent on a woman. But, oh, hell, he couldn't bear the thought of losing Liza, either.

With a muttered curse, he got up and went outside. It was nearly dawn, so he went across to the rough shelter he called a kitchen and started building a fire.

'You're up early!'

He turned to see the man who had become a friend watching him, nursing the injured hand. 'So are you.'

'I had something on my mind.' Fergal hesitated, then decided to put things to the test. 'What would you think if I – if I began living with Dinny? Maybe brought her here? Would you mind?'

'Live with Dinny!' Benedict cut off further comment as he saw the defensive expression on his friend's face. 'She wants to come and live here, leave Liza?'

'We haven't discussed the practicalities yet, but we're interested in – in being with one another.'

'But you already have a wife back home.' Even as he uttered the words, the irony of his saying such a thing made guilt shoot through Benedict.

'A wife who wants nothing more to do with me.' Fergal started poking at a drift of gum leaves with one toe, making them crackle and shift, so leathery they were, so unlike the fragile fallen leaves in Ireland's autumn. 'Am I to live the rest of my life alone because of that?'

'It's hard on a man. Does – um – does Liza know about this?'

'No. Not yet. You're the first I've told. We've only just started thinking about it.'

Benedict began fiddling with the fire. 'What about Dinny's – well, her colour?'

'It doesn't matter to me.' Fergal looked up at the sky. ''Tis kindness and human warmth I crave – and so does she. Someone to share my life with. Have you seen her with that child? She's wonderful. And her eyes are so gentle. I feel right when I'm with her, right and comfortable.'

'But if she – if you two had children – her colour might matter then.'

'She wants them. And I'd like another child or two, I must admit. I often wonder how my little Sean is, what he looks like.' Fergal's voice broke as he said that and he turned away till he had his emotions under control again. Another pause, then, 'Anyway, what about me being an ex-convict? That makes me just as much of an outsider to society as she is. I'll pay for my youthful rashness for the rest of my life, won't I? Most people are not like you. So – so I think we'll be good for one another.'

Benedict let out a long, slow breath. 'Well, it's up to you. I wouldn't mind at all if Dinny came to live here, of course I wouldn't, but you should talk to Liza as well. She depends on Dinny a lot. Maybe you should go and live over there instead?'

'Maybe. We'll see.'

Afterwards, as he was working, Benedict couldn't get the thought of what Fergal was planning out of his mind. The other man had more courage than he had: the courage to strive for happiness in the face of society's disapproval, the courage to live with the woman he loved.

As dusk began to fall Benedict set his work aside but was too restless to settle so went for a walk, not even seeing the beauty around him because his heart felt so heavy with pain. He did not want to abandon Liza and his child, but the thought of abandoning Grace upset him, too. He hated the thought of treating a decent woman like that, of going back on his word.

When he found himself near Liza's house, he tried to walk

away and couldn't, could only stand there feeling a sense of homecoming flooding through him. He loved this place, loved the water nearby, which could become a lake one day if they continued to work on it. This whole place was more his creation than Josiah's – just as Liza was his woman.

When she came out on to the verandah, she didn't notice him at first and he watched her hungrily. She had grown from a lovely girl into a beautiful woman in the years since he'd first seen her. The baby was only just beginning to show and she had one hand on her belly in that protective gesture pregnant women often make unconsciously. But this time it was *his* child and that touched Benedict's heart. He took a step forward.

Liza turned at the sound of gum leaves rustling beneath his feet and froze when she realised who was standing there in the gathering darkness. She half-opened her mouth as if she was going to speak, then closed it again and waited.

He walked across to her slowly, savouring the moment, seeing how she studied him, still holding herself back, waiting for him to make the first move. When he reached her, he stopped and simply held open his arms, and she flung herself into them with a sob.

'I can't live without you, Liza,' he admitted, his voice muffled by her hair. 'I still dislike the thought of using your money – I can't lie about that – and I still feel dreadful about abandoning Grace, but I can't imagine spending the rest of my life without you. You're part of me now.' Then he bent his head and kissed her, at first gently, but with growing hunger until they were pressed as closely together as was possible.

They broke apart to search each other's faces, then, her eyes bright with tears of joy, she tugged him towards the house. No need for words. He didn't hesitate to follow her inside. His decision was made. His future lay with Liza.

A few days passed, golden days in which the two of them spent most of the time together, learning each other's ways and laying the foundations for an enduring love as they started making plans for leaving. Benedict did not move into the farm, however, for all Liza's urging, spending most of each night in his own home. He didn't want to harm her reputation if someone turned up by chance, nor did he want Cathie to wake and see him there, so they never made love in Liza's bed and took great care not to disturb the child. Living together properly would have to wait until they'd left Western Australia.

After much discussion they decided to travel to Melbourne first, then settle somewhere in the countryside where they were not known. He had no doubt they'd be happy together for Liza had a great capacity for generating happiness. He loved to see it bubbling out of her, as it was now, listen to her humming as she went about her daily work, see the sparkle in her eyes as she talked to Dinny, gesticulating and throwing back her head to laugh. She had not glowed quite as brightly as this since he had known her.

Then, one day late in the afternoon, the idyll ended with earth-shattering abruptness.

There was the sound of wheels rumbling along the track from Brookley, the most unexpected of noises in this secluded place now that there was no longer a magistrate living here. Benedict looked up from where he was working on the roof of a shed with Fergal, who was not too hampered by his injured hand to pass things and generally make himself useful.

Inside the house, Liza set down her chopping knife and walked towards the door, while Cathie tugged Dinny to follow.

A small vehicle came into sight with a stranger driving it, a young man with fair hair. It was neither cart nor passenger vehicle, but the sort of hybrid that amateur colonial coachmakers created sometimes to answer several needs. Benedict narrowed his eyes, squinting against the sun. The driver looked vaguely familiar, but it was hard to see the man's face properly. 'Good excuse for a break,' he said, grinning at Fergal. He climbed down from the ladder, stretched his aching shoulders and waited.

As the cart drew nearer, a woman's head appeared behind the driver. Her outline looked familiar as well, but the sun was at the worst angle for looking in that direction. Then the cart bumped into the shade beneath a tree and Benedict could see her face more clearly. It looked like – oh, no, it couldn't be!

But it was! He groaned aloud.

Grace!

A wave of black misery washed through him. Fate had

intervened yet again to keep him and Liza apart. He could not tell Grace he no longer considered her his wife after she had made the long journey to Australia! No one could be that heartless, certainly not him. Swallowing hard, he whispered hoarsely, 'It's my wife.' From behind him, he heard Fergal's shocked intake of breath.

'Ben!' Grace called, waving and beaming. 'Ben, it's me!'

He couldn't move, not an inch, couldn't even lift his hand to wave back.

Liza was standing in the doorway of the house holding Cathie's hand with Dinny behind her. As she looked across at Benedict, her smile vanished for his expression showed clearly that something was dreadfully wrong.

Grace's smile faded as she looked at her motionless husband.

Seeing how uncertain and worried she looked, Benedict summoned up all his willpower and managed to start moving towards her. He tried to smile, but failed, so took a deep breath and forced out her name. 'Grace.' A quick glance sideways showed him the sudden shock on Liza's face. 'Grace, you're the very last person I'd expected to see!'

She scrambled down from the cart and ran towards him, laughing. 'Oh, Ben, I've so much to tell you! Please don't be angry with me for coming. I couldn't bear to wait any longer.'

He put his arms round her and let her bury her head in his shoulder because that avoided the need to kiss her. But Grace's plump body felt wrong in arms which had now learned to expect Liza's slenderness. Grace smelled different, too. 'I – I can't believe it's you.' He could hear his voice shaking. 'Tell me I'm not dreaming?'

She took a step backwards, smiling, and linked her arm in his, drawing him towards the cart. 'Ben, there's more. Prepare yourself for an even bigger surprise!'

His steps faltered. He wanted no more surprises. This one was the worst thing that had ever happened to him. As they passed the doorway of the house, he saw that Liza had moved back into the shadowed interior. Dinny was now standing in front of her protectively, holding Cathie back by the apron strings.

At the cart Grace paused to say, 'Do you remember Nicholas Rawley, Josiah Ludlam's brother-in-law? He's come to visit his sister. Nick, this is my husband – at last.'

'I'd never have recognised you, Nick,' Benedict muttered, then blew out a long, shaky breath and glanced over his shoulder as he realised this meant another unpleasant surprise for Liza.

Nick leaped lightly down, proffering his hand, looking young and fit and happy. 'Well, it's not surprising. I was hardly more than a lad when I last saw you.'

Numbly, Benedict took the hand of a man almost the same height as him, though more slender in build, shaking it automatically. 'I'm sorry. I – I still haven't taken all this in.' Should he say something about Catherine's death or leave it to Liza?

Before he could decide, Grace tugged him round the back of the cart, which had an awning over it and a rough wooden bench seat. As she tied the canvas back she said softly, 'This is the reason I came, Benedict – to bring you your son.'

He closed his eyes for a moment, while inside his brain a thousand banshees screamed their derision, then he took a deep breath and opened them again. His wife was backing carefully away from the wagon carrying a small child who had been asleep and was now waking up. As Benedict stepped forward to help her, his throat closed with emotion and he held out his arms for the son who already had the dark Caine looks and was big for his age.

The boy rubbed his eyes, then began pushing away from the strange man who was holding him. Benedict set him down gently, squatting beside him to say, 'Hello, there, lad.'

The child stared at him, frowning, unsure.

Above them, Grace chattered on, seeming unaware of her husband's shock. 'I've called him Lucas, after my great-uncle, I hope you don't mind – Lucas Newton Caine?'

'It's a – a good solid name.'

When he spoke, the child lost his shyness to ask, 'Are you my daddy?'

Benedict nodded, his throat aching with tears of both anguish and joy. He did not dare turn to look at Liza so concentrated instead on his son, the child of a few secret nights of marriage and that last stolen farewell. 'Aye, I'm your father,' he said, the words sounding thick and strange. He looked up at his wife, still standing by the cart. 'Why didn't you write and tell me about him before, Grace? Why keep his existence from me?'

She flushed. 'At first I tried to hide it from everyone. Then, when my mother found out, my parents were so angry about – about everything that I went to stay with my great-aunt Mary. And – well, I didn't go back home, so Lucas was born there. Then my aunt fell ill. She'd been so kind to me, I simply couldn't leave her to die alone. So I stayed until she passed on.'

'But you could have *written*!' The words exploded from Benedict. 'The child is – what? Getting on for three now. You could at least have *told* me I had a son!' Then he would not have hurt Liza so. He doubted anything could have stopped him loving her, for that feeling had begun to grow in him on the ship, taking him totally by surprise – but if he'd known he had a child by his wife, he'd never have risked making another with Liza.

Grace began sobbing. 'I'm sorry. I just – I couldn't write it down. I'm not good at writing letters, never have been. And this was so important.'

Benedict realised he had hurt her and she didn't deserve that. 'I'm sorry. I didn't meant to upset you. But you will admit I had a right to know, and – and it's a shock for me.'

'Yes, I suppose so.' Her eyes were searching his face again. 'Not an unpleasant one, though, I hope?'

Footsteps approached and Liza's voice sounded behind him, tight and unlike her usual tone, but the newcomers weren't to know that. 'Why don't you bring your wife inside, Benedict? She must be tired after all that travelling. I'll make us some tea.'

He turned and for a moment their eyes met, then she looked away, speaking to the other stranger who was staring at her in open puzzlement. 'You're Catherine's brother.'

'Yes. Nick Rawley.' He looked sideways, clearly expecting an introduction.

'I'm sorry to be the one to tell you,' Benedict said gently, 'but your sister died on the voyage out here. This is Josiah's second wife, Liza.'

The young man's eyes widened in shock, then they filled with tears and his fair complexion flushed with emotion. 'No!' he whispered. 'Oh, no! Cat *can't* be dead!'

Liza stepped forward, throwing an angry look at Benedict. 'You could have broken the news more gently.' She took Nick's hand and clasped it in both hers, patting it with her top hand. 'I didn't realise until recently that you hadn't been told—' She had never understood Josiah.

His strange love for his dead wife had been almost an obsession, as if he couldn't quite let her go, couldn't quite admit to those he had left behind that she was dead. Did these Ludlams never act openly and honestly? She could see this poor young man was devastated by the news. To come all this way for nothing, as well! Her heart went out to him.

'No. We'd heard nothing. We wondered why she hadn't written – and that's partly why I came.' A pause, then, 'Why? Why didn't he *tell* us?'

'Who ever knew why Josiah did things? Not me, that's for sure.'

'Is he here? I think he should—' Something in her face made him stop and stare down at her.

Liza took a deep breath. Of course, the news of Josiah's death would not have reached England yet.

Benedict intervened again. 'Josiah's dead as well. He was killed in a fire last month. Half the house burned down.' He gestured to the blackened ground beyond the house, for though he and Fergal had cleared away the remains of the building, soot and ash from the blaze had darkened the sandy soil.

Wide-eyed with shock, Nick continued to stare at Liza, then his eyes focused on her belly. 'How dreadful for you! I'm so sorry. I didn't mean to – to . . .'

'That's all right. I've grown accustomed – and it wasn't exactly a love match between us, more a matter of convenience.'

There was silence for a moment, then he said hesitantly, 'You speak as though you knew Cat?'

Liza nodded. 'I was her maid on board ship. Her other maid ran away in Liverpool rather than come to Australia, so I took on the job.' She did not intend to pretend about herself.

'And *Josiah* m—' He cut off what he had been going to say, flushed bright red and swallowed hard.

Liza finished it for him. 'Yes, he married me, his wife's maid. There were circumstances which made it practical for us both. But we'll talk about that later, shall we, Mr Rawley, after Benedict has taken his wife and child home?'

He looked round, as if searching for other houses, a village. 'Is there an inn nearby where I can get a room for the night?'

'No. You'll stay here with me.'

'But that wouldn't be – wouldn't be—'

'We keep open house for travellers here in Australia. We have to.'

Benedict came to join them. 'Grace tells me you hired this vehicle, Mr Rawley, and have helped her and Lucas in many ways. I'm grateful for that. We'll have an accounting about the expenses tomorrow, but could I please borrow the wagon tonight to get them home?'

'Of course. Just let me get my things out.'

'Come and have a cup of tea first.' Keeping a tight hold on her emotions, Liza led the way inside, where she and Dinny dispensed tea and refreshments, then packed some food to see the Caines through until the following morning.

And all the time her heart was throbbing with pain, so that her whole body felt raw with it. How she managed to function at all, she didn't know, but Grace at least didn't seem to notice anything wrong. Liza tried not to look at Benedict, not to think about him even – or of what she had lost with such cruel suddenness.

After they had eaten, Benedict helped Nick unload his luggage. His eyes met Liza's a couple of times, pleading for understanding, but she looked quickly away and stayed by his wife's side, so that he couldn't even attempt to talk to her.

Dinny kept Cathie and the little boy occupied. Benedict's son closely resembled his father. If Liza's child was a son, would he look like that, too?

When the Caines had got on the cart, Benedict gave her one last pleading glance, then told the horses to 'Walk on'.

Only when she heard them begin to move away did Liza look up, seeing the cart through a blur of tears. She didn't need him to tell her that it would now be impossible for them to be together. Their relationship was over before it had really begun – and she was on her own again. Furtively she flicked away a tear, then turned to face Nick. 'I hope you'll stay for a few days, Mr Rawley?'

'Are you sure? I don't want to impose or intrude on your grief.'

She shook her head. 'In the colonies even complete strangers expect to stay the night if they arrive anywhere near dusk and you're – well, almost a relative.'

'But you're on your own here. It wouldn't be—' His voice trailed away and he flushed slightly.

'I have Dinny.'

'The native woman?'

'Dinny's my friend, and a good one, too.' Liza changed the subject. 'I have some things of Catherine's which you may like to have as keepsakes.'

'Thank you.' He smiled at her, but there was sadness behind the smile and he still looked shocked. 'Will you tell me what happened? We knew Cat wasn't well but we all thought the sea voyage would help her – had helped her – especially when we heard that she and Josiah had a child. I can't—' his voice broke for a moment '—still can't believe she's dead or that he didn't tell us.'

'Your sister knew she was dying when she left England. She was a very brave woman and very kind to me.' Liza hesitated then, since his expression was so sympathetic, found herself telling him the story of how Catherine had wanted her to marry Josiah since he had been subject to bleak moods and Catherine had feared for his life. But she didn't tell Nick Rawley that her children were not Josiah's. She did not intend to tell anyone that.

'And now he's dead, too.'

'Yes. He died a hero, saving Cathie's life in the fire.'

'Jos did?' Nick sounded dubious.

'Yes. He was very fond of his daughter.'

He inhaled deeply, clearly finding it an effort to speak calmly. 'I must let his family know. And my parents – oh, dear God, how am I to tell them that Catherine's dead?' His voice broke. 'There are – were only the two of us. My mother will – she'll be devastated.'

'My lawyer has already written to tell them. I didn't find out that they didn't know until after Josiah's death.'

'Oh, I see.' He looked at her compassionately. 'Well, at least you have your children to remind you of Jos. We have nothing of Cat left now. Nothing.' His voice faltered for a minute and he had to swallow hard before he could continue. 'Are you – I hope you don't mind my asking, but you're not in want of anything?' He avoided her eyes as he said this.

Only in want of the man I love, she thought bleakly. That's all I lack. But at least Mr Rawley had accepted the idea that her little daughter and unborn child were Josiah's. 'No. Josiah left me with enough money and there's this farm as well, though I'll have to find someone to run it for me now.'

Nick wiped away some tears, then stood up. 'I don't want to sound discourteous but I'd like to be alone for a while. Would you mind if I went for a walk?'

'Not at all, but do keep to the track. It's easy to get lost among the trees.'

He nodded and walked away, a graceful athletic young man with the sun shining on his gilded hair. But his shoulders were drooping and every line of his body seemed to radiate sorrow. Liza had always thought it strange that Catherine had not attempted to write any farewell letters to her family, but her mistress's thoughts had been all of Josiah towards the end.

Pulling herself together with a huge effort, she got on with some chores, chatting quietly to Dinny and trying to keep an eye on Cathie. The child was getting into a great deal of mischief these days and tended to wander away if not watched carefully, having little sense of her own safety. But at one stage, as they were talking about the arrival of Benedict's wife, Liza could not help weeping and Dinny put her arms round her for comfort.

Inevitably, the child seized this moment to slip away and the next thing they knew, Nick was standing near the outdoor kitchen, holding her in his arms. His eyes were red, for he had the sort of fair complexion that betrays every emotion, but he seemed calm again. 'I found this little miss wandering down the track.'

Liza brushed her own tears away. 'I'm so sorry! She loves to go for walks. Thank you for bringing her back.'

He jigged the little girl up and down and she gurgled with

pleasure. When she leaned her head sleepily against his chest and cuddled up to him, he smiled. 'She's a pretty child. Doesn't take after the Ludlams, though.'

'No. I – er, think she takes after my side of the family.'

'It must be hard for you to be left on your own like this.'

She realised he had seen her weeping and nodded. Best if he assumed the tears were for Josiah. 'Yes. It gets me down sometimes.'

'If you really don't mind my staying, I could perhaps help you. And I'd like to talk about my sister. Would you tell me of her last days? My parents will wish to know – and I do, too.'

'Yes, of course. And you're welcome to stay for as long as you like, Mr Rawley. Fergal has been giving me a hand but there's always too much work. I'm thinking of asking him to manage the farm for me and perhaps hiring someone else to work with him. I was going to ask Benedict about that, but he'll no doubt be busy for a while.'

'Fergal is the man who's bringing back the cart, I presume. Who exactly is he?'

Liza hesitated, but if she didn't tell him he'd find out anyway. 'He's a ticket-of-leave man, though we're hoping he'll get a conditional pardon soon. He's Irish and it was a political offence, so he's not really a criminal.' But Nicholas's face had gone rigid and she could see that he had already judged poor Fergal. 'He's been very good to me, has helped a lot since Josiah's death.'

'I suppose you have to find help where you can in a place like this.'

On his face was the inbred arrogance that had been so much a part of her late husband and Liza realised it was no use attempting to defend Fergal to him. 'You'll have to sleep on the sofa, I'm afraid, Mr Rawley.'

Nicholas looked round. 'For tonight, I thank you. When Mr Caine brings the cart back, it might be better if I slept on that. Mrs Caine and the child did so on the way down here, while I slept underneath. There's plenty of room.'

'As you wish. I have a spare mattress you can use and blankets, and we can make sure you're sheltered from the rain. Before the fire we'd have had a spare bedroom for you, but just now we're a bit cramped, I'm afraid.'

'You're very brave,' he said suddenly.

'Am I? I don't feel brave. I just have to get on with living, look after my child. The new one isn't due for a few months yet, thank goodness.' She could feel tears threatening again and tried to blink them away but failed. 'I'm sorry.' And suddenly the tears were pouring down her cheeks, and Nick was holding her hand, patting it, thinking she was weeping for her husband, when actually she was weeping for this new loss, for Benedict who now belonged to another woman, for the years of loneliness she would have to face, for the child who would not know its father.

Would she ever stop weeping for him?

CHAPTER TWENTY-ONE

During the next few days Nick Rawley tried to help around the farm, though he was better with the animals than with other tasks, especially the horses. He spoke enthusiastically of the mounts he had left behind, of the hunts in which he had taken part, of the difficult jumps he had taken. When he found that Liza did not understand anything at all about hunting, he spent many enjoyable hours explaining it to her.

She let him talk about his passion because it was easier than thinking up topics of conversation herself. Besides, she liked to see his excitement, the way his pale blue eyes sparkled. She thought him a nice boy, though he was two years older than she was. But he had had an easy life, been spoiled as the only son of wealthy parents, while she had lived from one crisis to another for the past few years – and was still doing so. All she wanted now was peace, time to have the new baby and then a quiet life raising her children. She had felt very tired and dragged down since Grace's arrival, something not normal for her.

Nick was scrupulously polite to both Dinny and Fergal, but there was a distance in his tone and manner when dealing with them which upset Liza sometimes. When she tried to apologise to Fergal, he shrugged it off.

'That's how most people speak to me now.' He hesitated then took the opportunity to add, 'Dinny understands that because they speak to her in a similar way. She and I – you ought to know – we're getting very close.'

Liza stared at him in shock. 'You mean—'

'I mean we'd like to live together as man and wife, if you don't object? My own wife has disowned me but Teresa is young and healthy so there's little chance I'll ever be able to marry again. Dinny understands that. We just want to be together, to find a little quiet happiness if we can.' He smiled.

'She's teaching me about the plants and animals. I've been here for years and not noticed some things.'

'Well,' Liza struggled to find the right words, 'you must do what seems right, Fergal, of course you must.' She gave him a bleak smile. 'Who am I to prevent someone from being happy?'

He touched her hand briefly, but didn't put his understanding of what Grace's arrival had meant for her into words. 'We could live here, build a small house not far away – if you agree – then I could take up your offer and manage this place for you. Benedict is agreeable and I could also work with him, since the properties adjoin. We could hire someone else to help us both. We have quite a few plans for what we'd like to do once we've cleared more land, actually. I'd like to settle here permanently. I'm badly in need of a permanent home. But only if you agree?'

'It'll be a very lonely sort of life for an educated man like you,' she said quietly. 'Are you sure it'll be enough, Fergal?'

'I've no desire to go out into the world again. Didn't I make a sorry mess of it all before? And for what? For stupid idealism, that's what. And through it I lost Ireland.'

When he fell silent, struggling to master his bitterness, she waited a moment then said, 'Show me where you want to build your house and I'll deed the land it stands on to Dinny and her children.'

He stared at her, shock on his face. 'You can't mean that?'

'I can and do. She'll need the security. Women can be very vulnerable. I have enough money now to give her that at least. She's certainly given a lot to me.'

Fergal's voice was gruff and he hugged her without thinking. 'Ach, thank you, thank you. I can't tell you what this will mean to us.'

Nick's voice came from behind them. 'Are you all right, Liza? This fellow isn't annoying you, is he?'

Fergal took a quick step backwards, his face expressionless again. But his hands were clenched into fists and there was anger behind his eyes.

Liza forced a smile on to her face. 'No, of course he's not annoying me.' She gave Fergal a nod of dismissal. 'You go and tell Dinny about my offer and I'll explain things to Mr

270

Rawley.' She took Nick's arm. 'Let's walk down to the lake, shall we?'

Like Josiah, Nick seemed to enjoy strolling with a woman on his arm, helping her over the rough bits of ground as if she couldn't manage without him – which amused Liza. These well-bred gentlemen wanted their women to behave as if they were fragile, which was against her nature. However, since she needed to put him in a better mood, she let him guide her along.

'Whatever his background, Fergal has become a friend,' she told Nick quietly but firmly, 'and he would never even think of annoying me in the way you mean. Like you, he is a gentleman. Indeed, I don't know what I'd have done without him since Josiah's death.' She saw his expression become somewhat cynical and added, 'He has never, ever made advances towards me, only behaved in a brotherly manner. He's interested in Dinny, not me, and certainly not my money. And I'm not, and never could be, interested in him in that way.'

'Dinny? But she's—' Nick broke off and stopped walking.

'She's part aboriginal, yes. But she's part Irish, too. That forms a bond between them, I think – as does the way people treat them both. And like Fergal she has been a good friend to me, helping me through some difficult times. I take people as I find them, Mr Rawley, and treat them accordingly.' She could hear herself using some of the longer words she had learned from Catherine and Josiah, and almost smiled to think of how much she had changed in this respect.

Nick was silent then surprised her by asking, 'You find me snobbish?'

'Just very English and – and a typical man of your class. As Josiah was.'

His smile was rueful. 'And yet I'm here because my father was displeased with my behaviour, said I was letting my class down.'

She had guessed there was something more behind his visit than a mere desire to see his sister. 'They send a lot of their unruly sons out here, like the Ludlams sent Josiah.'

'They didn't send me. I came of my own accord. My father is very autocratic and I had some money of my own, so I decided to see a little of the world – against his wishes.'

They walked along without speaking for a few moments, then Nick asked, 'Were you very fond of him? Josiah, I mean.'

The silence went on for too long and when Liza glanced sideways, she saw a knowing expression on his face.

He gave her hand a little squeeze. 'You weren't, were you?'

'No. He'd never have married me in England and even here mostly treated me as if I was still his wife's maid. It was your sister he loved, you see. He never stopped loving her or missing her. That didn't make for – well, easy relations between us.'

They walked on, reaching the lake, and when Liza sat down on her favourite log, Nick followed suit, sitting beside her with sunlight lighting his untidy fair hair into a halo.

They both fell silent, enjoying the beauty of the scene. A kangaroo came to drink delicately from the water, with a joey peering out of its pouch. A couple of galahs started shrieking at one another and Liza smiled. 'Such quarrelsome creatures, parrots. And to think I'd never even seen one before I came to Australia.'

When the birds flew away, Nick said quietly, 'I saw Josiah's mother before I left. She sent him her dearest love and a letter. I think it has money in it, so I suppose I should give that to you now?'

Liza felt uncomfortable at the thought of reading it or of taking any more money from the Ludlams. 'Maybe you should just take it back to her. The Ludlams will have received the lawyer's letter by then, and – and I have enough money. You must tell them how bravely he died, how Cathie owes her life to him. It may comfort them a little.' She stared across the small stretch of open water and changed the subject. 'Josiah wanted very much to make a lake here, you know. We've started digging it out, because it has a practical purpose as well, and will give us a water supply in the dry summers. I'd like to see it finished as a kind of memorial to him.'

'A lake would look good, open things up.' Nick glanced round, frowning. 'Do you not find the bush rather oppressive, though?'

She could not hide her surprise. 'No, I love it. I grew up in

Pendleworth in a grey street just off Market Road. My father had a shop there – probably still does.'

'Do you not keep in touch with your family?'

'No. I ran away. My father was trying to force me to marry a neighbour, you see – a widower, much older than me and very rough in his ways.' Her voice quavered as she added, 'But I wish I could see my mother and the younger children again.'

He answered obliquely, 'You've not had an easy life, have you?'

She didn't know what to say to that. As far as she could see, few people had an easy life, even when they were rich. Josiah certainly hadn't had. Or Catherine.

Walking back, she found herself again expected to link her arm in Nick's while he told her a little about his own family, the father who had such rigid standards of behaviour and who tried to impose his ways on everyone else, the gentle mother, very like Catherine in both appearance and nature, and the uncle whom he loved. 'I was so angry with my father this time that I just left. I wrote them a letter, of course, but by the time they read it, it would have been too late for them to stop me.'

'They'll be worried about you.'

'I sent them another letter when I arrived in Fremantle, mainly for my mother's sake. I met Mrs Caine on the ship and when we found we were both coming to the same place, it seemed sensible to travel together. Otherwise I'd have bought myself a riding horse.'

'That was kind of you.'

He grinned. 'Wasn't it? But the cart's come in useful. I never expected it to become my bedroom.'

'Are you uncomfortable there?'

'No. It's an adventure. I'm enjoying myself.'

When he fell silent, she recounted some anecdotes from her time with Catherine and Nick seemed to enjoy hearing them. He was a pleasant companion and talking to him took her mind off her own troubles.

They had not seen Benedict and his wife since the day they'd arrived. Fergal said Grace had settled in without a fuss, not complaining about the tiny house and getting on with making it more homelike. Benedict had bought some dressed timber and was adding on more rooms.

'He looks sad, though, Liza,' Fergal wound up.

'Does he?' She managed to keep her voice cool. When she did not pursue the point, Fergal said nothing more about Benedict and, perversely, she wished he had done.

Nights were the hardest time. Liza found it difficult to sleep, but did not like to go outside and wander round her property now that Nick was sleeping in his cart. The first time the baby fluttered delicately inside her, she wanted to weep not rejoice for it would never know who its real father was. Once she had wanted to stay here, but now she wished desperately that she could get away. To think of living near Benedict and Grace for the rest of her life horrified her. She supposed they would have other children because Benedict was a lusty man. But she didn't want to watch.

A growing fear was that this coming child of hers would resemble its father, as his other son did. People would notice, Grace surely would – and what would everyone say then? They might ostracise her and the child. As her thoughts beat through such tangles, the hours of darkness passed slowly. In the mornings when Liza stared at her face in the mirror, she noticed dark circles under her eyes and knew she was moving lethargically. Sometimes, when the pain of her loss nearly overwhelmed her, it seemed like a miracle she could keep going at all.

She would definitely have to get away once the baby had been born, though where she would go, she could not think. Not back to England. She didn't want to go anywhere near her elder brothers, hoped never to see them again as long as she lived. Perhaps she could go to Melbourne or Sydney, where no one knew her. Only what would she do there? How earn a living? Josiah's money wouldn't last for ever if she sold up and moved away. You had to be practical, however much it hurt. Well, you did if you had two children depending on you.

Dinny and Fergal spent a day or two looking for a place to build a small house for themselves, deciding in the end to site it further along what would one day be the shore of the lake, though in the opposite direction to the cemetery with its single occupant. Once Liza had approved their choice, she sent a letter to her lawyer asking him to deed the land to Dinny, though she used her friend's Irish name Davnat Fitzgerald to avoid complications.

Dinny and Fergal worked together in the evenings to clear the land since neither of them felt comfortable in Nick Rawley's company, however polite he tried to be. If it rained, they took refuge in Fergal's tiny hut.

'It's kind of Liza to offer you the land, isn't it?' he said idly one evening.

Dinny smiled. 'My mother would say that no one can own land, that we belong to it.'

'And do you feel like that?'

She shrugged. 'Sometimes. But since she died, I've spent most of my time with white people, so I don't always know what to think.'

He came to sit beside her and put his arm round her. 'Ah, Dinny girl, you're such a comfort to me. I don't always know what to think either. I just know that I like being with you. That your quietness brings me peace as nothing else has done since they captured me.' He touched her face then moved to hold her in his arms and kiss her.

She did not return to the farm that night but stayed with him.

A week later, on a sunny winter's day, Grace walked across to see Liza, bringing little Lucas with her. 'I'm so sorry I've been remiss in calling on you. You must think me terribly un-neighbourly, but there's been so much to do, so much to learn, and Ben's been building on a new room – isn't it amazing how you can do that so quickly with timber houses?'

Liza wished the woman hadn't come, but could hardly say that. 'Do sit down, Mrs Caine,' she stumbled for a moment on the name, 'and we'll share a pot of tea.'

Cathie broke the ice by coming forward and patting Lucas's cheek. 'Dolly.'

'He's not a dolly, he's a little boy,' Liza told her, quickly stopping her daughter from poking at his eyes. 'He's come to play with you. Show him your rabbit.' She had sewn the creature herself and Cathie loved it.

The child's lower lip pushed forward the way it did when she was unsure of herself, but Lucas saved the situation by offering her a ball he was clutching. 'For you, girl.' He pushed it into her hand.

Cathie snatched it and hid it behind her as if she thought he might want it back.

'She doesn't know how to play,' Liza apologised to Grace. 'She's never had anything to do with other children.'

'Lucas will win her over. He's a little heartbreaker already,' Grace said placidly. 'And we brought the ball over 'specially for her. It's a present. He has plenty of other toys.'

It was warm enough for the two ladies to sit outside on the verandah and within minutes Dinny had brought them a tea tray.

'She makes a very good maid,' said Grace, who had been talking non-stop. 'She wouldn't have a sister looking for work, would she? I'm going to need some help when I set up my dairy and start cheese-making.'

'Dinny's not a maid – well, not exactly. She's more of a friend. And, no, she doesn't have a sister. I don't think she has any relatives now.'

Grace stared at her. 'Well, I'm sure you know your own business but it doesn't do to make *friends* with servants, you know. You'll never keep them in order if you do.'

Liza bit her tongue, and continued to keep her thoughts to herself as they chatted. Grace did not seem to be a perceptive woman, which was probably a good thing, and her mind seemed to run only on domestic matters, which made conversation easier than Liza had expected – but still awkward.

When her visitor stood up to leave, Liza's only feelings were of relief.

'I'll invite you round to afternoon tea as soon as we have the new rooms finished,' Grace promised, 'Ben's putting in long hours on them. I don't know where he thought the children and I were going to live, I really don't.'

'Children?'

'Oh, I hope to have others,' she glanced fondly at Lucas, 'now that we're together again.'

Together? Liza thought in shock. Did that mean they were sleeping together? Had he forgotten her so quickly?

As she was leaving, Grace stopped suddenly. 'There – I almost forgot. Ben asked me to tell you that he'll be over to discuss the future of the farm with you in a day or two.'

'Tell him to sort all that out with Fergal,' Liza said hastily. She had no desire whatsoever for a tête-à-tête with her former lover. 'I trust them both.'

'Oh, I think you should understand what's going on,' Grace said in her placid way. 'It's your farm after all, your children's inheritance. Though you can indeed trust Ben. He's always been a very reliable sort of person. I'm so glad I married him. He was worth waiting for.'

Liza breathed in and out very slowly and hoped she had not shown how this remark upset her. She caught an assessing glance from her companion and wondered suddenly whether Grace suspected something and was warning her off. Surely not?

When her visitor had gone strolling back down the track, Liza left Catherine in Dinny's care and went down to the lake. She didn't think she could bear regular visits from Grace Caine.

Nick found her there later and saw at once that she was upset. 'Oh, my dear!' He took her hands. 'This is such a hard time for you. Even if you didn't love Josiah, you're all alone now and must miss his support. I wish . . .' He broke off suddenly. 'But it's too soon to speak. Only let me tell you how very much I admire you, Liza – you will let me use your first name from now on, won't you? It's how I think of you.' He broke off, hesitated, then said bitterly, 'There was another reason for my leaving England that I didn't tell you about. It was a bit like yours, actually. My parents were urging me to marry a certain young woman. Only I felt nothing for her, less than nothing. She was vain, idle, couldn't even treat a dog kindly. She would not have lasted a week out here and she didn't have half your courage.'

Liza stared at him in shock because there was no mistaking his meaning. His eyes were fixed on her with undisguised tenderness and he was holding her hand in both his. As she stared at him in shock, he raised that hand to his lips and pressed them against it in a gentle kiss.

She drew it back with a gasp, clasping it in her other hand as if to protect it. 'Mr Rawley, please, I can't—'

'Nick,' he corrected. 'Please call me Nick from now on.'

'It's too soon! I can't think of—' She broke off, feeling confused and upset. She wanted to get away but didn't want to marry again, and certainly not another man whom she didn't love, however much she liked Nick and enjoyed his company.

He nodded and clasped his own hands together loosely, letting them dangle between his legs as he continued to sit beside her. 'I know it's too soon. And if we were in England I wouldn't dream of speaking during the period of mourning, but as you've said to me many times, things are different here in Australia and – and people seem to behave more naturally with one another. Surely you've guessed how I feel about you?'

'I – I hadn't even considered—' She could not help a sudden thought that if she married him, she could leave Pendleworth and not have to watch Grace and Benedict building a life together. No, what was she thinking of? That would be very unfair to Nick.

'Think about it,' he urged, his eyes searching her face. 'Promise me you'll give me a chance to woo you at least?'

'I don't know what to say.'

He smiled. 'I'll take that as permission granted.'

She could not find an answer, and as Cathie ran up to them just then, turned in relief to her daughter.

Weeks passed and still Nick didn't speak of leaving. Life had fallen into a pleasant enough routine and the weather added to this as spring approached, such a beautiful season with wild flowers blooming everywhere in the bush in carpets of colour. Liza still felt lethargic, still wept for Benedict at night, but she was glad of Nick's company in the daytime. He was young, light-hearted, and he made her feel young again, too, in spite of her troubles. They played cards and chess – though he had to carve rough wooden figures before they could do that and then teach her the rules. Best of all, they could laugh together over small things, something she had never been able to do with Josiah.

When Benedict walked over to speak to her one day, Liza saw him coming and took refuge in her bedroom, telling Dinny she was too ill to see anyone. But she could not resist peering out of the window and noting how dejected he looked as he turned away. Well, he deserved to be dejected. She was feeling the same.

Twice Liza sent Nick up to Perth, saying he should meet people, not just stay in the country She gave him an introduction to Agnes Fenton and he stayed longer than he had planned, confessing when he returned that he had enjoyed the social round, especially as someone had lent him a pretty decent horse and they'd had some cracking rides.

'Did you miss me, then?' he teased.

'Yes.' It was out before Liza considered the implications.

'Aaaah!' His eyes twinkled down at her and when she would have turned away, annoyed at revealing her feelings, he grasped her arm and gently turned her back.

'You did miss me, didn't you?'

She shrugged. 'A little.'

'I missed you a lot. Your friend Agnes introduced me to several young ladies.' He pulled a wry face. 'But they were too like the ones back home. They didn't have your courage and honesty.'

Guilt surged through her. She hadn't been honest with him, didn't dare be honest with anyone. 'They didn't have this, either.' She patted her belly, which seemed to be growing larger by the day. She watched his smile fade. He was always a bit uncomfortable with open references to the coming baby, though at least he didn't show revulsion to her condition.

Liza had been thinking what to do for the best and this was her opportunity. 'Nick, you've spoken of visiting Sydney, seeing the rest of Australia – why don't you go and do that?'

'Because I want to be with you, that's why.'

'At the moment, it upsets you to see me in this condition – and I'm only going to get larger. Besides, I do need time to recover from Josiah's death. I know things are different here, but not that different. So I've been thinking – why don't you go on to Sydney and Melbourne, as you had planned? You can come back again in a few months, after I've had the baby – if you still want to.' She didn't think he would return, and wasn't even sure she wanted him to.

'How can I leave you alone, with no one to protect you?'

She laughed. 'I have Dinny and Fergal. Benedict and Grace are only a short walk away, and there are the Pringles in the other direction and several other families in Brookley, too. It's not nearly as lonely as it was when we first arrived.'

Nick pulled a face. He had not taken to Kitty Pringle who had set her cap at him quite blatantly, then been particularly spiteful when he made his preferences obvious.

Within the week Liza had persuaded him to leave. And without him loneliness seemed to weigh down on her. The days dragged on as her body grew heavier – and yet she still couldn't think what to do with her life after the baby had been born.

If she hadn't had Dinny, she didn't know what she'd have done. But even there she felt guilty, for she was well aware that her need was keeping Dinny and Fergal apart.

CHAPTER TWENTY-TWO

Liza's second child, a son, was born in October. She had only Dinny to help her this time, but things went well. At the first sight of the baby Liza's eyes filled with tears for she could see Benedict's features in his little face so clearly. The likeness faded within a day or two, as is often the case with new-born infants, but it left her with an increased fear that the resemblance would be obvious when he grew older and that other people would notice it.

In spite of her worries, she was delighted with the child and called him Seth.

After the birth she felt very placid and lay contentedly on the bed feeding her son with a fascinated Cathie sprawled by her side. On the second day after the birth she heard footsteps on the verandah and looked up to see Benedict standing in the doorway. Liza swallowed hard, not knowing what to do or say, then turned to Cathie. 'Go and find Dinny, love. Ask her to – to get me something to eat.'

Benedict did not speak until the child was out of hearing, then said in a low voice, 'Fergal told me about the baby. I had to come.'

'Does Grace know you're here?'

'No, of course not.' He moved forward. 'Can I see him?'

She shrugged and indicated the cot, digging her fingernails into the palms of her hand to stop herself from bursting into tears.

'Seth,' said Benedict in a hushed voice. 'I like the name.' He stood there staring down at the infant in silence, then looked across at her. 'Oh, Liza, my darling. I'm so sorry for this dreadful mess.'

'That doesn't help. And – and now you've seen the baby, you can just go back to your wife and your *other* son! It does me no good you coming here and stirring up old feelings.' She could feel tears welling in her eyes and hoped he would go before they started falling.

Benedict stared at her with love showing clearly in his face, but when she said nothing, bent to kiss his son and walked out without another word. Only after he'd left did Liza let the tears fall freely, and then found she could not stop weeping. But deep down she was glad he had come, glad he had at least seen their son, had wanted to see him.

When Cathie brought Dinny back, Liza managed to stop crying and pretended she wanted a cup of tea. But later she told her friend what had happened and wept again. 'I'm always weepy after I've had a child, it seems.'

'You have good reason.'

Dinny's hand was gentle on her shoulder and Liza laid her head against it for a moment with a sigh.

A couple of times during the first few days Dorothy came over to see if she could help but Dinny had everything under control, so they just sat and chatted, not mentioning Benedict.

'Kitty's begging me again to send her to England,' Dorothy said abruptly on the second visit. 'She wants to go desperately and is so bitter and angry that I'm thinking seriously of doing it. Only it'd cost so much!' She stared blindly out of the window. 'We manage to earn a living, Andrew and I, with the garden and the inn, but I never seem to have much spare money. He took most of my other savings and wasted them, investing them in a carting business, though Jem Davies insists he'll pay us back one day – but I doubt he'll be able to. And – and Andrew still spends what's in the till if I leave anything there, especially if people are down on their luck. I tell him we can't afford to give our money or food away, that we're poor as well, but he simply won't listen.'

'I can let you have some money if you're short – but I'm only paying for a steerage passage for Kitty.' And it wasn't for the daughter's sake Liza was making the offer.

Dorothy looked round as if to check that no one could overhear and whispered, 'It would take all I have saved to send her to England and I can't bear to be left with nothing. I'm grateful for your offer, but she won't even consider travelling steerage, insists she's not going to arrive at her Aunt Nora's stinking of poor people. She gets more selfish, not less, as she grows older, but I can't help feeling for her. She's only young and has a right to a better life than this. How is she ever to find a husband stuck out here in the bush? Andrew was so wrong to insist she come.'

Liza nodded sympathetically but privately wondered if Kitty would ever find anyone to marry her. She was quite pretty in a sharp-featured way but her expression was always sour.

Dorothy sighed. 'I'll think about your offer of help, though. I may have to accept it.' After a few moments she changed the subject. 'Have you heard from Mr Rawley since he went across to Sydney?'

'Once.'

'Is he planning to come back, do you know?'

'Maybe.' The letter she'd received had been short, penned by a man who was not good with words, for all his wealth and breeding.

'He's asked you to marry him, though?' Dorothy pressed.

Liza stared down at her son. 'Not in so many words, no. He's just said he wants to woo me when it's appropriate.'

'It might be the best thing for you now that Benedict's wife has come to live with him.'

'I suppose so. I can't seem to think clearly yet. And there's no hurry to make a decision, is there?' She had been hurried into marrying Josiah, and wasn't going to be rushed again.

When Dorothy got home she found Andrew out working in his beloved garden, even though he hadn't been feeling well that morning. Inside the house, Kitty was staring listlessly into space.

Dorothy went to put on her pinafore. 'Did the bread rise well?'

'What? Oh, it wasn't bad, but you know I don't make it as well as you do. I made an apple pie, though.' She jerked away from her mother's kiss. 'You had no need to go looking after *her*. She can manage perfectly well on her own because she always finds someone to help her – usually the nearest man.' And Kitty flung out of the house.

Dorothy sighed and began to tie the strings of her pinafore, but dropped them at a scream from outside. As her daughter called to her to come quickly, she picked up the bread knife to defend herself with and ran out, only to let the knife fall on the boards of the verandah. Her daughter was kneeling beside Andrew, who was lying motionless among his early lettuces. 'Oh, no!' moaned Dorothy, rushing over. 'Don't let him be dead!' She knelt beside him and breathed a sigh of relief as she found a pulse.

'What's wrong with him?'

'I don't know. Can you help me carry him inside?'

They were both surprised by how light he was.

'He's lost weight,' Dorothy whispered. 'Why didn't I notice?'

'Because you're too busy working from dawn to dusk!' snapped her daughter, with a return of her old sharpness.

It was a while before Andrew regained consciousness and then he seemed dazed, as if he didn't quite understand what was happening around him.

'You'll have to go for the doctor, Kitty,' Dorothy said abruptly. 'I'll help you harness the horse.'

'I can do that myself. You stay with Father.' The girl went out without her usual fuss and soon there was the sound of the horse clopping down the track with the little cart rattling behind it.

The doctor was away and did not come until the following morning. Andrew was querulous, but still weak and had made no attempt to get up. He responded to the doctor's bracing greeting with a scowl and his voice was slurred when he tried to speak.

Dorothy waited outside for a private word after the examination. 'Is he going to be all right? He seems very vague.'

The doctor patted her hand. 'That's in the hands of the Lord, but I doubt he'll ever recover his old vigour. It's a seizure of some sort, I'm afraid.'

Panic filled Dorothy and she could not hold back a soft whimper of distress.

The doctor backed away from her hastily. 'Must be off. Other calls to make.'

'What are we going to do?' she asked. 'How can we manage without Andrew's work?'

'Trust in the Lord,' he repeated, which was his stock phrase in such circumstances. When she began to weep he left without asking for payment. Sometimes the most unsuitable people came out here to settle. You needed strength to clear and farm land, and some money behind you for the bad times. Pringle had been too old for all this hard work and had not been a well man for some time. The doctor had noticed a slight tinge of blue to the fellow's lips sometimes when they met at church and had drawn his own conclusions.

That same afternoon two travellers stopped at the inn and, since her mother was upstairs feeding her father, Kitty went outside to greet them. They were both well dressed but not gentlemen by any means. Quite good-looking, though. She made her position here clear, as always. 'Welcome to my family's inn. May I serve you with something?'

'Aye. A drink of beer if you have some, lass, then a meal.'

'I'll get you a jug of beer. We have some stew if that'll suit, with fresh bread and a piece of apple pie, perhaps, to finish?'

The burlier of the two nodded. 'That'd suit us just fine.'

'I'm afraid my father's ill, so you'll have to tend your own horses, but we can sell you some feed.' Kitty showed them where everything was, surprised they didn't unsaddle their mounts, just left the poor things standing under the rough shelter. They must be in a hurry to leave. When they had fed and watered the horses, she led the way inside and indicated seats as if she were greeting a guest in her aunt's house.

As they sat, hardly saying a word to one another, she watched them covertly. The burly one looked older than the other and she didn't like the expression on his face, not at all. Brutal was the only word for it. The one who looked younger and had done most of the talking was slim and far better looking, to her mind, in spite of needing a bath and a shave. He had smiled at her a couple of times as she measured out the horses' feed, but Kitty hadn't smiled back because she didn't want him taking liberties. As she drew a jug of beer from the barrel, she wrinkled her nose in disgust and scowled down at it. How she hated the stink of this stuff!

A voice right behind her said, 'Careful! You'll spill it!' and she jerked in shock.

The younger man took the jug from her, holding it steady under the tap. 'Let me see to that, miss. It doesn't seem the sort of job a young lady like yourself should be asked to do.'

She felt flustered. His body was blocking the way, so she could only stand close to him as he expertly drew a jug.

'There,' he said with a smile. 'I haven't lost my touch.' He handed it to her, winked and walked back to his companion.

Taking a deep breath, Kitty set the jug and two glasses on a tray and carried them across to the rough scrubbed table. 'I'll – um – go and heat up the stew.'

'Good big helpings, mind,' called the burly man. 'We're hungry.'

She took the opportunity to ask, 'Are you travelling south?'

'What business is that of yours? You go and get us that food.'

Kitty flushed and backed away.

'My brother always gets grumpy when he's hungry,' the man who had helped her called across the room. 'I apologise for his rudeness.' He dug his brother in the ribs.

'And *he* always likes to talk softly to the ladies,' countered the burly man with a scowl. 'You'd best be ignoring his blandishments if you know what's good for you.'

Kitty went across the yard to stir the stew and swing it over the hottest part of the fire. Remembering the harsh expression on the older man's face, she shivered. There was something about him that made her feel nervous and she'd be glad to see the back of him. Afraid of angering him, she rushed back, cut some pieces of bread and set them out before the men.

'What's your name, then?'

The friendly one's gaze was openly admiring, but there was nothing you could take offence at and she found herself smiling back at him, enjoying his admiration. 'Pringle. My parents own this inn.'

'Talks like a lady, but doesn't live like one!' the other mocked, glancing round.

'Oh, shut your face, will you, Niall! It wouldn't hurt you to remember your manners.'

But the mood was broken. Kitty left them to bicker and

went to stir the stew carefully, making sure it didn't catch on the now blazing fire. She ladled big helpings on to plates, deciding to charge them extra for it because they didn't look short of a penny or two.

While they ate, she kept an eye on them, something they had learned to do with all customers, wiping the small counter unnecessarily and pretending to tidy the ale pots. They shovelled the food into their mouths without any signs of table manners. Pigs! When they had finished, she went across to ask if they'd like another helping.

'You mentioned apple pie?'

'Yes.'

'We'll have some of that, then.'

All the time she served them, the younger brother kept watching her, smiling at her occasionally. Usually she gave such men short shrift, because she didn't intend to waste herself on a common working man. But there was something about this one that attracted her, she had to admit. At that thought she clicked her tongue in exasperation at her own stupidity. You could easily get taken in by a good-looking face and then where would you be? Slaving in some god-forsaken settlement like Brookley for the rest of your life with a house full of brats, that's where. Well, she intended to get home to her aunt and find herself an English husband, a gentleman, though she had not yet sunk so low as to travel steerage, whatever anyone said.

She'd been searching for her mother's savings but so far hadn't found the new hiding place. When she did, though, she'd take what she needed and be off, because if she had to endure this place for much longer, she'd go mad.

Fingers snapped in front of her face and Kitty came out of her reverie with a start. 'Oh, sorry!'

'How much, love?'

The younger man paid what she asked, then added a coin, accompanied by another of those smiles. 'This is for you. To cheer you up. I don't like to see a pretty woman looking so unhappy.'

More tears welled at the sympathy in his voice.

'Are things that bad, love?'

'Yes, they are! I hate it here. It's like – like being buried alive.'

'Aye, I suppose it would be for a lass like you. No gentleman friend to brighten the evenings?'

'No friends of any sort.' Her voice came out husky with unshed tears. She wasn't used to sympathy.

'Eh,' his voice was soft and he caressed her cheek briefly with one rough fingertip, 'life can be a bugger sometimes, can't it?'

She looked up at him, feeling confused, wishing suddenly he were more of a gentleman. As he stepped back, she tried to return his smile but failed. 'Safe travelling.'

'Oh, we're not going far. Mebbe we'll see one another again. Would you like that?'

And Kitty, sharp-tongued Kitty, blushed. 'Yes.'

The other man gave his brother a shove towards the door, scowling. 'Which way to the Ludlams', miss?'

Wondering what they wanted with Liza, she indicated the direction they should take and told them where to turn off to Pendleworth – a name that seemed to amuse both of them – then watched them mount their horses. As she cleared up, her mind was in turmoil. Who were they?

The younger man had glanced over his shoulder and smiled at her again. He had such a warm smile that she raised one hand to wave, then grew angry with herself for being stupid about someone she'd never see again. She banged the dishes around, muttering to herself, but nothing drove the picture of the man out of her head.

Not even her father taking a turn for the worse that afternoon.

The day started badly for Liza and it didn't improve. Seth was fractious and woke early. By afternoon his crying had set Cathie off grizzling, too. Liza stood by the door for a moment's break from the noise, then braced herself to go back inside and attend to her screaming son.

Before she had settled Seth, Cathie fell over a wooden toy Benedict had made for her, the sight of which never failed to upset Liza, and began to wail even more loudly than her brother, so Dinny picked her up. The two women didn't hear anyone approaching. The first they knew was when someone stood in the doorway and cast a dark shadow across the room.

When Liza looked up, she froze, blinking hard because she was sure she was seeing things. But the figure didn't go away and as she realised that it was definitely Niall standing there, she found it hard to breathe. It wasn't possible. Oh, heavens, it couldn't be them!

But it was.

'Well,' he said, with the malicious smile that was peculiarly his own, 'we've come to the right place, then. You've grown up, little sister, but I'd still know you anywhere.'

She couldn't speak. Not a single word. Could hardly draw breath, her chest felt so tight.

'Not got a welcome for your brothers?' He took a step forward. 'We've come a long way to find you, girl. We're expecting a really *warm* welcome.' But his eyes were hard and even more calculating than they had been when he was younger.

Dermott gave him a push and followed him into the room, smiling at her more normally. 'You look well, Liza lass.' He cast a cursory glance at Seth, and saw Cathie peering from behind her mother. 'Yours, are they?'

'Yes.'

'Where's the husband, then?'

She swallowed hard, ignoring the question. 'How did you find me?'

It was Niall who replied. 'You wrote to Mam. We came across the letter after the funeral. You didn't say the exact address, but we found you easy enough.'

Only one of his remarks got through to her and Liza's voice came out as a hoarse whisper as she said, '*Mam's dead? When? How?*'

Dermott's voice was gentler than his brother's. 'Six months ago it'd be now. She just faded away, Nancy said. Da found her dead next to him in bed one morning. We heard about it from a fellow as knew where we were and got back in time for the funeral. Da gave her a good send-off, I'll grant him that, but he got rotten drunk afterwards.'

Ignoring Niall, who was wandering round fingering her possessions, Liza stumbled towards the nearest chair and collapsed into it, covering her eyes with her forearm and letting the tears flow. 'I hoped – I really wanted to see her again.'

Dermott shrugged. 'Not likely, was it, with you living here?'

She raised her head to glare at him and say with something of her old spirit, 'I could have gone back for a visit, couldn't I? Ships sail both ways, you know.'

Niall came round to stand in front of her and demand, 'Where is he?'

'Who?'

'Your bloody husband, that's who. The rich one. You did well marrying a Ludlam – even one like him.'

Liza looked up quickly at that. 'What do you mean?'

'A Nancy boy. Think folk didn't know about him?' Niall chuckled. 'He was well-known in certain parts of Manchester.' He leaned forward, thrusting his face at her. 'I reckon we know enough about your fellow to get a generous payment out of him.'

She laughed, a thin sound that ended in a hiccup. 'You're too late.'

'What do you mean, too late?'

'Josiah's dead. He died a few weeks ago – a real hero, saved our daughter's life in a fire.'

Niall swore comprehensively, then stopped and stared at her thoughtfully. 'If he's dead, who gets the money?'

Her heart sank as she realised where this was leading. 'It's not money that's left, it's land. You don't think old Saul Ludlam gave him *money* when he sent him out here, do you? He was an old miser, as I found out to my cost.'

The two men exchanged glances, then Niall picked her up by her bodice and shook her. 'You're not answering my question. Who – gets – the land?'

In the bedroom, Dinny decided to go for help and slid the window gently open. The two men heard the noise and since Niall was still holding Liza, Dermott ran across the room and flung open the door. Dinny was already climbing out of the window. He dragged her back by her skirt, though she struggled and kicked against him.

'Be still, you stupid bitch!' he roared, clouting her across the head. 'Now, who the hell are you?'

'She's my maid,' Liza said quickly.

'Shut up, you. I want *her* to answer. Can she speak English?'

Dinny said, 'Speak – little bit.'

Cathie, who had been staring at the two strangers, suddenly launched herself across the room, beating her tiny fists against Dermott's leg and screeching at him to let go of Dinny. He laughed and shoved her away with one hand so that she fell over backwards. 'Proper little firebrand, you are. What's your name, pet?'

She began to sob and when Dinny reached out to pick her up, he let her take the child.

'So you've got a maid now,' he mocked. 'My, you have come up in the world, little sister. Pity you can't afford a proper girl to help you, though, instead of a black one who can't even talk properly.'

'I've come up and gone back down again,' she said, avoiding Dinny's eyes. 'Now that my husband's dead, I don't know how I'm going to manage.'

Niall laughed and shoved her into a chair. 'I do. You've got two brothers who are going to manage everything for you – until we sell the land – though after that you'll have to manage on your own, I'm afraid.' He eyed her up and down. 'You're pretty enough to find another gentleman protector, mind, and we might help you do just that. We can get more money for your services than you ever would.'

'I'm not signing my land over to you!'

'Aren't you? I think we have the means to persuade you here.' As his eyes lingered on Cathie and Seth, an expression of horror crept over her face. He chuckled. 'And to make sure neither you nor her,' he jerked his head towards Dinny, 'go telling tales to anyone else, we'll keep one of the dear little children with us at all times. We are their uncles, after all. Fond of kids, we are. If they behave themselves. Tell *her* that. Make sure she understands.'

So Liza told Dinny, slowly and loudly, not to go out, not to tell anyone about her brothers.

Silence followed, then Niall asked for water and she poured him a drink. Neither of the two women said anything, but each took one child. Liza was still desperately trying to think of a way to let Dinny escape and go for help. She wouldn't put anything past her brothers, including murder, but maybe if she pretended Dinny hadn't understood her instructions properly, they wouldn't realise what was happening till help came. She had not forgotten how ruthless these two could be – nor had she forgiven Niall for handing her over to Teddy Marshall that day.

Dermott broke the silence. 'Tell us, little sister, did your dear departed husband have any booze? That thin beer they serve down the road doesn't satisfy a man.'

'You went to the Pringles'?' Would they realise something was wrong?

Niall answered. 'We went to that little inn – well, some might call it an inn. Poor sort of place if you ask me and only a sulky, stuck-up bitch to serve you. Pretty, though, or she was when she smiled at our dear Dermott here. She didn't smile at me – not that I wanted her to.'

Dermott's expression softened a little. 'Told us her father was ill and her mother was looking after him. All she needs is a good rogering, that one, and she'll brighten up a bit. If we stay around long enough, I wouldn't mind being the one to give it her either.'

He had always been a ladies' man, Liza remembered, and they seemed attracted to him, too, though she couldn't understand why. He wasn't as bad as Niall, or at least he hadn't been in the old days, but he was still a nasty piece of work.

She rocked Seth and shushed him as he started to cry, still trying desperately to think of some way to let Dinny escape. But they were big solid men, very much in charge, and one of them stayed near the open door at all times. She cast a quick despairing glance at her friend then forced herself to weep. Heaven knew, she had little trouble producing tears.

Niall seemed to find it amusing, but Liza was glad because she wanted to seem weak. She didn't feel weak, though, only very determined. She was not going to give her inheritance away, if she had to kill them to keep it. That thought made her suddenly remember the gun. Josiah had taught her to use it and they kept it loaded and ready in case of vagrants, but hidden behind the door. The door was open, so of course it didn't show.

If she could get it, she would threaten to shoot them and order them to leave. But what if they wouldn't go? Could she actually shoot someone? She wasn't at all sure of that. She might hit Dinny or the children by mistake. All she knew was, if she got a chance she'd take it.

Dusk fell with its usual suddenness, and Liza, who had been sitting with her back to the others, feeding her son, got up to light a lamp. Just one tonight, in case she got a chance to grab the gun.

'Food,' Niall said, his voice harsh in the shadowed room. 'What have you got to eat, little sister?'

'There's a piece of kangaroo steak. One of the neighbours brought it over for us yesterday.'

'That sounds a bit better than bloody stew.'

She moved towards the back of the house.

'Where are you going?'

'Outside to the kitchen. Though the fire will be out. We don't cook inside the houses here. It's too hot.' He followed her outside and stood watching. Liza worked as slowly as she knew how, giving Cathie some bread and biting back angry words when Niall grabbed the loaf and tore a piece off for himself.

'Real men need a lot of good food,' he said, patting his belly. 'And other things, too. I daresay that maid of yours has all the usual equipment a woman needs to satisfy a man. She's nice and plump.'

Liza froze where she stood.

He roared with laughter at her expression, but something told her he hadn't been joking. As she cooked, he roamed up and down, boasting of some of his exploits, of things he had stolen, people he had attacked and his regret that Manchester had grown too dangerous for him as he got better known. From what he said, she realised it was the other criminals he was fleeing from, not the law which he seemed to hold in great scorn.

When the food was ready she carried it inside, not looking towards the place where the gun was hidden. Surely he didn't think he'd be able to keep her and Dinny quiet for weeks? Or months even. It could take a long time to sell newly settled land here.

While the two men made a hearty meal, Liza picked at some

food and Dinny pretended to serve them, getting things wrong on purpose to inconvenience the men.

'Is she really that stupid?' Niall asked once. 'I don't know why you put up with her, I really don't.'

Dinny said nothing, just started to clear the table. While she was passing Niall, he grabbed hold of her, his hands roaming over her body. 'She's built like a woman, though,' he said to Dermott. 'I'll try her out first.'

'No!' Liza tried to get between him and her friend, but he knocked her backwards with a quick swipe of his arm. She cannoned into Dermott and knocked him off the stool. He lay on the floor laughing. She could not imagine a better opportunity, so went for the shotgun.

She had it in her hand before either man realised what she was doing because Dinny distracted their attention by kneeing Niall in the crotch and getting away from him.

Roaring in anger, he grabbed for her, missed, then noticed Liza and the gun for the first time. For a moment he stopped moving, eyes darting here and there as he assessed the situation.

'Stand still!' she ordered.

He laughed and began to walk towards her. 'You wouldn't dare fire that at your own brother. If you even know how.'

She gulped. 'I will fire. Stay back.' She didn't want to pull the trigger, just wanted them to leave.

'I dare you.' He laughed again.

With only a couple of paces between them, she aimed and when he still kept on coming, pulled the trigger. The noise seemed deafening. She hadn't been holding the gun properly and it recoiled against her shoulder, bouncing her backwards against the door.

When Niall fell to the ground at her feet and did not stir, she could not at first move, just pressed back against the wood, breathing with sounds that were close to sobs.

She saw that Dinny had picked up a gnarled root from among the firewood and had gone to stand protectively in front of the bedroom where the children had been put to sleep.

Dermott, who had stayed on the floor, swore and started to stand up.

Liza forced herself to point the gun at him, trying not to

let him see that her hands were trembling. 'Stay where you are. There's another barrel still loaded.'

He stopped moving, his face dark with fury. 'Aren't you even going to help him?' he demanded. 'Just shoot a man and let him lie bleeding, is that the sort you are now?'

Since her oldest brother still hadn't moved, Liza took a quick glance in his direction, the first she had dared, because as long as he hadn't moved she hadn't even wanted to see his wounds. Nausea swamped her for a moment and she nearly dropped the gun, because where his face had been was a red mass of torn flesh. Blood was splattered around him and when she looked down there was some on her skirt, too.

Dermott suddenly lunged towards her.

Dinny darted forward to lash out with the chunk of wood. He fell to his knees, groaning.

'Hit him again if he moves,' Liza ordered. 'And make it harder this time.'

'I'd love to,' Dinny said.

'What about Niall?' he asked. 'Christ, you have to do something! Help him, you stinking bitch!'

'You help him. But you'd better not stand up or I'll fire.' Liza took a couple of steps away, swallowing hard on the greasy nausea that kept threatening to overwhelm her. She mustn't give in to it, for her children's sake.

Dermott crawled across the floor, keeping one eye on her, felt for a heartbeat and stared down, not moving or speaking.

'Well?' she asked. 'There's some water outside and—'

In a hoarse whisper he said, 'You've killed him.' It looked as if he would leap up and charge her then but Dinny darted forward, brandishing the gnarled root, and he stayed where he was.

'You should kill this one, too,' Dinny said. 'I'll shoot him for you, if you don't want to do it.'

Dermott edged away from her but stayed down. His eyes kept going to his brother, then back to Liza.

She shuddered. She would fire again if she had to, but she was hoping desperately that she wouldn't be forced to do that. 'I didn't mean to kill him. I didn't *want* to fire.' She had to force the words through the sobs that kept threatening. 'Why did you two come here anyway? Why couldn't you leave me alone? Hadn't you already done me enough harm?'

His eyes held hers as he said in a low, furious voice, 'You'll pay for this, Liza Docherty. One day I'll make sure you pay.' Hatred had twisted his face into ugliness. When he looked down again at Niall's body, that changed briefly to sorrow.

After a few moments of silence she took a deep breath and said, 'Tie him up, Dinny. We'll send for the policeman from Brookley.'

Dinny picked up a sheet from the laundry pile, slashed it with a knife and ripped it into lengths. After tying some pieces together, she moved carefully towards Dermott, who was still standing near his brother's body.

'Lie down on the floor and put your hands behind you!' Liza ordered.

Slowly he began to kneel down, but when Dinny tried to bind his hands together, he exploded into action, rolling aside quickly and pushing her towards Liza before they realised what was happening. As they struggled to get their balance, he shoved them away and hurtled through the door.

Terrified he would find some way to hurt her children, Liza followed him outside and aimed the gun at him. She could still have shot – and hit – him though she was not close enough to hurt him seriously, but she didn't want another death on her conscience so merely stood there, contenting herself with shouting. 'Take your horses and get out of here. And don't you ever come back, Dermott Docherty!' She stayed in the doorway, gun at the ready, watching him fumble with the horses' reins, seeing him glance towards her several times – though how she stayed upright she didn't know because the horror of what had happened was making everything waver around her. She could sense Dinny behind her and that helped a bit.

When Dermott was mounted, he stared at them from across the clearing. 'I'll be back one day, you bitch.' Then he galloped off down the track.

Unable even to hold up the gun any longer, Liza sagged against the door frame.

'You had no choice but to fight them,' Dinny whispered softly. 'No choice.'

'Niall is – he is dead, isn't he?' She couldn't bear the thought of examining that bloody mess of a face.

'Yes.'

'Are the children still asleep?'

Dinny walked across, opened the bedroom door and nodded.

'Then please will you go and fetch Benedict? I need him! Tell them there's – there's been an accident.' Tears were raining down Liza's face and she was shaking.

'You'll keep hold of the gun?'

'Yes.'

As Dinny set off running down the track, Liza went indoors and stood pressed against the wall, with the door to the bedroom open so that she could keep an eye on the children. She kept hold of the loaded gun and tried not to look at the corpse of her eldest brother sprawled near the door. It was the longest hour of her life.

Only when Benedict and Dinny came into the house did she let the gun fall and allow herself to collapse into his arms.

CHAPTER TWENTY-THREE

Dermott rode off, leading Niall's horse. Just before the track twisted out of sight between the trees, he slowed down and turned round. When he saw Liza staring at him, still holding the shotgun at the ready, he rode on with a muttered curse.

Further along the track he paused to listen for pursuit, wondering if the bitch had sent the black woman for help. Was there any to be had near such an isolated farm? When he heard nothing, he sat for a moment with his head bowed, trying to come to terms with what had happened.

Niall was dead! *Dead!* He shuddered, remembering the bloody mess that had once been his brother's face, and for a moment contemplated going back, circling round the farm and making Liza pay for what she had done. The thought was sweet. But no, she still had the bloody gun. When had she learned to shoot? Or to stand up for herself like that?

Anyway, if he killed her – as the shrew fully deserved – he would be the one pursued by the law. He wondered whether to find a policeman and report *her* for murder – they must have policemen in Australia – but shook his head and abandoned that thought. It went against the grain to have anything to do with the law. And besides, she'd know any policemen round here, so they'd be on her side. No, if there were revenge to be had, he'd see to it himself.

'One day,' he vowed softly, 'I'll be back, Liza Docherty! And I'll make you very sorry indeed, believe me.'

He nudged the horse into action again and the other one followed, still laden with his brother's things for they had not bothered to unpack the saddle bags. What was he to do now? For a while Dermott's mind went blank because it was usually Niall who decided such things, then he took a few deep, shuddering breaths and muttered, 'Think, damn you!' He had money, his own and Niall's, too. On that thought he reined in the horse and jumped off, going to rummage through his brother's saddle bags in the fitful moonlight.

When he found some money, gold sovereigns and other coins, he grunted in relief. There would be more in Niall's pockets, of course, but he could not go back for that. The bitch would get it all. They had both carried their money in two or three separate lots, so there was probably another stash hidden away somewhere among his brother's things. He'd check through them properly later. He hefted the soft leather drawstring pouch in one hand, then shoved it into his pocket and stuffed the rest of the things back into the saddlebag anyhow. Without Niall's gambling and rash spending, at least this money would last a lot longer. But that was no consolation.

He sucked in a painful breath as he kicked his horse into action again. What the hell was he going to do with himself now? Tears suddenly spurted and ran down his cheeks, leaving trails of moisture for the night air to chill. Dermott could not remember the last time he had acted on his own initiative in anything more important than choosing a woman or a new neckerchief. It had been Niall who worked out where to get more money, who to diddle, which houses to burgle – and he'd been good at it, too. Slowly they'd begun to save money, and if it hadn't been for Niall getting on the wrong side of a couple of important men one night when he was drunk – men who boasted that they killed anyone who offended them – the Docherty Boys, as they were commonly known, would not have had to leave Manchester in such a hurry.

He sighed and wiped away the tears. What he'd wanted to do for a while was go into a real business and turn respectable. He'd always fancied having a big house and servants to wait on him – and a pretty wife to do his bidding. He should have insisted on settling down in another English town instead of coming on this mad chase to Australia.

Scowling as he looked along the path ahead of him, he let the horses slow right down. What the hell was he going to do, though? He and Niall had planned to see how much money they could blackmail out of Ludlam – he should have been worth quite a bit – then go on to the goldfields in Victoria and fleece some more fools. But they hadn't realised how far

Melbourne was from Perth, that it'd mean another sodding voyage on a stinking ship. He sucked in air through a gap where he'd had a tooth knocked out when he was a lad. He might still go to Melbourne, do what Niall had wanted this one last time. Why not?

He sighed and slumped in the saddle, rubbing his wet face again. He hated being alone and always had. If he was in a town now he'd go and find himself a woman. You could forget your troubles nicely in a woman's soft body.

When he came to the inn where they'd had a meal, he stopped and stared at the darkened building, half inclined to wake the owners up and ask for a room, because he was exhausted. No, better not do that. He was still too close to his sister's. It wasn't safe to stop. He remembered the determined look on Liza's face as she had threatened to shoot him as well if he ever came back. She'd do it, too, the jade.

Another memory replaced that of Liza – the young woman who had served him at this very inn. She hadn't liked his sister, either. She hadn't liked anything hereabouts from what she'd said, the poor little biddy. He'd noticed how unhappy she was. No wonder! Who would want to be stuck here in the middle of all these sodding trees? Not him, that was sure. Give him a proper town, with streets and people walking about any day!

As he moved forward, he saw a light shining from the back of the house and on a sudden impulse slid down from his horse, tied it to a tree and went to see who was up at that hour! What he saw had him transfixed. The young woman had just taken a bath and was standing up in the tub, letting the water drip off her – and she had as bonny a body as he'd ever seen. Long white limbs, with just the slightest swell to her belly and firm young breasts. He felt a tightening in his groin at the mere sight of her and edged forward to get a better view.

As she reached for the towel, he sucked in a long breath and eased it out again slowly. It'd been a long time since he'd had a woman.

When she was out of the water, wrapped in the towel, he grinned and took a chance, rapping on the window then sliding it down gently because the silly fool hadn't even locked it.

Kitty squeaked and looked round in alarm.

'It's only me,' he whispered.

She clutched the towel round her, gaping. 'What are you doing here at this hour? Go away!'

'I'm leaving. Our dear sister didn't make us very welcome, I'm afraid.'

'Sister?'

'Aye. Liza Ludlam she's called now.'

'Her!'

'A right harridan she's turned into, hasn't she?'

Kitty stared beyond him, trying to see into the darkness. 'Where's your brother?'

'Dead.'

As she goggled at him, her mouth opened and shut, but no sound came out. Then she gasped, 'What do you mean, dead?'

'She killed him. Our beloved Liza shot her own brother.' Dermott swung one leg over the window sill and stayed there, keeping very still because his prey was nearly panicking and he didn't want her calling out for help. 'She threatened to kill me, too, but I got away.'

'I don't believe you.' Then she looked more closely at his face and said in a tone of surprise, 'You've been crying.'

'Of course I have. My brother's lying dead with his face blown off.' He willed a tear or two and they obliged, trickling down his cheeks.

Kitty sniffed in annoyance. 'That doesn't explain what you're doing here. And you'd better get out before I call for my parents. If you want a room, go and knock on the front door. Or there's a magistrate in Mandurah if you want to report your sister for murder.'

Seeing her eyes glaze over with pleasure at the thought of that, Dermott took the opportunity to edge his other leg over the sill without her noticing. 'No, I can't do that. Whatever she's done, she's still my sister. I can't turn her in to the police.'

'But—'

He covered his eyes with one arm as if nearly overcome and saw her take a hesitant step nearer. He managed a sob, thinking, *Come on, little bird! You're just what I need to take my mind off it all, Come closer.*

And she did.

He grabbed her and covered her mouth with his hand in one

swift action. As she struggled and made panic-stricken noises in her throat, he wooed her with words. 'I'm only doing this to keep you from crying out. Sure, you're the prettiest thing I've seen in a long, weary time.' He let his voice go softer. 'I'm not going to hurt you, lass, I promise, but if you make a noise your mother will come to investigate. You don't really want her to see us like this, do you? You're only dressed in a towel. She might get the wrong idea about what's been going on.' When Kitty stopped struggling, he whispered, 'See, I'll uncover your mouth.' He did so, watchful for that sudden intake of air that foretold a cry, ready to grab her again quickly.

Kitty didn't move an inch, didn't utter a sound, but her breathing had become rapid and shallow, and she was trembling against his arm. *Ah,* he thought with immense satisfaction, *you're more than ready for the catching, little bird.*

He cuddled her against him and whispered in heart-broken tones. 'I just want to – to hold someone who's alive and warm. Me and Niall, we've been close all our lives, and I can't believe—' He sobbed, then rested his head against her bare shoulder.

She took him in her arms and held him close, stroking his hair. 'Oh, you poor thing. How awful for you.'

He leaned against her with a sigh, then began to stroke her arm. When he kissed her, she stiffened, but he pulled away a little and said, 'Ah, you're so beautiful!' which made her relax again.

It took him a while to edge her across to the bed, longer still to kiss her into such a state that she'd let him touch her body. But it was worth it. Such a soft, white body it was, and so responsive to his caresses. When he started to press the act to its necessary conclusion, of course she changed her mind, and he had to hold one hand across her mouth to prevent her crying out. But hell, once he was in, she enjoyed it nearly as much as he did!

He had been right. He always was where women were concerned. This little virgin had been very ripe for it.

It was a few minutes before Kitty recovered enough to realise what they had done, then she panicked and he had to kiss her quickly to keep her quiet. 'Shh, now, little bird,' he murmured in her ear. 'Shh, now. Just let me hold you.'

Tears were trickling down her cheeks. 'What have I done? What have I *done*?'

'You've done what you were made for – and done it well, too.' Dermott had never been the first with a woman before and found he rather liked that. As they lay there with him stroking her hair, he took a quick decision. 'Look, why don't you come away with me? You know you hate living here.'

'Come away with you?'

'Yes. I'm going to Melbourne, to the goldfields.'

Kitty shook her head immediately. 'No. I want to go back to England. If I had the money, I'd have gone before now. My mother has some saved, but I haven't been able to find it.'

Dermott's interest was aroused. 'A lot of money?'

She gave a bitter laugh. 'No. My father's spent most of what we had – or rather lost it. He's a fool. But there's enough left to get me back to England, I do know that. She hides what she can save, has to. If she doesn't, my father takes it off her and spends it.'

It didn't sound like rich pickings to Dermott. Still, every little helped. 'You'd be poor when you got to England, though. What were you going to do then?'

'Go to my aunt's. She's not poor and she has no children.'

'Why not come to Melbourne first, then we can both go back to England – and with plenty of money in our pockets, beholden to no one?' If she was this good in bed now, she'd be even better with a bit of practice. He'd enjoy teaching her. It'd keep his mind off things.

'You mean, get married?'

He smiled as she lay there on his shoulder. Married! Why get married when you could have what you needed for free?

When he did not answer, Kitty said, 'You don't want to marry me! You were just using me!' Her voice was rising again.

'Shh, my little lovebird. Shhh! Of course I want to marry you. I just didn't think a young lady like you would want to marry a rough fellow like me.'

She raised herself on one elbow then and stared at him, the softness gone from her face. 'And do you have enough money to get us to Melbourne?'

'Oh, yes. And to set us up in a business of some sort when we get there, as well.'

303

'Aren't you going after the gold?' She'd heard so much about the various goldfields, about the fortunes to be made there.

'What, break my back digging! No, my pretty little inno‐cent, there's more money to be made fleecing the ones who're daft enough to do the hard work. You'll see.'

They lay there for a while, then he eased himself on to her again. She tried half-heartedly to resist, then sighed and gave in – enjoyed it, too.

Afterwards, feeling a lot better about the world, he asked idly, 'Where do you think your ma has put the money?'

'She had it in the back of one of her bedroom drawers till my father found it, but then she moved it. I don't know where. I've been looking for ages.'

'In the kitchen?'

Kitty made a scornful noise in her throat. 'You've seen what kitchens are like here – they're just outside shelters, with nowhere to hide anything. And I've been through all the things in the pantry. Several times. It's not in there.'

'It'll be in the parlour then.' He was sure of it. That was the favourite place for honest fools. 'Show me the parlour and I'll find the money for you while you pack your things.' He knew all the likely hiding places.

Two hours later, he helped her climb out of the bedroom window, took her roll of clothes and her bag of bits and pieces, and fixed them on the back of his horse, then led her away through the night. She didn't beat his ears senseless like some women would have done, just sat on her horse as if she were part of it, looking triumphant.

He grinned across at her as they rode side by side along a wider stretch of track. 'You won't be sorry you came with me, lass.'

Kitty stared at him solemnly. 'I'll make sure I'm not. I'll help you make money and I'll be a good wife to you, Dermott Docherty.' She broke off as he suddenly dissolved into helpless laughter. 'What's the matter?'

'I've suddenly realised I don't even know your name.'

She gave him her proper name. She wasn't going to be Kitty any more. A lot of things were going to change from now on. 'My name's Christina,' she said firmly. 'And it'll be Christina Docherty before we do that again.'

His laughter faded as he looked at her. 'Well, my girl, I'm beginning to think it's a good thing we met. Good for both of us.' Hell, he might even marry her and get himself a son or two as well as working towards respectability. Why not? You were a long time dead and what was left of Niall now? Nothing, that's what. But he'd wait till she was expecting. He wasn't going to buy a pig in a poke.

Edging his mount across, he reached out to her in the moonlight. For a moment their hands touched, then the track grew narrower and he took the lead again. But she had smiled at him, and she was very pretty when she smiled. He'd have to wait and see what she was like to live with as well. It didn't do to rush into marriage. That was the one thing about which he and Niall had differed. When he got married, it would be permanent, like the priest said: Till death us do part.

Benedict took Niall's body away to bury and Dinny cleared up the mess. Having wept herself to a standstill, Liza lay on the bed with a puzzled Cathie cuddled in her arms and Seth sleeping peacefully in his cradle beside her. When she woke towards dawn Benedict had left, the doors and windows were locked and Dinny was dozing in a chair by the kitchen table, with her head resting on her arms and the shotgun propped within reach.

Liza stood in the doorway of her bedroom for a moment, then as Dinny stirred and looked up at her, asked, 'What have you done with the body?' She had to know.

'Benedict took it away. He said it'd be best if we didn't know where he'd hidden it.' She came across to hug her friend. 'Are you feeling better now?'

'No, I feel terrible. I k-keep seeing him fall – seeing his face afterwards.' She put her forefinger sideways into her mouth and bit hard on it to prevent herself from giving way to the emotions that were churning inside her. 'Do I look any different?'

Dinny was puzzled. 'Why should you?'

'Because I killed someone.'

'You didn't mean to kill him – and you were doing it to save me.'

They looked at one another solemnly.

'No, you don't look any different at all,' Dinny said softly. 'And I'm grateful to you.'

'I couldn't let him do that to you. I – I know what it's like.' Liza shuddered as she slumped down on a chair. 'Do you think Dermott will go to the magistrate?' There was silence for a moment then she answered her own question. 'No, of course he won't. He hates the police.' She bowed her head. 'He said Mam was dead. I didn't even know. I used to picture her sometimes – doing the cooking, cleaning up, telling Kieran off. I can't believe that I'll never see her again.'

Suddenly they heard someone approaching, riding down the track towards the farm. Liza flew for the gun and Dinny grabbed the chunk of wood she'd set in a convenient place. But when the rider came into sight, they saw it was Tom, a man from nearby Brookley, and both relaxed a little. Until Liza said, 'Isn't that the Pringles' horse he's riding?'

Dinny came to stand beside her in the doorway. 'Yes.'

When Tom got to the verandah he didn't dismount, just said baldly, 'Mrs Pringle's sent to ask for your help. Her husband died in the night and the daughter's run off.'

The two women looked at one another aghast and Liza said in a shocked voice, 'Andrew dead! Oh, no! We must go to her.' She looked up at the rider. 'Will you wait for us, Tom?'

'Aye. I'll harness the cart for you, shall I?' In such a small community they all knew what sort of transport their neighbours had, and knew most of each other's possessions by sight, too.

Inside the house, Liza whispered. 'I'll drive the cart. We'll take the gun, just in case. You hold it ready and if Dermott attacks us, shoot him.'

When they got to the little inn, they found Dorothy sitting weeping beside Andrew's body, while Tom's wife was waiting in the public room at the front.

Dorothy clung to Liza for a moment. 'Thank you for coming! I d-don't know what to do.'

Liza went to stand with her beside the body. 'He looks very peaceful.'

'Yes.' There was silence for a moment then she added, 'Did they tell you? Kitty's run away. She doesn't even know her father's dead. There are the marks of horses' hooves outside, two of them, we think, but I can't work out who they belong to. Someone came in the night, some stranger, and – and she went with him – and, oh!' Dorothy broke down again, weeping hysterically. 'She ransacked the parlour and took all my money. She found where it was hidden and didn't leave me a penny. How am I even to afford a coffin? What am I going to do?' She began weeping again.

A little later a tired-looking Benedict drove Grace over, but didn't come inside with his wife. She was her usual calm, sensible self. 'Ben's gone back home to make a coffin but I thought you might need me here. What can I do to help? I'm used to laying people out.' Lucas was with her, a quiet child who much resembled his mother in nature and rarely misbehaved.

Today, Grace's calmness and sense were exactly what was needed. While she began the task of preparing Andrew's body, Liza went to ask the neighbours to dig a grave by the lake, near Josiah's. Dorothy was of no use whatsoever, weeping all the time and going to the front door every few minutes to see whether Kitty had come back.

Liza and Grace agreed quietly that they'd be surprised if she did return.

'Of course, I didn't know her very well,' Grace whispered, 'but she was a young madam, from what I'd seen. Never had a pleasant word for anyone and seemed to hate you particularly. Had the two of you quarrelled?'

'Not really. What Kitty hated was the fact that I'd found a husband and she hadn't. She felt she never would find one here, either, and it soured her.'

'Well, she was probably right. If I didn't have my dear Ben I'd not stay because you hardly meet anyone from one week to the next. But I do have him and he's such a wonderful husband. I think you're very brave living on your own, my dear.'

Liza let her talk – well, you couldn't stop her – but could not help noticing that every now and then her companion would plant a little barb about Benedict: how happy he was with his son, how kind he was to Grace, how much she loved him. Liza wasn't sure whether it was done on purpose or not, but she definitely couldn't stand years of this.

Tom helped Benedict manhandle the coffin into the inn and

lift Andrew's body into it, then two other neighbours helped them get it on the cart and carry it from the cart to the lake, where most of the people from Brookley had gathered for the brief ceremony. Even the children were quiet, awed by the solemnity of the occasion and the sad looks of the adults.

Dorothy was silent during the short service but when the coffin was lowered into the grave she burst into wild weeping again and Benedict had almost to carry her back to the inn, she was so distraught.

'She can't be left,' Grace said. 'I'd invite her to stay with us, but there simply isn't enough room.'

Liza sighed, but knew her duty. 'It's all right. She can come to me.' She stayed to help Dorothy pack a few things while Benedict arranged for the neighbours to keep an eye on the inn and animals, then they took her home to the farm. Evening was falling by that time and the forest was made beautiful by the low slanting rays of the sun shining through the breaks in the trees. The quiet drive seemed to bring a measure of peace to them all.

In the late evening, after they'd eaten, all three women sat together.

'Have you any idea what you want to do now, Dorothy?' Liza asked gently

Her face puckered. 'I want to go home to England. Only how can I when there's Kitty to think of as well? One day she's bound to come back and how would she feel if I wasn't there? Maybe I can manage the inn on my own, find a lad to help around the place.' She shook her head, eyes filling with tears again. 'I don't know. I can't seem to think.'

Liza put her arm round her friend's shoulders. 'There's no need to decide anything now. If you do decide to go back to England, I'd be more than happy to help you. I have enough money. Indeed, I'm thinking of going back myself.'

Before they went to bed, Liza said to Dinny, 'If I did go home to England, you could come with me, you know.'

'No. I have Fergal now – and anyway, I couldn't bear to leave this place.' She gestured around her. 'It's been a refuge to me, thanks to you. The land has bound me to it.' She looked down at her belly. 'And I want my children to be born here.'

When Liza went to bed, feeling utterly exhausted, she could

not sleep. She kept hearing the shot, seeing Niall fall, seeing his blood splattered all over the kitchen floor. She had scrubbed the floor and washed her apron to get the splashes out of it, but kept feeling as if something must still show. And every time she nodded off, she jerked awake again almost immediately, her heart pounding and fear shivering through her veins, thinking she'd heard footsteps.

In the middle of the night, the wind rose and rattled the windows. She woke up with a start and a cry of panic, terrified that Dermott had come back to attack them. But it was only the wind. Next to her Seth mumbled in his sleep, a habit he had developed recently, and as she looked at dark shape of the cradle, she was glad she had her two children. Poor Dorothy had lost both husband and only child in one day.

Who had come for Kitty the previous night? It couldn't be Dermott, surely? No, he had only met Kitty the day before and anyway, she wasn't likely to run away with a common fellow like him. But however much she racked her brains, Liza could not think of any other man it might be. She knew everyone in the immediate neighbourhood and there was simply no one Kitty would have considered marrying.

Perhaps she had just enlisted Dermott's help to get to Fremantle. She would no doubt use the money she'd stolen from her mother to take the first ship back to England, where she would seek her Aunt Nora's help. If Dorothy went back to her sister, she would probably find her daughter there already. Yes, that must be what had happened.

CHAPTER TWENTY-FOUR

For the next month, Dorothy dithered and changed her mind a dozen times about going back to England. Liza tried to be patient with her, but could not help thinking that her friend was not the only person to lose someone. She herself had recently lost the man she loved, and it was hard to see him regularly still and yet have to conceal her feelings about him. She knew she had to find some way of making a new life for herself – but how?

Seth was three months old and the only plan she had thought of was to sell up this farm as soon as he was weaned and move somewhere. Already he had a look of Benedict. She did not dare stay here. And yet how could she bear to leave? She loved this place, which seemed much more a home to her than the house in Underby Street had ever been. She even loved the whispering forest around the farm. But she was worried that Grace would notice something.

The trouble was, she could not think what to do with herself after she had sold the farm, how to earn her livelihood. She had to make a settled life for her children somehow, give them a proper home. The easiest thing to do, of course, would be to marry again. Life was hard without a man's protection. She still slept badly, worried about the farm being attacked, and knew that Dinny had not moved out to live with Fergal because her friend understood how she felt. But who could she marry? You ought at least to *like* the person. She had liked Nick Rawley, but he had not returned from Melbourne, had not even written to her after that first scrawled note, so she could only assume he had changed his mind about her.

When she could leave Seth with Dinny, she would go up to Perth and ask Agnes Fenton's advice. Agnes was a very shrewd person and would surely be able to help her.

One glorious spring morning there was the sound of a horse approaching, clopping slowly along the track. Such a noise still had the effect of making Liza go rushing for her gun and she did this now, taking up a defensive position with it just inside the doorway. As the rider came into sight, however, she recognised him and with a lifting of the heart propped the gun against the wall before moving out on to the verandah.

Nick swung down from the horse and for a moment they stared at one another, then he grinned and came striding across to scoop Liza up into his arms. She laughed in delight at seeing him. He might not be the love of her lifetime, but he had become a good friend while staying with her.

He gave her a cracking hug and swung her round in circles. 'Ah, Liza, it's wonderful to see you again. Wonderful!' Holding her at arm's length, he studied her face, beaming down at her. 'I'd forgotten how fresh and alive you always appear. I've never met anyone else with quite that air.'

Another moment's silence, then he said, 'And the baby? Did everything go all right?'

'Oh, yes. I have a lusty little son called Seth now. Oh, Nick . . .' She broke off.

'Oh, Nick, what?' he teased, keeping hold of her hand and threading it through his arm.

'I never expected to see you again. You didn't write after that first note, not a word.'

He frowned and stopped walking for a moment. 'I did write again. Two months ago.'

'We never received it.' She stared down at his hand as it lay on hers. It looked as if it had worked hard while he was away from her.

'I'm sorry for that. I said in the letter that I missed you very much, Liza, and it was true. I've never missed anyone as I missed you. You seem to have bewitched me.'

She swallowed hard. These were the words of a lover and his tone said he believed she reciprocated his feelings. She didn't. Couldn't. Benedict was still a fever in her blood. Liking someone was simply not the same. To gain a few moments and put her thoughts into order, she suggested, 'Why don't you see to your horse and then come inside? Are you hungry?'

He raised her hand slowly to his lips and pressed a lingering kiss on it, saying in a throaty tone, 'Only hungry for a sight of you, Liza. Only hungry to touch your beautiful soft skin.'

He was all male, so unlike Josiah, and she couldn't help responding to his touch. He had a lean, elegant body and his carefree boyish face touched something inside her. She realised suddenly that she was yearning for fun and pleasure, and stifled all her doubts, giving him what she could. 'I've missed you, too, Nick.'

'Good. It's my sincere hope that we won't be parted again.' He looked round with a rather contemptuous expression on his face. 'Don't you ever long to go back to England? Surely you can't be happy living all your life in an isolated place like this?'

She had to swallow before she could form any words and then she chose them very carefully, because here, if she took it, might be her best chance of escape. 'No, I'm not happy here, Nick. I've been very lonely since – since Josiah died. And yes, sometimes I long to return to England. Though,' she could not stop tears filling her eyes, 'I've heard that my mother is dead.'

'But you have a father – brothers and a sister as well.'

'Yes. But I didn't get on with Da – well, I'm not sure I even want to see him again. I do miss Nancy and Kieran, though.'

He raised one hand to brush away a tear she had not known was falling. 'Poor little Liza. All alone in the world.'

Cathie broke the mood by coming running out of the house, calling, 'Mummy, Mummy! Seth's crying.' She stopped dead at the sight of the man standing there and glanced at her mother uncertainly.

Liza removed her hand from his, glad of the interruption. 'Children! They don't give you much peace.'

Nick frowned, looking round. 'Where's the girl? Doesn't she look after them for you?'

'Dinny, you mean?' Liza had forgotten his attitude towards her friend. 'Yes, she does sometimes, but she's gone to see Fergal this morning. They're building a house together.'

His expression grew disapproving, reminding her suddenly of Josiah. 'You shouldn't condone that sort of behaviour in a servant, Liza.'

As Cathie tugged at her skirt again, she bent to pick up her daughter, glad of an excuse not to answer that remark. She settled the child on her hip, though Cathie was getting a bit heavy for carrying like that now. 'While you're seeing to your horse, Nick, I'll make you a cup of tea.'

As she went round to the kitchen, Liza frowned. What sort of life would it be for her with a man like Nick? There was as much distance between them socially as there had been between her and Josiah, although she was not nearly as ignorant now. She didn't want to spend her days being scorned again for her lack of breeding. Then she smiled and shook her head. Nick wasn't at all like Josiah. He would accept her for what she was. He had come out to Australia to get away from stifling convention. His stay in Melbourne must have given him more than enough time to consider everything, to be sure of his own feelings.

For once she set the tray meticulously with fine china on an embroidered cloth and donned one of Catherine's lace-trimmed aprons. When Nick came in, she sat down with him at the table and poured him a cup in her most ladylike manner.

He ate three of her scones and drank two cups of tea, then picked up her hand before she could stop him and examined it closely. 'I don't like to see your fingers so red and worn. In fact, I don't like to see you working so hard here, or living on your own like this.'

'I haven't had much choice, have I?'

'Well, you do have a choice now.' Keeping hold of her hand, Nick slid to his knees, moving with the grace and balance which were peculiarly his. 'Liza, dearest Liza, will you marry me?'

She hadn't expected him to say anything so soon and could not form a single coherent word in response, only gape at him.

He laughed and stood up, tugging her to her feet with him. Chuckling softly, he picked her up, ignoring her shriek to put her down this minute, and went across to sit on the sofa with her on his lap. There he proceeded to kiss her very thoroughly indeed and when he moved his head away his eyes were very blue and boyish, and something about them touched her. 'Liza, dearest Liza, you won't refuse me, will you?'

'I ought to.'

He was clearly stunned by this. 'Why?'

It seemed unfair to accept his proposal without making him

face facts. 'Because we're so different. You're gentry and I'm not. I don't even talk properly.' She exaggerated her accent. 'I'm a Lancashire Lass and it shows. In England, we'd never even have met. That sort of thing made a difference to Josiah, a very big difference indeed, and I don't want you scorning me like he did.'

'Well, I'm not Josiah and that sort of snobbery is why I *left* England. Oh, Liza, my darling girl, I fell in love with you within days – hours.' He grinned. 'And you're not indifferent to me, or you wouldn't have kissed me back like that.'

She stared at him. Did he not know the difference between love and mild physical desire? No, clearly not. 'I find you very,' she sought for words, 'attractive and I'm tempted to accept.' Even though he wasn't Benedict, he was such a nice man – but was that enough? Could they be happy together? 'We have to be sensible, though.'

'To hell with being sensible. I'm a man in love!' Nick laughed and claimed her lips again, smothering her words. 'Why do we have to be sensible, Liza? Why can't we just be happy together?'

She stroked the fine, soft hair back from his eyes. 'Oh, Nick, if it were only you and me, I'd say yes in an instant. But you have family and friends in England. What will they think of me?'

'I don't care what they think of you. It's me who will be marrying you, not them.' His face took on a slightly sulky expression. 'And I'm not going back without a wife or they'll be trying to choose one for me again – another ugly one. Another girl who's silly and . . .' he slid his fingers through the unruly mass of her hair and held her head steady for another kiss '. . . doesn't have the most beautiful hair on this earth. Ah, Liza, why do you make things so difficult? I love you, you love me, we want to marry – what's wrong with that? It seems quite straightforward to me.'

It didn't seem at all straightforward to her, but she doubted she could make him understand that.

He made a scornful noise in his throat. 'Anyway, I'm not close to my father – no one ever could be – so what does it matter? Now will you marry me, woman, or do I have to kiss you into submission?'

She sighed and gave in to temptation, vowing that she would

do everything she could to make him happy. 'Yes, of course I'll marry you, Nick.'

He let out a yell of joy, then kissed her again, but when he tried to caress her, she pulled gently back from his touch. 'Not until we're married.'

He let out his breath in an exaggerated sigh. 'Sorry. You're so soft and warm. Could we get married tomorrow, do you think?'

'Nick—'

'I love the way you say my name. Say it again.'

But just then they heard the sound of footsteps, and Dinny's low voice talking to Fergal, Liza scrambled off Nick's knee and straightened her clothing, blushing furiously. He chuckled, then when she tugged at his arm, consented to sit up straight and tidy himself up.

But he was just as cool to Dinny and Fergal as ever.

And that worried her.

Two days later Dorothy took it upon herself to tell Benedict that Liza was to marry Nick Rawley. She waited until he was on his own to do so, knowing it would upset him.

He stared at her in shock. 'You can't mean that!'

'Why should I lie to you? She's going to marry him and return to England. And I think it's the best thing she could do, actually.'

'But—'

'You don't expect her to stay unmarried for the rest of her life, do you? *You* have a wife after all.'

'I don't know what I expect.' He only knew that the thought of her lying in another man's arms as she had lain in his was unbearable.

'I think it'd be better if she left – not only for you two, but for Grace. It's a wonderful opportunity for Liza.' But it hurt Dorothy to see that ravaged expression on his face, and to tell the truth, she didn't know what she would do without Liza, either. Maybe . . . She let the thought go.

Benedict stared up into the trees, then groaned with anguish. 'I can't think straight. Sorry.' He strode off into the forest.

Dorothy went inside and tried to chat to Grace, telling her about the coming marriage.

'She's marrying Nick Rawley, going back to England?' Grace exclaimed, her whole face lighting up. 'Oh, that's wonderful! I mean – wonderful for her.'

Dorothy stole a quick glance at her. Did she know about Benedict and Liza, then? It sounded like it.

She drove the cart home slowly, realising she would find it hard to leave. Strange, that. She hadn't wanted to come here – and yet somehow she didn't want to leave.

Benedict didn't turn towards home until late afternoon, having wandered along the forest tracks for hours like a man who had lost his wits. He knew them well enough not to get lost, but today he wished he could lose his way, not have to return home, not have to smile at Grace and make conversation with her. Only that would mean not seeing Lucas again, and he had grown to love his little son dearly.

He passed Pendleworth on his way back and could not resist the temptation to stop and see Liza, to make sure she really did want to marry this man and leave Australia.

He was lucky. When he turned up at the farm, Nick was outside chopping wood, looking happy and enthusiastic as he tackled the task. 'Can't shake hands, but I'm delighted to see you. Go inside and I'll join you in a few minutes. Tell Liza I'm dying of thirst, will you?'

When Benedict stood in the doorway and cleared his throat, Liza looked up, jerking in shock. He saw her face turn white as she realised who it was, then she glanced quickly beyond him to where Nick was working.

'Is it true?' he asked harshly, knowing they'd have only a few minutes together.

'Yes.'

'Why?'

'Because I need to make a new life for myself and my children.'

'Can you forget what we had so quickly?'

Her eyes were swimming in tears as she whispered, 'I have to. What else can I do?'

Across the clearing he could still hear the sound of chopping, so he allowed herself to say it one last time. 'I love you, Liza. I always will.'

'I love you, too. I'll never forget you, Benedict, never stop loving you. You know that.'

'Ah, Liza!' He stepped forward to take her in his arms but she evaded him, moving to stand behind the table.

'Don't!'

The silence felt heavy with their pain and neither could speak for a moment.

He swallowed hard. 'Dorothy says you're leaving soon.'

'Yes. Nick wants to and – and I think that's for the best.'

'Not for me, if I never see you again!'

The sound of chopping stopped and they both turned to see Nick bend and start gathering up chunks of wood.

'I love you,' said Bendict again, because what else was there to say? 'Never forget that.'

But she did not say it back to him this time, only turned to swing the kettle over the fire. 'It'll pass.'

He strode across and grabbed her arm, shaking it angrily. 'It will never pass. *Never.*'

She stepped away from him once more. When she heard footsteps, she turned to see Benedict leaving, brushing past Nick in the doorway without a word.

'What's upset him?'

It took all Liza's strength to summon up a smile. 'He hadn't realised it was so late and was afraid Grace would be worried.'

Nick was still staring at the door, looking aggrieved. 'He didn't even say goodbye.'

'I – I think I upset him a bit.'

'Why? And even if you did, hasn't he the manners to hide his feelings?'

She sought desperately for a reason and relief made her feel dizzy for a moment as she found one. 'I told him I was looking forward to getting back to England again. It reminded him. You see, Benedict didn't want to leave Lancashire. Saul Ludlam forced him to come to Australia with Josiah, and now – well, now he's trapped here.' It was the truth, though not the reason for Benedict's behaviour today.

'He could always sell up and go back. Josiah's dead now. There's nothing to stop him returning home.'

'He's got land here. He's always wanted his own land. It's not as easy to buy land in England. And anyway, I don't think he can afford it.' When Nick came and put his arms round her, Liza forced herself to lean against him, hoping the tension in her body didn't show.

'Well, I feel sorry about him, of course I do, but I was thinking about us as I was chopping.' Nick grimaced and looked down at his dirty hands. 'I've done enough travelling and living roughly. I want to see England again, feel cool damp air on my face, see trees that are really green, not these leather-leafed things! We'll start packing tomorrow.'

'Yes, let's.' She could not bear another encounter like today's. Best if she never saw Benedict Caine again.

Dorothy turned up an hour later, having walked across from Brookley. 'I need to talk to you, Liza.'

Nick stood up. 'I'll leave you two together.'

She looked at him uncertainly. 'Maybe you should stay, Mr Rawley. Liza offered to lend me some money for my passage to England.' Her fingers were nervously pleating the fabric of her skirt. 'I don't have any, you see, though I do own the inn and a little land so if that can be sold, I'll be able to pay it back one day, I promise. I'll go steerage – anything – I don't want to be a burden to you but I can't stay here on my own.' She had promised herself not to cry but the tears would not be held back. 'My daughter's been gone for over a month now. I don't—' she gulped in some air '—don't think she's coming back.'

'Of course I'll lend you the money!' Liza rushed across to hug her friend. 'Anyway, you and Andrew paid my passage out here, so it'd only be fair exchange.'

Dorothy hugged her back then collapsed on to the sofa, weeping as if she couldn't stand up for a minute longer. When Cathie came to stand next to her, upset to see her 'Aunty Dorothy' crying, she absent-mindedly hugged the child and kept hold of her. The little girl leaned against her in the comfortable way children have with people they know love them.

Nick stared at her and snapped his fingers in the air. 'Got it!'

The two women stared at him.

'No need to go steerage, Mrs Pringle. We need a nursemaid for the journey home because I,' his eyes lingered warmly on Liza, 'want to enjoy my new wife's company. We wouldn't treat you like a servant, but if you would share a cabin with the children and look after them during the journey, it'd be just the ticket.'

Liza had realised already that he resented the demands the children made on her time, and knew she could trust Dorothy absolutely. 'Oh, yes! What a good idea, Nick!'

He looked questioningly at the older woman who gave a tremulous nod, unable to speak. But she gathered the child to her and gave her a hug, as if to demonstrate her willingness.

'Nothing to stop us now!' Nick exclaimed jovially. 'We only have to pack and leave. We can put your inn up for sale at the same time as this place, Mrs Pringle, and—'

'No.' Liza's voice was quiet but determined.

He blinked at her. 'What do you mean, no?'

'I mean I don't want to sell this place, not if I don't have to.'

'But we're going back to live in England.'

'Yes. But it's Seth and Cathie's inheritance. They're not your children, they're,' she hesitated for a moment on the words, avoiding Dorothy's eyes, 'Josiah's. I can't expect you to provide for them. One day they can choose whether to return here or whether to sell the farm. In the meantime, I'm sure if we ask Fergal he'll manage this place for me, and he and Dinny can live here.'

Nick protested, telling her if they sold the farm they could invest the money for her children instead, but he found his beloved inmovable on this point and finally conceded. What did it matter, after all? The brats weren't his, though he'd let them be brought up in his house and stand in place of a father to them. But he intended to get children of his own on his young wife – and the sooner the better.

On the final evening Liza slipped out to walk through the forest with Dinny. 'I shall miss all this. England is so crowded and cold.'

Funny how she had now started remembering all the things she didn't like about her old country.

'You'll come back one day.'

'I doubt it.'

'You will.' Dinny's tone was certain.

Liza shook her head, unable to believe that, then took her friend's arm and pulled her to a halt. 'I'll write to you.' They hugged one another and stood there rocking slightly for a long time, not saying anything. They had never needed words to know what the other was thinking. 'I'll miss you most of all.' Liza's voice was shaking with the effort not to weep.

'You'll miss Benedict most,' Dinny corrected. 'But you'll see him again one day as well.'

Again Liza shook her head.

Dinny didn't press the point but she felt quite sure of that, as she sometimes did.

They set off walking again, ending up by the embryonic lake.

'You'll tend Josiah's grave for me?'

'Of course.'

When the moon went behind some clouds, Liza shivered, though it was a warm evening. 'Come on. We'd better turn round. Nick will be worrying.' Taking a deep breath, she turned back to the man she was to marry in Perth as soon as it could be arranged. No use pining for what could never be. You made the most of what life gave you and if it wasn't what you wanted, you just had to accept that. She was going to make Nick happy, provide a good safe home for her children – and she simply wouldn't let herself pine for other things.

A week after Liza had left, Grace confronted Benedict after their evening meal. 'It's about time we gave Lucas a brother, don't you think?'

He avoided her eyes. 'You said you'd had a hard time with him. I didn't want to risk anything. We aren't near a doctor here.'

'I want another child, Ben. And I want to share my bed with you.'

He stood up. 'I have to check on that cow again.'

She moved swiftly to stand in front of the door, arms stretched out to bar his way. 'Liza's married to another man by now and she'll not be coming back.'

Shock held him very still for a moment. 'I – I—' But he couldn't think what to say and his voice trailed away, leaving only the sound of a breeze whispering round the house and Lucas humming as he played with his toys in the bedroom he shared with his mother, but not his father.

'I guessed almost from the start,' Grace, her voice calm but her hands betraying her agitation as they gripped the edges of the doorway, knuckles white. 'You loved her and she had your child – oh, yes, Seth looks just like Lucas did at that age. Did Josiah know about that? Did he mind? Why will no one *tell* me what he was like?'

Benedict took a step backwards and felt for a chair with one shaking hand. 'Oh, hell, I hoped you wouldn't find out. I'm sorry, Grace. I never meant to – to hurt you. It just – happened.'

'Well, you did hurt me. Very much. But surely we can make a new start now she's left? I've tried to – to be patient.' Her voice broke and she couldn't continue. Tears were dripping down her cheeks and her skin was blotchy with emotion. 'I love you, Ben. I always have. Can't you at least like me a little?'

He had never seen her weep before. He took a step towards her and then another. When he pulled her into his arms, she came willingly but could not stop sobbing so he drew her over to sit down. 'Give me a little more time, Grace. I promise you I'll get over it.'

Then he told her about Josiah and how unhappy Liza had been. When he had finished, she let her head drop on his shoulder and sighed. They sat there for a long time.

But it was the beginning of a closer relationship and when he started sharing the bedroom with her, Grace at least seemed very happy. He hoped he had never called Liza's name when in the throes of passion. He hoped he hadn't given voice to the dreams that would keep returning to haunt him, dreams of his time with Liza.

Grace didn't tell him that he did sometimes call out another woman's name in his sleep, just concentrated on making him happy and comfortable, on making him truly her husband.

321

CHAPTER TWENTY-FIVE

Liza shivered with cold as she stood on deck watching the buildings of Liverpool grow more distinct on the horizon. Everything seemed grey today — sky, sea and even the land ahead — and she had a sudden intense longing for her Australian home, for bright sunlight and warm breezes.

It had been a fast passage back on an auxiliary ship. Although the engines were only used from time to time, they made a difference of two to three weeks to the length of a journey. This time, knowing what to expect, she had brought books and embroidery with her — for Dorothy had agreed to help her improve her skills so that she would have one ladylike accomplishment at least.

She and Nick shared a cabin similar to the one Catherine had once occupied alone, with Dorothy and the children next door. Only Nick never sat reading and ignoring her as Josiah had, but wanted to be with her, talk to her, make love to her. Her face grew warm at the memories. He wasn't as skilled a lover as Benedict had been, or maybe she just didn't respond to him in the same intense way — she sighed at herself for making comparisons — but he was very enthusiastic about the activity and she was beginning to suspect she was already carrying his child. He seemed to have no idea of that and to be unaware, in more than the vaguest terms, of the workings of a woman's body.

She turned to look for him and saw him at the centre of a group of men who were laughing uproariously at something he had just said. She smiled. He had a gift for making people laugh, Nick did, and that sometimes helped make things right between them. If he had been more sensitive, more observant, he might have wondered about her sudden moods of silence and preoccupation. But he never did. He was easy to live with, accepting of what she said, and she thanked God for that every day.

Dorothy moved to stand beside her, carrying Seth with Cathie holding her skirt. 'We've come to look at England.'

Liza picked her daughter up and pointed to the city buildings then murmured to Dorothy, 'I need to talk to Nick alone. Could you manage to keep them busy for a while?' Receiving a nod of assent, she made her way towards her husband, smiling and nodding at the other cabin passengers as she walked but not stopping to chat.

The men fell silent as she approached and Nick frowned at her. She ignored that. 'I'm sorry to interrupt, gentlemen, but there's something important I need to discuss with my husband.'

They walked down to the cabin together.

'Is something wrong? It's not quite the done thing to interrupt a group of gentlemen, you know.'

'I'm sorry, but this is really important.' Liza didn't know how else to say it so blurted out, 'I thought you should know – before we disembarked, that is – that I'm going to have your – our baby.'

Nick stared at her and then swallowed hard. 'How long have you known?'

'I've suspected for a week or two, and then – well, this morning I felt nauseous and my breasts felt sore so – so I think it's fairly sure.'

He beamed at her. 'Oh, Liza, nothing could please me more! And it'll make everything so much easier when we get home again, too.'

She didn't comment on that remark because she had grown to realise that he was apprehensive about confronting his father again and not nearly as sure of being able to defy him as he had claimed in Australia.

He didn't scoop her up and swing her round, but led her to the bed and helped her sit down as if she were an invalid. She laughed at him and tugged his arm so that he plumped down beside her. 'I won't break, you know. I worked right until the last minute with Seth and—' She broke off as he scowled, realising suddenly that it would be a mistake to reminisce about her other pregnancies to him. He was very possessive of her, hated her even to mention Josiah's name.

'Well, you won't be working this time.'

323

She threaded her arm through his and snuggled against him. 'No, of course I won't. Are you – are you really so pleased about it, Nick?'

'Of course I am.' He raised her hand and kissed it reverently. 'My darling, you must rest a lot and never overexert yourself because this is the most important baby there ever was.'

Liza chuckled. 'I'd go mad if I had to lie around all day. But I'm glad you're happy. I want a lot of children, don't you?'

'Well, one or two. An heir, certainly, and a daughter with your glorious hair.' They sat together on the bed arm-in-arm for a while, then went back up on the deck to watch the ship docking, standing close together with his arm round her shoulders.

When the train drew into the railway station at Pendleworth, it was raining heavily and the town looked grimy and ugly to Liza. Nick summoned up a cab with a mere tilt of his head and then called another to carry their mountain of luggage.

As the horses clopped along, Liza saw the Ludlams' mill chimney smoking and marvelled at the way the houses seemed to huddle together for protection around the dark mass of the huge, square mill building. She seemed to be looking at them with new understanding.

Then they were in the countryside and that was more pleasant on the eye, but everything was so tidy, with no inch of the land unclaimed. No mysterious, whispering forests here.

As the cab turned through a gateway in a long stone wall, Liza peered out of the window and what she saw made her feel even more apprehensive. Rawley Manor, which she had never seen from close to before, seemed huge, set amidst vast stretches of velvety lawns. It was built of grey stone and was L-shaped, two storeys high along most of its length, but three at the shorter end, which was at a right-angle to the main part of the house. She counted eight windows in the two-storey part and wondered how many rooms there were inside.

Nick sighed with pleasure and turned to beam at her, but his eyes slid quickly back to the view through the splashed and muddy carriage windows. 'I'd forgotten how beautiful it is.'

Liza shivered. Grey skies foretold continuing rain and everything felt damp to the touch, even her own skin. She tried to control her nervousness, drawing in long calming breaths surreptitiously, and as they got out, taking comfort from Dorothy's understanding glances. They had decided that she would stay with the children until they found a nursemaid, and only then would they contact her elder sister Nora, of whom she seemed rather nervous.

Nick didn't even wait for the carriage to stop but flung the door open and jumped out. Liza waited for him to turn and help her but when he saw a woman appear in the doorway, he abandoned her to race across, shouting, 'Mother! Mother, you haven't changed a bit!' and sweep the woman off her feet, laughing.

'We'll wait here till he remembers us,' Liza said, glad of a few more moments to pull herself together.

Dorothy nodded. She knew how hard it was going to be for her friend to settle into this family. The Rawleys were noted for their pride in their lineage and their long history in this place, dating back almost to the Conqueror.

A man appeared in the doorway, tall, very thin and frowning. He shook Nick's hand briefly then gestured towards the house.

'That'll be the father,' Liza murmured. 'He's the one Nick quarrelled with. Funny, isn't it, how we all seem to quarrel with our fathers, rich and poor alike?'

Nick was speaking urgently and gesticulating towards the carriage.

'He's telling them about me,' Liza whispered. 'And they don't look very pleased, do they?'

Dorothy didn't answer for it was quite clear from their expressions that the Rawleys were unhappy with their son's news. However, they both turned and followed him across the gravel to the carriage.

'Darling!' Nick held out his hand and Liza stepped out, holding on to him tightly to give herself courage. 'These are my parents. Mother and Father, this is Liza.'

She shook hands with each of them, but as soon as she spoke, she could see disapproval deepen in their faces. Well, she couldn't talk fancy because she wasn't one of them and wasn't going to pretend about that. For some reason their sour expressions gave her courage and she turned back to the carriage.

Nick was already helping the children to alight. Dorothy took Seth from him, though the little boy was almost a year old now and getting quite big. Cathie ran to her mother and hid her face in her skirts, overwhelmed by everything.

Mrs Rawley turned towards the house. 'You must all be very tired. Do come inside – um, Liza. Is that short for Elizabeth?'

'No. Just Liza.'

'Oh, I see. Well, the children can use the old nursery – and since you don't have a nursemaid, we'll get the housekeeper to find us one.'

'I'll stay with the children until then,' Dorothy put in quietly. 'They're a bit bewildered by everything.'

Once the two of them were alone in their bedroom, Nick grinned at Liza. 'That went pretty well, didn't it?'

She didn't think it had gone particularly well but like all their class the Rawleys had excellent manners and were good at concealing their real feelings.

'Wait till I tell them about the baby,' he went on. 'They'll adore you then.'

'I hope so.'

He cocked one eyebrow at her. 'Nervous?'

'Yes.'

'Don't be. I'll be there to help.'

'Not after dinner, you won't.' She was quite sure Mrs Rawley would question her closely when the ladies left the gentlemen to their port.

'In that case, we'll have to make sure we tell them about the baby over afternoon tea. That'll put Mother in a good mood with you.'

Liza didn't contradict him, but there was something chill and disapproving in both his parents' expressions that she couldn't see herself ever overcoming. Thank goodness he didn't intend to come back to live in this big, cold house!

Over tea, conversation was very stilted until Nick told them about the baby.

Mrs Rawley clasped her hands together at her breast. 'Nicholas! Oh, how wonderful!'

Mr Rawley got up to shake his son's hand and congratulate him.

Liza scowled. She was the one who was doing all the work of producing a child, but it was him they congratulated.

'Do you – er – carry children easily?' Mrs Rawley asked when the men had started discussing horses.

'Yes. Nick wants me to rest and lie around, but I can't do that. Keeping active seems to suit me.'

'Then we shall assign a maid to you so that you may go for walks whenever you wish.'

Liza forgot to watch her words. 'Why do I need a maid for that?'

Mrs Rawley's expression became stiff again. 'It is not acceptable for a lady to go out on her own.'

'As you can see, I'm no lady.'

'Please bear with us in such matters. I shall – if you'll allow it – guide you in what to do, how to behave. We must make sure that you're accepted by our friends and neighbours.'

'Yes. I suppose so. Um – thank you.'

Nick insisted Liza dress for dinner in one of the prettiest gowns Catherine had given her, so she went up early to take a bath in the dressing room that adjoined their bedroom. It seemed strange to find everything waiting for her, but she enjoyed the luxury of having the hot water carried upstairs by someone else, and didn't want to get out of the tub again. The big house seemed so chilly and she hadn't really felt warm since her arrival in England.

Thanks to Dorothy's skill with a needle, the dress fitted well and the maid assigned to her had ironed it and unpacked all her other things. Mona was waiting in the bedroom to help her dress and do her hair. She indicated a pile of what Liza had used as working clothes in Australia. 'Do you wish to keep these, Madam?'

Tears suddenly gathered in Liza's eyes and threatened to betray how fragile her composure was today. 'Yes, I do wish to keep them. They have great sentimental value for me.'

Mona said nothing but her expression was surprised. 'Certainly, Madam. I'll have them washed, shall I? There's a strange smell to them, something I don't recognise – perhaps it came from the ship?'

Liza went over and lifted a faded cotton skirt to her nostrils. The faint scent of gum leaves brought memories rushing back. She had stood in the shade of a huge tree once wearing this skirt and talking to Benedict. There had been sunlight, parrots flying around, a warm breeze on her face. Nick's homesickness had been for England, but to her surprise hers was for Australia – only she could never go back there.

'Madam – are you all right?'

Liza found Mona guiding her towards the chaise-longue set in the window and didn't protest. 'I'm sorry. It's probably the baby. It's early days yet, but—'

Mona's scornful attitude vanished abruptly. 'Oh, Mrs Rawley, how wonderful for you! The mistress will be that pleased!'

'Yes, she is. And – and don't wash these things. They're not dirty, just crumpled. I like the smell. It brings back happy memories of Australia.'

'Wasn't it very dangerous out there?'

'I suppose so – but it was wonderful too. I miss it.'

'Oh, you'll soon forget all that when you have the baby to look after.'

'I have my other baby, too. Which reminds me,' Liza stood up. 'I want to see my children before I go down for dinner.'

Mona looked at the clock and pursed her lips. 'It'd be better if they came down here, madam. We still have your hair to do and – if you don't mind my saying so – the master does like his family to look well-groomed in the evening. He used to send Mr Nicholas back to his room to change sometimes if things weren't right.'

Liza stifled a sigh, didn't say that her children were more important than what she was wearing. She had vowed to do her best here and do it she would. 'Send for the children then, would you, please?'

When Dorothy came in, she was still wearing the clothes she had arrived in.

'You'll need to change for dinner,' Liza told her.

Mona looked sideways and bit her lip.

Liza threw up her hands. 'Look, just tell me straight out about things, will you, Mona? I know I've a lot to learn and I shan't be upset at anything you say, I promise you.'

'Very well, Madam. Mrs Rawley thought the children might

328

be frightened if they woke in a strange place so she sent word that Mrs Pringle could have her dinner up in the nursery.'

'No.'

The two women looked at her in surprise.

'Mrs Pringle is my friend, not my maid. If she isn't coming down to dinner, then I'm not, either.' Liza folded her arms and stared at them both.

'But I'm not ready.' Dorothy looked down at herself. 'And just look at me. If I'd been going down I'd have taken a bath and—'

'If you don't mind using my water, there's a bath full of hot water next door. Mona, help me find something for Dorothy to wear. We have to get her changed before Nick comes up. Where's her room?'

Within minutes Dorothy had washed and donned an evening gown that had once belonged to Catherine but been altered for her before the journey. She had lost a lot of weight since Andrew's death, though Liza suspected she was more upset at Kitty's disappearance than her own widowhood.

With Mona's help, they each pinned up their hair in a simple style and Liza lent Dorothy a necklace and bracelet to add a touch of discreet elegance to the gown. When Nick came into the room from his own dressing room on the other side of the bedroom it was to find the three of them laughing together.

'I'll go and tell them to set another place at table.' Mona bobbed a curtsey and left.

Dorothy followed her. 'I'll wait for you in the gallery and go down with you, if I may?'

'Yes, you do that,' Liza said warmly, going across to kiss her husband's cheek. When he would have taken her in his arms, however, she pushed him away. 'Don't! I daren't get my hair messed up.'

'I'd like to mess up more than your hair,' he said, looking at her hungrily.

She rolled her eyes at the ceiling. 'There isn't time.'

'Help me fix my cravat, then, will you, dearest?'

'Here.' She tied it carefully, having acted as his valet on the ship.

'I'll get a proper man to look after my things, but you're

329

right. We don't want to upset Father and he is a bit of a stickler for dress. Still, he'll approve of you tonight. You look very beautiful, my dear. Having babies must suit you.'

She smiled. 'Yes, it does rather. Nick – I took it upon myself to insist that Dorothy join us for dinner. Your mother had sent word that she could dine in the nursery.'

He stiffened. 'I wish you'd not done that. I hadn't realised . . .'

Liza paused near the door. 'If she isn't fit to dine with them, then neither am I. I owe a lot to Dorothy. She's been a good friend to me and I won't have her slighted.'

He turned sulky. 'She'll be slighted once she goes to her sister's house. Poor relations always are.'

'Then if it's too uncomfortable, she can come and live with us.'

'Live here? I don't think so.'

She stopped dead, tugging at his arm to stop him walking on. 'What do you mean, live here?'

'Well, where else should we live? I'm the heir. Need to keep an eye on things. Anyway, there's plenty of space, isn't there?'

Her heart sank. 'I thought we'd decided to get our own home?'

'It seems unnecessary.' He cast a fond glance around him. 'I hadn't realised how much I loved this place till we got back.'

Liza didn't say anything, because he wouldn't understand, but she didn't want to live here. What would she do with herself all day, with her mother-in-law running the household and maids to do all the daily tasks? Nick had said they'd get a house of their own, but had quickly changed his mind – and without even consulting her. That made her feel uneasy. What else was going to be different?

Dinner was a very formal affair. They sat quite a distance apart at a big polished table and made careful, polite conversation. When the desserts had been cleared away, Mrs Rawley led her daughter-in-law and Dorothy into the drawing room.

Here the conversation was equally stilted and faltered to a halt altogether when Liza innocently revealed that she had been Josiah Ludlam's wife, and the two children upstairs were his.

Mrs Rawley stared at her in horror. 'You were that man's wife?'

'Yes.'

'Does Nicholas know this? Well, of course he must do, but it's very strange and—' She broke off, flushing.

Liza did not intend to pretend about anything. 'Your daughter arranged the marriage with Josiah, actually. I nursed her through her final illness. I was her maid on the ship when the other one ran away.'

'You nursed Catherine? You were with her at the end?'

'Yes. Your daughter was very kind to me and I shall always be grateful to her.'

Mrs Rawley dissolved into tears then and just as Liza was bending over her, trying to comfort her, the gentlemen came in.

Mr Rawley looked at his wife in patent disapproval. 'My dear, please control yourself.'

But Mrs Rawley only sobbed more loudly.

'Perhaps you could escort my wife up to her room, Mrs Pringle,' he said coldly. 'I wish to speak to my daughter-in-law.'

Nick opened the door for his mother and Dorothy, closed it behind them, then came across to stand beside his wife, giving her hand a quick squeeze. He seemed nervous. His father again. Liza drew herself up and turned to face Mr Rawley. She didn't intend to flutter like a bird in a snare as his wife had done, just because he frowned at her.

'Please sit down, Liza. Are you sure that's your full name? Elizabeth would be much more acceptable.'

'Yes, it is my full name and I don't wish to change it.' She ignored Nick's nudge and warning grimace and sat down in the nearest chair with her hands clasped in her lap.

'Nicholas has informed me of your previous marriage. I cannot pretend to be pleased. That man made my daughter's life a misery, and I must confess to feeling surprised that he has fathered *any* children.'

Liza didn't say anything, just met his gaze calmly, ignoring the tremors of nervousness and waiting for him to continue.

'We must, of course, inform Saul Ludlam and invite him and his wife to meet the children. It may be that they will wish to bring them up and—'

'They're my children, Mr Rawley. I love them dearly and no one is going to take them away from me!' She turned to

Nick for support but he was avoiding her eyes so she gave him a pinch.

He looked at his father but his expression was pleading rather than firm. 'Liza is a very good mother, Father. The best. It wouldn't be fair to take the children away from her.'

'But you will have your own family soon, my boy, and—'

Liza stood up. 'I refuse even to discuss this dreadful suggestion. And if you try to take my children away from me, Mr Rawley, I'll leave as well.'

Only then did Nick come and put his arm round her. 'As I told you, Father, I won't be a party to forcing her to do anything.'

Relief flooded through Liza. For a moment she had thought Nick wasn't going to support her – was amazed and upset that he'd even allowed his father to suggest handing her children over to the Ludlams.

Mr Rawley breathed very deeply. 'You came back as disobedient as you went away, I see, Nicholas.'

'I was a boy when I left – a rebellious boy – but I'm a man now, Father, with a wife and family of my own. If I'm not welcome here, just tell me.'

When he jerked his head towards the door, Liza took the hint and moved out of his arms. 'I think it might be better for you to discuss this without me here.'

They didn't try to stop her and as she walked slowly up the stairs she heard Nick's raised voice behind her and sighed. She hated the thought of living here. The house was cold and dark, and all its occupants seemed terrified of Mr Rawley, including his own wife.

When Nick came up, he was looking downcast. 'It didn't take long for the old man to start trying to order me around,' he said gloomily. 'I'm sorry, Liza. It wasn't my idea to take the children away from you – though there might be advantages to be gained for them from Saul Ludlam who is, after all, the richest man in the town. We can't just dismiss the idea out of hand.'

'From what Josiah said, Saul Ludlam is a bully and any children brought up by him would be very unhappy indeed. Nick, I think we should get a home of our own, not live here.' She was suddenly, fiercely glad that she had insisted on keeping control of her own money when they married and that Nick had agreed to it. Ever since Catherine first gave her the hundred pounds, Liza had felt more confident, and with her inheritance from Josiah behind her as well, there was surely nothing they could do to take her children away from her.

She looked at Nick and realised suddenly how immature he was in some ways, and probably always would be. His life had been too easy. Well, she had grown up the hard way, and if she had to help stiffen her husband's backbone, she would.

In Australia, Kitty Pringle was enjoying life on the diggings, apart from one thing: Dermott was still refusing to marry her. Everyone thought they were man and wife, but *she* knew that they weren't and it galled her.

They had proved to be a good business team, running an inn for the more successful diggers in this newly discovered goldfield – though it was not like any inn she had seen before, since it was housed in a canvas tent. Dermott had been talking about giving it a tin roof soon to protect his stock and equipment from the rain. It was ironic, Kitty thought, looking round, that her experience in Brookley should come in so useful here.

When they closed that night she turned to him with a grim expression. 'We need to talk.'

He yawned and gave a great bone-cracking stretch. 'Ah, Kitty lass, you're not going to start that again, are you?'

'It's different this time.'

He snorted. 'You always say that. What the hell argument have you thought up now?'

'I haven't thought up any argument. This time you've given me the best of reasons for us to marry.'

'How the hell have I done that?'

'You've got me with child.'

His expression was not that of a man gladdened by the news. As the silence lengthened, she watched him carefully then added, 'I've spoken to Father Timothy about it.'

'You stupid bitch! Why did you do that?'

'Because I don't want my son to be born a bastard.'

'Jesus, Mary and Joseph!' Dermott ran one hand through his thick dark hair.

Kitty folded her arms and waited, face grim, then as he didn't speak, started to tell him the priest was coming round to see him the next day, but couldn't get the words out for tears.

He had seen her angry, petulant, happy, but never weeping and helpless – had not thought Kitty could be like that, so sharp was she most of the time. And her tears moved him more than he had expected – as did the thought of a son. For a few minutes longer he held out until she was shaking with the violence of her sobs and he simply couldn't bear it any longer. 'Ach, come here, you fool of a woman!'

But she turned and tried to run into the bedroom, so he had to catch her by the skirt and drag her back. Normally she'd have started screeching at him – Kitty had a fine strong voice, which had cowed many an unruly customer – but this time she just collapsed against him, still sobbing.

'When's it due?' he demanded.

'In just under seven months.'

'Then you'll have time to turn Catholic before we wed.'

She blinked and stared at him.

He tried to make a joke of it. 'The mammy would turn in her grave if I married a heathen.'

Kitty swallowed hard. 'You – do you really mean that? Oh, Dermott, don't torment me! I can't bear it if you're mocking me.'

'I'm not.' His voice was quiet and sure. 'We'll see Father Timothy together tomorrow and then you'll take instruction from him.' He was setting an ultimatum and they both knew it.

'Yes, Dermott.'

'When he thinks you're ready, we'll marry.' He looked her in the eye. 'But I'll have no more of your tantrums and scenes. I mean to be master in my own house and I mean my children to grow up in a proper family. We'll let someone else manage the inn now and move to Melbourne.'

'Yes, Dermott.'

He nodded and drew her into the bedroom, but he didn't make love to her, just held her close until she had sighed into sleep. Then he lay awake for a long time, wondering if he was doing the right thing. How Niall would laugh at him, turning into a respectable married man! Dermott grinned into the darkness. He'd soon discovered that Kitty had a head for figures and he a head for business. He doubted he'd find anyone more useful as a wife – and she was good in bed too. From now on they'd work more steadily towards a prosperous future for their children.

I'll call it Niall if it's a boy, he decided as he grew sleepy. And one day, me and my little Niall will make that bitch pay.

CHAPTER TWENTY-SIX

Breakfast at Rawley Manor was another stiff affair with Henry Rawley sitting at the head of the table, his wife sitting at the opposite end, too far away for comfortable conversation, and the young couple placed on either side between them.

Liza, who was feeling nauseous, ate very little, which drew disapproving looks and finally a sharp comment from her father-in-law.

'I do not approve of people picking at their food, Liza. Nor do I approve of the modern habit of eating snacks between meals, which leads to obesity. Please make a hearty breakfast, for I allow no food to be served in this house between meals.'

Liza turned to Nick, but he said nothing to help her, so she put down her knife and fork, and spoke for herself. 'Women in my condition often feel sick in the mornings, Mr Rawley, and if my previous experience is anything to go by, I'm afraid I shan't be able to eat a proper breakfast for another two months. Are you saying I must go hungry until lunchtime every day?'

He inhaled so deeply he seemed to swell up with indignation and Liza saw what was surely panic on her mother-in-law's face. 'If you do not wish to provide me with food,' she continued, trying to speak calmly, 'then I shall simply go into town each day and buy something to eat there.'

There might have been only her and the angular, white-haired man in the room. 'Young woman, do not try me too far! We have agreed to accept you into the family, in spite of your background, but you will conform to our ways while you are under this roof.'

And still Nick didn't speak, just sat staring down at his plate.

Liza glanced sideways at her mother-in-law, whose face was now white with apprehension, and suddenly she could not bear to stay here a moment longer. She clapped her table napkin to her mouth and stood up. 'Please excuse me – I have to go and be sick.' To her immense satisfaction, disgust etched itself across Mr Rawley's face as she hurried out of the room.

In the bedroom she slammed the door behind her, pacing up and down and muttering. 'How stupid!' and 'I'm not going hungry when there's no need!' When Nick did not come up to join her, she decided to go and see her children.

In the nursery she found Cathie sitting mutinously in front of a plate of dry bread, with Dorothy beside her, trying to coax her to eat – as if anyone could coax Cathie to do something she had set her mind against! – and a maidservant standing by looking uncomfortable.

At the sight of her mother Cathie scrambled down from the table and rushed to throw herself into the arms that were always there for her.

Liza looked across at her friend. 'What's the matter, Dorothy? Why has Cathie only dry bread? Has she been misbehaving?'

'No. They sent this up with orders from Mr Rawley that the child was to eat everything on the plate. And,' she jerked her head towards the maid, 'Jill has been ordered to wait and see that Cathie eats it.'

The maid bobbed a curtsey. 'Sorry, Mrs Nicholas. It's the master's orders.'

'Horrid bread!' Cathie stamped her foot. 'Not going to eat it.'

'I'm not giving my children nothing to eat but dry bread!' Liza exclaimed, outrage boiling up again. 'They need good food if they are to grow up healthy. Can they do no better than dry bread in this household? They're surely not short of money?'

The maid shifted from one foot to the other and offered, 'Mr Rawley believes in simple breakfasts, Mrs Nicholas. Dry bread is all we get in the kitchen of a morning, too.'

'Well *he* can eat dry bread if he wants to, but my children and I won't – not when there's no need.' Liza had gone without breakfast many a time as a child, and been glad of dry bread then, but she was not going to have her own children suffering needlessly from that horrible aching stomach and lack of energy. 'The man's a bully. I've just had words with him because he

337

informed me I was to eat a hearty breakfast as no snacks were served in between meals – just when I was feeling sick.'

The maid gulped audibly and looked down at her feet.

'I'm going into town to buy some food. If *he* won't feed my children properly, I shall do so myself.'

'Do you think it's wise to anger him?' Dorothy ventured.

'It's he who's angered me.'

When Nick came up to the bedroom, he found Liza waiting for him, eyes sparkling with anger. She didn't wait for him to speak but demanded, 'Are you really going to allow your father to treat us like this?'

He shook his head. 'No. I've been trying to reason with him. He always did expect to control every aspect of our lives, but he wasn't quite so – so gothic before. And he certainly didn't try to control what we ate.'

She went across to put her arms round him, relieved he was taking her side. 'No wonder you ran away to Australia.'

'Yes, my godmother's money gave me a freedom I'd never had before. Father was planning to take charge of that inheritance, of course, but I was over twenty-one by then and I refused to allow that.' He nestled his head against hers and sighed. 'I think we'd better pack our things and go to a hotel, my dear. I'm not having you treated like this in your condition. Then we'll find a house to rent. I'll go into town and ask our lawyer.'

'I'll come with you. I'm going to be hungry in an hour or so.' Liza grinned at him. 'And we'll take Cathie – she's hungry as well. Have you told your father we're leaving?'

'Yes.'

'I didn't hear any arguments.'

'My father doesn't shout or argue. He simply issues orders and expects them to be obeyed. Today he *almost* shouted at me but walked out of the room instead. It's my mother who's upset. She's weeping. When we have a house, I hope you won't mind inviting her to tea?'

'Of course not. But will your father allow her to come?'

'If it's a question of seeing her grandchildren, I think she will disobey him – but discreetly.' Nick sighed. 'I'll have to spend some time here, though, so that I can learn to run the estate. I think he'll still permit that, because the estate is entailed on the

338

heir and he can't leave it to anyone but me. And he *is* good at managing things. I can learn a lot from him if he'll let me. I was too young to care before but now,' he patted her stomach and grinned, 'with a wife and heir to look after, I'm going to turn into a sober man of business.'

She chuckled because whatever Nick did, he couldn't stay solemn for long. In that they were very alike, and she sometimes thought that if she'd met him before Benedict, she might have been perfectly happy with him, instead of being riddled with these useless longings.

They drove into town in the comfort of one of the family carriages.

On the main street, Liza suddenly exclaimed, 'Oh, stop! There's a bakeshop over there.' Nick pulled the checkstring as she smiled reminiscently. 'I used to look in the window of that very shop and long to try their cakes, but of course I could never afford them. They used to have some tables where you could sit and eat.'

The tables were still there, so they had a jolly time devouring a pile of assorted cakes while the Rawley carriage waited outside.

As they were coming out they almost bumped into a man who was striding along not looking where he was going. Liza froze at the sight of him.

He stepped back to let them pass, looked at her indifferently, then jerked in shock and remained where he was, staring at her as if he had seen a ghost.

'Is there some reason for you to gape at my wife so rudely, fellow?' Nick demanded, stepping forward.

Teddy Marshall's mouth dropped open as he recognised a Rawley, then he shook his head and took a step backwards to let them pass. But he didn't move on until the carriage had driven away.

Liza could not stop shaking. The sight of him had brought back that dreadful night which still haunted her dreams occasionally. She looked down at the child holding her hand, a child who had been fathered by Marshall, though Liza would never tell anyone that. Never.

'He's frightened you,' Nick said in amazement. 'You can confront my father, who makes grown men shake in their shoes, and this rough fellow makes you tremble. Who is he?'

She tried to pull herself together but her voice wobbled as she said, 'He's the man my father wanted me to marry, the reason I ran away to Australia. He used to terrify me and he's bound to tell my father I'm back.' She wasn't sure she was ready to see Da yet. The thought of him coming round to Rawley Manor made her shiver.

'We'll send a message round to your family today – or I'll go to see your father myself, if you prefer, to tell him we're married.'

Liza was suddenly ashamed of her own cowardice. 'We'll go to see him together – but not today, not till I've got somewhere to invite Nancy and Kieran to visit me.'

She was glad they reached the lawyer's office just then and the subject was dropped. The interior was dark with wood panelling, but felt warm and cosy. When Mr Patenby said he knew of a house for rent, a place belonging to one of his other clients, it seemed as though matters were on the mend and Liza relaxed. Awed by her surroundings. Cathie clung to her mother's hand and behaved well, especially when Liza whispered that they were here to find themselves a new house to live in.

The place that was available turned out to be Dorothy's old home, and the landlord was of course Saul Ludlam. 'Haven't you somewhere else, Mr Patenby?' Liza asked. She turned to Nick and whispered, 'I'd love to live in Ashleigh, I was always happy there, but I don't want to be in that man's power.'

Nick kissed her cheek. 'Don't be silly, dear. We'll go and look at the place on the way home.'

'My clerk will give you the keys. And, Mr Rawley, may I remind you that it would be appropriate for you to make a will now that you are married.'

Nick pursed his lips then nodded. 'Yes. I'll come back in a day or two and see to it. Please make some notes on what you think would be correct.'

Outside Liza murmured, 'I don't like to think of making wills.'

'But just think of you being left in my father's power if I didn't make one!'

'Why should I be in his power?'

'Because you're carrying the heir to the estate. I've explained about the entail before.'

'It might be a girl.'

He shook his head. 'Oh, no. I'm quite certain it will be a boy. And I shall make my will. I must appoint a guardian for the child, too – just in case.'

Liza clung to his arm. 'Don't talk like that, Nick! It upsets me.' Josiah had made a will and had died soon after. She'd be in real trouble if anything happened to Nick.

He patted her hand. 'I want to look after you, darling, and that means acting responsibly.'

But she still didn't feel happy about it.

When they drove into the tiny hamlet of Ashleigh, Liza stared round her with pleasure. 'It hasn't changed at all. Look, if you follow that path you come to a place where the earliest snowdrops bloom.'

Nick helped her out of the carriage and they went round the house together. 'It's a bit small,' he complained. 'Where would your lady's maid sleep?'

'It's big enough for us, and I don't need a lady's maid. Oh, Nick, I'd love to live here again. You should have seen how pretty this room used to be.'

'Oh, very well.' He escorted her out to the carriage, smiling at her joyful expression, but both their smiles faded as the vehicle turned into the gates of the Manor. Even before they entered the house, the oppressive atmosphere seemed to reach out and stifle them.

Nick was immediately asked by the butler to wait on his father in the estate office. He grimaced at Liza and pushed her towards the stairs. 'I'll join you as soon as I can.'

'Don't let him bully you,' she whispered. 'And don't change your mind about the house.'

'I won't.'

As Nick paused by the door of the austere room which had been the scene of so many scoldings, his father looked across at him coldly. 'I am seriously upset that you have not learned better sense while you were away, Nicholas. But I should have known when you came back with a wife who—'

'If you speak disrespectfully of Liza, I shall simply walk out of the room.'

There was a moment's frigid silence, then his father nodded. 'Yes. You are right to defend her, whatever her background, because she *is* your wife now. But it's an improvident marriage nonetheless. Did she bring you any money at all? Josiah must have left her something.'

'She brought a few hundred and the Australian farm. We are agreed that it will be settled on Josiah's children.'

His father considered this, thin lips pursed, eyes narrowed, then nodded. 'Suitable. You'd better give me the details and—'

'Patenby is seeing to it.' Nick took a deep breath. 'Father, I've decided it'd be best if we set up our own establishment. In fact, we've already found a house – one owned by Saul Ludlam, over in Ashleigh. We can move to the Railway Hotel until it's ready for us to move in but I'm not having my wife going hungry.'

Another of those over-long silences, then, 'It would be better if you stayed here till your house is ready. Your wife may order a tray to be taken to her bedroom later in the morning, though I still do not approve of such indulgence. If she had a little more fortitude she would control her body as I have learned to control mine. I eat no food in the middle of the day, and only a plain dinner at night, and am the better for it.'

He did not look the better for it. Indeed, it seemed to Nick that his father had aged greatly while he was away and was not looking at all well.

As soon as he could escape, he went to find his mother.

She dabbed at her eyes when he told her they would be setting up house on their own. 'Your father always was difficult – and unreasonable, too.' She glanced towards the door and lowered her voice. 'He's much worse lately, though. I think he's ill. He denies it, but I see him pressing his hand to his stomach sometimes as if he's in pain, and he eats so little.'

'Well, that's his business, but he needn't think we're going to starve ourselves. You'll come and visit us often, won't you?'

Her face brightened a little. 'Oh, yes. If you'll let me?'

'I'll insist on it. You'll get on well with Liza, I'm sure. She's always so cheerful and busy. There's no one quite like her.'

'I'm glad you're happy and I'm looking forward very much to the birth of my first grandchild.'

'We are, too. Liza loves children and we'd like several.'

'We'll be out of here in a few days,' Nick said to Liza when he had joined her in their bedroom. He picked her up, ignoring her squeals, and swung her round and round, laughing.

When he put her down again, she asked in wonderment, 'How did you grow up so cheerful in nature with a father like that?'

'Well, he wasn't always this bad, and there was my mother, you see, and her brother. My Uncle Alexander is her twin. He's never married. I used to visit him often and I am really looking forward to seeing him again. Pity he's in London at the moment. I believe,' his grin was back, 'it was suggested that as I was my uncle's heir, I should keep in well with him, so things were allowed that might not have been otherwise. My father has a passion for increasing our family fortune, you see, and he's always resented the fact that the Ludlams are richer than the Rawleys nowadays, when we were traditionally lords of the manor.'

It seemed to Liza that these rich folk thought too much about money. If you had enough to eat and could live comfortably, what did it matter if someone had more than you? But she was learning not to make comments like that.

Later that afternoon a carriage drew up outside the house. Liza was sitting with her mother-in-law, working half-heartedly on a piece of embroidery for lack of anything else to do.

Geraldine Rawley glanced out of the window. 'Oh, dear, it's the Ludlams!'

Liza's heart began to thud with apprehension for although she had seen Saul Ludlam driving by many a time when she was younger she had heard enough about his father from Josiah to dread meeting him face to face. When the parlour maid announced the visitors, she was shocked. Of course this man's hair was iron grey and his body thicker, but nonetheless the resemblance between him and Josiah was unnerving.

Frowning, he shepherded into the room a lady with a faded, kindly face, who was dressed in very fussy clothes, and waited with open impatience for her to finish greeting her hostess. When Liza was introduced to him, Saul shook her hand without saying a word and studied her quite openly – though he did not seem to approve of what he saw.

His wife gushed into speech, however. 'Oh, I'm *so* pleased to meet Josiah's wife – I mean, widow – at last, even if my dear boy is no longer with us.' She flourished a handkerchief that was more lace than substance. 'I'm simply longing to see his children.'

'Later.' Saul Ludlam saw his wife seated then turned to his hostess. 'I wonder if your son's wife and I could go into the library for a few minutes? There are a few matters we need to discuss privately.' He did not wait for permission but offered his arm to Liza, an imperative gesture that seemed to expect instant obedience.

After escorting her to the library in silence, he indicated a chair. 'Who are you?'

This seemed a very strange way to start a conversation. 'I'm Nick's wife.'

'You were Josiah's wife before that and you've brought his children back with you so I wish to know your background. Who were your parents? Where were you born? Are any of your family still alive?'

It took more courage than anything she had ever done before to look this man in the eye and say coolly, 'My mother is dead, but my father has a second-hand shop in Underby Street – he's one of your tenants, Con Docherty.'

He sucked in breath with a harsh sound, his face a mask of revulsion. 'Irish as well, then! Why the hell did Josiah marry someone like you?'

She told the simple truth. 'Because Catherine wished it.'

Dead silence greeted this remark, then he snapped out a curt command to: 'Explain that, if you please, young woman.'

When she had finished the brief explanation, she waited for him to comment but he didn't speak for a long time.

'How did you persuade Josiah to act the man and get children on you?'

Liza sat rigid, remembering the night she had tried to do just that and failed. 'It was Catherine who – who made him promise to try and he – he managed it. It was,' she could feel herself

344

flushing, 'not a pleasant experience for me. We were lucky that I – I seem to get children easily.' Her shudder was not feigned. 'I think he also wanted the money you'd promised.'

'Hmm. I had promised that money for Catherine's children. However, I suppose I must be grateful that he got children on anyone, even you.'

Liza gazed down at her hands, ignoring his rudeness and waiting to see what he wanted. When she could bear it no longer and looked up, she saw him staring out of the window, deep lines graven in his cheeks and his mouth a narrow, bloodless line of compressed flesh. For a moment she felt sorry for him, then he turned and stared at her with such open disgust that the feeling vanished to be replaced by anger, a much safer emotion.

'I suppose you expect money from the estate now for your brats?'

'No. I neither need nor want anything from you. I have some money as well as the farm in Australia. I'm not greedy and Nick will—'

He laughed, a caw of derision that sliced across the room. 'You may not be greedy, but you're a clever young woman. How the hell did you persuade Rawley to marry you?'

A voice from the door said, 'She didn't. I persuaded her. And I take leave to tell you, Mr Ludlam, that I do not appreciate anyone speaking to my wife in that tone.'

Saul shrugged. 'You're clearly besotted with her. Well, you've made your bed and must lie on it. I want to meet the brats now.'

Liza pulled herself together. 'I'm not having my children bullied.'

'How old are they?'

'Cathie is three and Seth nearly one.'

'Do they look like him?'

She had already thought out what she would say to this. 'Seth has Josiah's dark hair, but Cathie looks more like my mother – and perhaps a little like your wife.'

Nick intervened again. 'If you'll return to the drawing room, sir, we'll send for the children.'

When Dorothy brought Cathie and Seth down, Saul Ludlam did not attempt to greet them, just stared at them as he had stared at Liza. Assessing, judging. As Liza led Cathie across to her supposed grandmother and saw the joy on Sophia's face, guilt speared through her. I have to do it, she told herself, but she hated deceiving this gentle, unhappy woman.

With tears in her eyes, Sophia drew Cathie to her and kissed her cheek, hugging her so tightly the child wriggled. 'She looks just like my niece did at that age,' she whispered, then fumbled for a handkerchief and blew her nose several times.

'Would you like to hold Seth?' Liza offered.

'Oh, yes.'

'He's quite heavy.'

'I love children.'

To Liza's surprise both children took to her immediately. Restless Cathie consented to stand beside her 'grandmother' and tell her about the farm in Australia, which she remembered quite clearly, and Seth gurgled at her and tried to suck her necklace.

'Well, at least she's not a stupid child and the baby looks alert,' Saul said as he took leave of Nick, who had escorted him to the door. 'I intend to keep an eye on them. They're Ludlams and must be brought up properly, as befits their station.'

'They'll be well looked after, sir,' Nick said in his easy way. 'Liza is an excellent mother and I shall play the father's part.'

'I'm grateful to you, Rawley. If they didn't have a gentleman to show them how to go on, we'd have to do something about the situation.'

When he returned to his wife, Nick found her in tears, though she would not tell him why. Putting it down to her condition, he sent Dorothy and the children back to the nursery and took Liza to their room for a rest. 'If you don't need me, my dear, I'll go out for a ride. I've missed having proper horses.'

'You go. I think I'll lie down for a while.'

When she was alone, tears slid down Liza's cheeks. Sophia Ludlam was a kindly woman and did not deserve to be the object of such a deception. And this life was far more difficult than she had expected. Saul Ludlam terrified her. Why? She could not understand it. But a shiver ran through her at the memory of how scornfully he had looked at her and spoken to her.

CHAPTER TWENTY-SEVEN

Liza and Nick went to visit her da the next morning and found him standing in the doorway of the shop staring blankly into the distance. He didn't recognise her when she got out of the carriage at the end of the narrow street, but as she walked towards him, she saw his head turn away then jerk back and his mouth fall open as if he couldn't believe what he saw. He seemed much older, and he was leaning against the doorpost with a sagging posture as if he'd lost both fire and substance.

'Hello, Da. This is my husband, Nicholas Rawley.'

Nick held out his hand. 'Pleased to meet you, Mr Docherty.'

But Con was looking at his daughter and frowning. 'Teddy Marshall said he saw you with a nob.' He considered the name for a moment. 'Rawley?'

'Of Rawley Manor.'

Con blew out a gust of shocked, sour-smelling breath, studied the hand Nick was still offering, then shook it briefly with the tips of his fingers, as if afraid of dirtying it. 'A Rawley, eh? Well, you'd better come through to the back then, girl – if you're not too grand to sit with your family now, that is.'

'No, I'm not too grand.' Receiving only a grunt in response, she grimaced at Nick and followed Da into the house. Nancy came to the scullery door to see who it was and she, too, looked startled at the sight of her sister. However, she offered only a black scowl and made no attempt to come forward and greet anyone. Tears came into Liza's eyes and she took the initiative by going across to hug her. 'I'm so happy to see you again, Nancy! Where's our Kieran?'

'Out,' Da said sourly. 'He's allus out, that one is. Can't find time to help me in the shop, can he, these days?'

'You know he's been earning a bit extra by helping Mr Grey

on the farm,' Nancy snapped. 'And anyway the shop doesn't do enough business to keep two of you busy.'

'Ah, but he don't give any of his money to me, does he, so what's the use of him earning it?' But Con's voice was without heat, as if this was an old argument now.

'If he did give it you, you'd only spend it on drink. Instead we waste it on things like buying food.' Nancy's tone was bitterly sarcastic.

Con cleared his throat noisily and spat a big gob of phlegm into the fire. 'A man gets a thirst on him workin' wi' dusty old clothes like I do. And why are you goin' on about that now, Nancy Docherty? We've got guests and you haven't even offered them a cup of tea. Sit down, then, Mr Rawley.' He kicked a chair out from under the table and nodded his head towards it, then dropped into another and began to cough, hacking and wheezing for a long time.

Nick pulled out a chair for Liza and sat down himself but remained stiffly upright, as if mistrustful of the whole situation. His expression was calm, but she knew that was only a mask.

Liza turned to Nancy and bounced up again. 'I'll come and help you, shall I?' In the scullery, she hugged her sister, but the thin body was still unresponsive against hers. 'How are things going, really?'

Tears came into Nancy's eyes and she folded her arms across her chest. 'Bad. There's hardly any money comin' in and Da still goes off drinking with Teddy Marshall. Sometimes he's so rude to customers they walk straight out again and if it wasn't for our Kieran working on the farm and coming home with bits and pieces of food, I don't know how we'd eat.'

'I'll be able to help you out now.'

Nancy began to fiddle with the old brown teapot. 'Well, don't give *him* any money or he'll just booze it away. I'll take anything you can spare, though. We're hungry most of the time, so we can't afford to be proud or fussy. An' if you have any spare clothes, well,' she stared down at her shabby clothes then across at her sister's elegant gown, 'we certainly need them. He hasn't got any decent stuff in the shop these days. You can play Lady Bountiful to us, like Mrs Ludlam does sometimes.'

'Don't be so bitter!'

'I've a right to feel vexed with you. When you ran away it

was all left to me, wasn't it? Did you think about that at all? Mam was ill, an' as for our Niall and Dermott – they were allus trouble an' they didn't get no better. They went off to Manchester in the end. We haven't heard from them since the funeral. They used to slip me a bit of money sometimes, at least – well, our Dermott did. I reckon they must be in jail. They used to go thieving, that I do know.'

'They're not in jail. They came to Australia and – and they visited me, but they went away again when there was no money to be had from – from my first husband.'

Nancy's mouth fell open. 'Australia? They never!'

'They didn't get anything out of me. I don't know where Der— where they went to afterwards and I hope I never see them again.' She hated lying to Nancy but no one must ever know what had happened to Niall. Taking a quick glance over her shoulder to check that her da hadn't followed them, Liza fumbled in her purse and pulled out a gold sovereign. When she offered it, her sister laughed.

'You've forgot what it's like living round here, haven't you?' Nancy's tone became even more scornful. 'What do you think people would say if I handed 'em that? An' how would they give me change for it? Someone 'ud be bound to tell Da about it, then he'd have the rest of the money off me for his booze.'

So Liza emptied out her purse and they picked through the small change together.

'It must be wonderful t'be rich!' Nancy jeered as she wrapped the money in a cloth and pinned it to her single ragged petticoat. 'You'll hafta tell me how you did it. Or p'raps you could find me a rich husband, too. I wouldn't be choosy, I promise you. As long as he had enough money to feed me well, I wouldn't care what he looked like.'

'Oh, Nancy, don't be like that.'

But her sister just muttered something and went back to making the tea, then they poured it out and carried the brimming cups through one by one.

Liza noticed that Nick barely touched the black liquid in his cup, but her father slurped his down noisily and asked for more. When Liza sipped hers, it reminded her of the tea they'd drunk in Australia, strong and with milk in it only when a cow had calved. That inevitably brought back a memory of Benedict

349

who had looked after those cows so carefully. He wouldn't have just sat here with a glassy smile on his face like Nick was doing, she was sure. He'd have got Nancy talking, pulled them all together, made them feel more cheerful. He always did that when he was talking to folk.

After they had sat for a few minutes in an uncomfortable silence punctuated only by remarks from the two women, Nick pulled out his watch. 'We must go now. I've arranged to see my father at eleven.'

'You'll come and visit us at Ashleigh, won't you, Nancy?' Liza whispered as the men went into the shop.

'If I can. Da doesn't like me to go out because of the shop.'

'We'll find a way. Maybe on a Sunday? And bring Kieran.'

'Maybe.'

As they sat in the carriage, Nick said idly, 'Your sister doesn't look like you at all, does she? How old is she?'

'Eighteen.'

'She looks older.'

'She's had a hard time lately.'

'So have you, only you didn't let it sour you as she has.' A minute later he said abruptly. 'I don't want you going there again. They can come and visit you, but you're not to go there.'

'But I—'

'I mean it. I don't want you contracting some disease that'll harm the baby. They can come and visit you any time they like at Ashleigh, but you're not to visit them in that filthy little house. Blame it on me if you like, but if you try, I warn you, I'll take steps to prevent you.'

Liza had never seen him in such a determined mood before and her surprise must have shown, because he added more gently, 'I intend to look after my own and that's my child you're carrying, Mrs Rawley.'

A young maid was found to take care of the children, a sensible girl with a cheerful nature, and since staying in Ashleigh was bringing back sad memories, Dorothy nerved herself to write to her sister, who lived in Preston. Liza had urged her to do it several times already, thinking her friend would be worrying about Kitty, but Dorothy was strangely reluctant to meet anyone she had known before and had stayed inside the house most of the time since their move, seeming to have lost all her former energy.

Two days after the letter was despatched a carriage drew up to the house and a gentleman got down from it, turning to help a lady who shook out her skirts daintily and pulled a face at the state of the drive, which had not yet been regravelled, before taking his arm and picking her way towards the house.

'It's my sister!' gasped Dorothy. 'Oh, heavens, what am I to say to her?'

Liza felt as if she were the elder, not the younger. 'She's your sister. You can tell her the truth, surely? She knew Andrew was not good with money.'

When shown into the house, Nora Rowntree stared disdainfully around the parlour before condescending to sit on a chair. 'I don't know why you didn't come straight to me, Dottie. We can't have you living off other people's charity, you know. And how strange that you're back here. I never did like this house.'

As the conversation limped along, with Mr Rowntree barely contributing a word, Liza took a strong dislike to Nora, who was distinctly spiteful as well as patronising towards her poor sister, reminding her very much of Kitty. And it hurt her to see how subservient Dorothy had become.

'Where is Kitty?' Nora demanded just then. 'Is she not at home?'

Dorothy began to twist her handkerchief. 'I'm afraid – well, she was very unhappy in Australia and one day she just – ran away. I thought she'd have come to you. She was always talking about returning to England.'

'*Ran away!* What can have got into the girl? You should have left her with me in the first place. Why Andrew wanted to drag you all halfway round the world, I don't know. And see what it's led to! I might have known he'd die and leave you penniless. Well, I know my duty so you can pack your things and come home with me today. We can't have you imposing on strangers like this. And if Kitty comes to England, I'll take her in, too. I know my family duty.'

Liza wanted to beg her friend not to go but Dorothy was already leaving the room so she stayed behind and tried to chat to Nora Rowntree, who was more gracious with her than with her sister, at least. Liza found it very heavy going. By the time Dorothy came downstairs again an hour later, the silences were growing longer and longer.

'Ah, there you are, Dottie. Goodness, you've taken an age and you can't have much to pack if that fool of a husband lost all your money.'

As Liza embraced her friend, she whispered, 'If it gets too much—'

Dorothy's voice was dull. 'I'm used to her ways. I'll be all right.'

But she didn't look all right and afterwards Liza missed her friend greatly. Her mother-in-law became a frequent visitor but somehow she could not feel close to Mrs Rawley. And to her relief, her father-in-law never crossed the threshold. She also received regular visits from Sophia Ludlam, with whom the children were greatly taken, and enjoyed her company.

Liza tried several times to get on better terms with Nancy, but her sister remained deeply resentful of her 'good fortune' – as if things had come to her easily! – as if she was now totally happy, with Nick growing increasingly autocratic about what he wanted her to do. He'd gone ahead with the will and only the other day had taken her to sign a pile of legal papers, all to do with it. They were so full of long words that Liza hadn't even tried to read them, nor had she embarrassed him by asking to have the will read to her.

Her brother Kieran was much pleasanter to deal with than Nancy, thank goodness, and she enjoyed his company greatly. He had grown into a sturdy young man, very much aware of how important he was to the little family with his father increasingly lost in a booze-induced stupor. He accepted money from Liza with no qualms, though he came back sporting a black eye once because Da had seen the money and tried to take it off him.

'He didn't get it. I'm not going hungry again if I can help it and nor is our Nancy. I just wondered,' he hesitated, 'well, I wondered if that husband of yours would come and have a word with Da – tell him not to take things off us? He found some of the clothes you gave Nancy the other day and put them in the shop. She was that upset. I took 'em out again, but Da's got his eye on 'em still, says they'll have to be sold if business doesn't pick up.'

Nick sighed in exasperation but went to warn his father-in-law sternly about taking away any of the new clothes Liza had given Nancy or confiscating the money: 'Which is for food, not alcohol, Mr Docherty, and I hope you'll remember that in future.'

For some reason, Da always went very quiet in Nick's presence, calling him 'sorr' and not treating him anything like a son-in-law. He had come over to Ashleigh once, but had not stayed long and had not been to visit since – which suited Liza just fine.

After Nick's visit, however, although there was no talk of selling the clothes, Da stopped giving Nancy any money for food, saying there was no need now he had a rich daughter to feed them all.

After some persuasion she told Liza about Mam's last days, her happiness to have received a letter from her distant daughter, and ended, 'I couldn't find the letter afterwards, though. I think our Niall might have had it away an' that's how he found you. He went through her things, you know, before she was even cold.' Nancy sniffed and wiped tears from her eyes as she added, 'And I'd promised her to destroy that letter. She asked me particular. I've always been sorry I didn't manage to do it.'

That confidence was the nearest they got to being close. Apart from that, Nancy always wore a sulky air when she came to visit, never seeming to be at ease – unlike Kieran, who ate heartily of anything offered and spoke of his daily life and his enjoyment at working in the open air. He looked like Niall, though not as big, but was always so cheerful the resemblance wasn't as worrying as it might have been.

The worst part of Liza's new life was the insistence of Saul Ludlam that she bring the children to the Hall to visit every week or so. Nick took her there himself the first time or two, but managed to find some excuse for not going after that. If there had only been Jos's mother Liza would have quite enjoyed herself, but the other daughters-in-law were sometimes there and always spiked their conversation with remarks which made her feel uncomfortable. Saul insisted on being informed when she was coming and joined them but the children grew very quiet in his presence, even little Seth seeming to sense that this man was not to be upset.

As Liza grew bigger with Nick's child, she stopped visiting, making the excuse of her condition. Then Saul came to Ashleigh occasionally with his wife and seemed not only to dominate the smaller house, but to leave the dark shadow of his presence behind him.

'When Seth is older,' he said one day, 'we must see about a school for him, a good boarding school. I'm not having him grow up like his father.'

'I'm not sending my son away to school,' Liza declared, sitting upright and looking him straight in the eye. 'You can be sure he won't grow up like that with Nick as his stepfather.'

Saul gave her that patronising smile which she hated so much. 'We'll see about that when the time comes. In our class things are done rather differently, young woman, and I rather think the Rawleys will agree with me on this matter.'

The last month of Liza's pregnancy seemed to last for ever and Nick grew very fussy, wanting her to lie down all the time when she was nearly bursting with suppressed energy. She was relieved when her pains began. As with her other births, matters progressed quickly and within four hours she had borne a second son, a fine lusty little fellow with blond hair who bore a great resemblance to his father.

After it was all over Nick came tiptoeing into the bedroom to kiss her and hang over the cradle. 'Thank you, darling,' he said, tears welling in his eyes. 'He's a fine infant.'

'Do you still want to call him Francis Alexander Stephenson Rawley?' she teased. 'He's much too small for all those names.'

'He'll grow into them, don't you worry. All first sons in the family are either called Francis or Nicholas. Using her maiden name will please my mother, and calling him after my uncle will please him.'

Liza would have preferred something simpler, but let him

have his way. 'Just as long as you don't let people shorten it to Frank,' she warned. 'I've never liked that name.'

'Don't worry. They won't.'

She had met Nick's uncle several times now and had not really taken to Alexander Stephenson. Oh, he had been civil enough to her, but there was always a constraint between them and she was sure he considered her unworthy of marrying a Rawley – well, they all did and she was fed up to the teeth of it, wished sometimes she hadn't done so because of all the complications that came with it. Only it was too late now to change matters, and at least she had a loving husband who would look after her and the children, though he was less fun to be with since their return to England.

That week, for the first time ever, Mr Rawley came to visit them at Ashleigh. Liza had got up and come downstairs the day after the birth, to everyone's horror, because she didn't see why she should lie in bed when she felt so fit and well, and was sitting in the parlour with Cathie and Seth beside her when the Rawleys arrived. She lifted her chin defiantly at Mr Rawley's first words.

'I did not expect to see you up and about so soon, daughter-in-law. Are you sure this is wise?'

'I feel perfectly well. I always do.' Liza had difficulty hiding her own sense of shock, because he had changed so much since their last encounter. He was skeletal now, his fine broadcloth suit hanging on him as if it had been made for someone else. 'Come and meet your grandson.' She indicated the cradle which had been brought down to stand beside her – another thing which had scandalised the maids and made Nick frown, but Liza didn't care. She loved to cuddle her children, was feeding the baby herself and had no intention whatsoever of handing him over to a nursemaid more often than she had to.

Geraldine was already hanging over the cradle beaming down at the baby, who opened his eyes and blinked back at her.

'Oh, he's so like Nick! Just look at him, James! Isn't he a darling?'

'Would you like to hold him?' Liza asked.

'I'd love to. Is it all right?'

'I do not believe in holding babies too often,' Mr Rawley announced.

'Well, I believe in giving them lots of cuddles,' Liza snapped. 'I think they're happier for it.'

'We're not put on this earth to be happy, but to do our duty.'

'Well, my duty is to see that my children flourish and you can be sure I'll do that.'

There was silence as he studied the child in his wife's arms, making no effort to touch Francis or even move closer. 'He's a real Rawley,' he said at last, which was the nearest he'd ever got to expressing approval of anything connected with Liza.

After they'd left, Nick found her in tears. 'I wanted our children to have grandparents they could love,' she wept into his chest, 'and I don't see how anyone could ever love your father.'

'No.' He patted her on the shoulder, but she could feel that his thoughts were elsewhere.

'Is something wrong?'

'No. Well, no more than usual. It's difficult working with him. I think I'll buy myself a hunter and get out for a good gallop occasionally, blow away my frustrations. Would you mind? Father sold mine while I was overseas and the horses he has now are rather placid mounts. I fancy something young and lively, which can take hedges and walls in its stride.'

'I don't mind at all.' Liza wanted him to be happy in every way possible.

Nick was delighted with his new horse, and she could see why. It was a huge grey with a steady look to it, without the wildness or skittishness she had seen in the eyes of some animals.

Geraldine turned up at Asheigh one day accompanied by her brother, who always seemed to be looking down his nose at Liza. She felt very depressed at the thought of spending the rest of her life with people who disapproved of her so markedly. But at least, like his sister, he was pleased with little Francis.

When Nick walked out with the two of them to the carriage, the men stood talking for a long time before his uncle got in, then Nick returned to the house in a thoughtful mood.

'Is something wrong?' Liza asked as his silence continued right through dinner.

He looked into the distance, as if wondering what to say.

356

'We-ell, my uncle wishes me to change my will and appoint him Francis's guardian, just in case anything happens to me.'

'What could happen to you here?' England felt so safe after Australia.

Nick grinned. 'Nothing much. But he's right, I hadn't thought of that aspect of things. I certainly wouldn't want my father as the child's guardian, would you?'

'I don't see why Francis needs anyone as guardian except me. I'm his mother. That should be enough.'

Nick sighed wearily because they'd had arguments like this before. 'Just oblige me, will you, my dear? I'll bring home the papers for you to sign in a day or two.' He didn't tell Liza that one reason for this guardianship was so that young Francis Rawley could be raised as a gentleman if anything did happen to him – something his young wife, for all her charm and vitality, could never do on her own.

In Australia, Grace Caine discovered herself to be with child at last and was utterly delighted. Benedict tried to enter into her enthusiasm but must have failed because she turned on him sharply. 'Can I do nothing right for you? She isn't coming back, yet still you hanker after her! It's me who is your wife, the mother of your children and – and—' She ran into the bedroom and threw herself on the bed, sobbing wildly.

Benedict followed her and drew her into his arms, shushing her and patting her until the tears dried up. 'I'm pleased about the child, Grace, you know I am, but I can't help being worried about you. This has nothing to do with Liza and I don't know why you go on about her. You said you had difficulty bearing Lucas and I care about your welfare far more than that of an unborn child.'

She pulled herself together, knowing she had betrayed too much understanding of his lack of love for her and that to go on like this would surely alienate him. 'I'm s-sorry, Ben. I just – I get emotional when I'm like this.'

'Of course you do. But we'll have to be careful to get help for you when the baby is born.'

Grace shuddered but said nothing. He could only guess how the first birth had been for her.

The following day he went to see Dinny, who had just borne a second child to Fergal without any problems. 'You seem to know about these things. What should I do to help her?'

Dinny frowned. 'Well, it's no use expecting to get the doctor. He takes his time about coming to births – and I wouldn't have him touch me with his dirty hands, anyway.'

'Will you come and help her, then?'

'I'd be happy to. But would she be happy to have me? Would she trust me?'

When he suggested it to Grace she flew into another temper and raged at him for thinking she'd trust herself to an ignorant black woman, so Benedict went with her to see the doctor who recommended a local woman to come and stay for the last month and see Grace through the birth.

When they met Mrs Cherton she was very pleasant and assured them she'd had a lot of experience, but Benedict continued to worry. It had been so different with Liza, who had glowed with health when she was carrying a baby. Grace looked pale and ill all the time.

CHAPTER TWENTY-EIGHT

When little Francis was six months old, a frantic note arrived from the Manor to say that Mr Rawley was desperately ill. Nick rushed off and stayed there for two days as his father slowly sank towards death.

Liza called once, uncomfortable at having to go and see the man she disliked lying helpless in his bed. She was sure he wouldn't have wanted her there, either. She had sharp words with Nick about bringing Francis, who was, she felt, too young to understand what was happening, and since her other two children were not connected to the dying man, refused point blank to bring them to a death bed. At this, Nick's face tightened into a grim expression that surprised her, it was so like his father's, but he did not press the point.

When the old man died, Nick became owner of the Manor and Liza, standing beside him and his mother to receive their neighbours on condolence visits, found herself being eyed critically by all the visiting ladies. Life was going to be even more difficult for her from now on because try as she might she could not behave in the stiff, formal manner required of the mistress of Rawley Manor. Sometimes Nick grew annoyed with her for her impulsiveness and hated to see her doing her own gardening, but her abundant energy was not being used and sometimes Liza felt she might explode if she didn't *do* something.

She made the preparations to move to the Manor with a heavy heart and when Nick suggested hiring a governess to teach the children, acquiesced in that reluctantly, because she knew she was too ill-educated to do it herself. They all seemed to want to separate her from her children, and she could see no way to stop it, but Cathie was old enough to learn her lessons now, and even Seth was getting to an age where he could do simple tasks and needed a careful eye keeping on him.

The new Nick made Liza nervous sometimes, because he seemed to have changed so much since his father's death and she suspected he was beginning to regret their marriage. Endearments were rare now and love-making a cursory, dutiful affair. She knew he wanted more children but she had not so far started another one. Maybe when she did things would improve between them.

After the move her mother-in-law took her in hand at Nick's request and together the two women bought mourning clothes and did the appropriate things. Liza refused point blank to wear a thick veil over her bonnets, however, because it made her feel as if she was suffocating – and she absolutely hated the crinoline skirts she now had to wear, because they hampered movement so much and you didn't dare run with one on. Later, before the clothes were showing any wear, Mrs Rawley insisted on them buying a whole lot more so that they could change to half-mourning. It seemed a ridiculous waste to Liza, but she was learning to hold her tongue about such things. What difference did it make to a dead person whether your handkerchiefs had a two-inch or a half-inch black border?

Sometimes she would sit by the window of her bedroom and indulge herself in dreams of Australia: the warmth of the sun on her arms, paddling barefoot in the lake, the shrieks of parrots quarrelling in the treetops and the way kangaroos sometimes paused while hopping through the bush to stare at you, as if they were trying to understand the strange creatures who had invaded their territory. And always, whatever she did, Benedict was there, occupying a special place in her heart. In fact, her thoughts had been turning to him more often now that Nick had grown so cool and serious about life. Her husband was trying to make her into something Liza knew in her heart she could never be and however much she pleaded, he would not stop doing it.

She and Dorothy exchanged letters often and for both of them it was the only opportunity they had to express their true feelings, since they were equally unhappy in their present lives. Once Dorothy came to stay for a few days and the two of them sat for hours reminiscing.

'You still haven't heard anything from Kitty?' Liza asked, knowing how her friend grieved for the loss of her daughter.

'No. I sometimes wonder if I should go back to Australia and search for her. I miss it more than I had expected – the warmth, the wildflowers in spring and having my own home. Benedict is keeping an eye on the inn for me and says it's making a little money – that there's more than enough for a passage back if I want it.' Dorothy brushed a tear away. 'Only I can't decide what to do. My sister grows no easier with age, but she *is* still my sister, my only living relative apart from Kitty. I'm finding it hard to keep up the appearance of a lady to her satisfaction on my annuity.' She gave a bleak smile. 'She's very mean with her money, you know, although they have plenty.'

Then Dorothy pulled back and studied the younger woman's face. 'You're not happy, either, are you, Liza? You've lost weight and your eyes look sad. They used to sparkle with happiness.'

'I ought to be happy. Other ladies envy me my position.' She waved one hand at their surroundings and her expression was scornful. 'But I'd give anything to live in a smaller house again.'

After another companionable silence, Dorothy asked, 'How's your sister going? Is she still intending to marry that young man?'

'I think so. Nancy doesn't talk to me much, though. She's having a hard time with Da lately. He's stopped working in the shop and if it wasn't for her and Kieran, the place would have closed down long ago.' And Liza was the one supplying them with money, because the shop's takings didn't even earn enough to cover Da's boozing now. As for Nancy's young man, he was a rough type and had already thumped her sister a couple of times. But it was hard to help someone who refused to talk to her and only came to visit when she needed money. Kieran came over to the Manor at least once a month, refusing to be daunted by the people he called 'them nobs' and chatting cheerfully to his sister about his life and hopes. Nick complained about the frequency of his visits, but for Liza they were one of the few good things in the tedium of her new life.

'I reckon if you were still in Australia,' Kieran told her one day, 'I'd have gone out there to join you. It sounds a good place for a fellow as wants to make something of hissen.' He looked round the dark room, with its heavy old furniture. 'Don't you ever miss being outside? You always seem to be sitting indoors these days.'

'I miss it all the time.' Liza clapped one hand to her mouth and looked over her shoulder. 'Don't tell anyone here, though.'

'Nay, why should I do that?' He grinned cheekily. 'Any road, them nobs don't talk to me if they can help it. They put me in the back parlour an' ignore me.'

'You could still go out to Australia, if you're serious, Kieran. I have friends there and I'm sure they'd help you. There's always a need for experienced workers.'

'Aye, well, if our Nancy marries yon Charlie Heffell, I may just do that.' He looked at her thoughtfully. 'Would you lend me the money for the fare, then? I've tried to save up, but it's hard with *him* drinking away all he can get his hands on. I'd pay you back, you know.'

'I wouldn't want paying back. After all, I've got everything I could want here, haven't I?' Liza could hear the bitter echo to her words and could see that he'd caught the tone, too.

'You're really unhappy.' His tone was flat.

'Yes. This place is . . .' She shrugged and didn't even try to put it into words.

Kieran stared round. 'Too bloody gloomy. I allus feel glad to get out into the fresh air again.'

'Yes. So do I.' But even when she went for walks, Nick insisted she took a maid and the housekeeper grew huffy if they stayed out for too long.

'Still, that friend of yours is coming for a visit soon, isn't she? That allus cheers you up.'

Liza smiled. 'Yes, Dorothy's coming next week. Her sister and husband are going to London, so they're letting her visit me while they're away.'

When Dorothy arrived a few days later, she was clearly brimming with news but didn't say anything until she and Liza were alone.

'Well, what's happened? You look full of yourself.'

'I had another letter from Benedict.'

'Oh?' Liza was longing to hear how he was going. He and

Dorothy corresponded regularly and it seemed he was doing well for himself, making and selling beautiful furniture embellished with his carvings now, as well as running the farm.

'It's sad news, really. Well, sad for him, but good for me.'

'What's happened?'

'Grace is dead.'

Liza stared at her in shock. '*Dead?* But how?'

'In childbirth, poor thing. He says she was very brave, but she lost too much blood afterwards.'

'And the child?'

'Is a little girl and is being looked after by Dinny.'

'Well, she's in good hands then. Oh, I do miss Dinny! I wish she could write to me. Fergal wrote once, but Nick didn't like it. He's grown very conscious of *doing the right thing* and he always disapproved of my knowing an ex-convict. But you haven't told me your good news yet.'

Dorothy looked almost her old self as she said, 'Benedict has asked me to go out and act as his housekeeper, help him raise the children. He says he'll never marry again,' she lowered her voice, 'and we both know why.' There was a pause, then her voice rose joyfully. 'Oh, Liza, I'm going to do it. Nora will be furious, but Benedict has arranged my passage and given me a bank draft for my expenses. There are more people in Brookley, the inn is doing better and so, apparently, is Jem Davies. That might be the one good investment Andrew made. Your farm's doing well, too. Weren't you pleased with the last accounting?'

'The what?'

'Benedict sent you the accounts. Surely you—'

'I haven't received them. I – I daresay Nick took care of that' But the thought that he had kept them from her, as if she couldn't understand such things, made Liza furious though she didn't say so now. She tried to feel happy for her friend but could only think that once Dorothy left she'd be totally alone here in England, with no real friends. The years ahead were beginning to seem very bleak. 'I'm glad for you. When do you go?'

'Next week.'

'So soon!'

'I intend to leave before Nora gets back from London

because I know she'd try to prevent me from going – so I can only stay a day or two with you, I'm afraid. But I wanted to tell you myself, say goodbye properly, and anyway I can do my shopping for the voyage just as well in Pendleworth as in Preston. I shall know better what to take with me this time.'

The two women spent the short visit shopping and talking of old times. When Dorothy had left, with many promises to write often, Nick found Liza uncharacteristically in tears.

'I'm sorry you're losing your friend, but maybe it's for the best.'

It seemed a cruel thing to say. 'What do you mean? How can it be for the best to lose my only friend like this?'

'Well, it's more than time you stopped dwelling on your period in Australia – and time you made friends among our own sort. You can do it if you try. Look how much better you're speaking nowadays, and with my mother to help you choose clothes, you're avoiding some of those over-bright garments.'

'Is that why you kept the accounts of the farm from me?' she asked sarcastically. 'So that I didn't *dwell* on Australia?'

His expression became stiff and wooden. 'I think it's up to the husband to deal with business matters. I'm sorry now that I ever agreed to let you manage your own affairs. It's time you handed them over to me and—'

Anger about many things overflowed suddenly and Liza threw the nearest object at him, which happened to be a vase, and screamed at him to get out of her bedroom. With a look of utter disgust, he left.

When she joined him and his mother for dinner, Liza hardly said a word. In bed she turned her back on him.

'It's not like you to sulk.' He touched her shoulder tentatively and she shrugged his hand off.

'Oh, please yourself!' he snapped.

When he turned over and went to sleep, she could not stop the tears trickling down her cheeks.

The following morning she confronted him. 'The farm in Australia is my children's heritage. I will neither sell it nor hand it over to you.'

'You'd be better cutting all connections with Australia now.'

'It's their inheritance,' she repeated.

'Which they won't want.'

Anger at his remarks still rankled she went into town, found another lawyer and handed over her children's affairs to him, asking Mr Lorrimer to write to Benedict to tell him to communicate with her through him in future. She had to produce the agreement Nick had signed before their marriage before the lawyer would deal with her, though. Men! They were not the only ones who could add up and make plans.

Liza's action caused another quarrel with Nick when he found out what she had done, but she didn't care, and at least he didn't try to take things back into his own hands because he knew Lorrimer was a decent fellow and would handle things properly.

'If it had been my son's inheritance,' he said angrily, 'I would not leave matters like this, I promise you.'

In the weeks and months that followed, although the overt breach between them healed, she and Nick were never even half so close as they had been in Australia and on the ship coming back. Liza devoted herself to her children and even tried to learn to ride in an attempt to get on better terms with him, but that was a total failure. It seemed ridiculous – and indeed, downright dangerous! – for women to sit perched sideways on horses and she soon gave up the attempt to ride. Nick told her she was better sticking to walking, but he spent more and more time hunting in the season or hacking through the countryside out of season. They only met at mealtimes now.

Dorothy's first letter from Australia brought tears to Liza's eyes. It had been posted in Fremantle upon her friend's arrival and was a diary of life on board ship, which brought back many memories of her own voyage back to England, a happy time. A second letter followed a few weeks later, describing in satisfying detail the thriving farm and furniture manufactory that Benedict and Fergal now ran, and talking about a visit Dorothy had made to Dinny, who was still living in Liza's old home. The description of that and of her friend's two children brought tears to Liza's eyes and she wished desperately that she could go back there herself.

If it hadn't been for her children, she didn't know what she'd have done. They were her only consolation and Liza loved them dearly. She was surprised she hadn't fallen for another baby, and knew Nick was growing increasingly anxious about that. He had increased his rate of love-making, but it seemed a hasty matter nowadays and she did not really enjoy it. Anyway, she didn't want to bring up another child in this stifling atmosphere.

A governess now took up the two elder children's days and a nursery governess looked after Francis much of the time. Mrs Rawley insisted on calling him 'our little heir', but for all her devotion to her grandson, her visits to the nursery were very short.

When Liza went to the nursery, the staff were nothing but polite. However they made her feel like an intruder, and clearly did not like her interrupting their routine, while for her part she hated to see Cathie's high spirits quashed into meek behaviour and Seth being corrected over nearly everything he said or did.

Whatever Nick said, she wasn't going to stop seeing her children so often, or taking them for walks on sunny days instead of leaving them indoors doing lessons.

In 1863, when Francis was two, the winter was very stormy. Tiles were blown off the roof, trees came crashing down everywhere and branches littered the roads nearby.

Nick continued to ride out in all weathers, saying he enjoyed a good blow. He complained this wasn't good country for hunting, however, and once or twice went to stay with friends near Leicester for several days, returning with boring and often incomprehensible tales of 'rattling good chases', describing in tedious detail the high hedges his horse had sailed over and how people had admired his mount's strength and endurance.

He never asked Liza to go with him, though from what he said other wives went to these house parties. She knew that was because he was ashamed of her, and that hurt her.

When he didn't return from one visit on the day he'd specified, she thought nothing of it, admitting to herself that it was something of a relief to have him away from home and unable to complain about the time she spent with the children. He had changed so much from the carefree young man she'd married that she didn't even like him sometimes. And when she felt like that, she could not help remembering that Benedict was free now – so they could have got married if she'd only stayed in Australia.

But would he still have wanted her? Nick didn't want her now and had clearly grown tired of her. Josiah hadn't really wanted her either. Perhaps no one would ever want her again. Liza shook her head and told herself not to be silly, then lost herself in daydreams of her little house in Australia, a favourite reverie.

The maid had to speak to her twice before she answered. 'Mrs Rawley needs you downstairs, Mrs Nicholas. She's really upset about something.'

Liza checked her appearance in the mirror so that she wouldn't have to face recriminations about untidiness, then walked slowly down the wide staircase that always smelled of beeswax and lavender. *A lady doesn't run around like a hoyden, Liza!* Nick had said to her several times. When she heard sobbing from downstairs, she forgot propriety and quickened her pace. In the drawing room a gentleman she didn't recognise was standing next to Mrs Rawley who was sitting on the sofa, sobbing into her handkerchief.

As Liza paused in the doorway the stranger stared across at her. 'Mrs Nicholas Rawley?'

'Yes.'

'I'm afraid I have some terrible news for you. Perhaps – perhaps you'd better sit down.'

'Nicholas is dead!' wailed her mother-in-law. *'Dead!'*

Liza could not move and everything seemed to go distant, so that she stood wrapped in her own cloak of silence and the sounds the others made only registered as a faint buzzing. Gradually she became aware of a hand under her arm and looked up to find the stranger at her side.

His voice was gentle. 'Mrs Rawley, this must be a dreadful shock. Please come and sit down.'

She found that her legs would not move easily and was glad of the arm he offered to help her across to the sofa. But even as she sank on to it, she realised that her first duty was to the hysterical woman beside her. 'Ring the bell for her maid,' she ordered, gathering Geraldine into her arms and rocking her to and fro, patting her back and making shushing noises as if she were a baby.

When he had done that, the stranger came back to hover nearby and Liza asked, 'What happened? How – how is it possible that Nick . . . ?' She let the words trail away.

'It was a hunting accident.' He went across to stand with one hand on the mantelpiece, staring into the fire. 'Happened out of the blue. A bird flew out of the hedge just as his horse was about to jump. He shied and took off awkwardly and – and Nick was thrown. We think his stirrup must have been a bit loose. He fell heavily. Broke his neck, I'm afraid. Shockin' affair. I had to shoot the horse myself. Poor thing was screaming.'

What did she care about a stupid horse? 'Was Nick – was he in much pain?'

'No, no. Killed instantly. All over in a minute.'

Geraldine moaned and began to utter incomprehensible sounds in between racking sobs.

When the maid came down, a sensible woman who had looked after her mistress for many years, Liza explained quickly what had happened, then together she and the maid half-carried the distraught woman up to her bedroom.

The maid whispered, 'She has some laudanum, Mrs Nicholas. Uses it sometimes when she can't sleep. Shall I prepare a dose?'

'Yes, I think so.' Liza stood there, her mind a blank. 'I don't know what to do next,' she said without thinking.

'I don't mean to speak out of place, but you should perhaps send for Mr Alexander. He'll know exactly what to do. He'll have to be informed anyway. Very fond of his nephew, he was. Miss Geraldine and him are very close, being twins. They always were. He'll be able to help her better than anyone.'

'Yes. Yes, of course. I'll do that. Thank you.' Liza walked slowly downstairs, intending to pen a note, then remembered that the stranger was still in the drawing room, so went to apologise to him and explain what she was doing.

'I'll take the note to Stephenson for you. We're members of the same club, though I don't know him well. He's not often in London these days. I've got a cab waiting outside. Just tell me how to get to his place.'

An hour and a half later, Alexander Stephenson arrived and took over completely.

At first Liza was very glad to leave everything to him. She

suppressed her own grief and thought only of getting through this sad time as best she could. *After the funeral*, she kept telling herself, *after the funeral I'll sit down and think what to do with my life now. And I'll never rush into anything again as long as I live.*

But when the funeral was over and the gentlemen who had followed the hearse rejoined the ladies at the house, Liza was allowed no time to herself. First the guests must be spoken to, then there was the will to be read.

'Tomorrow will be best for the reading,' Alexander decreed. 'My sister is overset by all this and must be put to bed now. You will see to that, Liza, my dear, won't you?'

'Yes, of course.' Since Geraldine turned more to her maid than her daughter-in-law in her time of grief, Liza escorted her to her bedroom, then wandered downstairs and slipped out into the garden, going to sit in the summer house, absent-mindedly shredding the leaves of a bush that was tumbling over the low wooden walls.

She wept for a while, seeing Nick as he had looked in the coffin, so still and white, his face unmarked and handsome, his hands crossed on his chest. The corpse had looked like a statue and not at all like the easy-going man she had married. She found herself remembering the good times, the fun they'd had together at first, his joy in his small son.

It was here that Alexander found her, her lap full of shreds of leaf and twig and traces of tears on her cheeks. He came in and sat down opposite. 'How are you bearing up, my dear?'

She looked at him and wished he had left her alone. 'I'm managing.'

'I came to ask if you know about the terms of the will?'

Liza frowned, not understanding why he wanted to discuss this now when it was to be read the following day. 'Yes. Well, I think so. Nick made you joint guardian of Francis with me, didn't he? And the estate is entailed on the male line, so Francis will inherit everything.'

'I'm the sole guardian, actually.'

She didn't like the sound of that. 'Exactly what does that mean? I'm still Francis's mother. How can you be sole guardian.'

'Because that's how Nick arranged it. This means I'm in charge of making decisions about my nephew's life and

369

upbringing, a charge I'm happy to assume. I've already promised my sister that I'll move here, so that I can help you both and supervise his upbringing.'

'There's no need for that, surely? Francis will have me and I assure you I'll take great care of him.'

'You're a good mother.' He hesitated then said gently, 'But let us speak frankly. You were not born into our class and you have certain – shortcomings, shall we call them? Nick arranged things this way because he wanted to make sure that if anything happened to him, his son would be raised a gentleman.'

'You're not taking him away from me!' gasped Liza, terror on her face.

'No, no, of course not! But I shall take my guardianship very seriously. It's my *wish* to do so, as well as my duty. And I'm sure you'll allow yourself to be guided by me, hmm?'

Liza didn't know what to say and compromised with, 'I shall always do the best I can for my son. For all my children.'

'And you'll not make a fuss at the will reading tomorrow?'

'Why should I do that?'

'Well, there are further provisions which Nick perhaps did not explain to you.'

She drew herself upright. The words sounded so ominous. 'What other provisions?'

'Concerning your other children who are Ludlams, not Rawleys. Apparently Saul Ludlam was happy to leave them here while they had a step-father who was a gentleman to bring them up, but he asked for a provision in the will – just in case. Don't look at me like that. This is how we do things in our world.'

'How could Nick make provisions about *my* children? They're nothing to do with the Rawleys now.'

'You signed a consent form making him their legal guardian, remember? Their sole guardian. That gave him the right.'

Fear cut through her. She had signed a lot of papers without really understanding them when she first came here, with Nick beside her pointing to where she should sign. She had not wanted to betray her ignorance of the long words and legal phrases and in those days he had been very loving, so she had trusted him. She had not seriously thought he might die, nor had she understood the papers' implications. 'That gave him the right to do what? Tell me again.'

'It gave Nicholas the right to name Saul Ludlam their guardian if anything happened to him. So your other father-in-law will have the main say in what happens to them from now on.'

'But they're *my* children!' Liza repeated. Suddenly she couldn't bear to be shut in the summer house with its dim light and the shadows falling like prison bars across her face. When Alexander barred the way out, she tried to push him aside and, failing that, beat frantically at his chest. 'Let me go!'

'Not until I'm sure you'll do nothing to upset my sister.'

'I'm not giving my children up to that man! I'm not!' She almost blurted out that Cathie and Seth were no relation to the Ludlams, but bit back the words just in time.

'We shall discuss the matter quietly and sensibly after the will has been read – and if you don't promise me not to make a scene, I shall make sure you are locked in your bedroom during the reading until Mr Ludlam and I have come to certain decisions.'

Liza stumbled backwards, staring at him in horror. 'You're going to take my children away from me, aren't you?'

'Not necessarily. But we are going to do what's best for them, rather than you. That is our duty as guardians.'

She sat down abruptly on the wooden bench that ran round the walls, her head spinning with shock and terror. He didn't move and when she looked up, she saw him staring at her coldly as if she were a child who was misbehaving.

'I shall require your promise to behave,' he insisted.

'I shan't make a scene tomorrow,' Liza promised dully. She knew by now that making a public fuss would be the worst thing she could do. These people set a great deal of store on keeping calm and behaving in what they considered to be a civilised manner. Well, she would keep calm, difficult as it was going to be, because she wasn't going to be shut away like a naughty child.

Alexander's eyes searched her face, then he nodded. 'Very sensible of you, my dear Liza.'

When he left, she was too upset for tears, could only sit there with a chill of sheer terror on her. They were powerful, these rich people. Without Nick to protect her, they wouldn't heed her desires. Why had he done this to her? Had he despised her so much that he couldn't even trust her to raise their son? Couldn't he trust her to raise her other children, either? That hurt. Dear heaven, that hurt so much!

Liza found herself praying, repeating under her breath the prayer she had learned in her childhood. 'Hail Mary, full of grace . . . pray for us sinners now . . .' Only she wasn't a sinner – was she? She had killed her brother, but not intentionally, and she had prayed for forgiveness for that many times. She had tried to be a good wife to both her husbands. She knew she was a good mother. Everyone said so. But apparently that wasn't enough for these people.

It was a long time before she went back to the house. When she began to walk up the stairs, Alexander came out of the library to gaze at her and say, 'Are you all right?'

She forced herself to nod. 'Yes. I'm just – going to lie down. It was the – the shock that upset me so.'

'Yes, I dare say.'

But she could see that he was still suspicious of her. She didn't know how she was going to cope with the next few days. Or face living here with him afterwards.

The following morning, Saul Ludlam drove up to the Hall and joined them in the library for the reading of the will. He nodded to Liza, looking at her in such a cool, assessing way that it made her heart pound with fear. These men were planning something. Whatever it was, she'd get nowhere by opposing them and making a fuss, she had to remember that.

Should she tell them that the children were not Josiah's? No, for then they'd brand her as immoral and might take little Francis from her. She had gone to play with him in the nursery before she came down, holding him close and burying her nose in the soft soapy-smelling flesh of his neck, blowing on it to tickle him and make him giggle. Then she'd hugged Cathie and Seth to give herself courage.

She sat down in the chair Alexander pointed out, clasping her hands together on her black silk bell of a skirt with its frills and ruching, waiting to hear what they had decided.

Alexander studied her, nodded once, then turned to the lawyer.

The will was full of those long legal phrases that made little sense to Liza. When the lawyer had finished reading it, she turned to Alexander Rawley, not saying anything but hoping he would explain.

He did so in his thin, dry voice. 'As I told you yesterday, my dear Liza, this means that in effect I am the guardian of Francis and Mr Ludlam is the guardian of your other two children. And, as you already knew, Francis inherits everything here.'

The lawyer nodded.

Saul Ludlam cocked his head slightly to one side and continued to stare at her.

'That needn't make a difference to – to how we live, need it?' she asked, hating the way her voice fluttered with nervousness.

'We'll speak of this a little later, shall we?' Alexander said smoothly. 'Perhaps you ladies will leave us to finish up here and then we'll join you in the drawing room?'

Liza wanted to resist, to say they weren't going to make decisions about her without her being present, but she knew that would be unwise, so she stood up, put an arm round her mother-in-law's shoulders and guided the older woman out. Geraldine was weeping again. She had done nothing but weep since Nick's death. Liza's pain and fear for her children went too deep for tears, and she was too angry with Nick now to weep for him. She felt that he had betrayed her trust totally.

Inside the library, the men signed some papers then the lawyer took his leave. The two others sat down in the big armchairs to either side of the fire and looked at one another.

'What I'd really like to do is get rid of her,' said Saul.

'I think that would be unfair. She loves her children and is a good mother in her own way. No, I don't think I can agree to that.'

'What can you agree to, then?'

'Well, I think it will give my sister a purpose in life if she is allowed to raise her grandson without interference. It's a question of what you want to do about the other two?'

'I prefer to raise them myself, make sure they don't grow up like their father, who was a fool – and worse.'

Alexander nodded slowly, several times. 'Yes. I don't blame you for feeling like that.' He saw that Saul looked angry and said apologetically, 'It's not generally known but I couldn't help suspecting what he was like. And what Catherine let slip confirmed it in my mind. Having lived in Italy, I've encountered similar types a few times. You were wise to send him overseas. But the children seem normal and healthy at least.'

Saul swallowed his chagrin at his private shame being known by this man. 'I think Josiah's children should come to live with me.'

'And their mother?'

'If she behaves herself, she can come too.'

'I could agree to that.'

'Young Seth can go to boarding school as soon as he's old enough. That'll knock any nonsense out of him and get him away from *her* influence. I should never have allowed Sophia to persuade me to educate Josiah at home. I shan't make that mistake again.'

More nods were exchanged.

'So – shall you tell her or shall I?'

Alexander smiled. 'I think we should both do it.'

'She'll make a fuss.'

'Yes, but she'll come round when she's had time to think things over. She's too afraid of us taking all the children away from her. And she's not stupid, I will grant her that.'

CHAPTER TWENTY-NINE

Liza stared at the two men in horror when they told her what they'd decided. She knew better than to appeal to Saul Ludlam so looked at Alexander pleadingly, but received only a quick shake of the head in reply.

One protest escaped her. 'I don't deserve this!'

They exchanged weary glances, then Alexander spoke in his soft, gentleman's voice. 'My dear, please keep your voice down and think before you speak.'

She heard the warning he was sounding, so pressed her hand against her mouth and bit hard on her forefinger. After drawing in several deep breaths, she managed, but only just, not to shriek at them, but was unable to keep a slight tremor out of her voice, 'Please, please don't take my son away from me! I love him so.'

Saul Ludlam looked down his nose at her and made a scornful noise in his throat. 'We're not taking Francis away from you. You'll be able to visit him any time you like. My house is only a couple of miles away, less if you walk across the fields.'

'But I want to be with him all the time, to bring him up myself. Oh, please! I'm his mother.' Liza's voice broke and she fought again for the self-control she knew to be so necessary when dealing with these men.

Alexander came across to where she was standing and pressed her shoulder, his fingers digging in so cruelly she realised he was giving her another warning. 'Legally you have no rights, as I've already explained to you, Liza. We've found a solution where you can be with your other two children—'

'Until the lad goes to school, at least,' Saul said callously.

Alexander threw him an angry glance at this gratuitous provocation, then squeezed the shoulder again and continued smoothly, '—and you'd be wise to accept it. Legally, Mr Ludlam could take your children away from you. You'd have no recourse, then.'

'And I shall still not hesitate to do so if I think it's in their best interests,' Saul said, not mincing his words. 'I'm not at all sure you'll be good for them.'

Nothing, not even Teddy Marshall's rape, had hurt Liza as this did, but from somewhere deep inside herself she found the strength not to give way to hysterics, not to rail at them or attack them with fists and hands. Instead she sat very still and fought the biggest battle of her life, that of keeping her body and voice under the control these cold-hearted men required.

When she raised her head again, she said, 'I think your solution is unkind and ungenerous, too.' She stared at Alexander. 'I'm sure that Nick would never have meant you to treat me like this.' She had the slight satisfaction of seeing a flush on his cheekbones. Turning back to Saul Ludlam, she asked, 'When must I move to your house?'

'Tomorrow.'

'It would be better if we waited until next week. If my mother-in-law is to take charge of Francis, there are things I should show her, things we should discuss.'

But they wouldn't allow her even this much.

'Better to do it quickly, my dear,' said Alexander. 'We don't wish to prolong your distress. And after all, the nursery maid will know the child's ways.'

Saul moved towards the door. 'I'll go back and tell my wife to have Catherine and Josiah's old rooms prepared for you. Your children can join the others in the nursery. We already have a governess, a woman I chose myself.' He paused at the door to add, 'And see that you don't try to undermine her authority in any way.'

Liza looked him directly in the eyes as she nodded. To her, his nature showed in his face, the flesh hard, like granite, eyes dark and totally devoid of any kindness or humour. He was like a statue come only partly to life. And this man was to mould her Seth and Cathie? Never! He had made Josiah into a darkly unhappy soul. He would not do that to her children and – she swore a solemn vow to herself – he would not find her as easy

376

to vanquish as he expected. She would find a way to take them away from him.

'You might like to start packing now,' Alexander prompted as the silence dragged on. 'Saul, could I just have a further word with you?'

Liza rose, obedient as a marionette because she had no other choice at the moment but to acquiesce in their wishes.

'I shall look forward to making your better acquaintance,' Saul said mockingly as she passed him. 'I'm sure you won't find it too difficult to adjust to my ways. You will have my wife and daughters-in-law to guide you.'

To her shock the look he gave her this time was that of a man assessing a woman's charms physically, as if deciding whether he wanted her or not. Liza had seen that look too many times to mistake it. She was relieved that he seemed to find her lacking, for the interest faded from his face almost as quickly as it had arisen. Or had she been mistaken? No, definitely not.

Before she left the house, Liza wrote a letter to Dorothy, telling her friend exactly what had happened. She hoped – oh, she didn't dare think what she hoped. As she was about to take it downstairs and lay it on the hall table to be taken to the post office, it occurred to her suddenly that if this fell into the wrong hands, they could use it as an excuse to take her children away from her. She tucked it into her pocket and went down to find Alexander, to ask his permission to visit her brother and sister in the town so that she could let them know what was happening.

'I need time to adjust to what is happening,' she finished. 'It's going to be difficult for me to leave my son. I think a walk in the fresh air would be beneficial.'

'Better if you use the carriage. Our womenfolk do not tramp the countryside. And if you'll take my advice, you'll tell your family not to visit you until you've settled in. No doubt Mr Ludlam will allow you to make some arrangements for seeing them – if you insist.'

Liza inclined her head. From his tone she doubted she'd be allowed to see her family at all while staying at the Hall.

She asked the coachman to stop the carriage in town, went into the shops and made a couple of trifling purchases, ducking out through a side door of the shop to post the letter herself.

She let out a sign of relief as she passed the envelope across the counter and paid the requisite amount.

In Underby Street her brother Kieran was out and Nancy was minding the shop on her own. When Liza explained what had happened, her sister was for once sympathetic so Liza dared to say, 'Don't marry that man Charlie, Nancy. You'll have just as bad a life with him as you do now with Da. Believe me, an unhappy marriage is a living hell. The things a husband can do to you are—' she had to gulp back the tears '—terrible. Even when he's a rich husband and you live in comfort. And it'll be worse if he's poor and you and your children don't even have enough to eat.'

Nancy stared at her in shock, looked down and squeezed her hand in sympathy. 'What are you going to do?'

'I don't know. They'll be watching me every minute, looking for an excuse to send me away from my children. They – they may not even let me see you and Kieran again. If they don't, remember, it's not by my choice.'

By the time she got back to the Manor, Liza was thinking of this as a war – and the first battle was about to commence.

If Liza had thought life difficult living with the Rawleys, she soon realised it was going to be far worse with the Ludlams. Saul was a stern dictator and even his two grown-up sons did his bidding without question. Their wives were spiteful women, who banded together to make Liza's life miserable in numerous petty ways, but to her surprise she found Josiah's mother willing to be a real friend to her. At first Liza was suspicious of this, but soon realised that gentle Sophia could not have deceived anyone for more than a minute or two.

Together the two women visited Cathie and Seth in the nursery, entertained them at little tea parties and took every opportunity to spend time with them.

Saul sent for Liza a month after her arrival. The summons was enough to send shivers of apprehension rippling through her, but she took a deep breath and followed the maid out.

He indicated a chair and played his usual trick of making her wait until he was ready. She fixed her eyes on the gardens, only turning back to him when he began to speak.

'I'm pleased to see that you're settling in here, Liza, though I do feel you spend too much time with the children. They have lessons to learn – lessons which you cannot teach them.'

She swallowed her pain and panic, but was afraid they had shown on her face.

'However, I am glad to see you spending time with my wife. So long as you do nothing to upset her, I shall be pleased to see this continue because she is enjoying your company. You can learn much about how a lady should behave from my Sophia.'

That afternoon when Liza went to take tea with her mother-in-law, Sophia poured her a cup then sat twisting her handkerchief into a damp ball, before blurting out, 'Saul does not wish us to spend as much time with the dear children, I'm afraid.'

Liza could not hold back her tears and let them trickle silently down her cheeks, not saying anything, not knowing how far she dare go in expressing her feelings, even with this woman who seemed to be her friend.

Sophia's voice was low, as if she didn't want to be overheard. 'I'll do the best I can, Liza – I enjoy seeing them, too. They're delightful children and a great credit to you, my dear. But we'll have to be careful, I'm afraid. My husband is a fine man, but he doesn't always understand a woman's heart.'

Liza didn't think him a fine man at all. From what she had overheard the maids saying, he wasn't even faithful to his wife. But she nodded, let the soft hand pat hers, and listened with a show of interest as her mother-in-law spoke determinedly of other subjects.

To entertain themselves the ladies of the house had many little hobbies and Sophia made a big effort to find something which Liza could do as well as the embroidery, seeming to feel that it was important for her to occupy her time 'usefully'. In the end they settled for sketching, at which Liza proved to have some small talent. An impoverished gentlewoman was brought in from Pendleworth to give her lessons and when she found she was allowed to go out sketching alone on fine days, so long as she kept to the grounds, Liza applied herself in earnest to the task of mastering this useless skill. Even that short time away from the house and out in the fresh air helped her

379

cope, and she felt very frustrated when rain kept her penned indoors.

She'd so much rather have been doing real things, looking after her own home, baking and washing and gardening. It seemed ridiculous to invent activities to pass the time, but at least the embroidery with which she occupied herself in the evenings kept her fingers busy and prevented them from curling up into fists or claws when Saul aired his views on 'the poor' or other topics as he took tea with the ladies after dinner.

There was never any question of her visiting her brother and sister, or of them visiting her. Saul Ludlam simply informed her one day that he had sent word to them to stay away from his house as their sister was too busy to see them.

'I've been giving them money,' she said. 'Without it, they won't have enough to eat.'

Saul considered this. 'Hmm. Well, as their connection with me is known, I shall make them a weekly allowance, but only on condition that they stay away from you.'

One day, however, Kieran sneaked into the woods and found Liza sketching. He crouched behind some bushes to talk to her and she bowed her head over her work and wept with joy to hear from him.

'They told us to stay away,' he said.

'I know. It wasn't by my choice, Kieran, believe me.'

'Are they ill-treating you?' he asked, angry at her distress.

'Not in the eyes of the world. But,' she had to gulp back the tears, 'they won't let me spend much time with my children, either.'

'Why the hell not?'

'Because Saul wants to – to keep them away from my low connections.'

He swore under his breath.

When he said he must go, she begged him not to come too often, because she was terrified of what might happen if Saul found out, but could not resist agreeing to his coming on the first Saturday of the month, late in the afternoon, as now. She sent her love to Nancy, who had now stopped associating with Charlie and was attending night classes at the local church in order to better herself.

'I walk her there and back because that sod is still hanging round. Wants to get some of Ludlam's money,' Kieran said. 'Eh, it's a right old mess, all this.'

'One day,' said Liza fiercely, 'I'm going to escape and go back to Australia.'

'Will you take us with you, our Liza?'

'You'd really like to come?'

'It can't be worse than the life I've got now, can it? No one makes any money in this town but Saul bloody Ludlam.'

When she got back to the house, Liza was worried that someone might have seen them speaking but no comments were made, nor was she prevented from continuing with her sketching – though Saul occasionally asked to see her work, as if checking that she really was doing what she said, and even commented on her improvement.

When Dorothy's next letter arrived, it was passed to Liza after dinner with the envelope slit open. She stared at it in shock. 'What happened to this?'

There was a gasp from her sisters-in-law and Sophia flapped one hand at her in warning.

Saul stared across the room at her. 'The letter was opened by me. As master of this house, I read all communications which arrive here. If you object to that, we can always tell your friend to stop writing to you. When you have written your reply, you may give it to me and I'll see that it's sent.'

He spoke in such bored tones she felt furious, but had learned to keep not only her anger but her expression under control.

Dorothy's letter was the usual chatty exchange of thoughts and feelings, some of which were very personal, and Liza hated to think of that man reading it.

She tried to find an opportunity to send a letter to Dorothy privately to warn her what was happening but it rained the first Saturday so she could not go out sketching and meet her brother. She knew better than to confide in her poor mother-in-law. As well expect a reed to fight back against a foot stamping down on it as for Sophia Ludlam to defy her husband.

When Liza's father fell ill, Saul informed her of it himself, ending, 'If he seems to be dying, it would be fitting for you to pay him a final visit, much as I regret the necessity, and you will, of course, have to attend the funeral, though you will not linger with those people afterwards.'

Her father grew worse and Liza was given permission to visit him. Before she did, she hid the letter to Dorothy in her reticule and passed it to Kieran to post, explaining how carefully they kept an eye on her.

'Ludlam is a nasty devil,' he said. 'Every time his rent man brings round the money, he reminds us we've not got to see you. And the old sod has a nasty reputation with the women. If he ever touches you—'

'He doesn't. And *please* don't do anything to upset him, Kieran,' Liza begged. 'They'll take my children away from me as soon as look at me if you do.'

'Do you see much of the other little 'un?'

She shook her head and could not keep back a tear. 'No. Twice a week now and only for a short visit. Francis hardly knows me.'

'Eh, that's cruel.' He pulled her into his arms and gave her a hug. 'However do you stand it?'

'Because I have to. If I could think how to escape, I would, but there's someone watching me every minute.' She was beginning to wonder whether she should tell Saul Ludlam the truth – that neither of the children was related to him – but did not quite dare do this because heaven alone knew how he would react to this revelation! She was quite sure, now that she knew him better, that he would find a way to take his revenge on her for the deception.

When her father died, she was allowed to attend the funeral, but one of the daughters-in-law was sent with her and they did not leave the carriage.

Liza was beginning to feel despairing about her future, because she still had not managed to work out any way to escape, though she had racked her brain many times. How did you get away from a man who seemed to control a whole town?

When Benedict turned up at Ludlam House six months later Liza knew of it only because by a lucky chance she saw him arriving from the window of her bedroom where she often took refuge on the pretence of sketching. She was just settling on the window seat with her sketch book in her hand when she saw a man walking up the drive. There was something familiar about him, so she stood up to see better.

When she recognised him her heart began to thump with joy. He looked well. A little older than last time she had seen him, but a man in his prime still. And he had an air of confidence he hadn't had before, as if he was now used to commanding respect from others. She almost ran down to greet him in the hall and had got to the bedroom door before she realised how unwise this might be.

After she had heard him admitted, she checked that no one was around, then tiptoed out on to the landing in an attempt to listen to any conversation from below, but although she heard him ask to see her, he was shown into Saul Ludlam's office. As the door at the rear of the hall closed with a snap, she went downstairs to sit in the drawing room and wait for the summons she was sure would come, leaving the door slightly open.

But nothing happened. As the slow minutes passed, she could bear it no longer and crept across the hall. She had her hand on the door at the back when there was a cough behind her which made her jump in shock. She turned to find the butler standing there.

'May I help you, Mrs Rawley?'

'I was just – I had something I wanted to ask Mr Ludlam.'

'He has a visitor and asked me to ensure that he was not disturbed. I'll let you know when he's free, shall I?'

'I thought I recognised the visitor,' she said, feeling desperate. 'And I definitely heard him ask for me.'

'I can't say about that, madam. If you like to wait in the drawing room . . .'

They both broke off as angry voices were raised behind the door. Desperate to see Benedict, Liza tried to push past Mattley, but he was a big man, and although he apologised for the necessity to deny her entry to the rear of the house, he did not budge.

'I have to see Mr Caine,' she pleaded. 'It's important. He'll have news from Australia.'

'The master would wish you to wait in the drawing room, madam.'

There was more shouting from behind the door, then

silence. Shortly afterwards another door slammed somewhere at the rear of the house and Liza turned to rush outside at the front so that she could catch Benedict on his way down the drive. But before she could move, the door she had been trying to pass through was flung open.

In a towering rage Saul Ludlam strode through it, stopping dead when he saw her. 'What are you doing here?'

'I wanted to see Benedict. I heard him ask for me when he arrived.'

He grasped her arm. 'We shall discuss this in private, if you please. Thank you, Mattley.'

Liza tried to pull away, but he dragged her back down the corridor and into his office, thrusting her down on a chair. She got up at once and was pushed back so roughly she bumped her head.

'You'll stay there if I have to tie you down,' Saul roared.

So she stayed where she was, glaring at him.

'You are not to see Caine again. In fact, I've told him he's not welcome anywhere on my land. If he knows what's good for his family, he'll leave the district within the day.'

'But why? He's been managing my affairs in Australia. I *need* to see him.'

'It seems you've been hiding from me how much business you still have in Australia. I shall expect a full accounting from you tomorrow and then you'll put your affairs into my hands so that we can sell that land.'

'No. That's my children's inheritance.'

'They're Ludlams and they won't need a scrubby bit of ground in the Antipodes. I am quite capable of providing for my family, I assure you.'

He loomed over her and for a moment Liza thought he was going to hit her, but she was as angry as he now and flung at him, 'I won't do it.'

'You'll find I can enforce my will in this matter.'

'Oh? Not if I leave this house.'

'You're going nowhere without my permission.'

'I'm over twenty-one and I don't need anyone's permission to come or go. I've only stayed here for my children's sake.'

'And you'll continue to stay. I shall have you locked in your room if you try to leave. Mattley has his orders about that.'

At that moment Liza knew she would have to tell him the truth, and though fear began to curdle into acid in her stomach, she drew herself up. 'I suggest you sit down, then, Mr Ludlam, because there is something I need to tell you, something I should have told you before.'

He folded his arms and stayed where he was near the hearth, staring down at her with scorn in every line of his body.

She took a deep breath, then said baldly, 'Neither of my children is Josiah's. They are not in any way related to the Ludlams. And I'm glad of that.'

A vein began to beat in his forehead, pulsing rapidly, and his complexion darkened with a rush of angry blood. 'You slut!'

She drew herself up. 'I'm not a slut and I never have been.'

'Whose children are they, then?'

'That's none of your business. Josiah knew and he was the only one who needed to.' She waited and as the silence lengthened ominously had to swallow to moisten her lips for they felt dry – she had never in her whole life seen anyone as angry as this huge man.

'Well, you've made it my business by coming here,' Saul said at last. 'So now you can tell me as well.'

'No. But I shall be happy to relieve you of our presence within the hour. More than happy. Your house, Mr Ludlam, has been a prison to me.'

When she tried to walk past him, he grabbed hold of her again and shook her hard, before throwing her down on the chair again. Before she realised what he was doing, he had pulled out a handkerchief and was trying to tie her hands behind her. But it wasn't quite long enough and Liza began to struggle, then scream loudly. He tried to cover her mouth with his hand, but she bit him hard and then kicked him for good measure.

'Gutter bitch!' he panted.

The door behind them opened and without turning round, he ordered, 'Get out!'

'Saul! Oh, Saul, what are you doing?' Sophia quavered.

Liza opened her mouth and screamed again, as loudly as she could, following it up by shouting, 'Let me go, you bully! You're hurting me!'

He cursed under his breath, dragged his wife into the room and slammed the door shut again.

Looking terrified, Sophia collapsed into the nearest chair. 'Saul?' she asked in a wobbly voice.

'This lowbred gutter trollop,' he said, indicating Liza, 'has foisted two children on us who are not Josiah's, and now thinks to reveal this to the world and make a laughing stock of the family. Well, I'm not having that. Go and fetch Mattley, Sophia.'

She lingered to ask, 'What are you going to do? You're not going to hurt her. Oh, please don't hurt her!'

'I'm going to lock her up until I decide how best to save the situation.'

Liza managed to dodge behind a chair for long enough to say, 'Benedict Caine came to see me – your husband wouldn't let him, though. Benedict would take me and the children away from here, back to Australia. There's no *need* to cause any gossip. I won't say a word. We can just—'

This time Saul had hold of her firmly, his big hand clasped across her mouth from behind, so that she couldn't even kick him properly.

Sophia was looking horrified, her cheeks white and her whole body trembling. 'But Saul—'

'Ring the bell, damn you!'

She glanced from one to the other, then shook her head and tottered across the room to do as he ordered.

Hope died in Liza then and she stopped struggling.

When Mattley came in, gaping for a moment to see his master holding Liza prisoner, Saul said curtly, 'Help me carry this hellion out to the stables. We'll lock her in that empty storeroom until I can decide how to deal with the situation.'

Without questioning the rightness of this order, Mattley stepped forward.

Facing two large and very determined men, Liza wondered whether it was worth struggling any further and for a moment lay limply against Saul. She let them take her outside. But she chose her moment, waiting until there were people around before beginning to scream again, 'Help! Someone fetch Benedict Caine!' She managed to repeat this three times before the big hand clamped down on her mouth again, but she didn't stop struggling all the way across the yard at the back of the house and saw a maid gaping from the kitchen doorway and several people peering out of stables and shed doors as she passed.

The two men pushed her into a dark space, so that she fell heavily to the ground. Immediately, even before she had picked herself up, Liza began screaming again. The only light came from underneath the heavy wooden door and there was nothing in the storeroom except a few horse blankets.

At regular intervals she screamed some more and kicked the door, anything to make a noise. But time passed, her voice began to grow hoarse and still no one came to help her.

As night fell the line of daylight underneath the door vanished and darkness closed in, making Liza feel as if she couldn't breathe. When lamplight appeared under the door and she heard footsteps approaching, she jumped to her feet, facing it. The key turned in the lock and the door opened, but she sagged back against the wall in disappointment when she saw only the butler, flanked by the housekeeper and one of the maids.

'Someone tell Benedict Caine!' she begged. 'Mr Ludlam has no right to keep me prisoner like this. I've not done anything wrong.'

'It's like I told you, the poor thing has lost her wits,' Mattley said sadly. 'The doctor will be coming to see her tomorrow. It may even be necessary to lock her away for good.'

Liza stared at him in horror, then looked at the housekeeper. 'I'm not mad. I've defied Saul Ludlam, that's all. That's not a crime, is it?'

The maid shot her a startled glance as she set down a bucket of water and an empty bucket, which she covered with a worn piece of towelling. The housekeeper put a plate and a tin mug on the bare dusty floor. The plate contained only a piece of bread. All was done in complete silence, then both women turned to leave.

'If you have any mercy in you, send a message to Benedict Caine,' Liza begged. 'Surely you won't take part in this crime?'

The maid slowed down and glanced back, but the house-keeper pushed her quickly through the door and followed her without a word.

Mattley looked at Liza pityingly. 'It doesn't pay to anger

him, young woman, as you should know by now. There's nothing anyone can do to help you now. It's my guess he'll have you shut away for the rest of your life. You were a fool even to think of defying a man like him.'

When he had closed the door Liza sank to the ground and could not hold back the tears. They were going to lock her up and Benedict had been sent away so he would not know what was happening. Despair flooded through her and she kept seeing her poor children weeping for her, ill-treated, growing up under the shadow of that terrible man.

She wept for a long time, alone in the darkness, then she huddled in a corner under a blanket and slipped into an uneasy sleep.

When she woke, shivering from cold, it was still dark, so she went to the door and began to scream for help, again shouting for someone to go and fetch Benedict Caine. But there was not even a whisper of sound from outside, so she went back to her horse blanket and eventually managed to doze off again.

CHAPTER THIRTY

Benedict was woken in the night by someone banging on the front door of his father's farm. It sounded so urgent he was out of his bed and down the stairs before anyone else could answer it.

Outside he found a young woman he didn't know who seemed terrified and glanced over her shoulder as she whispered, 'Let me in, quick.'

In the kitchen he lit a candle and studied her face. 'Who are you?'

His brother's voice came from behind him. 'She's the sister of Jack Rodmell who got thrown out of his cottage last year when he upset Mr Ludlam. She's a maid at the Hall.' He turned to her. 'What the hell do you think you're doing, coming here in the middle of the night?'

'I've come to see your brother and I won't speak to no one else.'

Martin folded his arms. 'I'm not having folk banging on my door like this – nor do I intend to upset Mr Ludlam.'

'It's Father's house, not yours,' Benedict protested.

Martin smiled at him triumphantly. 'No, it's not! The lease has been signed over to me now because Mr Ludlam knows he'll get proper loyalty and respect from me.'

Benedict had heard footsteps on the stairs but at these words the person stopped moving and the conversation was punctuated with soft creaking sounds as someone went slowly back upstairs again.

'You took Dad's farm away from him!'

A bedroom door shut quietly upstairs and a bed creaked. Benedict guessed his father had been too ashamed to face him. 'You rotten, toad-eating sod!'

'Father's still living here, isn't he? Folk think he's master still. Only the family knows about it – and Mr Ludlam.'

A voice interrupted them from the doorway. 'You promised Dad not to tell our Benedict about that lease, Martin Caine.'

They turned to see their young sister Jenny standing at the door in her nightdress with a shawl wrapped round her shoulders.

'You get back to bed at once!' Martin shouted.

She scowled at him, made a huffing noise and disappeared – but Benedict didn't hear the landing floorboards creak and guessed she was still listening behind the door.

Martin glared at his brother, then glanced quickly sideways, remembering they were not alone. 'Never mind all that now. You get out of my house this minute! Any lass as creeps out of the Hall at this hour of the night is no better than she ought to be so I'm not having owt to do with you.' When she didn't move he took a step forward, fist raised threateningly, and she jerked backwards, looking at Benedict pleadingly.

'Wait for me at the gate, lass,' he told her. 'I'll go and put some clothes on.'

She nodded and opened the door. 'Well, fetch some money with you, 'cos I know something as'll interest you and I'm not telling you owt unless you pay me.'

When he joined her, after a short, sharp quarrel with Martin, Benedict was carrying all his luggage, two carpet bags with his possessions crammed into them anyhow. He set them down and stared back at the house sadly for a minute. Things were coming to a bad pass when brother threw brother out for fear of upsetting a landlord. 'Thanks for waiting for me, lass. Now tell me what this is about.'

'I want ten guineas first.'

'That's a damned lot of money.'

'I felt sorry for that poor young woman, I still do, but I've been trying to think how to find the money to escape from *him* for a while now.' The girl shivered, adding, 'And you'd better not argue for long 'cos you'll need to look sharp if you're to save her.'

'Save who?'

'Mrs Rawley. She's been living at the house since her husband was killed. Mr Ludlam's shut her in that storeroom off the stables now an' he's threatening to have her locked up for a madwoman. He'll do anything to get his own way, that one will.'

Even in the moonlight Benedict could see her cheeks flush and she wouldn't meet his eyes as she added, 'No one dares say owt about it, but he has us maids in his bed whenever he chooses – whether we want to or not. I hate him touching me, but he likes it better when you don't fancy doing it with him. That's why he let me stay on when our Jack were chucked out.' She shuddered. 'He likes to hurt folk, Mr Ludlam does. Laughs as he does it.'

Anger flooded Benedict. 'The hypocritical old devil! Tell me exactly what's happened to Liza and you'll get your money.'

When she had left, he went back to the farm but another argument with Martin led to nothing save the door being slammed in his face. Taking a quick decision, he set off towards Ludlam Hall. Maybe he could rescue Liza before anyone woke up. They could work out a way to rescue the children later.

The house was in darkness as Benedict crept across the stable yard. The door to the storeroom was locked, so he went to find something to break in with. He'd try to do it quietly, but even if they were caught, he doubted Ludlam would call in the police. If he did, Benedict and Liza would tell their story far and wide. You couldn't claim two people had gone mad.

When he tapped on the door, a voice from inside said, 'Who is it?' and he recognised it as Liza's.

'It's me, love. Benedict.'

There was a gasp, then she sobbed, 'Oh, Benedict, I can't believe you've come.'

'It'll take a minute or two to get you out. Stand back.' Throwing caution to the winds, he used a crowbar to break open the door, though it took more effort than he'd expected and he couldn't help making a noise.

When Liza stepped through the opening, he seized her hand. 'Come on. We have to get away quickly.'

'You're not going anywhere,' a voice said behind him, and he turned to find two of the stable lads standing there grinning in the moonlight, hefting cudgels in their hands.

'We've sent for the master. He'll have you locked up for this, Benedict Caine.'

'He was only trying to rescue me,' Liza cried. 'How can you let him shut me up when you all know I'm not mad?'

'The poor woman has definitely lost her wits, as I'm sure you'll all testify,' stated a deep, gravelly voice and they swung round to see Saul Ludlam standing there, flanked by the butler and one of the gardeners. 'I was afraid Caine might try to get her out, but it's in her best interest to be locked away so that she can't harm herself.' He eyed one of the stable lads. 'You'll bear witness to the way he broke down my door, won't you, Ned?'

'Yes, Mr Ludlam.'

'And you, Tom?'

The other one shuffled his feet and cast an apologetic glance towards Liza. 'Yes, sir.'

'Right, then, catch hold of that thief and tie him up. We'll send for the police in the morning. It won't hurt him to cool off in the feed room. Mattley and I will deal with the woman.'

He had a gloating look on his face which made Liza shiver. Benedict made no attempt to drop the crowbar and she snatched a piece of wood from the nearby pile before moving closer to him.

'We'll be dearly bought,' Benedict said. 'Someone might get hurt.'

'Then you'll both go to prison, instead,' Saul said, smiling broadly. 'Which would suit me very well.'

'If you can, you run away, lass,' Benedict whispered.

'I'm not leaving you,' Laza whispered back.

As the men began to move towards him, careful step by step, another figure moved out of the shadows holding a pitch fork, and went to stand beside the two at the centre of the conflict.

'I'm here as well, Benedict.'

'Jenny! Eh, lass, you should have kept out of this.'

'I'm not letting him lock you up,' she declared.

'Look at him!' Saul mocked. 'Hiding behind two women! Brave fellow, aren't you, Caine? Well, you'll all regret this for the rest of your lives, I'll make very sure of that.'

'You're going to have trouble keeping three of us quiet,' Liza said. 'People will wonder what's been going on.'

His voice lashed out like a whip. 'It won't matter to you, you slut! You'll be shut away in the asylum for the rest of your life. I'm one of the patrons there and they'll do exactly as I wish.'

Suddenly a voice behind him said faintly, 'I can't let you do that. Stop this, Saul! Stop it at once!'

It wasn't a loud voice and it quavered as it spoke, but they all recognised it and swung round to gape as Sophia Ludlam walked across the stable yard, a cloak over her nightdress and her waist-length hair gleaming silver in the moonlight.

'Get back to your room at once, madam!' Ludlam roared.

She shook her head and twisted sideways to avoid him as he tried to grab her. 'Not this time, Saul. I've stood by and let you hurt people for too long.' She went to range herself beside Liza. 'You'll have to shut me away as well, or kill me, because I think people will listen more carefully when I tell the same story as these poor young people. Liza is a good mother, and from what she's told me I believe she was a good wife to Josiah, even if the children aren't his.'

Saul lunged towards Benedict as if to attack him, but the butler dragged him back. 'There are too many of them, master,' he muttered. 'You'll have to let them go this time.'

There was utter silence in the yard, then Saul gestured to the stable lads. 'Clear off. And if you say one word about tonight's happenings, be sure you and your families will regret it.'

The three of them hurried away immediately, one of the lads slowing down to turn for a quick glance backwards until tugged along by one of his companions.

Saul folded his arms. 'Go on, then! Take her away, Caine. But if you set one foot on my property again, I'll have you taken up for theft, I promise you. And,' he jerked his head towards Jenny, 'you'd better make sure that your sister goes back to Australia with you. She takes after you, not your brother, and I'm not having disloyal folk living on my farms.'

'I'm not going anywhere without my children,' Liza declared.

'And how are you going to get them?' Ludlam asked in silky soft tones. 'If you try to push your way into the house, I'll have you arrested for burglary.'

'No one will believe you when I've been living there for months.'

'Are you prepared to risk that?'

Benedict stepped forward. 'Yes, we are prepared to risk it, because I wouldn't leave a dog in your hands, let alone a child.'

393

Again, Mattley held his master back, which was strange behaviour for a butler, but then Mattley had always seemed very close to his master. Saul shook off the restraining hand, but stayed where he was. 'You're not taking the children. I'm not having folk knowing about Josiah.'

When Sophia moved forward again, her voice was stronger than before. 'The children are already waiting for you at the front door, Liza dear. When I realised what Saul was doing, I brought them downstairs myself.'

'*What?*' He turned round and would have lunged towards the house but his wife rushed to stand in front of him.

'You're going to have to stop me by force,' she declared, trembling visibly but not flinching. 'Even if you get to the children first, I'll continue to help Liza and I'll swear to any judge that you're not fit to look after them on moral grounds.'

'Why?' he raged. 'Why are you doing this? Have I not given you everything you could want?' He gestured to the large brooding mass of the house.

'You didn't give me your love, and you took Josiah from me. I've watched you grow more and more cruel as the years passed, and lately I've seen you hurting this decent young woman, keeping her children from her. I can't stand it any longer. But most of all,' Sophia was sobbing as she spoke, 'I'm doing it because of all the maids you've hurt over the years. I've been weak. I should have stopped you, but all I did was make sure they had money to live on when you turned them out. You have several other children, Saul, but you'll never know where they are. I've made quite certain of that, for you're not fit to be a father.'

He stood like one poleaxed then snarled, 'You'll regret this, Sophia.'

'No.' Her words were punctuated with sobs, but she did not let that stop her defying him. 'No, I won't. The only thing – the one and only thing I'll regret is not doing something earlier. I must live with my conscience about that, but nothing you do to me – nothing! – will make me regret helping Liza get her children back.' She looked across at the younger woman. 'Go now, my dear. Go as far away as you can. And I hope you have a happier life from now on. I shall miss the dear children.' She

394

began to weep, but clung to her husband, preventing him from moving, and Mattley did not try to pull her away.

Liza and Benedict ran through the gardens, followed by Jenny, and found the children huddled together at the front door, quite mystified about what was happening. When they saw their mother, they began sobbing.

Lights were going on inside the house even as Benedict snatched up Seth and Liza took Cathie's hand, saying, 'Run! Run as fast as you can!'

Jenny picked up the bundle of clothes that had been flung down next to them and said, 'I'm coming with you, our Benedict.'

'I wouldn't dare leave you behind, love.'

As they hurried through the grounds and began to make their way towards the town, he asked, 'Do you think he'll follow us?'

'I don't think so.' Liza sniffed away a tear. 'Who'd have thought Mrs Ludlam would stand up to him like that?'

'She was very brave tonight.'

'She's very kind, not at all like him. I'd grown fond of her. She's always tried to help me, as much as she was able.'

His eyes met hers across their sleeping son's head. 'It's been bad, hasn't it, love?'

'Very bad.'

'I came as soon as I heard you were free.'

'I hoped you would. So you haven't received any of my other letters?' She smiled at him, her eyes lit up with love.

'No. I just knew I must find you, ask you to marry me. You will, won't you?'

'Oh, yes.'

Behind them, Jenny smiled to herself.

Cathie stopped walking, scowling down at her feet, still clad only in house slippers. 'I'm cold.'

'We'll soon get you warm, love,' her mother promised.

'I'm out with only my nightie on,' she giggled, 'and Seth hasn't even got his slippers.'

'You'll just have to keep on walking, Cathie darling. It's not far now, but I can't carry you, you're too big. We'll buy you both some new shoes tomorrow, don't worry.'

The child looked back fearfully in the direction from which they had come. 'We're not going back there?'

'Never,' Liza said quietly. 'I promise you that, love.'

They had been walking for a few more minutes when Cathie suddenly asked, 'Where are we going, then?'

Benedict and Liza both spoke at once. 'We're going to Australia.'

Liza looked at Jenny as she added, 'You'll like it out there, I'm sure.' She gasped and stopped walking for a moment. 'Oh, heavens, there's my brother and sister to think of as well! We'll have to take them with us, Benedict, or he'll find a way to get back at them.'

'Then we'll go straight to their house now – but we're not lingering in this town for an hour more than we have to.'

But when they had woken Nancy and Kieran, and were waiting for them to pack their things, Liza tugged at Benedict's arm. 'I can't go without saying goodbye to Francis. I just can't.'

'But the risk! Darling, you know how powerful Saul Ludlam is in this town.'

Tears welled in her eyes. 'Francis is my son. I love him dearly. I know . . .' she gulped and had to pause before she could speak again, '. . . know they won't let him come with me. And – and it's in his own best interest to live here, take up his inheritance. But I have to see him, Benedict.'

He pulled her to him and cradled her close. 'I understand, love, though how we're to manage it, I don't know.'

Kieran came into the room, stopped and would have gone out again, but Benedict gestured him to join them. 'Liza needs to say goodbye to her other son but I'm afraid Ludlam might still take it into his head to have us arrested and claim we've stolen something. Or take the law into his own hands – he has enough men working for him and I'd not put anything past him. You and I aren't going to be enough to defend the women.'

'You could always hire a few lads yourself,' Kieran suggested. 'I know a few likely 'uns who'd be glad to stop Ludlam. Trouble is, it's going to take time to round 'em up.'

Benedict hesitated, glanced down at Liza's anguished

expression and jerked his head towards the door. 'Go and fetch them.'

'You've the money to pay 'em summat for their trouble?'

'Aye.'

Kieran grinned and moved towards the door. 'Give me an hour, then.'

The children were put to sleep and the three women came to join Benedict in the kitchen. As the old clock on the mantelpiece ticked the minutes slowly away, Jenny and Nancy rested their heads on their arms and dozed, but the others could not sleep.

'He's been gone two hours now,' Liza worried.

'I'll just go and look down the street,' Benedict said.

Liza stood up. 'I'll come with you.'

Outside everything was dark still, but there was just the faintest hint of grey in the sky towards the east. One of the street lamps wasn't working, so there were deep shadows near it. He put his arm round her. 'Eh, love, I'm beginning to think we should have left when we could.'

A voice from beside him said, 'Aye, you should have done.' Mattley stepped forward into the circle of dull light cast by the one remaining street lamp. 'Mr Ludlam sent me to check whether you were still here. He's angry. Very angry.'

Behind him two other men moved forward, hefting cudgels.

'Get him, lads!' Mattley said.

The three men rushed forward and grabbed Benedict, who yelled, 'Get inside!' But there wasn't time for Liza to shut the door and one of them shoved it back to crash against the wall, setting the little bell tinkling widly. She began to scream for help, desperate to save Benedict, and her voice echoed loudly down the shadowed street.

Windows slammed open and voices called.

Benedict knocked one man to the ground and Mattley drew back for a moment to shout, 'Anyone as tries to interfere will be in bad trouble with Mr Ludlam.'

The windows slammed closed again, and though there were now lights behind some of them, none of the doors opened and no one came to their aid.

The noise had brought Jenny and Nancy to join Liza and with their help she fought off her attacker, who proved to be one of the stable lads from the Hall. The three women then rushed outside to stand behind Benedict and for a moment no one moved.

'I see I shall have to wait for the others to join us,' Mattley said. 'Mr Ludlam is sending reinforcements. He's very keen to see justice done.'

Then there was the sound of running footsteps from Market Road.

'Justice? To take a woman's children away from her!' Benedict exclaimed, edging backwards; trying to get the women into the shop, from where they'd be able to fight off their attackers for a while longer. Where was Kieran? Had he not found anyone willing to help them?

Then the first of the dark figures came into view in the light of the gas lamp.

'Kieran!' Liza moved forward again.

Her brother came to a halt beside Benedict. 'Having a bit of a wrestling match, are you?' he asked in a mild voice. 'Eh, I'm a pretty good wrestler myself. What do you say, lads? Want to join in the fun?'

Several young men came into view, their faces covered by scarves. They ranged themselves around Kieran and Benedict.

Liza sagged against Jenny. 'Thank goodness,' she whispered. 'Oh, thank goodness.'

'You lot will be sorry you poked your noses in where they weren't wanted!' Mattley snarled at the newcomers. 'Very sorry.'

'Mebbe,' said one. 'But I've seen the lass I loved come away from that bloody Hall with her belly swelling an' bruises on her body.'

'And I know another as hung hersen for shame,' said the man next to him. 'Yon Ludlam's had things his own way for too long – an' he's got a lot to answer for.'

'We were too late to help them others,' said a figure at the back, 'but mebbe we can help this lot.'

Mattley began edging away. 'The best way you can help them is to get them out of town.' There was the sound of more footsteps and three men appeared at the end of the street, hesitating. He waved them away, shouting, 'Hold on!' then turned to smile grimly at Benedict. 'There's other ways to do things. Mr Ludlam is ready to swear he's been robbed. He's already sent for the police an' magistrate. You'll not be free for long.'

'We can't fight Ludlam, lass,' Benedict said quietly. 'What time's the first train?'

'The milk train's not left yet.' Kieran looked at his friends, then at Benedict. 'I promised 'em five bob each to see us safely out of town.'

'I'll pay. But they'd better not attack the police.'

'No, but they can see us safe to the station if them others try to stop us.'

In grim silence they went inside. Liza roused the two children and everyone picked up their bundles before walking off down the street.

The station was already lit up and a sleepy ticket clerk took their money.

They sat on the platform waiting. The children huddled together on a bench beside their mother, Nancy and Jenny sat nearby, whispering to one another, seeming already to have formed an alliance. Benedict paced up and down, muttering to himself, and Kieran waited with his friends by the entrance.

'Where the hell's that train?' Benedict muttered, glancing at the station clock.

Liza didn't say anything, but she too kept glancing at the hands moving with agonising slowness across the clock face. Would they get away? Or would Saul have them arrested?

When a carriage rolled up outside the station, everyone tensed and looked at one another.

Liza stood up and went to join Benedict. 'I can't believe this is happening. How can a man have such power?'

He shook his head. 'He's mad, I reckon.' He braced himself to face Ludlam, but someone else got out of the carriage. 'Who the hell is that? I feel I ought to know him.'

'He's Nick's uncle and Francis's guardian.'

Alexander Stephenson, immaculate as ever, strode towards the station. When the group of young men blocked his path, he stopped and called, 'Liza, I need to speak to you.'

Benedict offered her his arm. 'We'll do this in style, love.'

As they moved forward together to meet him, she drew herself upright and stared Alexander Stephenson in the eyes.

She was not going to behave as if she'd done something wrong.

'I wish to speak to Mrs Rawley privately,' he said in his chill precise voice.

'As Liza's fiancé, I think I have a right to be part of any discussions.'

'Fiancé?' He stared from one to the other, then shrugged. 'Very well!' Turning, he led the way towards the First Class Waiting Room and gestured them inside.

'What has been happening tonight?' he asked them. 'I must hear your side of things.'

Liza explained.

When she had finished, Benedict asked, 'Why are you here, Mr Stephenson?'

'I received a visit from Mrs Sophia Ludlam. Her husband had locked her in her bedroom, but her maid let her out and she ran across the fields to the Manor. She was extremely distressed and very fearful for your safety. And,' he glanced from one to the other, 'her story tallies with yours.'

There was silence then he said slowly, 'I'm afraid Ludlam has gone beyond reason in this. I have never approved of the way the fellow conducts his business but I had not thought he would go so far in his private life. I am therefore prepared to help you, so long as you leave the country.'

Benedict gave a snort of anger. 'That's what we're trying to do.'

'Mattley told us he'd send the police after us and swear that we'd robbed him,' Liza said bitterly. 'And Mr Ludlam said he'd have me locked up in the asylum.'

'I'm surprised you didn't leave the town immediately, then.'

'I wanted to say goodbye to Francis.' Liza could not prevent her voice from quavering. She knew she would have to leave her child behind, and that thought filled her with such anguish she could hardly speak.

'I'd rather you didn't. I don't want you upsetting him or Geraldine.'

'But he's my son!'

'Even so. I'm afraid I cannot help you if you insist on seeing him.'

Liza felt Benedict's arm go round her. She could not help sobbing and begging, 'Please, Mr Stephenson! *Please!*' But there was no softening of his expression and even as she stared at him, she heard more footsteps approaching the station and a voice calling, 'Police! Move away from there.'

'Well, Liza?' Alexander might have been discussing the weather, so calmly did he speak.

She sagged against Benedict. 'You leave me no choice.'

The door crashed open and the Chief Constable strode inside, stopping abruptly when he saw who was there.

Alexander stepped forward. 'I believe there has been some confusion tonight.'

'Mr Ludlam has laid a complaint that these people have stolen his property.'

'Yes. And Mrs Ludlam is presently at my house, having come to see me and explain that it was all a mistake. Allow me to explain.' He turned to Liza and Benedict. 'Please wait outside.'

'I hate this,' Benedict said as he took Liza outside. 'Hate feeling helpless to protect you.'

'They have all the power here.'

'Aye, well, I'm damned if I'm coming back here again, I can tell you.' He looked round with loathing. 'At least in Australia I can make something of myself without such as him breathing down my neck. Eh, lass, I'm sorry about your Francis, though.'

She swallowed hard. 'I knew I couldn't t-take him, but – not to say goodbye to him. Oh, Benedict!' She could not help weeping.

He held her close and gradually her tears stopped. They stood there, waiting, until the door of the room opened and the two men came out.

It was Alexander who spoke. 'We feel it'll be better if you all leave Pendleworth immediately. The Chief Constable will see you on to the train. You should not return.'

'What will you tell Francis about me?' Liza asked.

He stared at her. 'That you left him behind when you returned to Australia. It's the truth.'

At that, she gave a cry and collapsed against Benedict, sobbing again.

'I hope you can live with your conscience,' he told Rawley, his voice harsh with suppressed anger and disgust.

'Quite easily. Ah, there's the train. I believe I'll wait and see you off myself.' He took a few steps back and folded his arms.

The others were looking towards them, uncertain what had been decided.

'They're letting us go,' Benedict called out. 'See to the children, will you, lasses? Kieran, can you help me get the luggage on the train?'

Steam blew around them, bringing that sour smell that only railway engines seem to produce. It added to the sense of unreality as they walked through the vapour towards the train.

Liza stumbled along supported by Benedict's arm, not caring who heard her sobbing. She did not turn round. The Rawleys had stolen her son and there was nothing she could do to prevent it. She sat with her eyes closed until she felt the train begin to move again, then shuddered and tried to stop weeping.

Benedict was desperate to offer her comfort, any comfort, for he felt he had failed her. 'You could write Francis a letter,' he said after a while.

'Even if he could read, they wouldn't let him have it.'

'Not now, maybe, but if you sent it to a lawyer, with instructions to give it into Francis's own hands when he's twenty-one – well, at least he'd know the truth then.'

Liza looked at him numbly. 'And I'll have missed all his childhood, will never even see him as a young man.'

He shook his head, bitterness scalding him at their helplessness.

She could tell what he was thinking. 'Benedict, it's not your fault. There was nothing you could have done.'

'Aye, but . . .'

'And I shall write him a letter. It'll be a – a small comfort.'

She leaned back, closed her eyes and let the train carry her away from Pendleworth. She hoped she would never come back here as long as she lived.

She pushed her grief at losing her son to the back of her mind. It would always be there, a pain she would have to live with, but it would do no good to dwell on it. And she would at least have her other two children – her brother and sister, too. Besides, had she not learned years ago that when bad things happened, you just had to bear them as best you could and get on with your life?

'I'm looking forward to going home,' she said softly. 'I've missed Australia.'

'Me, too.' Benedict looked at her with a surprised expression. 'It's become home to me as well, now.'

Three weeks later, five adults and two children stood by the rail of the ship and watched Liverpool fade into the distance.

'Eh, I'm looking forward to seeing this Australia of yours,' Kieran said jubilantly.

'You would be!' muttered Nancy, who wasn't sure about anything now except the need to get away from Mr Ludlam.

'We'll make things come right for us,' Jenny told her bracingly.

'You're as bad as our Liza,' Nancy grumbled. 'Always thinking things will turn out well. And they don't.'

Kieran gave her a sharp nudge.

Jenny chuckled. 'Come on, silly! Cheer up.' She linked her arm in Nancy's and got a reluctant smile.

The recently wed Mr and Mrs Caine didn't say anything, just gazed at one another and smiled. He was holding Seth in his arms, she was holding Cathie's hand, but for a moment they might have been the only two people on the deck.

'Happy, now?' asked Benedict.

'Very happy indeed.' Liza lifted her face to sniff the salty breeze. 'I hope we get a quick passage back.'

He hugged her close, forgetting where they were, his eyes smiling down at her, full of the love that seemed to be overflowing in both of them. Neither of them noticed Seth wriggling and trying to get down.

'Are you going to kiss her again?' Cathie asked in an interested voice.

Liza blushed, then laughed. 'No, love. We'll keep our kissing for when we're alone from now on.'

'We will not!' said Benedict. He thrust Seth into his uncle's arms and proceeded to prove that. And Liza did not protest.

CONTACTING ANNA JACOBS

Anna is always delighted to hear from readers and can be contacted:

BY MAIL

PO Box 628
Mandurah
Western Australia 6210

If you'd like a reply, please enclose a self-addressed envelope – stamped from inside Australia or with an international reply coupon from outside Australia.

VIA THE INTERNET

Anna Jacobs now has her own web domain, with details of her books and excerpts to read. She'd love to have you visit at http://www.annajacobs.com

She can also be contacted by e-mail on anna@annajacobs.com

If you'd like to receive e-mail news about Anna and her books (once every few weeks only) you are cordially invited to join her announcements list. Your e-mail address will not be passed on to anyone. E-mail Anna and ask to be put on the list, or there is a link from her web page.

ANNA JACOBS

RIDGE HILL

It's 1848 and preparations are underway for Annie Gibson's wedding to Bilsden's wealthy millowner, Frederick Hallam. But not everyone is as pleased as they are.

Frederick's daughter, Beatrice, is horrified at the prospect of a new attractive stepmother arriving at the house on Ridge Hill. Even Annie's own family feels threatened. The only person who seems pleased is Tom, Annie's brother.

Soon, however, real troubles begin to pile up for the Gibsons. Tom's happiness is jeopardised by the news that he is father to a child he never knew about. Annie's son, William is devastated to find out that his real father is not the man who brought him up. And even Annie's joy cannot last. Because someone has uncovered the secrets she has fought so hard to keep hidden.

HODDER AND STOUGHTON PAPERBACKS

ANNA JACOBS

LIKE NO OTHER

Rachel Smedling is not like the other women in her isolated Pennine village: she is taller, stronger and weaves cloth like a man. Without her, the household would fall apart, for her mother is ailing and her vicious drunkard father seems to hate her so much, he would happily offer money to any man who would wed her.

When Rachel's mother dies, she is at the mercy of her increasingly violent father. Her only escape is by marrying a kindly man with whom she finds happiness, if not passion, and her life begins to seem complete. Rachel's growing prosperity infuriates her father and his cronies, however, and they will stop at nothing to see her destroyed. It begins to seem as though she will lose everything – but other people's lives cross hers, bringing pain and hope and uncovering a long-buried secret.

HODDER AND STOUGHTON PAPERBACKS

ANNA JACOBS

SPINNERS LAKE

It is 1860 in Bilsden, the Lancashire mill town, and Frederick Hallam is dying. But first he makes secret plans to smooth the future path for his beloved wife Annie. Her sister, Joanie, is fed up with everything until a dashing new admirer crosses her path. But a spurned suitor is determined that Joanie will be his, whatever the cost. And he is not the only one who wants to harm the Gibson Family.

Meanwhile the Civil War in America cuts off cotton supplies, so that times are hard in Bilsden and unemployment is rife. Annie has to rebuild her life after her husband's death and plans to create Spinners Lake, an extraordinary project that will keep her workers from destitution and assuage her own grief.

Tian Gilchrist is caught up in the American war and nearly dies there. He fights his way back to Bilsden, to Annie, whom he has never forgotten.

And the plans that Frederick made for Annie will change her life in unforeseen ways, bringing her hope and happiness once again . . .

HODDER AND STOUGHTON PAPERBACKS

ANNA JACOBS

HIGH STREET

In 1845 Annie Gibson can finally leave Salem Street. Her dreams of being able to open an elegant dressmaking salon in the High Street of Bilsden, a Lancashire mill town, have come true. And she is going to take her father and his second family with her, away from poverty, away from the Rows.

But Annie has not left trouble behind. Someone is trying to undermine her business. Her family have their own ideas about what they want to do with their lives. And several men are persistently trying to win favour with the beautiful young widow – including Frederick Hallam, the mill owner, and Daniel O'Connor, her childhood friend.

As Annie gets better acquainted with both, she becomes increasingly confused about her feelings. Can she really be in love? And can she risk trusting any man again?

HODDER AND STOUGHTON PAPERBACKS

ANNA JACOBS

HALLAM SQUARE

In 1858 Annie Hallam has at last found complete happiness. She has three healthy children and adores her husband Frederick. After years of struggling to make a living in the small Lancashire town of Bilsden, Annie knows she deserves to sit back and enjoy her life – after all, she's not yet forty, and still in her prime.

But worries – at first faint clouds on the horizon – are imminent. Frederick has been looking pale and ill lately, Her brother Tom hasn't moved on after the death of his wife. Rebecca, her half-sister, is longing for something more than work in the salon. And William, her son, isn't happy at university. In spite of Frederick's gentle urging not to take the entire burden of the Gibson family on her shoulders, Annie can't help feeling concerned.

And something much more dangerous is looming – a threat not only to Annie's peace of mind, but to her life . . .

HODDER AND STOUGHTON PAPERBACKS

ANNA JACOBS

A Pennyworth of Sunshine

Keara Michaels doesn't want to leave her family in Ireland, but fate sends her first to Lancashire, then across the sea to Australia, pregnant and penniless. And Theo Mullane, the man who loves her, is married, with an ailing baby son, so cannot follow her as he longs to.

Mark Gibson leaves Lancashire to avoid marriage. But gold prospecting is a dangerous pursuit, and when his gently young wife dies in childbirth, his father-in-law kidnaps the baby. So Mark runs away again, this time to Western Australia, where he employs Keara in his country inn.

But danger threatens them all, even in the bush, as Keara searches for her lost sisters, Theo comes looking for the woman he loves, and Mark at last confronts his past.

Anna Jacobs' new saga is a breathtaking panorama of Ireland, Lancashire and Australia in the 1860s.

coronet

CORONET BOOKS
Hodder & Stoughton